STEPHANIE LAURENS

"When it comes to dishing up lusciously sensual, relentlessly readable historical romances, Laurens is unrivaled."
Booklist

"Another mesmerizing read. A fascinating historical romance blended with an intriguing mystery."
Night Owl Reviews, Reviewer Top Pick, on *The Lady Risks All*

"(A) masterful, eloquent storyteller..."
Romantic Times

"Laurens's writing shines..."
Publishers Weekly

"(The) Regency setting is brilliantly detailed and the romance heated and passionate..."
BookPage on *The Capture of the Earl of Glencrae*

And Then She Fell

He was a past master at the art of circling a ton dance floor, of using the waltz to his own ends . . . but tonight, he discovered, the shoe was on the other foot, and the waltz used him. Worked on him, certainly, and on her, too; he couldn't recall ever being so immersed in the moment, so caught in the effortless action, in the swooping glide, the swirling turns, the sheer power that flowed when he had her—Henrietta—in his arms.

It had never been like this; no waltz had ever captured him before. His senses had coalesced and locked, fixed, so deeply engaged with her and the moment that there was nothing left of him, of his awareness, for anything else. The world fell away, and they were the only two people revolving down the floor, and he was lost, trapped, in her eyes.

Caught, ensnared, by the effortless way she matched him, light on her feet, instantly responsive to every subtle direction he gave. He hadn't expected her to be . . . such a perfect match.

She, and the waltz, took his breath away.

By Stephanie Laurens

Stephanie Laurens

And Then She Fell

AVON
An Imprint of HarperCollinsPublishers

AVON BOOKS
An Imprint of HarperCollins*Publishers*
10 East 53rd Street
New York, New York 10022-5299

Copyright © 2013 by Savdek Management Proprietary Ltd.
Excerpt from *The Perfect Lover* copyright © 2003 by Savdek Management Proprietary Ltd.
ISBN 978-0-06-206864-4
www.avonromance.com

First Avon Books mass market printing: April 2013

10 9 8 7 6 5 4 3 2 1

Acknowlegments

Titles for books are fickle things—the right one might pop into my head even before I start writing, and at other times it's like pulling teeth, finding a suitable set of words that "fit." Normally, my agent, my editor, and I brainstorm, tossing possibilities back and forth until something clicks, and we sing, "Eureka!" But when it came to Henrietta's book, my fifty-first, we came up blank. Yes, we had titles, but none of them sang. So we decided to turn to my readers for inspiration via the Cynster Sisters Title Challenge, inviting title suggestions for both Henrietta's and Mary's books, selecting a final five for each, and letting readers vote on which one worked best for them. Out of that, it's my pleasure to acknowledge Joyce Marie Verellen for her brilliant suggestion of *And Then She Fell* as the title for this book. Thank you, Joyce—you hit the mark, not just for me, but for an overwhelming number of my readers.

The Cynster Family Tree

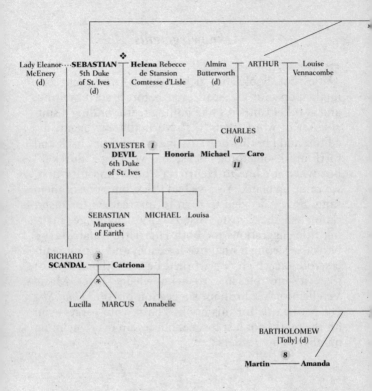

Lady Eleanor····**SEBASTIAN**──**Helena** Rebecce   Almira──**ARTHUR**──Louise
McEnery   5th Duke   de Stansion   Butterworth   Vennacombe
(d)   of St. Ives Comtesse d'Lisle (d)
                     (d)

CHARLES
(d)

SYLVESTER *1*
DEVIL──**Honoria** **Michael**──**Caro**
6th Duke   *11*
of St. Ives

SEBASTIAN   MICHAEL   Louisa
Marquess
of Earith

RICHARD *3*
SCANDAL──**Catriona**
        *

Lucilla   MARCUS   Annabelle

BARTHOLOMEW
[Tolly] (d)
                    8
          Martin──**Amanda**

MALE Cynsters in capitals   * denotes twins
CHILDREN BORN AFTER 1825 NOT SHOWN

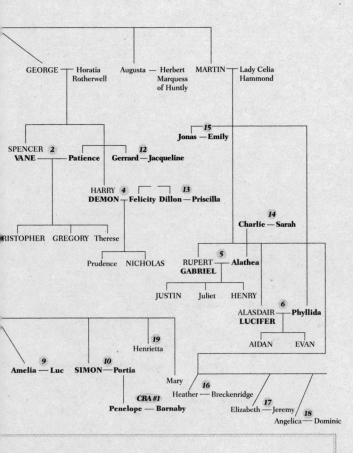

GEORGE — Horatia
Rotherwell

Augusta — Herbert
Marquess
of Huntly

MARTIN — Lady Celia
Hammond

SPENCER — Patience   Gerrard — Jacqueline
VANE *2*   *12*

15
Jonas — **Emily**

HARRY   *4*
DEMON — **Felicity**   Dillon — Priscilla
                        13

14
Charlie — **Sarah**

RISTOPHER   GREGORY   Therese

Prudence   NICHOLAS

RUPERT   *5*
GABRIEL — **Alathea**

JUSTIN   Juliet   HENRY

ALASDAIR   *6*
LUCIFER — **Phyllida**

AIDAN   EVAN

9   *19*
Amelia — **Luc**   **SIMON** — **Portia**   Henrietta

Mary   *16*
Amelia — **Luc**   **SIMON** — **Portia**
Heather — Breckenridge

CBA #1
Penelope — **Barnaby**
Elizabeth — Jeremy   *17*
Angelica — Dominic   *18*

Chapter One

April 1837
London

It was time to dress for what was sure to prove a trying evening. As she climbed the stairs of her parents' house in Upper Brook Street, Henrietta Cynster mentally rehearsed the news she would have to impart to her friend Melinda Wentworth when they met as arranged at Lady Montague's ball.

Henrietta sighed. Reaching her bedroom door, she opened it and halted on the threshold, arrested by the sight of her younger sister, Mary, riffling through the jewelry box on Henrietta's dressing table.

Mary acknowledged Henrietta's arrival with a flick of her eyes and continued pawing through the jumble of chains, earrings, brooches, and beads.

Movement drew Henrietta's attention to the armoire beside her bed. Her maid, Hannah, was lifting out Henrietta's new royal-blue ball gown, simultaneously shooting disapproving glances at Mary's slender back.

Stepping inside, Henrietta shut the door. Like her, Mary was still in her day gown and hadn't yet changed. Curious, she studied Mary's intent expression; the baby of the family, Mary had the single-minded focus of a terrier when it came to anything she wanted. "What are you looking for?"

Mary threw her an impatient glance. Shutting one drawer, she reached for the last, the bottom drawer in the box. "The—*aha*!" Inserting, then withdrawing, her fingers, Mary's face transformed as she held up her find, suspending it between the fingers of both hands. "I was looking for this."

Eyeing the necklace of fine gold links interspersed with polished amethyst beads from which a faceted rose-quartz crystal hung, then noting that Mary's expression now held the satisfaction of a general who'd just learned his troops had captured a vital enemy position, Henrietta waved dismissively. "It's never done anything for me. You're welcome to have it."

Mary's vivid blue eyes swung to Henrietta's face. "I wasn't looking for it for me." Mary held out the necklace. "*You* have to wear it."

The necklace had been gifted to the Cynster girls by a Scottish deity, The Lady, and was supposedly a charm to assist the wearer in finding her true hero, the man by whose side she would live in wedded bliss for the rest of her life. Pragmatic and practical, Henrietta had always had difficulty believing in the necklace's efficacy.

More, in the same pragmatic vein, she'd always considered it was unreasonable to expect that all seven Cynster girls of her generation would find love and happiness in the arms of their true heroes, that it was in the cards that one, at least, would not achieve that outcome, and if that were the case, then the Cynster girl destined to die an old maid would, almost certainly, be her.

As she and Mary were the only two Cynster females of their generation yet unwed, her prediction of her spinster-forever state seemed well on the way to becoming fact. She was already twenty-nine and had never been even vaguely tempted to consider marrying any gentleman. Conversely, no one in their right mind would imagine that twenty-two-year-old Mary, dogged, determined, and unswervingly set on defining and forging her future life, would not achieve her already trenchantly stated goal—namely finding and marrying her hero.

Sliding her shawl from her shoulders, Henrietta shook her head. "I told you—it's never worked for me. You may take it with my blessing. I presume that's what this is about—that you want to use it to find your hero?"

"Yes, exactly." Mary's expression hardened. "But I can't just take it. It doesn't work that way. *You* have to wear it and find your hero first, and then hand it to me just as Angelica handed it to you, and Eliza handed it to Angelica, and Heather handed it to Eliza before that—on the evening of your engagement ball."

Turning to set the shawl on a chair, Henrietta hid a smile—that of an older, more mature sister at her little sister's enthusiastic belief in the charm. "I'm quite sure it's not that specific. There's nothing to say it has to work for us all."

"Yes, there is." There was no mistaking the crisp certainty in Mary's tone; as Henrietta turned back to her, she went on, "I asked Catriona, and she asked The Lady, and it's The Lady's charm, after all. And according to Catriona, The Lady was very clear. The necklace has to go from one to the other of us in the stipulated order. Specifically, the necklace won't work for me if it hasn't already worked for you and you haven't had your engagement ball. So!" Mary drew in a breath and, jaw set, held the necklace out to Henrietta. "You have to wear this. From now until you find your hero—and pray to The Lady and all the gods that that will be soon."

Frowning slightly, Henrietta reached out and reluctantly lifted the necklace from Mary's fingers. Refusing it . . . wasn't really an option. Henrietta might be older, more mature, more experienced socially; she might be taller by nearly a head, and she certainly wasn't any weak-willed miss, but the entire Cynster clan knew that attempting to deny Mary something she'd set her heart on was a fool's endeavor, and that was doubly true if she had a logical argument to bolster her case.

Letting the links slide through her fingers, Henrietta once again studied Mary's face. "Why are you so eager to have the necklace now? You know I've had it since Angelica's engagement ball, and that was nearly eight years ago."

"Precisely." Belligerently, Mary narrowed her eyes back. "So you've had eight years to wear it and find your hero, and instead you've put it in your jewelry box and left it there. That didn't matter while I was still in the schoolroom. Even after I was presented, I wanted to look around myself, so you not wearing the necklace wasn't a problem. But I'm twenty-two now, and I'm ready to take the next step. I want to find my hero forthwith, and start my marriage and set up my own household, and all the rest that comes with marrying. Unlike you, I don't want to spend the next seven or more years doing other things, which means"—Mary jabbed a finger at the necklace—"that you have to wear that now, find your hero, and then pass it on to me. Only once I have the necklace can I get on with my life."

Others might have accepted that at face value, but

Henrietta knew her little sister just a little too well. "And . . . ?"

Mary held her gaze, vivid cornflower-blue eyes steady and unyielding.

Henrietta tipped her head, arched her brows, and waited. . . .

"Oh, all right!" Mary flung up her hands in surrender. "*And* I think I might have found my perfect hero, but I need the necklace to be sure. The necklace is supposed to come to me, work for me, and then go to Lucilla, so it seems I'm supposed to wait for the necklace before I decide on my hero, and, well, it would seem to be flying in the face of fate and The Lady to make any final hero-decision *before* I get the necklace, and I have to have it in the proper way." Mary's expression firmed; her eyes bored into Henrietta's. "Which means *you* have to wear it and find your hero first."

Henrietta looked down at the necklace, at the innocent links draped over her hand. And sighed. "All right. I'll wear it tonight."

Mary uttered a whoop of delight.

Henrietta held up a staying hand. "But I don't expect it to work for me, so don't get your hopes up."

Mary laughed and darted in to plant a quick peck on Henrietta's cheek. "Just wear it, sister-mine—that's all I ask. As for it working"—eyes twinkling, Mary swung toward the door—"I'll put my faith in The Lady."

Smiling, Henrietta shook her head.

Mary paused at the door. "Are you joining Mama and me at Lady Hammond's tonight?"

"No—I'm expected at Lady Montague's." Given Henrietta's age, she often attended different events than those to which their mother escorted Mary. "Have fun."

"I will. I'll see you tomorrow." With a wave, Mary went out of the door, shutting it behind her.

Still smiling, the necklace in one hand, Henrietta turned to discover that Hannah had put her new gown back in the armoire and instead laid out a gown of purple silk.

Catching Hannah's gaze as the maid turned from the chest of drawers, a purple-and-gold silk shawl in her hands, Henrietta arched a brow.

Correctly interpreting the gesture, Hannah assured her, "The royal blue won't do, miss, not if you're wearing that." Eyes bright, Hannah nodded at the necklace. "And if you're going out looking for your hero, we want you to look your best."

Henrietta inwardly sighed.

Two hours later, Henrietta joined Mr. and Mrs. Wentworth by the side of Lady Montague's ballroom. After exchanging greetings, they stood and watched the Wentworths' daughter, Melinda, who was dancing a cotillion.

Melinda's partner was the Honorable James Glossup.

It was James's motives in paying court to Melinda that had brought Henrietta there; she found herself studying him, absorbing all that his appearance and his expertise in the dance conveyed, and wondering—as she had for the past several days—why, given his transparent attractiveness and accomplishments, James had taken the tack he had with respect to finding a bride.

Mrs. Wentworth, a short, comfortably rotund lady in brown bombazine, sighed. "It's such a shame—they make *such* a handsome couple."

"Now, now." Mr. Wentworth, a solid, conservatively

dressed gentleman, patted his wife's hand where it rested on his sleeve. "There'll be other handsome bucks that'll come sniffing around, and as Mellie's of a mind to find a gentleman who loves her . . . well, I'm just grateful to Miss Cynster for finding out what she has."

Henrietta smiled faintly and quashed an impulse to squirm. She didn't know James well, but he was her brother Simon's closest friend; James had been Simon's groomsman when Simon had married two years ago. Consequently, James's and her paths had crossed at several family functions, but beyond what she'd gathered through his association with Simon, she'd had no reason to look more closely at James.

Until he'd grown so particular in his attentions to Melinda that his intention to offer for her hand could not be doubted. At that point, Melinda, with her parents' approval, had turned to Henrietta for, as they'd termed it, "clarification of James's motives."

From her early twenties, Henrietta had found a calling in assisting her peers, the other young ladies of the haut ton, to discover the answer to the critical question every young lady had of the gentleman who sought her hand: Does he love me, or is there some other reason he wishes to marry me?

It wasn't always easy to tell, or, sometimes, to discover the true answer. Henrietta, however, born into the powerful Cynster clan, with all the connections and associations that afforded her, had long ago learned the ways of finding out almost anything.

She wasn't a gossip; she rarely told anyone anything they hadn't specifically asked to know. But she'd always been observant, and her acuity had only sharpened with the years, with constant application and the resulting experience.

While mamas, matrons, and chaperons guided their charges through the ton's shoals, acting as matchmakers for those young ladies, Henrietta provided a countering service. Indeed, certain disgruntled gentlemen had labeled her "The Matchbreaker," but to the female half of the haut ton, she was the person young ladies set on marrying for love turned to for reassurance as to their would-be fiancés' matrimonial motivations.

With tonnish sentiment over recent years shifting in favor of love-matches, Henrietta's insights and expertise had been much in demand.

It was entirely possible that her extensive experience was the reason behind the nebulous niggle in her brain, the suspicion that *something* about James Glossup's situation didn't quite fit. But Melinda had asked, and Henrietta now knew, so despite that niggling but irritatingly unspecific reservation, she would oblige and tell her friend the truth.

Watching James turn elegantly with the music, surveying his broad shoulders, his long, lean frame, the ineffable grace with which he moved, his impeccable and stylishly subdued attire and fashionably ruffled brown hair, and the smile of true gentlemanly gentleness he bestowed on Melinda, Henrietta wondered yet again why he'd decided to take the tack he had and marry merely to secure extra funds, rather than searching for some lady to love.

He could, of course, simply be a coward too wary of love to take the risk, yet to Henrietta that explanation didn't ring true.

As an acknowledged wolf of the ton, James had prowled the salons shoulder-to-shoulder with Simon, but since the summer of Simon's marriage two years ago, James had drawn back and been little seen in London, not until the beginning of this Season. Regardless, as one of the Dorsetshire Glossups, one of Viscount Netherfield's grandsons, there were any number of suitable young ladies who would be entirely agreeable to falling in love with him, but instead he'd fixed very quickly on Melinda.

And Melinda was one of Henrietta's friends.

The measure concluded. James bowed; Melinda curtsied, then rose. Melinda glanced toward her parents, saw that Henrietta had arrived and, albeit with due courtesy and smiles, dismissed James, parting from him to thread her way through the crowd.

As Melinda drew near, Henrietta schooled her features into an expression of uninformative blandness, but after one good look at her face, Melinda glanced at her mother's—and knew.

Melinda's face fell. "Oh." Halting in front of her parents, she took her mother's hand, then looked at Henrietta. "It's not good news, is it?"

Henrietta grimaced. "It's not the news you wanted to hear."

Melinda glanced over her shoulder, but James had melted into the crowd and was no longer visible. Drawing in a breath, Melinda clutched her mother's hand more tightly and, head rising, faced Henrietta. "Tell me."

Mrs. Wentworth glanced meaningfully at the other guests. "This really might not be the best place to discuss this, dear."

Melinda frowned. "But I have to know. How can I face him again otherwise?"

"Perhaps," Mr. Wentworth suggested, "we might return home to discuss the matter in private." He looked at Henrietta. "If we could impose on Miss Cynster to oblige?"

Henrietta hadn't intended to leave the Montagues' house until later, but faced with three earnestly entreating expressions, she inclined her head. "Yes, of course. I have my parents' carriage. I'll follow you to Hill Street."

She trailed the Wentworths as they made their way to Lady Montague's side. While Melinda and Mrs. Wentworth thanked her ladyship for the evening's entertainment, Henrietta stood back and idly scanned the crowd. There were few present she did not know, few she couldn't immediately place in terms of family and connections.

She was absentmindedly surveying the heads when her gaze collided with James Glossup's.

Standing across the room, he was watching her intently.

The Wentworths took their leave and moved toward the door. Wrenching her gaze from James's, Henrietta smiled at Lady Montague and made her farewells, then followed the Wentworths.

She told herself not to look, but she couldn't resist glancing back.

James was still watching her, but his eyes had narrowed; the austere planes of his handsome face seemed harder, his expression almost harsh.

Henrietta met his gaze, held it for an instant, then she turned and walked out of the ballroom.

On the other side of the room, James Glossup softly swore.

What I've learned is that Mr. Glossup needs to marry in order to release additional funds from his grandaunt's estate." Ensconced in an armchair by the drawing room fire in the Wentworths' Hill Street house,

Henrietta paused to sip the tea Mrs. Wentworth had insisted they all required.

Seated in the armchair opposite, with his daughter and wife on the chaise to his left, Mr. Wentworth frowned. "So he's not a fortune hunter after Mellie's dowry?"

Setting her cup on its saucer, Henrietta shook her head. "No—he has funds enough, but to release the balance of his grandaunt's fortune he has to marry. As I understand it, the old lady wanted to ensure that he did, so she made it a condition of her will."

Mr. Wentworth snorted. "I suppose that's one way an old lady can force a whelp to the altar, but not with my girl."

"No, indeed!" Mrs. Wentworth agreed, then, clearly recalling that it was Melinda's opinion that, in this instance, carried the real weight, turned to her daughter. "That is . . . Mellie?"

Cup and saucer held in her lap, Melinda had been staring into the fire. Now she blinked, glanced at her mother, then looked across at Henrietta. "He's not in love with me, is he?"

Henrietta adhered to the absolute truth. "That I can't say. All I can tell you is what I know." She held Melinda's gaze, then gently said, "You would be a much better judge of that than I."

Melinda stared back for several moments, then her lips firmed. She shook her head. "He likes me, but no—he doesn't love me." She paused and took a long sip of her until-then neglected tea. Lowering the cup, she went on, "Truth be told, that's why I asked you to learn what you could of him. I already suspected from the way he behaved that there was some motive other than love behind his approach . . ." Lips twisting, Melinda waved and looked away.

Henrietta drained her cup, then set it on the saucer and shifted forward to place both on the low table before the chaise. "I should go. There's nothing more I have to add, and you'll want to think things through." She rose.

Melinda set down her cup and saucer and rose, too, as did her parents. "I'll see you out."

"Thank you again for being such a good friend to Mellie." Mr. Wentworth gruffly patted Henrietta's hand.

Henrietta took her leave of the senior Wentworths and followed Melinda into the front hall. As soon as the butler shut the drawing room door, Henrietta murmured, low enough that only Melinda, just ahead of her, could hear, "I'm truly sorry to be the bearer of such tidings."

Halting, Melinda swung to face her. Meeting her eyes, Melinda smiled, albeit weakly. "I admit I was hoping to hear I'd misjudged him, but, truly, you've been a godsend. I *don't* want to marry a man who doesn't love me, and all your information has done is confirm what I already suspected, and for that I'm truly grateful. You've made my decision so much easier."

Clasping Henrietta's shoulders, Melinda touched cheeks, then drew back and continued, "So yes, I'll be glum for a day or two, but I'll come around soon enough—you'll see."

"I hope so." Henrietta smiled back.

"I know so." Melinda sounded more certain with every passing minute. "You've helped so many of us now, and I'm sure none of us know what we would have done without you. You've saved countless young ladies from disappointing marriages—quite honestly, you deserve an award."

Henrietta humphed. "Nonsense. I just have better-than-average sources of information." And, although in the present circumstances she wasn't about to mention it, she'd confirmed countless other matches as being soundly based on love.

She allowed the butler to settle her cloak about her shoulders, then he opened the front door.

Melinda accompanied her out onto the front step, and immediately shivered as a chill breeze whipped up the street.

Henrietta caught her hand and pressed it. "Go inside. You'll catch your death—and my carriage is right there." She nodded across the street to where her parents' second town carriage stood waiting by the curb.

"All right." Melinda squeezed back. "Take care. No doubt we'll meet again soon."

Henrietta smiled, waited until Melinda retreated and shut the door, then, still smiling to herself, reassured by Melinda's ready acceptance that she truly hadn't been in love with James, either, she started down the steps.

While she might have no faith in finding love herself, she was staunchly in favor of love-matches per se; to her mind, love was the one protection that guaranteed a lady a happy and contented married life—

A man barreled into her, moving at shocking speed. The collision sent her reeling.

"Oh!" She would have fallen, but the man whirled and grasped her shoulders, holding her before him, steadying her.

From the corner of her eye, she glimpsed a silver-mounted cane grasped in one gloved hand, registered that the glove was exquisitely made, of soft, pliable leather. She blinked and glanced at the man's face, but he was wearing a cloak with the hood up; with the street-lights behind him, his face was shrouded in shadow.

All she could see was the tip of his chin. As she watched, it firmed.

"My apologies. I didn't see you." The man's voice was deep, the diction clipped, but cultured.

Catching her breath, she replied, "I didn't see you either."

He paused; she sensed he was studying her face, her eyes.

"Miss! Are you all right?"

She raised her head; the gentleman glanced over his shoulder. They both saw her groom dropping down to the street, intent on hurrying to her aid.

Even as she called out, "It's quite all right, Gibbs," the gentleman looked back at her, released her, brusquely nodded, then swung away and strode quickly on down the street, disappearing into the gathering fog.

Henrietta mentally shook her head, briskly straightened her skirts and cloak, then crossed to where her groom stood waiting to hand her into the carriage.

The instant the door shut, she sighed and sank back against the leather seat. The carriage rocked into motion; Upper Brook Street was only minutes away.

Relaxing, expecting to feel the usual uplifting swell of satisfaction at another motivation-investigation successfully concluded, she instead found her mind unexpectedly focusing on something else entirely.

On the image of James Glossup standing in Lady Montague's ballroom, watching her intently. On his expression as he'd realized she was following his intended out of the room.

He was Simon's friend; he would know her reputation.

She wondered what he was thinking now.

Chapter Two

"Do you have *any* idea what the hell you've done?"

Henrietta started, then glanced over her shoulder—into soulful brown eyes that were, at that moment, not at all soulful. Indeed, the look on James Glossup's face suggested he was contemplating murder.

Lips thin, his expression stony, he went on, "I'm sure it will come as no shock to you that Melinda Wentworth just handed me my congé, essentially refusing my offer before I'd even made it. After seeing you leaving Lady Montague's last night in the Wentworths' train, Melinda's new attitude came as no great surprise—but that leads me to ask, again, if you have any notion—any *concept*—of just what, in this case, your meddling has achieved?"

His tone, condemnatory as well as accusatory, pricked Henrietta. She swung to face him. Her mother had insisted that together with herself and Mary, Henrietta had to attend Lady Campbell's soiree, but there was little to interest her in her ladyship's drawing room; most of those attending were of the younger set, young ladies only just out and young gentlemen only just come up to town, along with their mothers. But Lady Campbell was a close friend of her mother's, so, after dutifully circling the room once, Henrietta had taken refuge in an alcove partly screened by a large potted palm, which was where James had found her.

Cornered her; she couldn't get out unless he stepped back.

Not that that bothered her, but her pulse had sped up—she wasn't sure why.

"All I did was tell Melinda the truth—that you need to marry to release part of your inheritance." She narrowed her eyes in warning; she was not going to be held responsible for his shortcomings. "You hadn't thought to inform her of that. Melinda has her heart set on a love-match, but although she asked, I specifically refused to comment on that aspect. I left that to her own judgment, and if you failed to convince her of the emotional foundation of your suit, I do not believe you can lay the blame for that *at my door*."

He narrowed his eyes; normally so soft a chocolate brown that drowning in all that lusciousness wasn't a silly thought, they currently resembled chips of adamantine agate. "As I thought—you have no notion of the havoc you've caused, not just for me, but for so many others."

She blinked, frowned. "What do you mean?"

He seemed not to hear her; his eyes continued boring into hers, his face a mask of reined anger and frustration. "Simon had mentioned your interfering interest, of how you dabble and meddle in other people's lives to keep yourself amused."

His tone sent her temper soaring. "You *aren't* in love with Melinda!"

"No, I'm not—but did I ever claim I was?"

He'd lowered his head so they were speaking face-to-face with only inches between them, his diction so clipped he all but flung his words at her as if they were darts, or possibly javelins.

She searched his eyes, the hard, austere planes of his face. His emotions were close beneath that rigid surface; anger and frustration reached her clearly, but so, too, did an underlying current of concern, of anxiety, worry, and trepidation. And underneath all lay a lick of fear, but it wasn't fear for himself; there was a distracted quality to it that she recognized—his was fear for someone or something he viewed as in his care. Abruptly, she felt out of her depth. "What—"

"Did it *never* occur to you that some gentlemen might, just might, be subject to other pressures—reasons that have nothing to do with love—that might dictate that they have to marry? How the devil do you expect such gentlemen to proceed, matrimonially speaking, if they have to contend with the likes of you, meddling where you have no right to interfere?" He dragged in a breath, then even more forcefully, albeit quietly, ground out, "If you learn nothing else from the mess you've just created, if I can convince you to stop intruding in matters you neither understand nor that are any true concern of yours, at least I will have accomplished something."

The look he cast her held an element of disgust, along with a degree of disappointment; he started to step back, to leave.

She caught his lapel. Curled her fingers and clamped them.

He froze, glanced down at her fingers locked in his coat, then slowly raised his gaze to hers and arched a supercilious brow.

She didn't let go but belligerently met his gaze, returning his anger and frustration in full measure. "What," she enunciated, the word as bitten off as his had been, "are you talking about?" She wasn't about to let him cast such nebulous yet hurtful aspersions and then just walk away.

He held her gaze for a long moment, then glanced down at her hand. His anger had abated not one jot, yet with outward, almost languid calm, he said, "Given you've chosen to interest yourself in my matrimonial situation, perhaps you deserve to learn the full story." Raising his gaze, he met her eyes. "And the full scope of the problems your ill-advised interference has caused."

A burst of laughter from the other side of the palm had them both glancing that way; a group of young people were gathering beyond the palm, eagerly swapping secrets.

"But not here." James looked back at her.

Releasing him, she boldly met his eyes. "Where?"

He shifted, glanced around the room, then tipped his head to the right. "This way."

He led her out of the drawing room, through a side hall and down a corridor. She followed, walking quickly, keeping pace just behind his right shoulder.

Somewhat to her surprise, the necklace—the amethyst beads and especially the rose quartz pendant hanging just above her décolletage—felt oddly warm. Mary, of course, had checked to make sure she was wearing it, and Henrietta suspected her little sister had been whispering in Hannah's ear; her maid had gone searching through all her gowns to find the creation she was presently wearing—a well-fitted gown in the palest pearlescent pink silk with a sweetheart neckline—purely to properly frame the blasted necklace. The flaring skirts of the gown swished about her legs as she followed James down the corridor and into another.

Finally pausing by a door, James held a finger to his lips, then turned the knob and quietly opened the door.

The room beyond was his lordship's study. A lamp on the table had been left burning, but turned low. They both looked in, searching, but the room was empty.

James waved Henrietta in, then followed and shut the door.

He wasn't surprised when she went straight to the chair behind the desk and sat. It was an admiral's chair, and she swiveled to face him as he walked to the fireplace to the left of the desk and fell to restlessly pacing. In his present mood, sitting held little appeal; he wanted to rant and berate, but beneath the roiling surface of his anger ran a disturbingly swelling well of helplessness. What the devil was he going to do?

And why was he wasting more of his steadily shrinking time explaining anything to Henrietta Cynster? To Simon's younger sister?

He honestly wasn't sure, but something about her interference had pricked him on the raw. On some level he saw her actions as a breach of trust—more, as a disloyal act. He'd expected better from his best friend's sister. He might not know her well, but surely she knew what sort of man he was, namely one who followed the same creed as her brother. He was irritated and disturbed that her actions could only mean that she viewed him in a dishonorable light. That she thought he would have lied to Melinda, or at least tried to pull the wool over her eyes, that he wouldn't have made his situation clear. Instead, Melinda had dismissed him before he'd had a chance to explain said situation.

"So." Henrietta fixed her blue-gray eyes on his face. "What in all this don't I understand? What is your 'full story'?"

He met her gaze for an instant, then, still pacing, replied, "My grandaunt, as you clearly know, died not quite a year ago—on the first of June last year, to be precise. I was her favorite of all the family and she wanted to ensure that I married. That had always been a goal of hers, one she pursued as well as she could over the last decade and more. However, she then learned she was dying, and so in her will, she left me her estate—a country house and surrounding grounds and various farms in Wiltshire, and a large house in town, all staffed and in good order. She also left me the income for upkeep of same—but for a year only. Beyond that, in order to access the continuing income needed to keep the houses and farms and all the rest operational"—he halted and met Henrietta's eyes—"my dear grandaunt stipulated that I have to marry within the year following her death, which means before the first of June this year."

Henrietta blinked, then her eyes searched his face. "What happens if you don't?"

"The estate, houses, farms, and all, remain mine—my responsibility—but there is no way in all the heavens that I could possibly fund them from my own pocket, without access to the income. A fact my grandaunt well knew."

"So what would happen?"

"What would happen is that I would have to let all the staff go—close up the houses, perhaps keep caretakers, no more, and as for the farms, I have no idea what I might be able to keep functioning, but it won't be much. Oh, and in case you imagine I might sell any part of the estate to keep the rest going, my grandaunt made sure I can't."

"Ah." She paused, apparently working through the reasoning, then said, "So in order to continue to support all the people dependent on your grandaunt's estate—your estate now—you have to marry by June the first?"

He didn't bother answering, just curtly nodded.

Still considering him, she frowned slightly. "You've left it a trifle late, haven't you?"

The look he bent on her held no patience at all. "In leaving me a year to find a suitable bride and tie the knot, what my grandaunt didn't allow for was, first, the change in social mores that has occurred since she was a young lady—in her day, all marriages within the ton were arranged on the basis of material concerns, and love never entered into the equation. So she imagined me finding a suitable bride was simply a matter of me looking and offering, and not very much more. She also failed to allow for the period of mourning my father and grandfather felt the family should observe, or for the months it took to sort out the current state of affairs with respect to the estate. Although it's in Wiltshire, not that far from Glossup Hall, and I've visited there many times over the years, I had no notion she intended to leave the whole to me, and so I haven't in any way been trained as to how the estate functions . . ."

Unable to stand still any longer, unable for some reason to continue to conceal his agitation, he ran a hand through his hair and fell to pacing once more. "Do you have any idea what a mess this now is?" He flung out a hand. "I spent a month looking into all the likely candidates, and Melinda Wentworth stood out as the best—the most likely to accept an offer that wasn't couched in love. She wasn't, as far as I could see, enamored of anyone else. She's twenty-six, and must be fearful of being left on the shelf. And she's sensible, too—a female I could imagine having by my side, working alongside me in managing the estate. I spent the last month and more courting her."

He swung back and trapped Henrietta's gaze. "But now that's all gone—useless wasted effort, wiped away." He gestured broadly, sweeping a slate clean. "Which leaves me with a bare four weeks in which to find and woo a suitable young lady as my oh-so-necessary bride."

Halting before Henrietta, he looked down at her. "And the blame for such a fraught situation, one that could dramatically and adversely affect the livelihoods of so many innocent people, lies equally as much at *your* door as it does at mine."

A chill washed through Henrietta. Eyes locked with his, burning with anger, shot with concern, all she could think of to say was, "Oh."

The control he'd maintained shattered. Incredulous, he stared at her. "Oh? Is that all you can manage? *Oh*?"

Swinging violently around, he paced away from her, then paused, whirled, and came charging back. "But no—it's *worse*." He looked truly appalled as he halted before her, staring down at her. "I just realized—everyone in the ton, certainly all those with marriageable young ladies under their wing, will now know that on the issue of Melinda Wentworth's hand, you've passed judgment on me and found me wanting. Found me *not worthy*." Sinking both hands into his hair, he ran his fingers back through the dark locks, clutching with both hands as he turned away. "*Aargh*! What the devil am I to do? How in all Hades am I to find my necessary bride *now*?"

Silence greeted his questions. He started pacing away from her.

"I'll help you."

She hadn't even known she was going to say the words; they formed and fell from her lips without conscious direction.

Purely in response to what she'd heard, what she could see—what, inside, she knew.

His back to her, he halted. Several more heartbeats of silence ensued, then he slowly turned his head and, frowning slightly, looked at her. "What did you say?"

She moistened her lips, and stated more definitely, "I said I'll help you."

He slowly turned to face her fully. His frown deepened. "In case you didn't know, you're known as The Matchbreaker. You break up matches of which you disapprove, just as you did with me and Melinda."

"No." She drew breath and evenly said, "I only tell young ladies who've asked me to learn the truth about their prospective fiancés what I find. For your information, I confirm as many matches as I disrupt, and contrary to the generally held belief, not all those matches I confirm are love-matches." She held his gaze levelly. "Not all young ladies wish to marry for love. These days most do, but not all."

She hesitated, studying his eyes, his face; neither gave all that much away, but she thought she detected a glimmer of hope, which was encouragement enough for her to say, "I didn't know your situation, but now I do . . . I can help. I can tell you which young ladies might suit, and if the ton's ladies see me assisting you, they'll know that the reason Melinda drew back was not in any way a reflection of any substance on you, but rather lay in her expectations, her wants and wishes. In other words, that she and you didn't suit in that regard, but my . . . championing of you will lay all other adverse speculation to rest."

Pausing, she tipped her head, regarding him steadily as she considered. "I admit it'll be a challenge—finding you a suitable bride in barely four weeks—but if I work with you, we might just manage it."

It was his turn to tip his head as he regarded her, in his case through slightly narrowed eyes. "You'd do that?"

Righting her head, she nodded decisively. "Yes, I would. I'm not apologizing for disrupting your pursuit of Melinda, because such a match wouldn't have worked, but given your situation and, as you correctly point out, the implications of my involvement over Melinda, and you've always been a good friend to Simon, too, then given all those circumstances, helping you to find your necessary bride seems the least I should do."

He stared at her as if he couldn't quite believe what she'd said, and didn't know how to reply. Eventually, he ventured, "So The Matchbreaker will turn matchmaker?"

She tipped up her chin. "I only disrupt matches that won't work, but, assuming you can leave that aspect aside, if we work together, we might just have a chance to meet your deadline."

He studied her for a moment more, then he slowly nodded. "All right. So . . . where do we start?"

They arranged to meet in Hyde Park the next morning.

Handsomely garbed in a walking dress of sky-blue twill, Henrietta was waiting some yards inside the Grosvenor Gate, not far from her parents' house in Upper Brook Street, when James came striding along Park Lane and turned in through the pillared gateposts.

At the sight of him, her heart tightened and an inexplicable band constricted about her chest, restraining her breathing. The effect was so marked, and with no one else about she couldn't pretend it wasn't occasioned by him. Which was nonsensical.

Admittedly, he was dressed in his usual impeccable fashion and was therefore the epitome of an elegant ton gentleman; his coat of Bath superfine was exquisitely cut, his waistcoat of blue and muted silver stripes a study in understated elegance, and his superbly tied cravat would doubtless engender envy in all the younger blades. Nevertheless . . . faintly irritated by such missish susceptibility—she was twenty-nine, for heaven's sake, too old to be affected by the sight of any man— she bundled the sensations aside, and when that didn't work, banished all awareness of them from her mind.

Spotting her, he strolled across, his stride all long-limbed predatory grace; joining her, he smiled and inclined his head in response to her polite nod. "Good morning."

"Indeed. I thought we could sit on that bench over there." Keeping a firm grip on her wayward senses, with her parasol she indicated a park bench, presently unoccupied. "We'll be far enough from the fashionable areas to ensure we won't be interrupted." Starting for the bench, she continued, "I need to get a better idea of the sort of young lady you're looking for, and then we need to devise our campaign to locate her."

Large, lean, and powerful, he strolled beside her. "I can see the sense in the latter, but as to the former, I suspect beggars can't be choosers."

"Nonsense!" Reaching the bench, with a swish of her skirts she sat, and frowned up at him. "You're a Glossup—you can't marry just anyone."

The expression in his eyes suggested he wasn't so sure

about that. "I'm desperate, remember?" He sat beside her and looked out over the manicured lawns.

"Desperate time-wise, perhaps, but not, I fancy, desperate choice-wise."

"I bow to your greater knowledge of my options. So"—he glanced at her—"where do we start?"

Henrietta paused to consider. She'd spent half the night wondering why she'd offered to help him—why she'd felt such a compulsion to do so. Yes, she'd felt obligated, given that the difficulty he now faced was a situation her actions, albeit wholly justified, had inadvertently contributed to. Yes, he was Simon's best friend, and she felt another form of obligation on that score, but she'd finally decided that the greater part of what had moved her had been simple guilt. She'd misjudged him, in her mind even more than via her actions; she'd failed to recognize, let alone credit him with, any sort of honor, yet as a Cynster she knew honor was a sterling quality that not only men valued—ladies, if they had any sense, valued it, too.

And it was very easy to see that the greater part of what was driving him—the primary source of his desperation—was his unquestioning devotion to the welfare of people whose well-being was an obligation he'd unexpectedly inherited. He didn't have to take up that burden, yet he had, and from all she could see, it hadn't even occurred to him to shrug it aside, even though, in reality, he could. His grandaunt's estate aside, he was wealthy enough in his own right to walk away, but he hadn't. He hadn't even thought of it. It was difficult to get much more honorable than that.

Although she wasn't, even now, totally certain as to the entirety of her motives, guilt had, at the very least, weighed heavily in the scale.

Settling more comfortably on the bench, she commanded, "Tell me what traits you don't want, or alternatively that you specifically require, in your bride."

His gaze on the trees and lawns before them, he took a moment to think, then replied, "No flibbertigibbets, no ninnyhammers. And preferably not anyone too young. Whether she has a dowry or not is of no consequence, but as you observed, she should be of good family, preferably of the haut ton. If she can ride, that's a bonus, but social aptitude is, I suspect, a must." He paused, then asked, "What else?"

Henrietta's lips quirked. "You forgot the bit about her being at the very least *passably* pretty, if not a diamond of the first water."

"Ah—but you already knew that." From under heavy lids, he slanted her a glance. "You know me so well."

She humphed. "I know your type well enough, that's true." She mentally reviewed his responses, then asked, "Are there any physical characteristics you prefer? Blond rather than brunette, tall rather than short—that sort of thing."

Dark brown hair, taller than average, soft blue eyes—rather like you. James kept the words from his lips and substituted, "In all honesty I'm more interested in the substance than the package—on what's inside, rather than outward appearance." He glanced at her. "In the circumstances, it's more important that I marry a lady of sound character who accepts me as I am, and accepts the position that I'm offering for what it is, and is willing to devote herself to the position of my wife."

She'd caught his gaze; she searched his eyes, then inclined her head and faced forward. "That's an admirable attitude and an excellent answer." After a moment, she blew out a breath. "So we know what manner of lady we're looking for."

"Now, how do we find her?"

"Did you bring your invitations as I asked?"

He fished in his pocket and drew out the stack of cards he'd received.

She took them, placed them in her lap, and started leafing through them . . . and stopped, frowning. "These aren't sorted."

No . . . "Should they be?"

She glanced at him, perplexed. "How do you keep track?" When he blinked, not quite sure what she meant, she huffed and waved. "No—never mind. Here." She regathered the stack and gave it back to him. "Sort them by date, starting with tonight. And we're only including events at which marriageable ladies of the ton will be present."

"Hmm." That cut out a good half of the invitations he held. Somewhat reluctantly laying the others—the invitations to dine with friends at clubs and the like— aside, he combed through the untidy sheaf, extracting and ordering as she'd instructed.

Meanwhile, she opened her reticule, rummaged inside, and drew out a medium-sized calfskin-bound book. She opened it, smoothed the page, then set it in her lap.

He glanced over and realized the book was her appointment diary. It was roughly five times the size of his and, he noted, had roughly five times the entries for each day.

She waited—with reined patience—for him to reach the end of his sorting. "Right, then," she said as he neatened the pile. "Let's start from this evening." She tapped an entry in her diary. "Do you have an invitation to Lady Marchmain's rout?"

He had. They progressed through the next two weeks, noting those events she deemed most useful for their now-shared purpose for which he already had invitations; where that wasn't the case, she made a note to speak to the relevant hostess. "There's not a single hostess who will refuse to have you, especially if she suspects you're bride-hunting."

"Ah . . ." A horrible vision flooded his mind. "We're not going to make any public declaration of my urgent need for a bride, are we?"

"Not as such." She looked at him—as if measuring how much to tell him, or how best to break bad news. "That said, as you've already been courting Melinda but have parted from her, most will know, or at least, as I said, suspect that you're actively looking about you, but as long as you're with me, under my wing so to speak, I seriously doubt you'll be mobbed."

"Oh—good." He wasn't sure whether to feel reassured or not. After a moment, he added, "I purposely haven't let it get about that I'm under any time constraint. I imagine that if I let my desperation become known, I won't be able to appear in public without attracting a bonneted crowd."

She chuckled. "Very likely. Keeping your deadline a secret is indubitably wise." Returning to her diary, she flipped through the next weeks. "But as to that, as *I* didn't learn you had a deadline even though I learned the rest, I can't imagine any other lady will readily stumble on the information, so you should be safe on that score."

He nodded, then realized she hadn't seen. "Thank you."

She glanced at him, her soft blue eyes glowing, her delicately sculpted, rose-tinted lips curved in an absentminded smile, and he felt a jolt strike his chest, reverberating all the way to the base of his spine, even as he realized just how deeply he'd meant the words.

He trapped her gaze. "And thank you in the broader sense, too. I honestly don't know what I would have done—how I would have forged on—if you hadn't offered to take me and my campaign in hand."

Her smile deepened, her lovely eyes twinkled. "Well, it is something of a challenge, and a different challenge to boot." Shutting her diary, she slipped it into her reticule, then nodded across the lawns. "Now we've defined the essential elements of our campaign, we should make a start on assembling a short list."

He rose as she did. He would have offered his arm, but she lifted her parasol, shook it out, then opened it, angling it to shade her face. Then she looked at him and arched a brow, distinct challenge in her eyes. "Shall we?"

He waved her on, then fell in beside her, strolling bravely, with no outward sign of his inner trepidation, across the lawns toward the Avenue and the carriages now crowding the verges, and the surrounding hordes of fashionably dressed young ladies and elegantly garbed gentlemen chatting and taking the air.

He paced slowly, adjusting his stride to hers. While some wary part of his mind still found it difficult to accept that she—The Matchbreaker—really had agreed to help him, she was indeed there, and was indeed helping him, and he was absurdly grateful for that.

Regardless, he hadn't expected to dream about her last night, yet he had. He couldn't remember the last time he'd dreamed about a specific woman, rather than a womanly figure, yet last night it had definitely been Henrietta in his dreams; it had been her face, her expressions, that had . . . not haunted, but fascinated. That had held his unconscious in thrall.

The dream—dreams—had not been salacious, as most of his dreams of women were. Which was just as well; Henrietta was his best friend's sister, after all. But the tenor of the dream had puzzled him and left him just a tad wary, a touch wondering. His attitude in the dream had felt *worshipful*, but perhaps that had simply been his gratitude manifesting in a different way.

Assuring himself that that was most likely the case, he focused on the rapidly nearing crowds. Dipping his head closer to hers, he murmured, "What should I do?"

"Nothing in particular." She shot him an assessing glance; he appreciated that she was taller than average, so he could easily see her face. "Just relax and follow my lead."

Her tone made him smile. Raising his head, he looked forward. "As you command. Onward—into the breach."

As it transpired, the interactions, the exchanges, flowed more easily than he'd anticipated. Henrietta was so well known she could claim acquaintance with virtually all the older ladies and matrons present, and could thus introduce him, in turn gaining him introductions to the ladies' unmarried charges.

The next hour passed in steady converse. As they were walking between two barouches, temporarily out of hearing of others, Henrietta tugged his sleeve; when he glanced her way inquiringly, she tipped her head toward a knot of people gathered on the lawn twenty yards away. "That's Miss Carmichael. She would have been a good candidate, at least for you to consider, but the latest on-dit is that Sir Peter Affry has grown very particular in his attentions. That's him beside her. As you don't have time to spare, I see no sense in wasting any on Miss Carmichael—I suspect we'll have enough candidates to assess without chasing after one some other perfectly eligible gentleman has all but settled on."

Curious, James looked over Henrietta's dark head, peering past her parasol's edge at the group in question. A fair-haired lady with an abundance of ringlets stood surrounded by a bevy of gentlemen, a much less well-favored young lady by her elbow. The gentleman on the fair beauty's other side was presently scanning the Avenue, but then he looked down at her and smiled. He was a touch older than most of the gentlemen strolling about and had a striking, dark-featured face. James faced forward. "Even I've heard of Affry. Up-and-coming Whig, by all accounts."

"Indeed, but he is only an elected member, after all." Henrietta frowned. "I'm really not sure what all the fuss is about him, but he does seem quite charming."

"Ah, well—charming is as handsome does, or however that saying goes." With a wave, James indicated the group they were approaching. "So, centurion, who do we have here?"

Henrietta smothered a laugh and told him. She continued to guide him about the various groups and was favorably impressed by his behavior and his style. He made charm seem effortless, and his attitude was all relaxed urbanity, polished to a gleam. She might have made the mistake of thinking him a superficial sophisticate—and indeed, that had been her previous, half-formed view—but in the times in between, when they left one group and traveled to the next, he dropped his mask. As they compared impressions of the young ladies they'd encountered, his comments revealed a dry wit and a keenly observant eye, both of which struck a chord with her. Regardless, he was never unkind, not by word or implication, and his behavior never strayed from what she mentally characterized as the quiet, honorable, gentlemanly type.

He had depths she hadn't known he possessed.

Which was distracting enough, but nowhere near as disturbing as the continued insistence of her senses on registering and dwelling on every little nuance of his physical presence. She could only hope that the effect would ease on further acquaintance.

If she'd thought he was in any way affecting her on purpose, she would have cut the connection and left him to find his own bride. But he wasn't doing anything—the silly susceptibility was all hers—and despite his excellent performance that morning, he definitely needed her help.

And, all in all, despite the unsettling repercussions, she was enjoying herself—enjoying the challenge of finding him a bride, and simply enjoying being in his company.

After several further forays into the groups of young ladies parading about the Avenue, they headed for Upper Brook Street. It was half past eleven, and she had a luncheon to attend at noon, and James, apparently, was meeting Simon and their mutual friend, Charlie Hastings, somewhere in the city.

As they turned into Upper Brook Street, she said, "I believe we've made an excellent start." She glanced at James. "Did you see any young lady who you think might be suitable—anyone we should put on your short list?"

Yes—you. Keeping his eyes forward, James scratched his chin and wondered where the devil those words had come from. After a moment, he offered, "Miss Chisolm seems a good sort. And Miss Digby wasn't too far from the mark."

"Hmm. You don't think Miss Digby might be too . . . well, giggly? She does giggle, you know."

"Good God—I hadn't noticed. Strike Miss Digby. But what about Miss Chisolm?"

Henrietta nodded. "On the face of it, I agree—I know nothing about Miss Chisolm that would count against her." She glanced at him. "So Miss Chisolm should go on the short list?"

He hesitated, then forced himself to nod. "Just Miss Chisolm for the nonce." Miss Chisolm was a buxom, good-natured young lady with, he judged, few false notions of life. That said, she wasn't . . . anywhere near as engaging as the lady currently walking by his side.

They reached Lord Arthur Cynster's house, and with a suitable smile and an elegant bow, James parted from Henrietta, promising to meet her that evening at Lady Marchmain's rout. He stood on the pavement and watched her go inside; when the door closed behind her, he turned away and, sliding his hands into his pockets, started strolling toward Grosvenor Square.

As he walked, he consulted his feelings, not something he often did, but in this instance it wasn't hard to define the uncertainty that was itching just under his skin. He really would like to find some way to suggest Henrietta put her own name on his very short short list, but . . . he was deeply aware of just how beholden to her he was. If she took it into her head to take offense at his suggestion and withdrew her support, he'd never find his necessary bride, of that he had no doubt. That morning's excursion had proved beyond question how far out of his element he was in the matter of conventional bride-hunting; if Henrietta had not been there, he'd have managed to gain perhaps two introductions, while with her beside him, he'd lost count.

And he only had four more weeks to find his bride and get the knot tied.

He grimaced. "No—in this, sadly, I have to play safe."

Raising his head, drawing his hands from his pockets, he lengthened his stride. Given he'd spent most of the morning by Henrietta's side, he really should explain to Simon just what he was doing with his younger sister.

She's *what*?" Simon Cynster stared across the table at James, then burst out laughing.

Beside Simon, Charlie Hastings chortled, valiantly attempting to stifle his laughter, then he caught James's long-suffering look and lost the battle; Charlie laughed until tears leaked from his eyes.

Seated at their regular table tucked away in an alcove toward the rear of the main room of the Horse and Whip tavern off the Strand, James waited with feigned patience for his friends' mirth to subside. He'd expected as much, and he could hardly claim to be surprised that his news had been greeted thus.

Eventually catching his breath, Charlie gasped, "Oh, my giddy aunt! Or in this case, your grandaunt."

Still grinning, Simon added, "Who would have believed The Matchbreaker would consent to turn matchmaker—your powers of persuasion, dear boy, continue to impress." Simon raised his ale mug in a toast, then sipped.

"Yes, well." Turning his own mug of foaming ale between his hands, James grimaced. "I suppose you could say my situation is now so desperate, and what with me being so relatively helpless, my appeal engaged her sympathy."

"Hmm." Simon pulled a face as he considered. "I

wouldn't have said Henrietta had much sympathy to spare, at least not for gentlemen of the ton."

So James had gathered from the references Simon had made over the years to his younger sister, only two years younger than Simon's thirty-one yet still unwed, which, now James thought of it, for a Cynster miss was nothing short of extraordinary. Simon himself had married two years ago, when he'd been the same age as Henrietta was now.

The waitress brought the platters they'd ordered, and they settled to eat. Companionable silence reigned for several minutes.

Charlie broke it, glancing up from his pie to confirm, "So it's all off with Melinda, then?"

James nodded. "Completely and utterly. Nothing further for me there. Seemed she was set on a love-match, so, as Henrietta pointed out, we really wouldn't have suited."

Simon nodded. "A lucky escape, then." He chewed, swallowed. "So what has Henrietta suggested?"

James inwardly sighed and told them.

They guffawed again.

James rolled his eyes and thought of how much more they would laugh if he confessed to the rather more particular thoughts he'd started to entertain regarding The Matchbreaker.

But even after Simon and Charlie sobered, neither suggested that following Henrietta's plan was unwise.

Simon waved his fork. "There is, after all, the time element."

"Indeed." Charlie nodded. "You can't afford to dither, and Henrietta, at least, will have no burning desire to steer you in one direction over any other."

Simon nodded, too, looking down at his plate. "She'll have no particular agenda of her own."

Which was precisely the point James would like to alter. While they turned their attention to cleaning their plates, he revisited all Simon had ever let fall of Henrietta's attitude to gentlemen of the ton.

By all accounts, she held a rather low opinion of gentlemen like him, albeit in general, rather than specifically. However, he'd already shown her he was the sort of gentleman who would approach marriage cold-bloodedly, and, despite her agreement to help him, she'd viewed his approach to Melinda as him being less than truthful. Although he'd had sound reasons for that, not all of which he'd explained, the die had been cast; Henrietta's view of him was now likely fixed. As for her own expectations, being a Cynster, and regardless of her revelations of having supported non-love-matches for others, for herself Henrietta would want what all Cynster young ladies wanted—a marriage based on love.

Cynsters married for love. That was, apparently, an unbending law of fate, one that could not be, and never had been, broken. Simon, for instance, was very definitely in love with his erstwhile social arch-nemesis, now his wife, Portia. Even James had known that Simon had long been in love with Portia; only Simon and Portia had apparently failed to notice, and it had taken them years—and two dead bodies and a murderer—to open their eyes.

Simon stirred and pushed aside his empty plate. Charlie followed suit; James had already set his plate aside. Without a word, they drained their mugs, then rose, paid their shot at the bar, tipped the smiling waitress, and strolled out into the early afternoon sunshine.

They ambled along the Strand, back toward Mayfair. They'd been friends for so long that they didn't need to talk constantly; their silences felt comfortable to them.

Sauntering along shoulder to shoulder with Simon, James let his gaze roam while inwardly weighing his options. He understood, or at least he thought he did, what Henrietta's view of him currently must be. Was there any way he could rescript that view and get her to see him in a better light?

A light sufficiently flattering that she might entertain an offer from him to fill the position he had vacant?

At least she already knew all the details, and as she was a Cynster, he could trust that she would be reasonable and amenable to rational persuasion, but . . . the not-so-small hurdle of falling in love remained.

No more than the next man did he have any idea how one accomplished that—how one fell in love—but given it was Henrietta who, even among the competing claims of the hordes of young ladies along the Avenue, had remained the unwavering focus of his attention, he was increasingly inclined, admittedly recklessly, to give love a try.

Who knew? It might suit him.

It might get him where he wanted to go, might gain him what he most truly wanted of life but had thought—given his grandaunt's will—that he no longer had any hope of attaining.

For all he knew, the possibility might be there.

If only he could fathom how to make her look at him—truly look at him and see him for what he was—and then fall in love with him . . .

Who was he deceiving now? She wouldn't fall in love with him, not spontaneously, not unless he made an obvious push to gain her regard, but in doing that, in making such a push, he would risk losing her help with his quest, his search for his necessary bride.

Simon glanced at him. "So how do you feel about this latest tack?"

"Stymied." He didn't meet Simon's eyes.

Charlie clapped him on the shoulder. "Never mind—it'll all work out. You'll see."

James hoped so, because, regardless of all else, he had the futures of a small army to ensure.

Chapter Three

Lady Marchmain's rout was one of the traditional highlights of the Season. That said, it wasn't an event patronized by the very young ladies only just out, but rather by those no longer caught up in the first flush of the Marriage Mart. Among the sea of well-coiffed heads gleaming beneath the crystal chandeliers, in between the black-clad shoulders of fashionable gentlemen in evening attire and the stunning gowns in more intense hues worn by dashing matrons and more mature ladies, could be glimpsed the definite-yet-still-pastel-colored creations favored by young ladies with several Seasons under their belts but as yet no offer for their hands.

"Just as I thought." Clad in blue silk in a shade deeper than her eyes, Henrietta tipped her head toward the melee, then leaned closer to James, standing alongside her, the better to be heard over the din created by hundreds of wagging tongues. "We're sure to find several good candidates in this crowd."

James eyed the shifting throng with a jaundiced eye. "The trick will be winkling them out from the herd."

"Never fear." Eyes sparkling, Henrietta grinned, transparently in her element. "Trust me—it won't be that difficult."

They were standing by one side of the massive ball-room, with a wall of long windows at their backs. Beyond the windows lay a wide lawn rolling down to a stream; the darkening shadows of extensive gardens stretched into the distance beyond.

Marchmain House stood outside London proper, at a bend along the river near Chiswick. James had arrived reasonably early, wanting to be there when Henrietta walked in. He'd assumed she would be attending with her mother and sister, but instead she'd appeared at the top of the steps leading down into the ballroom alone; a slender figure in the blue silk gown that echoed the soft shade of her eyes, a gold-spangled shawl draped over her elbows, she'd instantly commanded his attention. He'd watched her greet Lady Marchmain, a motherly lady of the grande dame variety, with open affection, then move on to peck Lord Marchmain's cheek before, with a laugh, descending to the ballroom.

James had been waiting for her by the bottom step.

The smile she'd bestowed on him when her gaze had alighted on him—the quick glance she'd sent skating over him and the approval that had flared in her eyes—had left him feeling a tad off-balance. Knocked askew. How he was supposed to command his unruly senses to focus on any other young lady was beyond his comprehension.

But . . . "There's Miss Alcock." Henrietta shifted closer still to point out a young lady in an apple green gown. "We should definitely consider her. And . . ." She wove away, then back, peering past the shoulders, simultaneously playing havoc with James's distracted senses; her perfume, a subtle blend of citrus and rose, wreathed his brain and trapped his wits. "Yes, that's

Miss Ellingham over there—I had hoped she would be here."

Henrietta turned to him. "Come along. I'll introduce you, and then, unless I miss my guess, and I rarely do, the musicians will start playing and the dancing will begin, and there's no better opportunity to assess a young lady than while you're waltzing with her."

Inwardly grim, he nodded. Wondering just what she meant by "assess"—what criteria did she think he might explore?—he manfully accompanied her into the crush.

Within ten feet, he'd been forcibly reminded just why he normally avoided such events. It was heavy going, tacking this way and that through the shifting mass, trying to keep alongside Henrietta while simultaneously not taking her arm. Time and again, when they paused to exchange greetings, occasionally stopping to chat, he was forced to clasp his hands behind his back simply to stop himself from reaching for her arm and drawing her protectively nearer.

Many young ladies would have shrunk toward him, would have relied on him to steer them through the throng, but Henrietta was entirely at home amid the surging bodies and forged ahead unperturbed; in this arena, she needed no protection. If anything, the shoe was on the other foot, and he needed hers.

That was a reality played out again and again, one that subtly grated on some heretofore unregistered instinct.

Yet she was as good as her word, and he found himself standing beside her in the circle in which pretty Miss Alcock stood animatedly chatting. When the first strains of the violins floated out above the heads, it was a simple matter to request Miss Alcock's hand. With a sweet smile, Miss Alcock accepted, and he led her to the dance floor—all too conscious of Henrietta's encourag-

ing smile following him into and through the resulting
waltz.

From there, the evening progressed with Henrietta
steering him into circle after circle, guiding him to one
potential candidate after another. He danced with Miss
Chisolm, whom he'd met in the park that morning, and
also with Miss Downtree and Miss Ellingham.

By the time he drew Miss Swinson into his arms and
started them revolving, his conversational gambits had
grown somewhat tired. At least to him. Luckily, Miss
Swinson found his deliberately charming smile and his
pleasant inquiry as to how she was enjoying the evening
entirely appropriate.

"It's the devil of a crush, isn't it? Oh!" Her eyes
rounded, then filled with rueful laughter. "Pray excuse
me! I know I shouldn't say that—devil, I mean—but
with so many brothers, it just slips out."

James grinned quite sincerely. "Pray don't censor
your words on my account."

She tipped her head, regarding him, then asked, the
laughter still in her eyes, "In that case—are *you* enjoying the evening? It seems an unlikely event to attract
one such as you."

"You are clearly perspicacious. I have to admit that
I'm finding the crush rather draining."

"Yes, well, it is one of the main events of the Season,
at least for all those not immersed in the Marriage
Mart." As they whirled, a ripple of reaction among
the other dancers distracted Miss Swinson; she looked
across, then returned her gaze to James's face. "A case
in point—that was Sir Peter Affry and the lovely Dulcimea Thorne waltzing by. Word is that he's dangling
after Cassandra Carmichael, but Dulcimea isn't one to
let any other steal a march on her."

The revolutions of the waltz brought the couple in question into James's sight. He recognized the gentleman Henrietta had pointed out that morning, and took due note of the predatory way Miss Thorne had all but draped herself over Sir Peter, the niceties of proper waltzing etiquette notwithstanding. "Miss Thorne certainly appears to be making a strong argument for Sir Peter's attention."

As they whirled again, Miss Swinson craned her neck to see. "It'll be all over the at-homes tomorrow morning, no doubt."

James could almost find it in him to be grateful to Sir Peter and his pursuit of the beauteous Miss Carmichael; with all eyes, however discreetly, watching the developments between Sir Peter and Miss Thorne, no one was inclined to pay all that much attention to the strange circumstance of one of the ton's acknowledged wolves running on The Matchbreaker's leash.

Henrietta watched from the sidelines. Although she maintained her part in a steady stream of conversations, she was aware that James remained the true cynosure of her senses, even while he was circling the dance floor with another lady. She wasn't sure she approved of her senses' apparent fixation, but she wasn't particularly adept at lying to herself; that moment when she'd seen him as she'd walked down the stairs . . . if she'd been carrying a fan, she would have used it.

James Glossup in evening attire, looking up at her, his lovely brown eyes, their soulfulness tonight entirely unmarred by temper, fixed on her, was a sight designed to make her heart leap, then speed into a ridiculous cadence, to make her lungs seize and her wits grow giddy . . . luckily he couldn't know the effect he had on her. She was perfectly sure no good would come of him gaining such revealing knowledge.

Indeed, when it came to that, she wasn't at all sure *she* wanted to know—in fact, she wasn't at all certain what her strange reaction implied.

The waltz currently in progress ended. James bowed to Miss Swinson, raised her from her curtsy, and escorted her back to the group where Henrietta, still chatting easily, waited. As he released Miss Swinson and took up his previous position by Henrietta's side, she surreptitiously arched a brow at him. He saw it, but other than briefly meeting her eyes, he didn't respond.

Once the group had re-formed, at her instigation they excused themselves and moved on into the, if anything even denser, crowd. "Now . . ." She looked about her with what was fast becoming feigned interest. "Who can we assess next?"

She felt James glance at her, then he murmured, leaning close so she could hear, so the waft of his breath swept the shell of her ear and sent shivery tingles coursing down her spine, "Perhaps we should take a moment to compare notes—before I forget which of my observations refer to whom."

"Yes, of course. An excellent thought." Her voice was weak, nearly breathless. She cleared her throat and dragged in a breath. "I could do with a break from the relentless conversations. Can you see a spot where we might talk without being overheard?"

The next instant, his fingers closed about her elbow. She very nearly startled, shocked by her instant response to his touch, totally innocent though it was. Heat and a sensation that strung her nerves tight streaked up her arm, then spread in a slow wave through her, dissipating, yet in its wake leaving her aware as she'd never been before. Aware of the heat and solidity of his body close beside her in the crush. Aware of the strength in his hand, his fingers, even though he was barely touching her gloved arm.

She glanced at him. He'd straightened and was looking over the heads, searching for a solution to her request. She could only hope he'd missed her odd reaction entirely; she didn't think she'd actually jumped.

Once again, she rued the fact she'd long ago given up carrying a fan.

"There's an alcove over there. Not large, and no potted palm to hide behind, but at least it should get us out of this accursed crush."

She summoned enough strength to say with passable normality, "Lead on."

He didn't, of course—he steered her on—but he knew what he was doing, and in short order they'd laid claim to the shallow alcove at the end of the room, and could breathe more freely. Even though the long windows had been propped open to the night, with so many now crammed into the ballroom, fresh air was in short supply.

"I'd forgotten how the perfumes rise with the heat, then coalesce into a miasma." James glanced at her, straight-faced. "You're not feeling faint, are you?"

She almost bridled. "Good heavens, no! It's only a ball."

She saw his lips twitch and realized he'd been teasing her.

But all he said was, "Good to know that you're not the fainting sort. Miss Alcock, however, apparently is, so I think we can leave her name off our short list. Swooning females can be distinctly wearying."

"Indeed. But what about Miss Chisolm, now you've danced with her?"

"She . . . can remain on the list, at least for the nonce."

They went through the other young ladies with whom he'd spent time, but other than Miss Downtree, none had passed muster with him. Henrietta frowned. "I had hoped we'd find more candidates here, but at least we still have two."

"Hmm."

She glanced sharply at him; he was looking out over the crowd and didn't seem overly concerned with what she considered their still too short short list. She wondered what was distracting him; he certainly seemed to be thinking about something else.

As if he'd read her mind, he murmured, "Actually, I'm rather amazed the pair of us, given the unlikeliness of my appearance here, let alone what by now must have been noted as your assistance, haven't raised more eyebrows."

"Ah—that's because I took care to plant the right seeds at luncheon and at the three teas I attended this afternoon."

He glanced down at her. "*Three* teas?"

She shrugged. "I wanted to spread the word widely enough."

"And what was that word?"

"That I've agreed to help you look over the field because your mother is so rarely in town these days and isn't here at the moment, nor expected up this Season, and as your next nearest useful connection—correct me if I'm wrong—is Lady Osbaldestone?" She paused and arched a brow at him. When he looked appalled, but nodded, she went on, "Well, given that, it wasn't all that hard to suggest that after your retreat from Melinda Wentworth, you turned to me, Simon's sister and someone very well acquainted with the unmarried young ladies of the ton, for assistance. Mind you, I took care to paint your interest as being merely idle—the sort of thing a gentleman might do at a certain age, that sort of thing."

"So you concealed that I have a deadline looming?"

She nodded decisively. "You were perfectly correct in thinking it won't do for the matchmakers to get wind of that. If instead they believe you have nothing more than a vague interest in matrimony, they won't rush you all at once in case you balk, fling up your hands in horror, and run away to the country."

"Ah—I think I'm getting the hang of this now. They'll happily parade their charges before me in the park and at whatever events I attend, but they won't see any pressing need to force their charges' claims to my attention down my wolfish throat."

"Precisely." She paused, then allowed, "Actually, it doesn't hurt at all that you are an acknowledged wolf. It makes them think twice before offering up any of the very young and truly innocent."

James laughed—he couldn't help it. "What a very nice way of putting me in my place—and ensuring I remain tame."

"I wasn't so much thinking in terms of 'tame'—more of a wolf in sheep's clothing."

Before he could reply to that piece of impertinence, the strains of a waltz filled the air—and his response was there, ready-made, before him. He turned to her, bowed, and held out his hand. "I believe that's our waltz."

"What?" She looked stunned. "No . . . that is—" She dragged in a breath. "You should waltz with one of the possible candidates for your short list."

He watched as she looked about, searching the throng

almost desperately. "Henrietta—it's just a waltz. And I'm tired of having to converse appropriately and otherwise assess my partners. Come and put me out of my misery, and let me enjoy one waltz for the evening." He made the last words sound almost whiny, a plea for relief—all pretense, of course. The notion of this waltz—of waltzing with her—had been fermenting in his brain since he'd first set eyes on her as she'd descended the ballroom steps.

He'd promised himself this in payment for his earlier toeing of her line. He'd done as she'd asked, now it was her turn to play to his rules.

She glanced at him uncertainly, then her resistance fell. "Oh, very well." She resettled her shawl, then reached out and set her gloved hand in his.

He closed his fingers about her slender digits and felt triumph surge inside. But it was such a small win—just a waltz, nothing more.

Holding her hand high, he led her onto the clearing dance floor, then turned and swept her into his arms, and into the swirling pleasures of the dance. Capturing her gaze, letting his own lock with the soft blue, he let his lips curve, appreciative and encouraging, sensed the lithe tension in her svelte form, and gave himself up to the heady delight—and drew her with him.

He was a past master at the art of circling a ton dance floor, of using the waltz to his own ends . . . but tonight, he discovered, the shoe was on the other foot, and the waltz used him. Worked on him, certainly, and on her, too; he couldn't recall ever being so immersed in the moment, so caught in the effortless action, in the swooping glide, the swirling turns, the sheer power that flowed when he had her—Henrietta—in his arms.

It had never been like this before; no waltz had ever captured him before. His senses had coalesced and locked, fixed, so deeply engaged with her and the moment that there was nothing left of him, of his awareness, for anything else. The world fell away, and they were the only two people revolving down the floor, and he was lost, trapped, in her eyes.

Caught, ensnared, by the effortless way she matched him, light on her feet, instantly responsive to every subtle direction he gave. He hadn't expected her to be . . . such a perfect match.

She, and the waltz, took his breath away.

He'd wanted a distraction from the other young ladies, a reward for his diligent application over the past hours, and she'd agreed and given him all he'd wished for; wholly focused on her, on the waltz, on the welling pleasure, he shut his mind to all else and enjoyed.

Henrietta couldn't catch her breath, but not breathing didn't seem to matter. She felt light as thistledown, floating and swooping in a deliciously delightful way—carried in his arms, swept along by his strength, cradled and protected and powerfully directed, yet free in a way she'd never felt before. As if her senses had expanded and broken their fetters and were no longer restricted to the mundane world.

The waltz was eye-opening on several fronts. She'd waltzed times without number, with gentlemen beyond count, but none before had held the key to this new and novel and wholly beguiling landscape. The sensations of his hand firmly clasping her fingers, of his other hand at her back, entirely correctly supporting her yet with his touch all but burning through the layers of fine silk, registered, impinged, yet they were only one set of waves amid a sea. The brush of his thigh between hers as they whisked through a tight turn, the sheer power of their movement up the floor, thrilled in ways she hadn't before experienced.

And she was enthralled. This was waltzing at a different level, of a different degree.

Some part of her levelheaded mind wanted to observe and catalog each aspect, yet his eyes were on hers, and the tug of the soul that shone through the brown tempted and lured, and she dispensed with all anchors to reality and let herself follow him, let her senses soar.

Let the dance, and him, sweep her away.

Into uninhibited enjoyment.

When the music finally ended and they whirled to a halt, and, breathless, she had to step out of his arms and curtsy, all she felt was disappointment that the moment had ended.

That they were back in the real world, with its attendant demands.

"Thank you." She could have waltzed with him for at least another hour; she smiled in honest and open appreciation. "That was indeed a pleasure."

He was watching her, as if seeing her anew, but he inclined his head and smiled easily in reply. "It was." He looked around, surveying the crowd about them. "Perhaps we could simply stroll for a while, without any defined agenda?"

She was ready enough to set aside looking for more young ladies, at least for the moment. "If you wish."

He offered his arm. She hesitated for only an instant before accepting and placing her hand on his sleeve; she'd managed to survive a waltz, after all. And if her fingers tingled at the feel of the hard muscle beneath his sleeve, and her still giddy senses purred at the sensations engendered by him standing so close, crowded even closer by the press of bodies all around, she would, she decided, find some way to cope.

They strolled easily, joining this circle, then that, stopping to chat with acquaintances—some hers, many his, most known to them both. Neither of them was all that young and, socially, they moved in similar circles.

Henrietta relaxed, and found herself enjoying the interactions, engaged and drawn in, both wits and senses more acute, heightened in an unusual way as she bantered with James, even outright flirted, exchanging views and barbed comments, her attention wholly focused on him . . . they'd been strolling and chatting for nearly half an hour before the warmth of the necklace, especially of the rose-quartz pendant dangling above her breasts, registered, and she remembered she was wearing the charm. . . .

Oh, God! She stared at James, who at that moment was speaking with George Ferguson and thankfully didn't see her sudden shock. But even as she tore her gaze away and schooled her features into a pleasantly smiling mask, her mind was scrambling, tripping . . . this couldn't be what she was thinking, could it?

Hell and the devil, could it be?

Was the damned necklace working on her after all?

She didn't know whether to feel aghast or ecstatic. But when she looked again at James . . . it was as if the proverbial scales fell from her eyes and she saw him in an entirely different light, from an entirely new perspective.

The shift in view was disorienting.

But before she'd done more than frame the obvious

questions—What should she do now? Should she act on her newfound understanding, and if so, how?—a stentorian bellow of "Ladies and gentlemen!" rolled across the room.

Conversations broke off and the crowd turned toward the source of the salutation—Lady Marchmain's butler, standing to rigid attention at the top of the steps leading down into the ballroom.

Alongside her butler, Lady Marchmain stood beaming. She raised both arms in a commanding gesture. "Friends, all, it's time for the highlight of our evening— the fireworks! If you could all make your way onto the lawn—and yes, the best view will, as usual, be had from the bridge over the stream. If you would?" Her ladyship made a sweeping gesture, directing the crowd out of the French doors that had been opened to the terrace and the lawn beyond.

As one, the crowd turned and obediently started shuffling out.

With James, George, and the others in their group, Henrietta had been standing not far from the long windows; they were among the first to gain the terrace. They descended quickly to the lawn and strode toward the wide stone arch that spanned the stream bordering the other side of the lawn.

On James's arm, grateful for his support amid the jostling throng, Henrietta leaned closer to say, "Head for the left side of the bridge—the fireworks will be set off from the gardens further down the stream on that side."

"Good notion," George, walking on James's other side, replied.

Their group, all much of an age, lengthened their strides, picked up their pace, and succeeded in claiming a prime position on the bridge, not as far as the top of the arch but along the raised stone side to the left. Although ancient, the bridge had been built wide enough to allow drays to pass, and so could accommodate quite a crowd across its span. There were, however, more guests than there was space on the bridge; as, eager to gain the best view, more people squeezed on, the crowd shifted and rippled, and Henrietta, James, and the others found themselves strung out in single file along the bridge's side.

While the bridge was solid enough, the low stone sides reached only to the top of Henrietta's calves; she shuffled into a better, more balanced stance. Beside her, the side of his arm pressed to her shoulder, James glanced at her, sharply assessing in a protective way; the press of the crowd had forced him to lower his arm. Settled and stable, she smiled reassuringly back. He met her eyes, then his lips curved just a touch, and together they looked out over the swiftly running stream to the swath of dark gardens further along the bank.

As if detecting some inexplicable sign, the crowd quieted.

A brief flare broke the darkness, then the first rocket hissed and surged into the sky, trailing tongues of flame as it soared into the velvet blackness before exploding in a corona of golden light, throwing out a shower of bright red and gold sparks that slowly fell, winking out as they trailed back to earth.

A communal "ah" of appreciative delight welled from the watching crowd.

They all stood with their faces upturned, watching successive fireworks light up the sky. A particularly bright rocket had just exploded when someone in the crowd behind Henrietta slipped and staggered, causing others to jerk and turn, some crying out in surprise.

Henrietta glanced around, started to turn—

A sudden shove sent the lady and gentleman behind her cannoning into her.

Henrietta tipped—fought for balance.

Lost.

On a gasp, she fell—desperately, she reached for help. For James.

She saw his shocked face, saw him reach for her, but they were both too late.

On her back, she hit the water with a splash, and sank into the racing stream.

In the instant before the waters closed over her face, she managed to get her lungs to work enough to haul in a breath. She held it and struggled to right herself and regain the surface.

But the stream was running high—there'd been rain earlier in the week—and this close to the river, the streamlets had coalesced and were racing strongly for the Thames; the tumbling waters tossed her like flotsam and dragged at her limbs. Her skirts trapped her legs; her spangled shawl tangled her arms.

I can swim!

She screamed that at herself, fought desperately to push away the enveloping panic.

But—oh, God!—the currents were so strong, and she could already feel the cold sinking into her flesh, feel heat and strength leaching away.

Still she fought.

On the bridge, horrified beyond thought, James dallied only long enough to toe off his shoes and jerk off his coat before diving into the swiftly running stream. Henrietta had already disappeared, swallowed by the darkness and the rushing, tumbling waters. The stream might be only ten yards wide, but this close to the river it was deep.

James struck out strongly, swimming downstream as fast as he could, trusting that she would be flailing at least enough for him to find her in the dark.

He didn't let himself think—couldn't afford to let the myriad thoughts shrieking in his brain distract him . . . he only allowed one through. He couldn't afford to lose Henrietta.

He didn't fight the current but harnessed it and let it sweep him on. Panic was nibbling at the edge of his mind when he sensed movement in the water ahead— and then he was on her.

Reaching for her, he scooped an arm around her waist, caught her firmly to him, then surfaced, hauling her up before him.

Her face broke free of the water and she gasped and dragged in air, and he all but sagged with relief.

"Stop struggling!" He had to shout to be heard over the noise of the stream and the cacophony coming from the shocked guests, many of whom were now streaming along the banks.

She gasped again, then he felt her fight her own instincts, trying to ease back from her panic.

"That's right," he encouraged, gathering her even closer. "Just relax—go limp—and let me get us to the bank."

She complied as best she could, but by the time he managed to angle them out of the raging currents and over to the bank, she was tense and shivering uncontrollably.

His feet finally found solid ground, but that wasn't the end of the ordeal. Kneeling in the shallows, holding her close, trying to impart some of his own fading warmth to her while simultaneously shielding her with his body, he had to wait while Lady Marchmain and her staff shooed the onlookers back and away. The staff had brought flares, the light from which James and Henrietta would need to climb the bank safely, but the water had turned her gown all but transparent, and on top of everything else she didn't need to feature in tomorrow's more scandalous on-dits.

Lady Marchmain wasn't a major hostess because she couldn't rise to the challenge of a near disaster averted. In strident tones, she ordered all her other guests back to the house and waited, hands on broad hips, until they complied. Then Lord Marchmain came puffing up with the blankets he'd clearly been dispatched to fetch. He handed them over to his wife with a meek "Anything else, dear?"

"Yes," her ladyship snapped. She pointed imperiously at the house. "Get all those malingerers inside, and then send them home. It was an accident, but thanks to James, Henrietta is safe, and they're both in my hands, so there's nothing more for the others to see, and they can all go home with my blessing."

In the weak light, James couldn't tell if Lord Marchmain smiled, but he sounded quite chuffed when he said, "Yes, dear. At once." Turning on his heel, his lordship strode away into the darkness, back toward the house.

Lady Marchmain came down the bank as far as she dared. Setting the blankets down, she shook one out and held it wide. "There, now. Out you get, Henrietta— we'll have you up to the house and into a hot bath in no time."

James glanced down at the bedraggled lady he was

still holding securely in his arms. He met her gaze, saw her lips weakly curve, then she nodded and, together, they struggled to their feet and clambered up the bank.

As Lady Marchmain decreed, so it was done. By the time, wrapped in the blankets but shivering hard, they staggered into the house—led to a private side entrance by her ladyship—carriages were rolling in a steady stream up to the front door, and then away down the drive and back out onto the road to London.

"I don't know what Louise will say if I allow you to catch a chill—either of you." Lady Marchmain shepherded them through the library, into a corridor, and around to a secondary stair, apparently unconcerned by the trail of drips they were leaving behind.

James still had his arm around Henrietta, and she was leaning against his side. She didn't think she'd yet regained sufficient strength to stand on her own, much less walk. Much, much less climb the stairs.

She'd never have made it if not for James . . . she shuddered as she realized just how true those words were. Whether she would have made it out of the stream alone . . . in truth, she didn't think she would have.

Once on the first floor, Lady Marchmain led her to a bedchamber ablaze with light and with a huge tub already half filled with steaming water. "There, now, dear—lean on me." Sliding her arm around Henrietta, her ladyship drew her away from James. "James, dear, there's another bath and some of my son's clothes waiting for you next door."

James nodded.

Henrietta met his gaze. She couldn't yet find the strength to say thank you, but she let her eyes say it for her.

He smiled slightly and nodded at her to go on.

Turning, she allowed Lady Marchmain to steer her into the room. Two maids were waiting to help her strip off her ruined gown. About to step into the tub, she remembered, and suddenly frantic again, raised a hand to her throat—but the necklace was still there. She sighed with relief and climbed into the tub.

On a soft groan, she sat, then slid deeper into the welcoming warmth.

Lady Marchmain, deeming herself in loco parentis, fussed. More than an hour passed before Henrietta, dressed in a warm day gown appropriated from her ladyship's daughter's wardrobe and further bundled up in a warm pelisse, with a knitted scarf about her throat and wound over her still damp hair, with someone's half boots on her feet, was allowed to walk down the main stairs to where James and Lord Marchmain waited in the front hall.

Henrietta noted that, although decently clad, the clothes James wore fell far short of his usual standards of sartorial excellence, a point over which he seemed supremely unconcerned.

His attention was all for her, his gaze streaking over her as if to reassure himself that she was indeed all right, taking close note of the way she moved, checking that she'd sustained no injury.

Beside James, Lord Marchmain beamed encouragingly.

James's gaze returned to her face; he caught her eye, then swept her a bow. "Your carriage awaits, my lady."

It was clearly an attempt to get things back on an even keel. She found a smile and inclined her head. "Thank you." Her voice was slightly gruff, a touch hoarse. Turning to Lady Marchmain, she made her farewells, assuring her ladyship for the umpteenth time that she was indeed entirely recovered, and by tomorrow morning would be fully restored to her customary rude health.

After various repeated assurances from both her and James, they were finally allowed to climb into her parents' carriage. The door was shut, the coachman gave his horses the office, and finally, finally, they were rolling home.

She sank back against the squabs with a sigh. "That was an adventure."

Seated beside her, James replied, "One I, for one, could have done without." After a moment, he asked, "What exactly happened?"

He'd taken her hand to help her up into the carriage, and had followed close behind; he hadn't released her fingers. His were still wrapped about them, his grip gentle, but warm and strong.

Reassuring. On multiple levels.

Making no effort to retrieve her hand, she thought back to the moments on the bridge. After replaying them several times, she shook her head. "Whatever caused it, it happened at least two people away from me. It seemed that someone tripped, or slipped and fell." She thought some more, then said, "It was an accident—unforeseeable and unavoidable."

"Hmm. Well, I heard Lord Marchmain giving orders to his steward to get an ironmonger in to look at putting up railings on the bridge, so I doubt that such an accident will happen again."

She let a mile roll past in the comfortable dark, then said, "Thank you. I . . . am not at all sure I would have managed to get out of the stream on my own. And the Thames was only a hundred yards away."

He glanced at her through the dimness. His thumb stroked gently, apparently absentmindedly, over the back of her hand. After a moment, he shifted and looked forward. "You don't need to thank me. You're helping me, so of course I helped you. That's what friends are for."

Friends? Is that what they were? He didn't, she noted, let go of her hand.

Would a friend still be holding her hand, as he was? Would a friend have held her so tightly to him, as he had held her in the stream?

Would a friend have been nearly as terrified as she had been that she might drown?

She was too exhausted to work out the answers, much less define what she would prefer them to be. So she sat in the dimness of the carriage, his hand wrapped about hers, his presence beside her reassuring and anchoring, and looked out of the carriage window, watching as the outskirts of London gradually gave way to the streetscapes of the capital.

Eventually, the carriage drew up outside her parents' house.

Reluctantly, James released her hand, opened the door and stepped down, then offered his hand again to help her to the pavement. He escorted her up the steps, using the moment to scan her face in the better light from the nearby streetlamp. She was still a trifle too pale for his liking, but otherwise she appeared to have recovered from her ordeal.

Inwardly, he suspected, she would still be shocked; he knew he was.

Gaining the top step, she turned to him. Drawing her hand from his, she met his eyes. "Again—thank you."

He inclined his head, unable, for once, to find a flippant reply. "I'm just glad I was there." *And so very glad I was able to reach you in time*.

Her lips curved lightly, then she gestured to the carriage. "Please—use the carriage to go home."

He shook his head, smiled faintly. "I'm only in George Street—the walk will clear my head."

She hesitated, but then nodded. "Very well. What have we organized for tomorrow . . . oh, I remember. Lady Jersey's alfresco luncheon. If we leave here at eleven we should make it in good time."

He frowned. "Are you sure you'll be well enough?"

"Of course." She looked faintly offended. "Falling into the stream was a shock, but I'll be entirely recovered by tomorrow."

He raised his brows, but capitulated. "If you're sure."

"I am—and we can't afford to dally in assembling your short list. We really should try to have the best candidate selected by the end of this week." She inclined her head in farewell. "Good night. And . . ." Holding his gaze, she paused, then softly said, "Thank you." Turning away, she opened the door.

He watched her go inside, raised a hand in salute when she glanced back as the door swung shut. When the latch clicked into place, he turned around and went down the steps. Waving off the coachman, telling him he'd elected to walk, James wriggled his shoulders, settling the not-so-well-fitting coat, then set off for George Street, striding briskly along.

He wasn't cold, yet he still felt chilled inside; the shock of nearly—so *very* nearly—losing Henrietta wasn't going to fade anytime soon. Still, he had found her, rescued her, and they were both hale and whole, and he was inexpressibly grateful for whatever fate had smiled on them.

Which fact very neatly led him to the question he was going to have to find an answer to soon: How long could he pretend—to himself, to her, and to everyone else—that he wasn't falling, in whatever way there was to fall, for The Matchbreaker?

Head down, eyes fixed unseeing on the pavement ahead of him, he strode quickly home.

Chapter Four

The next day, they reached Osterley Park, on the outskirts of the capital, just before noon.

Lady Jersey greeted them with open arms. "My dears! The hero and heroine of the hour—you *must* tell me all about your ordeal."

Henrietta exchanged a cynical glance with James; neither was surprised by her ladyship's demand. Nicknamed "Silence," Lady Jersey was an inveterate gossip and, not having been present at the rout the previous evening but overseeing a ball at Almack's instead, she was simply avid to hear the story from the best possible source.

"It was merely an accident," Henrietta informed her. "There were too many of us squeezed onto the bridge— the one over the stream that gives the best view of the fireworks—and I was accidentally tipped off."

"And James here jumped in and rescued you." Lady Jersey sent James an arch glance, then drew back to examine Henrietta. "Well, you don't appear to have taken any lasting harm, which is the main thing." Her ladyship's somewhat protuberant eyes shifted again to James, and she smiled. "And James had the chance to play knight-errant to your fair maiden." Lady Jersey's smile deepened and she looked back at Henrietta. "Excellent! Now you must come and join the others—we're gathering in the conservatory. Once everyone arrives, we'll head off on our ramble."

They allowed themselves to be ushered into the conservatory, then Lady Jersey whisked back to greet more arrivals, leaving them to the mercies of those already assembled.

Immediately, they were besieged, not just by matrons willing to be appalled by the horrors of a near brush with death but even more by the many unmarried young ladies present, all eager to vicariously experience a real life-and-death rescue.

James would have slunk away, would have run away if he'd been able—*anything* rather than face the bright eyes of the young ladies so eager to ooh and aah over his manly exploits—but even though Henrietta seemed to be bearing up well, he didn't want to, couldn't make himself, quit her side. Even when she cast him a sidelong glance, then embarked on a more colorful rendition of his rescue of her for the edification of Miss Chisolm, Miss Griffiths, and Miss Sweeney, he stoically endured and remained beside her, and pretended not to hear.

When, finally, everyone had heard the tale and the surrounding hordes thinned enough to let them wander, he caught Henrietta's hand, anchored it on his sleeve, and strolled down one of the many avenues of palms and potted plants arranged about the well-stocked conservatory. He glanced at her face. "Are you all right?"

Reliving the horror again and again could hardly be pleasant.

But she nodded. "Yes." Glancing up, she met his eyes. "I expected the interest, and with any luck, that should be the worst of it behind us."

"Hmm." He studied her eyes, then looked ahead.

"Next time we're about to walk into an inquisition like that, do, please, warn me."

She chuckled.

"And," he went on, "I'm not at all sure I approve of being labeled a Sir Galahad. I'm not even certain Sir Galahad could swim."

"It's the principle of the thing." She hesitated, then looked up at him and said, "And I assure you it will do your quest no harm to be painted in such a light."

"Hmm." How to break it to her that he wasn't all that keen on impressing even the buxom Miss Chisolm? Not now. "I'm . . . not sure that—"

Henrietta pinched his arm, then smiled amiably as Mrs. Julian and her niece, Miss Chester, walked by. Once the pair were past, Henrietta murmured, "They all have ears, you know. And, incidentally, what about Miss Chester?"

James glanced down at her. "She's too thin."

Henrietta blinked. "I wouldn't have labeled her thin—fashionably willowy, perhaps."

"Thin," James insisted; when she glanced up, he'd looked ahead, but she saw his jaw set. "And she's too young. Not Miss Chester."

She arched her brows and looked ahead, too. "Very well. Admittedly she is rather young."

They continued slowly strolling about the conservatory. When it came to him, she wasn't sure what she wanted anymore—no, she did know. She wanted to learn what he had meant by holding her hand all the way home last night. How was she supposed to interpret that? Yet this morning he hadn't alluded to those moments, or to any . . . connection between them, not in any way. When in the carriage on the way to Osterley Park she'd talked gaily about the prospects of gaining more names for his list, he'd only grunted and let her rattle on.

So what was she to think?

What was she to make of it all—of the necklace, and him?

After several minutes of silence, she drew breath and said, "Thus far we have Miss Chisolm and Miss Downtree on our list—we really need to expand our horizons. You can't have a viable short list with only two names." She'd offered to help him find his necessary bride, and she would fulfill her self-imposed obligation.

"I have to wonder if keeping as short a short list as possible isn't a sensible strategy. That way, I won't have to try to remember the attributes of too many females all at once. You must know that male brains aren't as capable as female ones when it comes to recalling details."

Henrietta would have scoffed, but Lady Jersey appeared and clapped her hands. "Come along, everyone! It's time to set out. We'll be using the bluebell dell today. I know several of you know the way, so please"—her ladyship waved them to the doors at the end of the conservatory—"do lead on."

The guests formed into chattering groups as they exited the conservatory.

"I take it you know the way to this dell?" James inquired as he and Henrietta brought up the rear.

"Yes. It's a frequent site for Lady Jersey's picnics." Henrietta looked ahead. "Not that there's any danger of anyone getting lost. We just follow the path and everyone else, and when we find the picnic hampers and rugs, along with the footmen, we stop."

James choked on a laugh.

But he quickly lost all inclination to humor; a Miss

Quilley and her mother, spying him and Henrietta ambling in the rear, dropped back to walk with them, and better display Miss Quilley's charms. Such as they were.

Not having any great fondness for artlessly vapid conversation, James wasn't impressed, but at Henrietta's warning glance, he hid his disapprobation behind his customary ready charm.

But the necessity irked. And the subtle abrasion of social demands trumping his inclinations, and his instincts, only grew worse.

They reached Lady Jersey's "bluebell dell," a large clearing dotted, it was true, with bluebells, albeit a little past their prime. Picnic rugs had been spread beneath the circling trees, and hampers lay with their contents enticingly displayed, inviting the guests to lounge and partake. But the current fashion for rustic charm extended only so far; the paths leading to and out of the dell passed through largely formal gardens and structured landscapes. The illusion of being in the countryside was wafer-thin—quite aside from the liveried footmen who stood beneath the trees, ready to assist with the opening of a wine bottle and the consequent pouring of libations, or providing any other help her ladyship's guests required.

James lounged on a rug beside Henrietta and suffered the company of a Mrs. Curtis, her daughter, and her niece while munching on chicken and duck, and sipping some rather thin champagne. He kept his charming persona to the fore, smiling and chatting with his customary facility, yet his mind remained distanced from the conversations, engaged with a far more pertinent consideration.

He didn't precisely *wish* to dwell on what he felt for Henrietta—in the manner of his kind, he felt thinking

too much about that subject only gave it more power—
yet he knew what he felt, and given he felt so, how could
he continue to pursue some other young lady to fill the
position of his necessary bride . . . as Henrietta, apparently, intended he should?

What did her encouragement in that direction mean?

Had she glimpsed his . . . *regard* for her, perhaps
through the fraught moments of the previous night,
and subsequently decided that encouraging him to look
elsewhere was a gentle way of dismissing his preten-
sions?

He felt her gaze, glanced at her, and saw she was
looking pointedly at him—one step away from a glare.

Correctly interpreting the blankness in his eyes, she
informed him, "Mrs. Curtis, Miss Curtis, and Miss
Mayfair are moving on."

Thank heaven! "Oh—sorry. Temporarily woolgath-
ering." Rising, he summoned his usual easy smile and
beamed it at the three ladies as he assisted them to their
feet. "It's been a delight chatting with you all."

All three smiled and made their farewells, but from
the look she cast him, Mrs. Curtis hadn't been fooled.

Henrietta opened her mouth—no doubt to upbraid
him—but instead had to shut her lips and smile as Miss
Cadogan and her aunt, Lady Fisher, arrived to replace
the Curtis party on the other end of their large rug.

And so it went, with group after group shifting around
the dell, chatting and sharing news, and assessing—as
he was supposed to be doing—with matrimonial intent.
There were several other gentlemen present patently engaged to varying degrees in the same endeavor, so he
didn't feel quite so exposed.

Regardless, courtesy of the revelations of the previous
night, he had precious little interest in pursuing their

campaign. Instead, he took every opportunity to try to see past Henrietta's expression—to discover some hint of what she thought in her fine eyes—but to no avail; she had a strong, well-developed social mask, and she kept it firmly in place.

He'd almost reached the point of deciding that any degree of revelation stemming from the previous night had been all on his part and none at all on hers, when they were joined by the too-thin and too-young Miss Chester and her aunt. Mrs. Julian engaged Henrietta, drawing in Mrs. Entwhistle, who'd been passing; the three ladies were soon deep in an exchange concerning the recent spate of political marriages, and the implications of King William's failing health.

At first James and Miss Chester pretended to listen, but then Miss Chester turned her bright eyes on James and shifted closer. "I'm not terribly riveted by politics, are you?"

He saw no point in obfuscation. "Not at the moment."

"Perhaps"—Miss Chester glanced around the clearing—"you and I might go for a stroll." She met his eyes. "Just the pair of us, as we aren't truly interested in all the gossip."

The avid light in her eyes set alarm bells ringing in James's head. Few others had left the dell, and from what he'd seen, those had been the older young ladies, like Henrietta, not the sweet young things like Miss Chester.

And call him old-fashioned, but he hadn't heard that it was yet common practice for young ladies to proposition gentlemen. Especially not gentlemen like him.

But how to refuse her without being overly blunt?

James glanced around for inspiration but found none. "Perhaps in a little while, if others are of a mind to ramble, too."

Miss Chester pouted. Literally pouted. James suspected she thought it looked endearing; it made him want to leave—he had not agreed to deal with spoilt, overeager young beauties.

"Oh, I don't think we need to wait." Miss Chester shifted closer still and laid a hand on his sleeve. "Why," she cooed, "I'm sure we can find something of interest to pass the time, away from all these others." She caught his gaze—rigidly unresponsive—and all but batted her lashes. "I've heard the gardens are extensive. I'm sure we can find some quiet path along which to wander . . ."

He honestly couldn't recall ever being so blatantly propositioned in his life. "I daresay." Enough was enough. "However—" He bit the word off, along with the rest of what was possibly a too-strongly worded rejection, and sent an entirely instinctive, helpless look Henrietta's way.

She was looking and caught it. Then her gaze dropped to Miss Chester's hand, lightly gripping his sleeve . . .

Henrietta noted in that part of her brain that had grown obsessed with James and his reactions that he'd stiffened, holding rigid against Miss Chester's entreaty, but it wasn't simply protectiveness that surged through her and had her turning to Mrs. Julian and Mrs. Entwhistle and saying, "Indeed, it's all quite fascinating, but sadly, Mr. Glossup and I must be on our way." An appropriately social smile curving her lips, she met Mrs. Julian's eyes, saw the flash of irritation therein, and evenly stated, "We have other engagements in town and should start back. If you'll excuse us?"

James promptly got to his feet, helped her to hers, and joined with her in making their farewells. As she turned from the three ladies—leaving two, at least, metaphorically gnashing their teeth—he offered his arm.

She took it. As they strolled away from the trio, he whispered sotto voce, "Are we really leaving?"

The hope in his tone was impossible to miss. Smothering a laugh, she replied, "Of course," and waved him toward their hostess.

Lady Jersey wasn't the least surprised to learn they had some other engagement. "Why, of course, my dears—you must be in *such* demand."

Duly taking their leave, Henrietta directed James down a secondary path. As he led her out of the clearing, she glanced up at him. "You really didn't enjoy this, did you?"

He grimaced. "The thing with being a wolf of the ton, you see, is that we avoid all such affairs when we're younger, so now I'm . . . well, you might say 'constitutionally unsuited' to such entertainments. I'm all the time thinking that I'd much rather be somewhere else."

She snorted. "Knowing Simon, I can believe that."

Looking down, she wondered if that was it—she was Simon's sister, after all. Was that why James had been so protective at Marchmain House? Was that why he'd held her hand all the way home—purely to comfort her? It had been a comfort, but . . . she'd thought it might have meant more, but perhaps that was just wishful, necklace-induced thinking.

The jewelry in question lay about her throat; she could feel the warmth that seemed to emanate from the beads and pendant. Strangely, she only ever noticed that when James was about.

Yet it was she who was wearing the necklace, not him; there was no reason to imagine it would have any effect on him. No reason to suppose he was thinking of her in any light other than as Simon's sister, The Match-breaker, who had broken up the match he'd arranged, and then, once she'd learned of his noble reasons for seeking a bride, had offered to help him find a suitable lady.

"Aah . . . do you know where we're going?" James glanced around, but the path they'd been following had led them into a long walk bordered by thickly growing laurel hedges taller than him. They could see down the walk, or look back to where they'd turned into it, but he couldn't see beyond in any other direction.

Henrietta glanced around as if only just noticing where they were. "This is a secondary route back to the house. If we just keep going, we'll reach there soon enough."

James wondered . . . "Secondary . . . so the others won't be coming up on our heels?"

"Probably not. The mamas and matrons will opt for the shorter way, taking most of the young ladies, which means most of the gentlemen will take that path, too."

So they were, for the moment, more or less alone. Out of sight of anyone. James drew in a breath. "Henrietta?"

"Mmm?"

He halted, and when she halted, too, and, drawing her hand from his sleeve, turned to face him, he . . . knew what he wanted to ask, but his courage abruptly deserted him. He'd been searching all day for some sign of her true view of him; when she'd leapt so decisively to his aid over Miss Chester, he'd thought—hoped that perhaps . . .

Moistening his lips, his eyes on hers, he heard himself say, "I was wondering . . . about kisses."

She stared at him. "Kisses?"

"Yes." He pointed at himself. "Wolf of the ton, re-member?" He'd had no idea his past would prove so useful.

She frowned. "I don't understand."

"Well, you see, there are kisses, and"—he lowered his voice—"*kisses*. I was wondering, with young ladies, what was acceptable? What degree, so to speak."

The look on her face told him more clearly than words that she had no clue how to answer him.

Which was exactly as he'd hoped. "Perhaps," he suggested, and prayed she'd swallow the line, "I could demonstrate. So you could see the difference between what I imagine a 'young lady' kiss might be, as distinct from a 'seducing an experienced matron' kiss."

Naturally, she looked suspicious, but he'd expected that. He sighed. "Yes, I know it's a bit much to ask, but you did offer to help me, and how else am I supposed to find out? If I get it wrong, I might shock some young lady out of her stays."

She snorted. "Most young ladies don't wear stays, as you very well know."

He widened his eyes at her and managed to keep a straight face. "Actually, I didn't know—wolf of the ton, if you recall. Experienced matrons are the standard fare for such as I—as you well know—and, in general, I assure you they do wear stays." His eyes on hers, he smoothly continued, "But we aren't here to talk about stays."

Eyes narrowing fractionally, she studied him, but then—*yes!*—gave a small nod. "All right. One kiss—one young lady kiss. Just enough for me to be able to tell you if you've judged it wrongly."

His lips curved—and if there was a greater degree of triumph in the gesture than there should have been, she didn't get a chance to register it. Looping an arm about her waist, he drew her close—not too close—as close as he judged she would allow, while with his other hand he tipped up her chin, and before she'd managed to catch her breath enough to even squeak, he swooped and set his lips to hers.

Gently.

Reining in the nearly overwhelming urge to taste her more definitely, to part her lips and claim her mouth—and go far too far—he fought and succeeded, because it was so desperately important that he did, in keeping the kiss light, in spinning it out into a fantasy of the most delicately exquisite sensation.

He knew exactly what he was doing, what he was aiming for, a seduction of an entirely different sort—at least for a wolf like him.

Never had he set himself to tempt with such a light touch, with the merest brush of his lips, a pressure so light it tantalized with near-crystal fragility.

He peeked from beneath his lashes; her eyes were shut—she seemed captured by the kiss, captive to the sensation. As he'd wanted her to be.

Henrietta couldn't breathe. She couldn't think, either, and for once didn't care. Thinking wasn't important; feeling—absorbing the sensations engendered by his kiss—was. She'd been kissed before, several times, yet those experiences had been nothing like this. Nowhere near as compelling as this.

Even though this kiss—James's "young lady" kiss—was as insubstantial as a fairy tale.

It was all about promise, and hope, and what might be.

The touch of his lips on hers . . . made them tingle. Made her nerves fizz delicately, like fine bubbles rising in the best champagne, with a species of anticipation. She was intensely aware of him, of his body and his strength, all around her and so close, yet not quite touching . . . except for his lips. His wicked, pliant, distracting lips.

Slowly, smoothly, he lifted his head.

Lips parting, barely breathing, she looked up at him.

His eyes—those pools of melted chocolate—looked utterly innocent. They slowly passed over her face, lingered for a moment on her still tingling lips, then he raised his gaze to her eyes. Arched a brow. "Well? Will that pass muster, or . . . ?"

She dragged in a huge breath and stepped back, out of the circle of his arms. Sought—bludgeoned her brains—for some suitable response. All she could come up with was a crisp nod and a breathless "You'll do."

Turning, she started down the walk, grateful her legs consented to carry her. She couldn't think about the kiss—about whether he'd been in earnest, or merely using his supposed pursuit of young ladies as an excuse—now. As he fell in beside her, she lengthened her stride. "We need to reach the house before the others do."

"Ah—of course. We don't want Lady Jersey, of all people, to start speculating on what might have detained us."

"No. We don't." Belatedly registering the quiet laughter in his voice, she shot him a glance as, entirely relaxed, he paced alongside her. "That's a truly evil prospect to raise."

He chuckled. "I know." Looking ahead, he smiled.

Henrietta was sitting before her dressing table that evening, watching in the mirror as Hannah curled and pinned her hair, when there was a tap on the door and Mary looked in. Spotting Henrietta, Mary entered and shut the door, then crossed to stand to one side of Hannah.

Mary's gaze swept over Henrietta and fixed on the necklace fastened about her throat. Satisfaction bloomed in Mary's eyes. "Good. You're still wearing it."

"Hmm."

At the noncommittal reply, Mary's gaze rose to fix on Henrietta's face. Henrietta avoided meeting her sister's eyes—which promptly narrowed.

"Is it working?" Mary asked.

Henrietta wished she could lie, but this was Mary, who was not simply her bossiest sister but also the most acute. Attempting to lie to Mary never worked well. Henrietta opted for caution instead. "Possibly."

"*Yes*! Wonderful!" Fists waving, Mary danced a little jig, then tipped her head back and said to the ceiling, "Thank you, Lady!"

Henrietta snorted.

Which brought Mary's attention swooping back to her. "So who is it?"

"I'm not telling."

Mary straightened. Folding her arms, she stared at Henrietta's reflection. Eyes narrowing, Mary tapped a finger to her lips . . . then stopped. "James Glossup. That's who it is—he's your hero, isn't he?"

Finally meeting Mary's eyes, taking in her little sister's triumphant expression, Henrietta narrowed her eyes direfully. "Under no circumstances will you *dare* say a word—not to anyone!"

Mary positively beamed.

Henrietta dragged in a breath, and remembered the one thing she held that would compel Mary's silence. "If you want to get your hands on the necklace in the right way, as soon as maybe, then you will make absolutely certain not one word of your *unconfirmed speculation* passes your lips."

Mary's smile widened, but she held up a hand and promptly said, "I do so promise—word of a Cynster."

"Humph!" Henrietta wanted to turn around to better study Mary, but Hannah was still working on her hair.

Mary, meanwhile, was still dancing—literally—with delight. She swirled in a complete circle, then headed for the door. "You have no idea how happy you've made me, Henrietta dear. And you may rest easy—I won't blab a word, and will do nothing at all to get in your way. Well—of course, I won't. I want that necklace in my hands—in the right way—as soon as may be."

Pausing with her hand on the doorknob, Mary glanced back, and, eyes alight, added, "I just can't wait."

Ignoring Hannah's efforts, Henrietta swung around, but Mary had already whisked out of the door. As it shut behind her, Henrietta sighed. "Do you have any idea," she said, speaking to Hannah, "what—or rather who—that was all about? Who she's got her eye on that she's so eager to have this necklace?"

"No, miss. Not a clue." Hannah paused, then asked, "But is it true? That Mr. Glossup is the one for you?"

Henrietta swiveled back and, in the mirror, caught Hannah's wide-eyed gaze. "It might be. But you, too, will breathe not a word."

"Not even half a word, miss." Her face showing almost as much excitement as Mary's, Hannah waved the curling iron. "Now do sit still, miss, and let me get this done."

The exchange with Mary had brought home to Henrietta that she had, indeed, started to believe. Started to hope.

Hope, she was discovering, was a very awkward feeling.

Descending the steps into Lady Hollingworth's ballroom, she saw James slipping through the crowd, making his way to the foot of the stairs to meet her—and she told her unruly heart to behave. Yes, he looked his usual polished, debonair self, every inch the wolf of the ton he so often claimed to be, and while he might be that . . . this afternoon, he'd been something else.

He'd been the gentleman who'd kissed her with such reverent delicacy that she still felt giddy whenever she recalled the moment.

They'd spent the drive back from Osterley Park discussing the various people they'd met there, but that had merely been a convenient smoke screen, one both of them had readily supported as a way to avoid having to deal immediately with what that deliciously simple kiss had revealed.

Had meant.

Truth be told, she still wasn't sure what it had meant, only that it had meant something. That the moment had marked a change, a shift in their interaction.

Exactly to what she wasn't sure, but as she looked down into James's face, upturned, his gaze locked on her as she descended the last steps, she knew very well what her heart was hoping.

"Good evening." With passable aplomb, she offered her hand.

He grasped it and bowed, then, straightening, brazenly raised her hand to his lips; meeting her eyes, he touched his lips to her knuckles.

Even though she was wearing gloves, she still had to suppress a shiver. The pressure of his lips on the back of her hand evoked the phantom sensation of those same lips pressed to hers. . . .

He'd been studying her eyes; now he smiled and drew her nearer. Tucking her hand in the crook of his arm, he steered her into the crowd. "Not quite as big a crush as last night, thank heaven."

"No." She glanced about.

Unsure of just what tack they would be taking, she was about to point out another young lady he might wish to meet and consider—if he was still considering other young ladies—when he said, "I believe the musicians are about to start a waltz. Ah, yes, there they are." Lifting her hand from his sleeve, he met her eyes and smiled—in an unshielded way she was beginning to realize he reserved just for her—then he drew her on. "Come along, my dear Matchbreaker. I want to waltz with you."

Finding herself stupidly smiling in reply, she opened her lips to make a token protest.

He saw, and twirled her—onto the floor and into his arms. "And no—don't start. I have no intention of wasting my time waltzing with other young ladies tonight." His gaze trapped hers, and he lowered his voice. "So you may as well save your breath." Then he whirled her into the dance.

James devoted himself to keeping her breathless and giddy, an activity that confirmed two things. One, that he could, if he put his mind to it, achieve such an outcome, and two, that he enjoyed doing it. Henrietta Cynster breathless and giddy was a sight that warmed his heart. Literally.

Which, he supposed, said more than enough.

But he wasn't yet ready to think more on that, on what she made him feel. On what he had felt when he'd kissed her so lightly in the walk at Osterley Park.

He was still coming to terms with that.

But she seemed as pleased as he to simply take tonight as they found it. There were enough guests crowding her ladyship's ballroom for them to keep to themselves without anyone truly noticing. The gossipmongers and the grandes dames tended to watch the sweet young things, or those for some reason in the limelight. At twenty-nine, Henrietta was long past the age when matrons kept a watchful eye on whom she was consorting with, and as for him, he'd never featured as a pawn in their matrimonial games.

So they had all the evening to laugh, and share anecdotes, and drown in each other's eyes. Had hours to spend discovering this and that, the minutiae of each other's characters that made them what they were, that made them themselves and fixed the other's attention.

That focused them, each on the other, to the exclusion of all else.

They waltzed again, and the ephemeral connection between them burgeoned and grew stronger.

On one level, he recognized it; on another, he didn't.

Familiar, yet not; known, yet unknown. Expected on the one hand, yet so much more . . . that summed up his reaction to her.

A reaction that escalated from curiosity to desire, and then to wanting.

They chanced a third waltz, but even that was not enough. He could see the same calculation in her eyes.

She glanced around, then met his gaze. "It's dreadfully stuffy—shall we stroll on the terrace?"

Where it was quieter and they stood an excellent chance of finding themselves alone.

He looked over the heads, saw the doors to the terrace standing open. "An excellent idea." He offered his arm. "Let's."

He steered her through the crowd of chattering guests. They'd reached the terrace door and were just about to step through when a young lady in a magenta gown appeared in a rush beside them.

"Miss Cynster." The young lady met Henrietta's eyes, then inclined her head to James before addressing Henrietta. "I'm Miss Fotherby—we met at Lady Hamilton's at-home a few weeks ago."

"Oh, yes." Henrietta lightly clasped Miss Fotherby's proffered fingers. "I remember." She introduced James, adding, "Miss Fotherby is Lady Martin's niece."

James bowed and Miss Fotherby curtsied, then, rising, spoke to them both. "I wonder if I might have a private word with you." She gestured to the terrace. "Outside might be best."

James met Henrietta's eyes, saw them widen slightly.

Miss Fotherby glanced back at the crowd, then looked at Henrietta, then at him. "Please," she said, and stepped over the threshold.

Mystified, James waved Henrietta before him, and followed.

They found Miss Fotherby, hands clasped nervously before her, waiting for them a little way from the door. She swung away as they neared. As Miss Fotherby was shorter than Henrietta, Henrietta went to one side and James to the other; flanking Miss Fotherby, they strolled deeper into the shadows further along the terrace.

"I hope you'll understand my reasons for approaching you like this, *but . . .*" Miss Fotherby paused to draw in a tight breath. "I have to marry. I live with my mother and stepfather, but for various reasons I wish to leave my stepfather's roof. My aunt has been all that is kind, and she's sponsoring me into the ton, as you know. I'm twenty-five, so finding a husband isn't all that easy. I have a decent dowry, but . . ." She paused to draw in another breath, then, fingers twisting, went on, "I've had one offer, and while everyone else is thrilled and I've been advised by many to accept, I simply don't trust the gentleman involved."

They'd reached the end of the terrace. Placing a hand on the balustrade, Miss Fotherby swung to face them. She focused on Henrietta. "And no, I'm not here to ask you to vet him. I know well enough not to trust a man such as he. However"—she transferred her gaze to James—"I have heard, Mr. Glossup, of your need for a wife. I realize that you are looking over candidates and would like to ask that you put my name on your list for consideration."

She glanced at Henrietta and smiled faintly. "Miss Cynster, I'm sure, will know how to learn all you might wish to know about me." Raising her head, Miss Fotherby met Henrietta's gaze. "I've heard that all Cynsters marry for love, but in my case . . . I know I'll be happier taking the other tack."

Turning to James, she met his eyes. "I distrust gentlemen who vow love too readily, Mr. Glossup, and infinitely prefer you and your honesty in approaching the matter as you have." She inclined her head, then simply said, "Please do consider me for your position." Her gaze traveling along the terrace to fix on the open ballroom door, she hesitated, then added, "And, if at all possible, I would appreciate some indication of your thoughts in the next several days."

With that, she nodded to Henrietta, then walked swiftly back up the terrace, leaving James and Henrietta staring after her.

Cynsters marry for love.

I distrust gentlemen who vow love too readily.

James felt blindsided—hit in the head by not one but two punches, neither of which he'd seen coming. He hadn't even thought that far . . . he looked at Henrietta. Shadows wreathed her face; he couldn't make out her expression, much less read her eyes. "Ah . . ." The coward's way out beckoned. "What do you think?"

She didn't say anything for several long moments, then, in a tone that sounded odd, faintly strained, said, "As far as I know, she would make an excellent candidate." She paused, then said, "I'll have to check, of course, but of all the ladies you've met thus far, I suspect she should be at the top of your list, even before I ask around."

So . . . she still thought he was searching for a bride? James's head reeled as he scrambled to revisit all they'd said that evening, all they'd implied . . . or had it only been him thinking? Imagining?

He honestly didn't know.

If he stated what he thought—what he'd assumed and hoped—would she laugh, and then balk and turn away?

"Perhaps . . . you can ask around." At least that would mean he would see her again, and soon, by which time he might have sorted out what was going on. What was *really* going on between them.

Henrietta forced herself to nod, inexpressibly grateful that the shadows hid her face. Sternly repressing her hurt—and her stupid, *stupid* heart—she forced herself to calmly say, "I can understand why she might feel a need to know sooner rather than later. I'll go and chat with the grandes dames—those who are here—immediately." She dallied only long enough to say, "Perhaps you can meet me in the park tomorrow—I'll be there with my mother and Mary in our carriage on the Avenue at eleven o'clock—and I'll be able to tell you what I've learned." In the park, with plenty of others about.

No more strolling with him alone; no more chance of another kiss to cause her further heartache.

She barely waited for his nod of agreement before turning and walking back up the terrace.

James forced himself to stay where he was and watch her go. And drink in the telltale signs—the elevated angle at which she held her head, the tension in her stride, the rigid line of her spine.

He'd got it wrong, hadn't he?

When she stepped over the threshold and without a backward glance disappeared into the ballroom, he turned, stared out at the night, and swore.

Chapter Five

As instructed, James presented himself in the park the following morning and located Lady Louise Cynster's carriage in the line of fashionable conveyances drawn up along the Avenue. Henrietta was sitting with her younger sister, Mary, on the rear-facing seat. Parasols deployed against the mild sunshine, both young ladies appeared to be idly scanning the lawns and the tonnish crowd strolling the sward while, seated opposite, their mother and old Lady Cowper chatted avidly.

Approaching from Henrietta's back and still a dozen yards away, James paused beneath an elm to take stock. He had ground to make up, which was why he was there, but exactly how he was to win Henrietta over he hadn't yet defined. His quest to find his necessary bride hadn't changed, but the campaign he and Henrietta had devised was no longer relevant. That had fallen by *his* wayside, but how to communicate that to her—a Cynster who would, he was perfectly certain, only consent to marry for love—was a problem to which he'd yet to find an answer. He'd spent most of the night bludgeoning his brain into providing one, but in this matter—critical though it was—his imaginatively inventive rakish faculties, his usual unerring wolfish instincts, had been strangely silent. Indeed, uncooperative; when it came to Henrietta, his instincts urged a different approach entirely.

That was a large part of his problem. His instincts viewed her in a different light from any other lady he'd previously set his eye on. His instincts insisted that she was his, and regardless of what was required to make that so, his inner self thought he should just grit his teeth and do it. Securing her as his was, to that instinctive inner self, worth any sacrifice.

But there were some sacrifices a wise man did not meekly offer, did not readily make.

Especially not to a lady of Henrietta's caliber, a strong-willed, intelligent, clear-sighted female.

Last night, quite aside from disrupting what had, until her appearance, been a highly encouraging evening, Miss Fotherby had reminded him of two immutable truths.

Cynsters married for love.

And gentlemen who vowed love too glibly were almost certain to be distrusted.

He had to somehow chart a course between those two rocks and convince Henrietta to smile upon his suit.

With that goal, at least, clear in his mind, he stirred and strode on to the Cynster carriage.

Henrietta knew James was approaching some moments before he appeared beside the carriage; she'd felt his gaze on her back and had had to fight the urge to look—too eagerly—around.

After the disappointment of last night, the dashing of her apparently unfounded hopes, she was determined to allow no sign of susceptibility to slip past her customary, no-nonsense façade. She intended to keep their interaction firmly focused on their mutual goal—on finding him his necessary bride.

Consequently, she met his eyes with an easy smile and inclined her head politely. "Mr. Glossup."

His eyes met hers, studied them; for a fleeting instant he hesitated, then he nodded in reply and, lips curving, murmured a greeting, then turned to greet her mother and Lady Cowper.

Hands clasped about her parasol's handle, Henrietta sat stiffly upright and watched critically as James deployed his usual charm, delighting her mother and Lady Cowper, glibly deflecting them from dwelling overlong on the incident at Marchmain House. But her mother would have none of it, roundly thanking him for his bravery in coming to her—Henrietta's—aid. James accepted the accolades but quickly steered the talk into more general avenues. For which she was grateful; she'd had her fill of having to assure everyone that the accident hadn't overset her nerves and scarred her for life.

With the older ladies satisfied, James turned to her and arched a brow. "Would you care to stroll the lawns, Miss Cynster?"

"Thank you, I would." She shifted forward.

As James reached for the door, Sir Edward Compton, who'd been standing nearby and, it seemed, biding his moment, stepped forward and made his bow to Louise and Lady Cowper, then inquired if Mary might like to stroll as well.

The implication being with Henrietta and James. While Henrietta could stroll alone with a gentleman, Mary was still too young to be allowed such license, at least not in the park, directly under the censorious noses of the ton's matrons.

Henrietta didn't expect Mary to accept; her sister wasn't one to waste time where she had no true interest, and Henrietta was sure Mary had no interest in mild-mannered Sir Edward, but after an instant's pause, Mary smiled and inclined her head to Sir Edward. "Thank you, Sir Edward. I would be delighted to stroll on your arm."

James opened the carriage door and handed Henrietta down, then Sir Edward stepped forward and performed the same office for Mary.

Mary smiled at him sweetly, placed her hand on his arm, and promptly steered him out over the lawn.

Mystified, her hand resting on James's sleeve, Henrietta strolled beside him as they followed Mary and Sir Edward across the neatly clipped grass. Her gaze on Mary, Henrietta murmured, "I wonder what she's up to."

James glanced at her. "Why would you think she's up to anything?"

Because otherwise Mary would not have done anything to interfere with Henrietta's time alone with James . . . Henrietta tipped her head toward her sister. "Just wait—you'll see."

Sure enough, they hadn't strolled far when Mary pointed ahead, spoke to Sir Edward, then looked over her shoulder to inform Henrietta and James, "Sir Edward and I are going to join that group over there. Miss Faversham and Miss Hawkins are there, too, and we'll still be within sight of Mama and the carriages."

Despite remaining unsaid, the words *so you don't need to play chaperon* could not have been clearer.

Henrietta scanned the group in question. As well as Miss Faversham and Miss Hawkins, it contained several eligible young gentlemen, chief among them the Honorable Julius Gatling and Lord Randolph Cavanaugh, second son of the late Marquess of Raventhorne, yet the company was suitable and innocuous enough. Henrietta nodded. "Very well. I'm sure Sir Edward can be trusted to return you to the carriage in due course."

Mary smiled beatifically at the clearly smitten Sir Edward. "You will escort me back in due course, won't you, Sir Edward?"

Henrietta inwardly snorted and didn't bother listening to Sir Edward's earnestly bumbling reply. She had business to which she needed to attend; meeting James's eyes, she arched a brow. "Might I suggest we stroll on and find a place where I can tell you what I've learned thus far about Miss Fotherby?"

Somewhat to her surprise, his lips tightened fractionally, but he nodded and led her on.

Once past the knots of younger ladies and gentlemen dotting the areas adjacent to the carriages, the lawns were much less crowded, and it was possible to stroll and converse freely without fear of being overheard. Turning her to promenade parallel to the avenue, now at some distance, James finally asked, "So what have you learned?"

"Miss Fotherby's case is exactly as she stated it. Apparently her mother has an unfounded and unreasoning fear that her second husband will be captivated by Miss Fotherby and transfer his affection from mother to daughter. No one who knows the family believes this to be the case, but as you might imagine it's made Miss Fotherby's situation very difficult. Consequently, she is seeking a husband so she may leave her stepfather's house, and Miss Fotherby's mama has, of course, insisted on remaining in the country, keeping her husband with her, and has packed Miss Fotherby off to find her own way forward under her aunt's aegis."

Glancing at James, Henrietta saw his lips twist.

Looking ahead as they strolled on, he murmured, "So Miss Fotherby is something of a damsel in distress who needs saving?"

Henrietta inclined her head. "You could paint her in that light."

And in so doing . . . Henrietta had no difficulty seeing that James might consider rescuing Miss Fotherby, while simultaneously rescuing himself and his people from the requirement imposed by his grandaunt's will, to be a reasonable bargain all around.

Yet she had to be impartial, and impartiality demanded she report on Miss Fotherby favorably. From all Henrietta had gathered in the short time she'd had the previous evening, Miss Fotherby possessed a spotless, entirely blameless reputation, and the difficulty she found herself currently facing was no fault of hers. Henrietta had heard not one adverse comment against Miss Fotherby, which left her with the unenviable conviction that both duty and honor dictated that she assist both James and Miss Fotherby by reporting the unvarnished truth, and subsequently, if James was so inclined, by fostering a match between them.

Both he and Miss Fotherby deserved no less.

Even if fostering a match between them was the very last thing she wanted to do.

They'd been strolling in silence. After a moment more, James asked, "Did you learn anything else?"

While Henrietta reported, in careful and neutral terms, what she'd thus far gleaned as to Miss Fotherby's standing, character, and personality, James found himself increasingly biting his tongue.

He wanted to ask Henrietta point-blank whether she truly wanted him to marry Miss Fotherby.

He wanted, badly, to ask the confusing female

walking so fluidly—so confidently and easily—by his side what she'd thought about the kiss they'd shared. Whether she'd felt anything at all—anything like the cataclysmic and ineradicable shift in focus that that kiss had imposed on him—and whether, just possibly, she might consider marrying him herself.

He wanted to ask her all those things—wanted to look into her soft blue eyes and say the words, direct and without any obfuscation—but he couldn't.

Not while she was strolling beside him singing Miss Fotherby's praises and all but specifically encouraging him to look at Miss Fotherby as his prospective bride.

Confusion wasn't the half of what he felt. Frustration roiled, mixing with a wholly unfamiliar panicky fear—a fear of not acting and through that losing her, which itself was solidly counteracted and blocked, stymied, by the weight on his shoulders and the horrible prospect raised by the question, What if she said no?

If he asked, and Henrietta refused him . . .

"I'll inquire further at the teas this afternoon, but I suspect Miss Fotherby really will prove to be the most outstanding candidate."

His temper snapped and flicked him on the raw. Goaded, he said, his tone terse and harsh, "All right. Enough of Miss Fotherby." He looked at Henrietta. "Who else should I look at?"

Me. Say, Me.

She'd been looking down while she'd been speaking; now she drew in a deep breath as if girding her loins—and his heart leapt in hope.

"Well, we still have Miss Chisolm and Miss Downtree on the list, so I'll ask after them, too."

Hope crashed and died on the rocks of futility. The

deflation that hit him left him feeling hollowed out inside.

"And you really should look further afield—we have Lady Hamilton's ball tonight, and that'll be another crush, so we may well find more suitable candidates there." Raising her gaze from the grass, Henrietta was about to glance up at James—unsure of what might show in her own eyes, she hadn't allowed herself to do so while speaking of Miss Fotherby—but as her gaze rose, she saw the lady in question standing a little deeper into the park and speaking with a very recognizable gentleman: Rafe Cunningham, gazetted rake, profligate gambler, and all-around hedonist.

The pair weren't conversing; they were facing each other, several feet apart, and Rafe was clearly arguing. Hotly. Miss Fotherby had her back to Henrietta and James, but from the angle of her head, and her gestures, she was arguing just as hotly back.

A swift glance at James's face confirmed that he, too, had spotted the pair.

Then Rafe spread his arms to his sides, hands open as he made some dramatic appeal.

Miss Fotherby threw her hands in the air, swept violently around, and strode swiftly toward the Avenue; all angrily swishing skirts, her face pale but with flags of color flying in her cheeks, her lips set in a trenchant line, her gaze fixed unswervingly ahead, she marched toward the carriages, where, no doubt, her aunt was waiting. She didn't glance back once, and she didn't notice Henrietta and James where they'd halted a little way away.

"Ah." Henrietta glanced at Rafe, then looked at Miss Fotherby's retreating back. "I suspect we can guess which gentleman has made Miss Fotherby an offer she doesn't trust." Rafe Cunningham was well-born and wealthy, the twin characteristics that, in a gentleman, made him eligible no matter his character.

Wondering how the information that it was Rafe who had approached Miss Fotherby might affect James's view of that lady, Henrietta refocused her attention on him—and registered the tension investing his long frame. Glancing at his face, she saw that he was studying Rafe.

Was James already feeling possessive over Miss Fotherby?

To Henrietta's dismay, her stupid heart lurched downward—which only proved that it hadn't yet come to its senses over James. Inwardly sighing, she looked back at the carriages.

James watched Rafe Cunningham—standing stock-still in the park, his hands on his hips, visibly exasperated and openly frustrated as he stared after Miss Fotherby, his dark features set in an expression of utter incomprehension—and experienced a deep and undeniable surge of fellow-feeling.

Jaw setting, he steered Henrietta away from Rafe and the revealing look on his fellow wolf's face. "Come on. We'd better get back or your mother will start getting impatient."

He escorted her back to her mother's carriage, handed her up, and made his good-byes.

With a brisk salute, and a last look at Henrietta, he forced himself to turn and stride away.

He'd hoped to regain some of the ground he'd lost last night, but instead . . . as far as he could see, he was further than ever from getting Henrietta to look at him as a potential husband. She seemed to have seized on the advent of Miss Fotherby as a solution to his problem, as a way of accomplishing her task of assisting him to find his necessary bride . . . but he didn't want Miss Fotherby; indeed, he wished Rafe the best of luck with her.

He wanted Henrietta.

As he crossed the lawns, he consulted his inner self, but the answer was unequivocal. He wasn't about to retreat, to back away and let Henrietta go—not now he'd found her, not now he'd finally recognized her as his.

So he was going to have to come up with some more definite way of reshaping her view of him.

Something powerful enough to change a Cynster female's mind.

From her seat in the carriage, Henrietta watched James go, watched him stride off without once looking back. As the carriage rumbled into motion, avoiding Mary's questioning gaze, Henrietta looked away across the lawns . . . and wished with all her unrepentant heart that Miss Millicent Fotherby had never crossed their paths.

Fate, Henrietta decided, was smiling on Miss Fotherby and her bid to become James's bride. Most helpfully, that afternoon saw Henrietta, along with her mother and Mary, attending an at-home at Lady Osbaldestone's house; her ladyship's drawing room was crammed with every last grande dame Henrietta might wish to question.

Reminding herself she was honor-bound to do her duty by James, she duly set about inquiring as to what the assembled ladies could tell her of Millicent Fotherby.

Of course, in the way of ton ladies, gaining information required offering information in return. In that

distinctly august company, her request for information
on Miss Fotherby necessitated explaining what had
caused what was, for her, a distinctly novel tack; as The
Matchbreaker, she more customarily inquired after
the bona fides of gentlemen, not young ladies. By and
large, as she worked her way steadily around the room,
going from group to group, she managed to excuse her
query by simply stating that she'd agreed to help James,
a friend of Simon's, with his quest to find a suitable
bride, and, if necessary, deflecting attention by asking
about Rafe Cunningham, who, as she'd suspected, was,
indeed, no better than she'd supposed. Most ladies
swallowed her half-truths whole and happily related
what they knew of Miss Fotherby, her family, her an-
tecedents, her expectations, and her present situation.

Sadly, what Henrietta learned wasn't *quite* definitive
and definite enough for her to deem her job done and
recommend that James make an offer for Miss Fotherby
without further ado. Even more unfortunately, again
and again she was directed to seek further clarification
from the very two ladies she'd hoped to avoid.

There was no help for it; if she wanted the last word on
Millicent Fotherby's eligibility for the position of James
Glossup's wife, she was going to have to approach Lady
Osbaldestone, who, as well as being a distant cousin of
Viscount Netherfield, James's grandfather, was appar-
ently also distantly connected to the Fotherby family.

Henrietta wasn't overly surprised by that; Lady Osbaldestone seemed to be connected to fully half the
ton.

Having to inquire of Lady Osbaldestone was bad
enough, but seated beside her ladyship was Henrietta's
aunt Helena—which meant the chaise on which the
pair of grandes dames sat held one too many sharp-

eyed older ladies than Henrietta was at all comfortable with.

Her aunt Helena, the Dowager Duchess of St. Ives, had the most lovely pale green eyes—and a gaze that seemed to see straight through any assumed façade. She was widely acknowledged as perspicacious to an almost mythical degree. Her son, Devil, Duke of St. Ives and head of the Cynster family, had similarly pale green eyes, but he had yet to develop the same perspicacity, much to the relief of the rest of the family.

Steeling herself, Henrietta presented herself before her hostess and her aunt. Both smiled with transparent delight and recommended she sit on a nearby chair and tell them what she wanted to know.

Henrietta obeyed and, despite her trepidation, felt she acquitted herself reasonably well in framing her questions and leading Lady Osbaldestone and her aunt to tell her what she needed to know.

It helped that, being connected with the Glossups, Lady Osbaldestone already knew the full tale behind James's need to wed. Which meant that Helena knew it, too; the pair rarely kept secrets from each other. Consequently, once they'd drawn from Henrietta the unadulterated story of how she came to be involved in James's quest, both older ladies fully concurred that James approaching Melinda Wentworth was entirely inappropriate for his situation, and confirmed that Millicent Fotherby was an excellent candidate for James to consider, *but* . . . it was at that point that Henrietta felt as if the conversation stepped sideways, into what arena she wasn't quite sure.

"Of course," Lady Osbaldestone said, "one needs to pay due attention to the reason James's hunt for a wife came to be."

"Indeed." Helena nodded sagely, her gaze growing distant. "It was . . . *peste*, what was her name? His sister-in-law, the one who was murdered?"

"Katherine—Kitty as she was called," Lady Osbaldestone supplied. "Precisely." Lady Osbaldestone caught Henrietta's gaze and continued, as if tutoring her, "Kitty is the reason James . . . how should I describe it? Pulled back from the general social round. In essence, pulled back from marrying or even socially consorting with suitable ladies of his class with whom he might form an attachment. Kitty, you see, was a much-indulged beauty, and she married James's older brother Henry for wealth and position, but once she had Henry's ring on her finger, Kitty set her sights on other gentlemen and, ultimately, her eye fell on James.

"The poor boy paid no attention, of course— Glossups are loyal to the bone. Kitty, sadly, understood nothing about such decencies and set herself to seduce James by whatever means possible—but then a previous lover murdered her. I was staying at Glossup Hall at the time, and it was all quite tawdry. We'll never know if Kitty's pursuit of James was in order to abrogate her pregnancy by that previous lover, but I strongly suspect that, when the whole sorry story came out, that notion did occur to James. It would have been a *dreadful* situation and would have torn the family apart—but that was Kitty. She was entirely self-absorbed."

"That was when Simon and Portia got engaged," Helena put in. "So all this took place nearly two years ago, just before they married, and since then James has . . . stood outside society, and only, at least as far as marriage and young ladies are concerned, looked in."

"Which," Lady Osbaldestone said, "is precisely why Emily, James's grandaunt, wrote her will as she did.

She was disappointed not to have been able to dance at James's wedding, but she did what she could to ensure that that wedding took place."

"Emily was, indeed, a loss." Helena smiled mistily, but then her gaze fixed on Henrietta, trapped before the chaise, and Helena's lovely smile took on a different shading. "And so now you are here, helping James to find his bride, and that is entirely as it should be."

Henrietta saw both older ladies glance at her throat, at the necklace that rested there; she waited for some comment, but none came. Instead, the pair exchanged a glance, then as one they sat back and regarded her.

"It occurs to me," Lady Osbaldestone stated, "that in your quest to assist James, and, indeed, Millicent, too, you would do well to dwell on the inescapable truth that in our circles, young ladies, these days especially, must be very clear in their own minds as to what they truly want."

"Yes, indeed." Helena nodded, her expression serious. "It is often the case that young ladies fail to question their own wants and desires—and even more specifically, their hearts—and so do not realize when fate steps in and hands them the chance to seize all they might wish of life."

Lady Osbaldestone snorted. "A common failing, that—to not stop and think enough to be sure of what one actually wants. How on earth any young lady can expect to gain the life she wishes without exerting herself even to define it, the heavens only know."

"Oh, the gentlemen are equally bad." Helena waved dismissively. "But in their case it is often willful blindness, which is rarely the case with young ladies. No, *their* problem is generally a lack of forethought—indeed, a lack of understanding that thought is required—combined with an assumption that life will somehow miraculously evolve in the way they wish it to without them having a clear idea in their minds what sort of life it is they wish, and *then* being prepared to actively go out and push and shove whatever needs to be pushed and shoved into place for that ideal life to take shape."

"Well said!" Lady Osbaldestone thumped her cane on the floor and caught Henrietta's eye. "And if you've a mind to be helpful, you might think to repeat that to your younger sister. She's hiding over there with the other young ladies thinking we haven't noticed what she's about, but she's one who definitely needs to put more thought into what she truly wants before she starts pushing and shoving."

"Being, as she is," Helena added, "so very good at pushing and shoving."

Henrietta found herself smiling and promising to pass on the message to Mary, who had spent the entire visit chatting in a corner with several other young ladies, then she happily accepted a dismissal and escaped from the two grandest grandes dames in the room.

Only later, when she was heading for the door in her mother's train and turned her mind to summarizing all she'd learned, did it occur to her that she wasn't at all sure who had been the principal target of Lady Osbaldestone and Helena's warning: Millicent Fotherby, Mary . . . or herself.

The thought distracted her, but once they'd settled in their carriage and it was rolling over the cobbles, carrying them to their next appointment, she mentally shook herself and refocused on the indisputable facts.

Rafe Cunningham notwithstanding, Millicent Fotherby appeared to be the answer to James's prayers.

And equally undeniable was her own welling desire to push Millicent aside and take her place.

Pushing and shoving?

Henrietta inwardly snorted, and stared out of the window as they rocked along.

Lady Hamilton's event that evening was a ball masque. Having realized that fact and recognized it as a godsend, James arrived at Hamilton House in good time to stand idling just inside the ballroom, indistinguishable from countless other gentlemen in domino and mask, waiting to pounce the instant Henrietta arrived.

When she did, shrouded in a hooded domino with a pale blue mask fixed across her face, he nevertheless recognized her instantly and swooped immediately she parted from their host and hostess and turned to survey the ballroom—already a sea of hoods, masks, and black cloaks.

He'd previously thought ball masques boring, their current resurgence in popularity distinctly ho-hum, but tonight . . . tonight, he hoped this ball masque would facilitate his salvation.

Halting beside Henrietta, grasping her elbow through her domino, he dipped his head to murmur, "Good evening."

She looked at his masked face, looked into his eyes, and smiled; relief tinted the gesture, which seemed almost absentminded. "I'd forgotten it was to be a ball masque until it was time to dress. I wondered how I was going to find you in all this." She waved at the anonymous crowd.

"Indeed—and speaking of that, I've had a revelation." He drew her aside, out of the press of incoming guests. Steering her toward the wall, he elaborated, "A ball masque is completely useless in terms of further assessing others—even if we think we know who someone is, we won't be certain, not until the unmasking at midnight. The odds that we might merely waste our time are high. Hence, for tonight, I propose that we set aside all thoughts of broadening my horizons and extending my short list, or even further discussing Miss Fotherby, and instead simply allow ourselves to enjoy the evening and the pleasure of each other's company." Halting by the wall, where the crush was less evident, he smoothly faced her and arched a brow, visible above his minimal mask. "What say you?"

She stared up at him, slowly blinked, then her gaze refocused and raced over his face. She hesitated, then glanced out at the crowd, surveying the shifting, anonymous throng before, finally turning back to him, she said, "I think . . . that's an excellent suggestion."

Henrietta wasn't sure what had most prompted that answer—her own inclination or the echoes of Lady Osbaldestone's and Helena's voices still ringing in her head—but the instant the words left her lips, she felt certainty and assurance well. She'd felt the lack of both in recent days, so she welcomed and embraced them, and beamed at James. "All right. So tonight it's just us, and all for fun." She spread her hands. "Where do we start?"

The answer was an exploration of her ladyship's rooms and the various entertainments offered therein. Neither felt drawn to the card tables set up in a minor salon, but they filled glasses at a fountain overflowing with champagne, and sampled the strawberries footmen were ferrying through the guests on silver salvers. The dance floor, occupying the half of the large ballroom before the raised dais on which a small orchestra labored, captured them. And held them.

"I'd forgotten that at a masked ball one can dance however many waltzes as one wishes with a single partner." Henrietta laughed as James responded by whirling her even faster through a turn.

"And," he replied, his eyes finding hers as they slowed and joined the stream of other couples more sedately revolving up the room, "at a masked ball, you can laugh and express delight without restraint." His eyes held hers for a moment more, then he murmured, "I love hearing you laugh."

He twirled her again. Henrietta was grateful for the momentary distraction; she'd suddenly lost her breath, lost her voice . . . lost touch with rational thought. He loved hearing her laugh . . . what did that mean?

She returned her attention to him, and fell into his eyes. And realized that her focus on him, and his on her, had deepened, had gained new depth.

And that mutual connection had gained even greater power to hold them both, to draw them in, heightening their awareness, each of the other, immersing them together in those moments of shared experience.

Weaving ribbons of mutual delight into a net that ensnared them.

They danced until they could dance no more, then wandered again, catching their breaths in the large conservatory into which countless couples had drifted to stroll in the moonlight streaming through the glass panes. Conversations there were muted, private exchanges that no one else needed to hear. Windows were open, so the air was fresher, and carried the scents of green growing things tinged with the exotic fragrances of night-blooming flowers.

To Henrietta, the night had taken on a magical quality. She'd lost track of time; since agreeing to James's proposal of how to spend the evening, she'd thought of nothing beyond the next moment, the next experience, the next aspect of their mutual enjoyment.

She'd allowed herself to be swept away—something she couldn't recall ever doing before. It was most unlike her, the practical and pragmatic one, to embrace a come-what-may philosophy and willingly plunge off the structured path. Tonight, she didn't have an agenda; she had no goal, no aim in mind. She wasn't pushing and shoving anything . . . but, she realized, she was learning.

Learning what she might desire in an arena she hadn't, until very recently, allowed herself to explore.

She felt the warm weight of the necklace circling her throat, the touch of the crystal pendant above her breasts. Strolling beside James in the moonlight, her hand on his arm, his hand lying warm over hers, she thought about that, and about what more she needed to learn.

James paused. She glanced at his face. He'd tipped his head and was peering past a collection of palms. Then he straightened. His teeth flashed in a smile. "I'd forgotten about that."

"What?"

He glanced around; she did, too, but there were no other couples near. Then he lowered his arm, caught her hand in his, and drew her around the palms—and through the door that had been concealed behind the large, strappy leaves.

The room beyond proved to be her ladyship's orangery. A narrow stone-walled chamber, it ran across one end of the terrace bordering the ballroom. Glass-paned doors could be opened onto the terrace but were presently shut. Two rows of potted orange trees marched neatly down the room, scenting the air. The only source of light was the moonlight slanting through the glass doors; the shafts struck the pale stone flags, resulting in a soft, diffuse illumination—enough to see by, but not enough for them to be seen by the few couples strolling on the terrace.

Releasing her, James shut the door.

Henrietta went forward, down the aisle between the rows of sculpted trees; glancing at the wall opposite the terrace, she spied a small sofa set against the wall beneath a rectangular window. Stepping out of the aisle, she walked to the sofa; curious, she peered out of the window, then sighed. "Oh—this is beautiful."

The window overlooked an ornamental lake. Sinking onto the chaise, she looked the other way—she could see all the way along the terrace—then she glanced at James as he prowled up to join her. "This sofa is perfectly set." She gestured with one hand to the rectangular window. "The view is simply lovely."

James looked down at her and smiled. "Indeed." After an instant of appreciating her upturned face, masked though it was, he turned and sat beside her.

Looking out along the terrace, she sighed. "It's been an unexpectedly delightful evening—thank you."

"It's been entirely my pleasure, for which I thank you."

He watched her lips curve, then she murmured, "Sadly, it's nearly over."

That was true, which meant . . . he was running out of time. The evening had gone perfectly to this point, but he couldn't risk not capitalizing on the opportunity Lady

Hamilton and fate had, it seemed, conspired to hand him. If he didn't take the risk, accept the challenge, and take one more step forward, tonight and all the ground he felt he'd regained might well be for naught.

He had to push on, or his advance, and all advantage, might dissipate like mist come the morning.

This, he suddenly realized, was the moment. His moment of truth with her. If he took the next step, he might be damned, but if he didn't, he almost certainly would be.

Yet if he took this next step, there would be no going back, at least not for him. And if she approved and accepted . . . then there would be no going back for her either, even if she didn't, immediately, recognize that . . . but he didn't have time to think and rethink.

His time was now.

Relaxing against the sofa, he glanced at her face. "There's one more thing we've yet to do—one more experience we've yet to enjoy."

"Oh?" Shifting to face him, she widened her eyes. "What?"

"This." He reached a hand to her nape, cupped the delicate arch, and drew her face slowly to his. They were both wearing half masks; they didn't need to take them off. He gave her plenty of time to resist if she wished.

She didn't. Instead, he heard her quick, indrawn breath, saw her gaze fix on his lips.

He lowered his gaze to her mouth, then drew her the last inch and covered her luscious lips with his.

And kissed her.

Properly, this time, yet still with restraint. He set his lips to coax, to tempt, to tease, and waited . . . until he sensed her tentative response, felt it well and swell and burgeon.

Until the pressure of her lips against his grew to be both invitation and incitement.

Only then did he take the next step, the first tiny step beyond innocent. Even then, he didn't want to frighten her with any too-precipitate glimpse of the passion he held leashed, yet this time he had a point to make, a claim to stake, and he wasn't going to retreat before he'd accomplished that. Slowly straightening, sliding his thumb beneath her jaw, he tipped her head up, angled his, and sent his tongue cruising over the fullness of her lower lip, tracing the seam . . . and she parted her lips, opened for him, and invited him in.

He wanted to plunge in, to dive deep into the heady delights she offered, but he hauled back on his reins, deployed all the expertise at his command, and smoothly, seductively engaged, traced, stroked, and tantalized.

Steadily, step by step, he led her deeper into the dance, into the subtle play of dueling tongues, the evocative delight of claiming her mouth, and the surprising pleasure of her questing response.

He introduced her to the complementary joys of him tasting her, and of her in turn tasting him.

Any thought that she wasn't enjoying this, that she wasn't as wholly engaged as he was, was shattered by her first more definite foray. Then she shifted; a moment later he felt her fingertips gently caress his cheek, and his awareness fractured.

Henrietta sensed it; she didn't know enough to put a name to what she sensed—a sudden break in his control, of his careful leading—but something in her leapt with a never-before-experienced delight, a sense of victory. Of feminine triumph.

Yes—this was right.

Kissing him and being kissed by him felt inexpressibly right, in a way that resonated to her bones. She wanted to rush ahead, to learn more—much more—all that he could teach her, yet simultaneously she wanted to linger, to savor this, to exalt in this, to drag every iota of simple pleasure from this—to learn the ways how.

He showed her. He didn't rush forward but lingered with her, savored with her.

They shared even that, openly and completely.

She had no space for thought in her mind, no scintilla of awareness left for reason, and certainly not for detached observation. She followed where he led, and when he paused, once she was certain she'd absorbed all there was to experience to that point, she pressed, and he responded, and they moved on.

So completely immersed in the kiss were they that neither reacted to the warning *swissh*.

But the explosion of the first rocket jerked them both back to the present—to the sofa in the orangery. They blinked across the shadowed room; looking through the glass doors, she saw the milling crowd now filling the terrace.

"Ah." With James's help, she sat up; she'd been leaning into him. His lips appeared softer than usual, his hair disarranged—had she done that?

He looked out at the gathering, then grimaced and met her gaze. "I just remembered—her ladyship has decided to enliven the countdown to midnight and the unmasking with fireworks. The twelfth rocket will be fired at midnight."

She sighed, but not unhappily; pleasured satisfaction sang in the sound. "We'd better go out."

"Sadly, yes." James settled his mask, then rose and held out his hand.

She resettled her mask, too, then laid her hand in his and let him draw her to her feet.

He met her gaze, then raised her hand to his lips, pressed a kiss to her knuckles, and said, "We can talk tomorrow morning. I'll meet you in the park."

"Earlier. I usually ride twice a week, at about eight o'clock."

The curve of his lips deepened. "In that case, I'll meet you at eight by Rotten Row."

She nodded, then faced forward and walked beside him as he led her to the glass doors, opened one, and escorted her through and into the crowd thronging the terrace flags. She needed to think about what they'd just done, of what it meant, of what she'd learned, and what they'd both intended. And then they needed to talk, yes, but as she couldn't yet corral her wits sufficiently to think at all, tomorrow was the perfect time for that.

As everyone else had their eyes on the heavens, oohing and aahing at the pyrotechnical display, no one noticed them joining the gathering. Still smiling with a species of reckless delight, she stood at the side of the crowd, and with James beside her, directed her gaze upward, too.

The second rocket soared into the firmament and burst in a glory of red and gold sparks.

A conflagration of other fireworks filled the moments between each rocket; the countdown steadily progressed, the guests taking up a chant, counting the rockets one by one.

Then, at last, to an eruption of cheers and applause, the twelfth rocket shot high overhead and exploded, raining silver and gold over the gardens.

Smiling, laughing, everyone threw back their hoods

and untied their masks. Gaily turning to each other, looking about, people started hunting for acquaintances in the crowd.

"No need for us to find anyone else." James smiled at Henrietta as she turned to him, her delicate features once more fully revealed.

She smiled back, but sighed. "I should leave soon. My parents will expect me home shortly."

"I may as well go, too." Flinging his domino back over his shoulders, he made a gallant show of offering his arm. "We can track down Lady Hamilton and take our leave together."

Henrietta grinned, placed her hand on his arm, and together they turned—

The young lady alongside Henrietta backed into her.

"Oh! I say!" The young lady whirled and proved to be the lovely Cassandra Carmichael. "I'm terribly sorry. Have I caused any harm?"

Smiling, Henrietta shook her head. "None whatever."

Cassandra introduced herself and Henrietta did the same, then she introduced James to Miss Carmichael, who smiled with transparently sincere delight; it was no difficulty to see why she was considered one of the catches of the season.

"And this"—Miss Carmichael waved over her shoulder—"is . . ." Glancing back, she broke off. "Oh."

The gentleman who had been standing with her had turned and was already some paces away, making his way through the crowd.

Cassandra smiled indulgently. "Someone must have summoned him." Shrugging, she laughingly shook her head. "It happens all the time—he's in such demand. You'll have to excuse him."

They shook hands and parted. Turning, Cassandra

started tacking through the crowd in the wake of her errant partner. Steering Henrietta toward the house, James softly snorted. "She'll make some politician an excellent wife."

Henrietta laughed. "We can only hope Sir Peter appreciates her."

"Was that him?"

"I assume so. I'm not that familiar with him, truth be told. Ah—there's Lady Hamilton."

Together they made their way through the crowd, waited in line to take leave of their hostess, then James handed Henrietta into her parents' carriage, smiled and saluted her, then shut the door.

As the carriage pulled away, Henrietta sank back with a sigh.

She was still smiling in a wholly revealing way—and she still couldn't think worth a damn.

Chapter Six

Despite her best intentions, by the time she reached Rotten Row the following morning, Henrietta had still not managed to adequately dissect what had taken place between her and James the previous night enough to come to any conclusion.

That said, when it came to him and her, something inside her seemed to push to the fore and make decisions—decisions based wholly on her emotions—and, to her wary amazement, thus far those decisions appeared to have been sound. Indeed, they appeared to be bearing fruit, for there James was, waiting at the beginning of the tan track, resplendent in an exquisitely cut riding coat and mounted on a heavy gray, and the light in his eyes when he smiled as she cantered up simply made her heart soar.

She'd never before had her heart behave as it did around him.

"Good morning!" She drew her mare, prancing in expectation, in alongside his gray. "And what lovely weather we have for our run."

James tipped his head, his lips curving appreciatively. "The sun isn't the only thing that's lovely enough to warm."

A blush touching her cheeks, she chuckled and felt a spurt of exuberant happiness inside.

Leaving her groom to wait by the tan, they took their place in the queue at its head. When their turn came, they thundered down the track, her fleet-footed black mare a good match for his stronger, but heavier, gelding. After three runs, punctuated by waiting for other riders to clear the tan, they turned away, letting the horses amble as they headed back toward Upper Brook Street.

For a while, she concentrated on slowing her breathing, on settling and finding her mental feet in the aftermath of the exertion. James seemed content to do the same. The horses walked on, then Grosvenor Gate neared. They clopped through, crossed Park Lane, and turned north.

They'd said that they would talk, but in all honesty she wasn't at all sure what they might say; it was too early, between them, for any declarations, and the moment . . . was perfect as it was, and she didn't want to wrestle with the question of whether, in the aftermath of last night, she should nevertheless tell him of what she'd learned about the excellent Miss Fotherby. She didn't want to bring up the subject of Miss Fotherby at all—but was that fair?

To Miss Fotherby, or to James?

They turned into Upper Brook Street, the clang of the horses' hoofbeats striking the cobbles echoing hollowly between the tall façades—and, dragging in a breath, she decided she couldn't *not* speak. If James no longer wished to pursue Miss Fotherby, or any other young lady, because he had shifted his sights to her, then he would have to tell her. They couldn't keep avoiding the subject. . . .

It suddenly occurred to her that she wasn't the only one who'd been avoiding the subject of Miss Fotherby.

She blinked, then glanced at James, riding easily alongside.

He was studying her mare. "Is that a horse from your cousin Demon's stables?"

"Yes." She paused, then, very willing to be distracted, went on, "Demon supplies all the family's horses. I think he'd be insulted if we got a horse from anywhere else."

James chuckled. "From what I recall of him, I can believe that. He always was a stickler over horseflesh."

Henrietta studied James's face, but all she could see was . . . the same enjoyment of the moment she felt.

Her horse screamed and reared.

Instinctively, Henrietta clamped her crooked knee tighter about her pommel; because she was riding side-saddle and was a strong rider, she managed to keep her seat.

But instead of coming down and settling, the mare plunged forward—straight into a bone-shaking, wildly careening run.

Gasping, jostled and shaken, Henrietta hung on and fought for control. She hauled on the reins, but the normally placid mare was frantic—and was far stronger than she.

Upper Brook Street was in Mayfair. It was cobbled, with stone gutters and pavements; if Henrietta fell, she'd dash her brains out.

That was the prospect that flared in James's mind as Henrietta's horse dove and wove through the carts and drays delivering produce to the houses of the wealthy. He'd clapped his heels to his horse's flanks before he'd even formed the intention of giving chase; within seconds he was thundering up in her wake, closing the gap to the black mare's back.

And Henrietta.

She was still clinging, white-faced and desperate, as he drew alongside.

Grimly, he used his own mount's weight to lean into the mare and force her to slow, but the panicked horse wasn't going to halt, and the wider streets surrounding Grosvenor Square lay just ahead.

"Trust me!" Dropping his reins, he reached for Henrietta. "Free your foot from the stirrup, unlock your leg, and let go of the reins—now!"

She didn't hesitate; if she had, he might not have had the balance to seize her, lift her, and haul her to him. To crush her in his arms and hold her tight while with his knees he slowed his gray.

Freed of her rider, reins flapping, the black mare flew on across the intersection and along the northern side of Grosvenor Square.

Belatedly, Henrietta's groom came racing up; he'd been dawdling far in the rear. "I'll get the mare!" he yelled and urged his own mount on.

James heard him through a buzzing in his ears. His arms were locked, convulsively tight. His lungs felt starved, and his pulse still pounded. Fear was a dull roar in his mind, even though the firm warmth of Henrietta in his arms, against his chest, assured him that she was safe. Still his.

Gulping in air, Henrietta clung to the solid pillar of male strength that was James, but as his horse halted, she drew her head from James's chest and looked toward the Square, where both the mare and her groom had vanished.

One of her hands had come to rest, fingers spread, on James's chest. Beneath her palm, she could feel his heart thumping heavily, running a race in rhythm with hers.

There were other people around, shocked merchants and delivery boys who had witnessed the drama, but her senses had drawn in; nothing around them felt real.

She looked up—just as James looked down.

They stared, desperately searching each other's eyes as if to reassure themselves she was indeed there, safe in his arms.

Then he swore beneath his breath, bent his head, and kissed her.

Hard. Voraciously.

Forget Miss Fotherby.

Henrietta closed a hand about his nape and kissed him back.

Henrietta was still shaking when James helped her into her parents' front hall.

The butler who had opened the door to them looked shocked.

"Miss Cynster's horse bolted and she was nearly thrown." As the butler hurried to close the door, James studied Henrietta's face. "Her groom's gone after the animal. Please summon Lady Cynster and Miss Henrietta's maid."

The butler snapped to attention. "At once, sir . . . ah, Mr. . . . ."

Henrietta pulled herself together; falling apart in a crisis never helped. Dragging in a breath, she bludgeoned her brain into cooperating. "This is Mr. Glossup, Hudson. He's a friend of Simon's, which is why he probably seems familiar."

"Ah, yes." Hudson drew himself up and bowed regally to James.

"Mama will still be upstairs. If you would send word

to her that there was an . . . ah, incident, and tell her I'm resting in the back parlor. No need to summon Hannah—I'm not about to faint." She made the statement with gritty determination, yet even as the words left her lips she felt a wave of weakness wash over her again.

James, one hand clamped about her elbow, had been watching her face. Now he muttered something harsh, bent, and swept her up into his arms.

Instinctively clutching his lapel, she blinked in surprise but felt too weak to protest. From Hudson's shocked face, she realized that spoke volumes.

"Where's the back parlor?" James demanded.

She waved limply down the corridor. "That way."

He carried her, trailing riding skirt and all—a feat she found quite impressive—down the corridor. Hudson came fussing behind; he opened the door and held it while James angled her into the room, then with swift strides carried her to the chaise before the windows and lowered her gently onto the comfortable cushions.

"Tea." The request was the sum of her contribution to her own recovery, but tea always helped and was the prescribed remedy for overset nerves. And her nerves, she decided, were definitely overset—far more than they had been when she'd been tipped into the river.

This time death—horribly violent death—had felt much closer.

"At once, miss." Hudson looked at James, who'd crouched by the chaise and—Henrietta belatedly realized—was chafing her hands. "I'll summon her ladyship."

Without looking at Hudson, without taking his gaze from her face, James nodded curtly.

Hudson left.

Henrietta tried a smile, but even she could tell it came out rather wan and weak. Drawing one of her hands from James's clasp, she lightly touched his hair, gently brushing the rumpled locks into better order. "Thank you." She met his eyes. "That was . . . frightening."

Running footsteps sounded in the hall.

Letting her hand fall, Henrietta looked toward the door.

James rose; squeezing her hand briefly, he reluctantly released it and stepped to the chaise's head.

The door burst open and Mary tumbled in, a maid, presumably Hannah, on her heels.

Mary's wide, cornflower blue eyes took in the scene in one sweeping glance, then she focused on Henrietta. "Are you all right?"

Henrietta's smile wobbled even as she said, "Yes, it was just"—she waved in weak dismissal—"a trifle oversetting."

From the looks on Mary's and Hannah's faces, James deduced that Henrietta saying she was a trifle overset was the equivalent of her admitting to being halfway to death's door; the pair swooped, enveloping Henrietta in effusive, if not smothering, feminine concern. Mary patted her hand and asked questions. Hannah shook out a knitted shawl and spread it over Henrietta's legs, then the tea tray arrived and, barely pausing for breath, Mary poured.

James stood beside the chaise, fielding Mary's questions, relieving Henrietta of that, at least. He watched all the fussing, listened to the chorus of exclamations, and saw Henrietta gradually relax.

Then the door opened and Henrietta's mother swept in. After a swift survey of her daughters, Louise's gaze rose to his face. James inclined his head. Louise smiled briefly in acknowledgment. "Mr. Glossup. I understand we must thank you again for rescuing Henrietta." Her expression turned wryly understanding. "You seem to be making a habit of it."

James glanced at Henrietta, caught her eye. "I'm just glad I was near enough to help." A chill touched his soul as he realized that, once again, being close enough to rescue her had been pure luck.

"So tell me—what happened?" Louise sat in an armchair, waved James to another, accepted a cup of tea from Mary, then fixed her gaze on Henrietta. "It's not like you to lose control of your mount."

Henrietta frowned. "I don't know what happened. Marie suddenly reared—I didn't see or hear anything that might have caused it." She glanced at James. "Did you?"

He shook his head. "And my mount didn't react."

Henrietta nodded. "True. But Marie screamed as if she was in pain and reared, and then she just shot off." Setting her cup on her saucer, Henrietta visibly quelled a shiver. "That would have been frightening enough in the country, but there I would have been confident I would have been able to ride it out. But in the streets here . . ."

James looked into his cup and decided no one needed to hear just how close to a fatal fall she'd come. With the barrows, drays, and carts cluttering the street, if a carriage had come the other way . . . raising his cup, he sipped, and glanced again at Henrietta, reassuring himself that she was indeed there, was indeed hale and whole, albeit a trifle overset.

Color was gradually returning to her cheeks, and her gaze was alert as she listened to her mother and sister debate her state.

James tuned in to their comments as Louise and Mary exchanged projections as to Henrietta's recovery, much to Henrietta's fond annoyance, but Louise was adamant in decreeing that Henrietta rest for the remainder of the morning and into the afternoon. In wholehearted agreement, James held his peace. If he could have, he would have wrapped her in the proverbial wool and sequestered her away somewhere out of everyone's reach, at least until he learned enough to soothe the protectiveness currently prowling, anxious and concerned, just beneath his skin. But, it seemed, he could rely on Louise and Mary to act in his stead.

Hannah, who had lingered, suggested a warm bath, as Henrietta wasn't going out again that morning. Henrietta agreed, and James approved; she was, apparently, taking the need to rest and recuperate seriously.

"And we can pack for the house party this morning, as well," Henrietta called to Hannah as the maid headed for the door.

"Yes, miss." Hannah bobbed and opened the door. "I'll get a footman to fetch your bag and bandbox from the box room."

James stared at the closing door, then looked back—first at Louise and Mary, sipping their tea apparently unconcerned—then at Henrietta. "You're not still going to Ellsmere Grange?"

Eyes widening, Henrietta looked at him. "Yes, of course I am." She looked faintly puzzled. "Why wouldn't I be?"

Because you've just had a too-close brush with death? James bit back the words; trapping her gaze, he said instead, "Under the circumstances, I imagine you might be better served by resting, at least until you're sure you've fully recovered from the shock."

The look she bent on him was faintly exasperated, as if she'd expected better from him. "I'm not such a weak thing—I'll be perfectly well by this afternoon, and I won't have to set out until then. Ellsmere Grange is only in Essex, after all."

"Yes, but . . ." He frowned. They'd originally agreed to attend the house party at Ellsmere Grange in order to pad out and ultimately to finalize the short list for his necessary bride; even though that was no longer their aim, he'd assumed they would use their time there—in a setting removed from the hubbub of the ton—to further explore their alternative path. However, he was now very aware that his concern for Henrietta's well-being trumped any consideration of his quest, however urgent. Setting down his cup and saucer, he met her eyes. "There's no pressing need to attend, is there? And a quiet few days would allow your nerves more time to settle."

Henrietta's expression turned stubborn. "My nerves are already well on the way to being settled again. The incident might have been a shock, but it was only an accident, after all. A poor thing I would be to allow that to affect me for more than an hour or two. Besides"— she glanced at Louise—"Lady Ellsmere is expecting us. It's far too late to cry off now."

James looked at Louise, expecting—at least hoping— that she would support him.

Both Louise and Mary, he realized, had been quietly sipping, and watching the exchange between him and Henrietta. Now Louise set her cup on her saucer and stated, "I have to agree with Henrietta." Louise met his eyes, her gaze that of the softhearted and kindly grande dame that she was. "I would be very surprised were any daughter of mine to need days to recover from an incident such as this, and Henrietta is correct in saying that for both of you to cry off at this late hour, with no broken bones or similar disaster to excuse you, would be seen as a snub to the Ellsmeres. I'm sure you wouldn't want that, and I certainly couldn't countenance it, certainly not for Henrietta, so she, at least, will be attending as expected."

Despite the kindliness, a spine of steel lurked beneath Louise's soft-seeming exterior. She held James's gaze for an instant, then arched her brows. "So, given Henrietta will be going, am I to take it you will attend as planned, too?"

He didn't look, but he could feel the weight of Henrietta's gaze, and Mary's, as well. He kept his gaze on Louise's blue eyes—very like Henrietta's—then, lips tightening, capitulated. "Yes. Of course." He glanced at Henrietta and was met by a brilliant smile. At least he'd made her happy.

Apparently his surrender had made Mary happy, too; her smile was simply dazzling.

Which left him feeling confused. Deeming retreat the course of wisdom, he rose. He bowed politely to Louise, then looked at Henrietta. After that kiss in the street, he would have liked to speak privately with her—just a word, a touch, perhaps another kiss—but at the same time, he didn't want her to bestir herself unnecessarily. He inclined his head. "I'll see you at Ellsmere Grange this afternoon."

She held out her hand, her face uptilted, her expression grateful and relaxed. "Indeed—and thank you again. I'm steadfastly *not* thinking about what would have happened had you not joined me this morning."

He wished he could do the same, but that thought was firmly embedded in his brain. However . . . he bowed over her hand, then, releasing it, nodded to Mary and strode from the room.

Henrietta watched him go. She really had no business feeling so very thrilled over the outcome of a potentially fatal accident, but what had been revealed by his responses and hers—that scorching kiss they'd shared in the middle of Upper Brook Street, which thankfully no one of any note socially had seen—had been their truth. In that moment, what was evolving between them had flared like a flame, indisputably true; to know that, to have been afforded that insight, was worth almost any price.

And she hadn't, after all, been harmed in the least.

Transferring her gaze to her mother's curious face, she smiled reassuringly. "I truly am fine."

Louise's lips curved with that deeper understanding only a mother possessed. "Indeed, so it seems. Now go up and have your bath, and you would be wise to take a nap. Mary and I will be out for luncheon, but we'll be back to see you off this afternoon."

After quitting the back parlor, James paused in the front hall, then glanced at the butler, Hudson. "Have you heard whether the groom caught Miss Cynster's mare?"

"Yes, sir. Gibbs caught up with the beast on the other side of Grosvenor Square, when some carriages blocked it in."

"So the animal's back in the stables?"

"Indeed, sir."

"And where might your master's stables be?"

Directed to the mews, James found the stables easily enough. The stableman, an older, experienced man, was walking the black mare, now perfectly placid again, on the cobbles before the stable doors, studying the horse's finely shaped black legs, no doubt checking for any wounds.

Hands in his pockets, James walked up and halted beside the man. "Good morning. Hudson told me where to find you. I was riding with Miss Cynster this morning—I'm a friend of Mr. Simon Cynster."

"Oh, aye." The stableman regarded him. "You're the one who saved our lassie." He nodded respectfully. "You have our thanks and more besides, sir. Miss Henrietta's a game rider, but from what Gibbs—her groom—said, she'd never have been able to rein in Marie here."

"Indeed. Miss Cynster told me the horse came from her cousin Demon's stable. And that, I admit, makes me curious." James tipped his head toward the horse. "Marie here was perfectly placid earlier, all the way until she screamed and reared, and I can't imagine Demon Cynster allowing any of his female cousins to possess a horse with an uncertain temper, or any other susceptibility that might result in what I saw this morning."

"No, indeed." The stableman's face darkened. "You're right there, but it's no wonder that Marie screamed as she did." Moving to the horse's rump, the stableman lifted a corner of the blanket currently draped over Marie's back. "Just look at what some bastard did to her."

James looked at where the man pointed. A small wound was still seeping blood. It took him an instant to realize what it meant. "A dart?"

Straightening, he looked incredulously at the stableman, who nodded grimly. "Aye—that's my guess. Some idiot boy out for a lark, I suppose—throw the dart and watch the fine lady flying off her horse." The stableman snorted. "If me or my boys could lay hands on the blighter, he wouldn't be smiling."

"No, indeed." But they'd have to get in line. James quashed the sudden impulse to violence, and nodded at the stableman. "Thank you for showing me—I thought it must have been something like that."

They parted with goodwill and good wishes all around.

James walked slowly back up the mews, lips twisting as he wondered . . . but there was no reason to suppose that the dart had been aimed specifically at Henrietta's horse, and not, as the stableman assumed, simply at the horse of some fine lady.

Chapter Seven

James left London early in the afternoon. Driving his curricle, he reached Ellsmere Grange in good time. After greeting his hosts, Lord and Lady Ellsmere, friends of his parents, and being shown to his room, he descended to the drawing room to lounge and chat with the other guests who had already assembled.

Miss Violet Ellsmere, the daughter of the house, had recently become engaged to Viscount Channing. James and Channing had known each other for years; James duly ribbed Channing over his soon-to-be lost freedom, which, James noted, Channing bore with the smugness of a well-satisfied cat.

Which only made James all the more restless as he prowled the gathering while constantly keeping one eye on the forecourt.

Finally, a black carriage rolled up the drive—the right black carriage; James recognized the Cynsters' coachman. By the time the coach rocked to a halt on the fine gravel of the forecourt, James was stepping off the porch, waving the footman back as he reached for the carriage door.

He swung it open. Henrietta blinked at him, then smiled. Happily. She was clearly suffering no ill effects from their morning's excitement.

Extending her hand, she let him help her down. "Thank you." When he offered his arm, with a laughing smile, she twined her arm in his. "Are you intending to monopolize me?"

He smiled back. "Why else do you imagine I came?"

Her soft laughter made him smile even more as he led her into the house.

She went through the usual process of greetings, then Violet escorted her upstairs to the room she'd been assigned, but soon enough they both returned, rejoining James and Channing in the drawing room.

The four of them sat and chatted while the rest of the company ebbed and flowed around them. Afternoon tea came, was consumed to the last tasty crumb, then they settled to an exchange of the latest ton stories.

Guests continued to arrive; by the time the dressing gong resonated through the house, James had counted twenty guests, not including their hosts, Violet, and Channing. All those lounging in the drawing room rose and, in couples and groups, headed up the stairs.

James ambled beside Henrietta, and thus discovered that the room she'd been given lay down the corridor to the left of the main stairs, three doors along on the right. After seeing her to her door, he walked briskly back through the gallery and on to the room he'd been given toward the end of the opposite wing.

While he washed and changed, he considered what they might make of the evening and decided they would have to play it by ear. While on the one hand he wanted to press ahead and secure Henrietta as his bride—and that compulsion had grown only more powerful in the aftermath of the incident that morning—simultaneously he was conscious of a fundamental desire to give her all and everything a young lady might wish for, including all she might wish for in a courtship.

"We have two full days," he muttered to himself, chin raised as he tied his cravat. Even though it was essential that they marry before the first of the coming month, he still had twenty-five days in hand. "She'll want some time to enjoy our engagement before we face the altar, but . . . we can afford at least a few days wooing. No need to rush." No need to shortchange her just because he was in a hurry and had an inflexible schedule.

With that resolution firmly fixed in his mind, he descended the stairs and strode to the drawing room. It was inhabited only by males; no ladies had yet made an appearance. Joining Channing, Percy Smythe, and Giles Kendall, James was quickly drawn into a discussion of that perennial topic of male regard—horses.

Five minutes later, Rafe Cunningham walked into the room. He glanced around, hesitated, then walked over to join James and the others.

"What-ho, old boy!" Channing shook Rafe's hand. "I didn't expect to see you here."

Rafe shrugged lightly. "Lady Ellsmere's my godmother." Rafe glanced at James and nodded. "Glossup."

James nodded back, wondering if he was correct in detecting a note of restrained animosity in Rafe's deep voice . . . and if Miss Fotherby numbered among her ladyship's guests. James hadn't seen her earlier, but he hadn't seen Rafe, either.

Eventually the ladies started drifting in. James was rather pleased when, upon his leaving the group to join Henrietta, she met him halfway. They shared a private smile, then together turned to engage with other guests; standing side by side, they chatted with Miss Finlayson and Miss Moffat, and were soon joined by Channing and Violet.

Miss Fotherby, James noted, joined the gathering a bare minute before they were due to dine. Even more telling, on stepping into the drawing room, Miss Fotherby looked swiftly around, saw Rafe Cunningham watching her from across the large room, and froze. For an instant, she looked like a deer poised to leap and race from a hunter, but then she stiffly looked away and, her features set and pale, walked across to speak with Lady Ellsmere.

Henrietta had noticed Miss Fotherby, too. She glanced at James, arched a brow.

Before he could reply, her ladyship's butler appeared to announce that dinner was served. Lady Ellsmere commanded their attention and told them the seating would remain informal for the duration of their stay, and recommended they oblige her and find their own partners. Everyone laughed, very happy to do so—except for Miss Fotherby, but Robert Sinclair was standing beside her and offered his arm, and she quickly accepted his escort.

With Henrietta on his arm, James dipped his head to whisper, "As she's here, I believe it would be wise for me to tell Miss Fotherby of my decision regarding her . . . ah, application as soon as may be."

Watching the byplay between Miss Fotherby and Rafe Cunningham, even though both were partnered with others, Henrietta nodded. "Be that as it may, I think tomorrow morning will be the earliest you'll be able to do so. If this event runs along customary lines, we'll have music or charades after dinner tonight."

James inclined his head in acceptance.

Once seated beside him at the long table, Henrietta

found herself enjoying the gathering more than she'd anticipated—certainly more than she had previously enjoyed such events. She'd attended innumerable house parties through the years, but she had never before had . . . a focus. A locus for her attention, a pivot about which she could circle. That, she realized, with a swift glance at James, currently chatting with Violet on his other side, was what was different. James's presence widened her experience of everything about her; the conversations, the sallies, the quick quips and repartee all seemed sharper, more engaging, when viewed through the expanded prism of his likely reactions as well as hers.

In the sense of scope, he opened her eyes. Never before had she viewed the world about her and considered how it might appear to, or might impact on, another.

That, she supposed, smiling and shifting so she could better hear something Miss Hendricks wished to impart to her, was what forming a relationship was all about; learning and empathizing with the feelings of one's other. Presumably that was what the affectionate tag "the other half" implied.

She was glad they'd agreed to include the Ellsmeres' house party on their schedule of useful events. Even though their quest might have been superseded, this was the perfect setting for her and James to spend time together, to get to know each other better out of the hothouse environment of the ton's ballrooms. Here, they would have time to ramble and talk without constraint or reserve, or the ever-present threat of interruption. As the covers were drawn and the company all rose, she realized she was looking forward to the next days with unalloyed expectation.

As she'd foreseen, at Lady Ellsmere's direction the

entire company repaired to the large music room on the other side of the old mansion. There, they passed an enjoyable few hours entertaining each other with ballads and song. Miss Fotherby was one of the first to take her seat at the pianoforte; she sang a ballad in a piercingly sweet voice. A few performances later, Rafe Cunningham sang, accompanied by Miss Findlayson; his baritone was rich and powerful, and held them all spellbound. Then Giles Kendall joined Rafe, singing tenor to Rafe's baritone, in what was quite certainly the most riveting performance of the evening. Somewhat later, Henrietta played the pianoforte and sang a sweet country song, followed by a duet with James, then Violet and Channing joined them for a rousing rendition of an old shepherd's song, a long and repetitive, subtly jocular composition of chorus and verses of extraordinary length.

She was out of breath, and so were the other three, by the time she played the last resounding chord. The audience gave them a standing ovation, then Lady Ellsmere called for tea.

Finally the evening ended, and in loose groups, the guests made their way down the corridors and up the stairs. Ascending the stairs beside James, Henrietta smiled at him and murmured, "I'd completely forgotten the brouhaha of this morning."

His eyes met hers. "No lingering effects?"

She shook her head. "None. I'm quite recovered, and this evening has been . . . the right sort of distraction."

"Good." They stepped into the gallery at the top of the stairs. James hesitated. The ladies were wandering off in twos and threes down the corridor to the left, while all the males had been housed in the opposite wing. Reaching for Henrietta's hand, trapping her gaze, he raised her fingers to his lips and lightly kissed. "In that case, I'll wish you a good night's rest. Sleep well."

She smiled brilliantly, lightly gripped his fingers, then drew her hand free. "You, too." She held his gaze for an instant, then inclined her head and turned away. "Good night."

He watched her walk away, then followed the other gentlemen down the corridor into the other wing. Just before he reached his door, he sensed someone watching him, felt the weight of their gaze on his back. Halting before his door, grasping the knob, he glanced up the corridor.

Rafe Cunningham stood in a doorway back along the corridor, watching him.

The light was too dim to make out Rafe's expression, but if James had to guess, he would have said that confusion dominated. Rafe, he realized, must have seen him part from Henrietta.

Opening his door, James went in and shut it. He paused, wondering if he should speak with Rafe now and put the poor devil out of his misery, at least with respect to James's intentions toward Miss Fotherby, which, from Rafe's reactions, Rafe at least partly knew, or rather, thought he did.

James considered, but the certainty of what Henrietta would say if he asked whether he should speak with Rafe decided the matter. She would say he should speak with Miss Fotherby first, then leave it to Millicent to decide what to tell Rafe.

Shrugging off his coat, James thought through the likely scenarios and decided that, after he'd told Millicent, if Rafe asked him directly he would tell Rafe, too. Rafe had the devil of a right hook. Explaining a black eye to Lady Ellsmere, let alone Henrietta, wasn't a scenario he wished to face.

As he slid beneath the sheets, his comprehension of and empathy for Rafe's situation shifted into a review of his own. On the one hand he wanted to give Henrietta all he could by way of courtship. She was twenty-nine; to his mind, she'd waited for him to come along, and he was abjectly grateful that she had, so it was only fair that he do his level best to woo her properly.

But simultaneously he wanted to speak; for him, the fright of the morning hadn't subsided but rather had transmogrified, adding to an unexpected compulsion to say something aloud, to stake a verbal claim. Even though he knew it was too early for a full-scale declaration, for some unfathomable reason his wolfish instincts had turned on him and were hotly urging him to make, at the very least, a statement of intent.

Why it was so important to his inner self that he tell Henrietta in plain English that he wanted her for his bride he didn't know. Settling to sleep, he closed his eyes—and wondered for how long he could stand against his surging inner tide.

Breakfast the next morning was a leisurely affair. Guests drifted downstairs and into the dining room from eight o'clock onward. The sideboard along one wall played host to an array of silver platters and chafing dishes offering everything from boiled eggs and bacon, to sausages, kedgeree, and a dish of boiled mutton, ham, and celery said to be a local delicacy.

James arrived reasonably early, helped himself to a selection of viands, then pulled out a chair midway down the long table. Settling next to Channing, he joined the discussion already raging between Percy Smythe and Dickie Arbiter over which company made the best pistols in this modern age. Dickie was all for the latest American guns, while Percy expounded the virtues of the English makers.

When appealed to, James admitted to the attraction of the new American mechanisms but, on balance, gave his vote to the English makers, "Purely on aesthetics." He looked at Dickie. "Have you seen one of their guns?"

Percy chuckled, while Channing erupted with his usual barking laugh.

Others arrived, and then Henrietta appeared, along with Miss Hendricks and Violet. They were the first of the female contingent to arrive, but other ladies quickly followed, and with their higher-pitched voices, the conversations changed in sound, tone, and subject.

James kept his eye on Henrietta as she progressed along the sideboard; in a golden-yellow walking gown she looked like summer sunshine to him. When she turned to the table, he immediately rose and drew out the chair beside him. With a smile, she accepted the unvoiced invitation and let him seat her. Channing had also risen and held the chair on his other side for Violet, while on the opposite side of the table Percy performed the same service for Miss Hendricks.

The ladies settled, and the talk turned to the one subject in which they all had an interest, namely what had been planned for the rest of the day.

"We'd thought to have a morning around the house—a croquet competition for those up to the challenge, with billiards for those gentlemen who would prefer it, and there's the library or the gardens for the ladies should they not wish to join those on the croquet lawn." As daughter of the house, Violet had been intimately involved in formulating the schedule. "And after lunch, we thought a ramble through the woods to the ruins would be nice."

"Ruins?" Both Miss Hendricks and Dickie Arbiter spoke the word simultaneously. They shared an arrested glance, then looked at Violet for further edification.

"They're the ruins of the original priory that the grange was attached to," Violet explained. "They're very old—no one knows how old, but old enough that they're half-buried. Not that we have to go into caves, or anything difficult—what we call the ruins are the walls and columns and altars and so forth that are exposed on the side of a hill. Goodness knows how much more of the original buildings are still buried beneath the hillside, but many of the walls are covered with moss and have ivy trailing over them." Violet smiled at Miss Hendricks. "Very atmospheric."

"The woods are old, too," Channing put in. "Huge old oak trees, that sort of thing. Easy to walk beneath, and the path to the ruins is relatively flat." He glanced up the table to where Lady Ellsmere and several friends of her generation sat breaking their fast and gossiping. "Even the older ladies would have no great difficulty reaching it, but it is a few miles away—it'll take us half an hour to stroll there, and another half hour back, so I'm not sure they'll want to waste the time."

Miss Hendricks looked positively enthused. "It sounds like a delightful excursion."

"Hmm." Dickie caught Miss Hendricks's eye. "I'm rather fond of old places. I, for one, will join the party for the ruins."

All their group voiced their intention to join the ramble, then Violet went on, "And this evening, as I'm sure you've all anticipated, there's to be a ball. Not a massive affair—we want to keep it a touch more relaxed. We're not in London, after all. But there will be musicians, so lots of dancing, and a few of our neighbors will be joining us, so there'll be several more people to meet."

"Excellent!" Percy beamed. "Sounds like my sort of day."

As Percy was an acknowledged social gadabout, everyone laughed and agreed.

They'd all finished their breakfasts. Together, they rose, the ladies gliding to the doors that opened to the sunlight terrace, the gentlemen sauntering behind.

Pausing to let Violet lead the way onto the terrace, Henrietta glanced at those still seated about the table. Miss Fotherby was sitting with Miss Findlayson and Miss Moffat, both of whom were gaily chattering, but Miss Fortherby had a hunted air. As Henrietta watched, Miss Fotherby darted a glance down the table to where Rafe Cunningham sat beside Giles Kendall. Rafe wasn't even pretending to listen to Giles or Robert Sinclair, seated opposite; he was watching Miss Fotherby.

As James joined her, Henrietta flashed him a smile, turned, and walked out onto the terrace. She hadn't been surprised to discover Rafe among the guests; she'd known of the connection with the Ellsmeres. Miss Fotherby, however, had looked shocked, almost stricken to discover Rafe there. From what Henrietta had gathered, Miss Fotherby's aunt, who had been among the older ladies seated with Lady Ellsmere, was an old friend of her ladyship's . . . which suggested that Miss Fotherby had been inveigled to attend, and both her aunt and Lady Ellsmere were playing matchmaker.

Which suggested that neither older lady knew of Miss Fotherby's offer to James.

They'd fallen into a loose group, strolling together in the mild morning sunshine. Reaching the steps leading down to a small parterre, Channing offered Violet his arm. She took it and they descended. James promptly offered Henrietta his arm. Placing her hand on his sleeve, she accepted his support down the steep steps.

And wondered if she should ask him what he planned regarding Miss Fotherby.

Courtesy of the incident with Marie, she and he hadn't talked—hadn't yet shared their thoughts on how each saw what was evolving between them. But clearly Miss Fotherby needed an answer—she had even requested one within a few days—and was there any reason, any justification, not to tell her how matters now stood?

Henrietta pondered that as they ambled along, into the rose garden and out again; she breathed in the fresh air, smiled and laughed with the others, and eventually decided she wouldn't yet prod. James knew how matters stood, and only he could give Miss Fotherby her answer.

They eventually found their way to the croquet lawn. The sun had risen enough to dry the grass, and they quickly set out the hoops and pegs, and distributed the mallets. Then came the matter of deciding teams and the terms of the competition. In the end, they agreed to play in couples, in a round-robin style of tournament. No one really cared whether or not they had time to complete the rounds, or, indeed, who won; it was all about fun and their enjoyment of the play.

Nearly an hour had passed, and most of the younger ladies and gentlemen had gravitated to the croquet lawn and joined the competition, and the older ladies had come out to sit on garden chairs in the shade of the nearby trees to watch and smile approvingly, when James, standing to one side with Henrietta, waiting for their next match, saw Miss Fotherby—whom Rafe had earlier attempted to solicit as his partner, but who had all but seized Giles Kendall instead—walking swiftly along the edge of the lawn, head down, coming his and Henrietta's way.

James waited until Miss Fotherby neared, then said, "Miss Fotherby?" When, startled, she halted and looked up, he smiled easily. "I wonder if I might have a word?" He glanced around, drawing her attention to the fact that, at that moment, the three of them were out of earshot of everyone else.

Miss Fotherby drew in a tight breath and nodded. "Yes. Of course." But her expression remained haunted; she glanced constantly around and appeared thoroughly distracted.

James inwardly frowned; he sensed that Henrietta, standing beside him with her hands crossed over the handle of her mallet, was also puzzled by Miss Fotherby's response. "About the suggestion you made on Lady Hollingworth's terrace."

Miss Fotherby's head swung his way and she stared—as if only just remembering. As if the matter had slipped entirely from her mind. "Oh—ah, yes." She colored faintly. "That is . . ."

He felt even more compelled to speak, simply to end the tangle the situation seemed to have become. "I've decided that my affections lie elsewhere, something I hadn't realized then. I must thank you for your suggestion, but I am no longer searching for a . . . convenient bride."

Miss Fotherby blinked, then her gaze seemed to focus. She looked at James as if finally truly seeing him, then she glanced at Henrietta, and her lips quirked in a fleeting smile. She dipped her head. "Indeed. I must thank you for speaking so plainly, and while you might not believe me, I sincerely wish you well."

But she was already turning away. "And now, if you'll excuse me . . ." Without waiting for any reply, with a vague nod she continued on her way.

"Well!" Bemused, Henrietta watched Miss Fotherby stride off. "I must say that wasn't at all what I expected."

"Oh, I don't know." James had spotted Rafe Cunningham stalking along the opposite side of the croquet lawn. "I suspect Miss Fotherby is feeling somewhat besieged at the moment."

Henrietta had followed his gaze. She humphed. "Goodness knows where that will end."

"Well," James said, turning to her with a smile, "that's entirely in their hands now, and no longer a concern of ours. Which, I admit, feels like a weight off my shoulders."

"Glossup—Miss Cynster!" From the starting peg, Channing beckoned. "You're up."

Saluting in reply, Henrietta lifted her mallet and walked with James down the side of the lawn. "We're never going to get a moment to *talk*, not while we're here, are we?"

James smiled. "I doubt it. But we have time enough to simply take these few days as they come, and just enjoy them." He caught her eye. "We're not in that much of a hurry."

She arched her brows. "I suppose you're right." Looking ahead, she swung her mallet experimentally. "All right then—let's see if we can defeat Dickie and Miss Hendricks."

With a laugh, James waved her on.

As anyone might have predicted, the ringing of the luncheon bell resulted in the croquet competition being declared incomplete and unresolved, and the company retired to the dining room for a rowdy luncheon, during which all those involved relived their exploits and aired their opinions on who would eventually have won.

After luncheon, a half hour passed while the ladies retreated to their rooms to don bonnets, spencers, and shawls, then the party foregathered on the terrace and set out in good order, Violet and Channing in the lead, to walk to the ruins in the woods.

Such a country ramble was standard fare for any well-run house party. Even the older ladies and gentlemen joined in, although all of the older generation parted company with the rest when they reached the lake. Those younger continued on into the woods, while their elders took a much less strenuous stroll around the lake and so back to the house.

The path through the woods cut a wide, wending swath beneath the spreading branches of the old oak trees. The crumbling detritus of last autumn's leaves lay thick on the ground; although sunshine slanted through the boughs and the air was a warm kiss, winter dampness still lingered in the heavier shade to right and left, the rich loamy smell of decaying drifts mingling with the crisp scent of new growth. Moss grew in a green carpet along the banks, cushioning the gray of the local stone that showed through here and there.

As Channing had said, the path was even, a very gentle downward slope leading them, somewhat deceptively, deeper and deeper into the old woods. The line of ramblers stretched out as they fell into groups, chatting as they walked. Topics were inconsequential; various guests stopped to point out a bird flitting through the branches, or to examine a fern, and gradually the group devolved into couples ambling companionably.

A full half hour had elapsed before Violet and Channing led them around a curve in the path, and the ruins rose all around them. Coming up behind their friends, Henrietta and James both stared, eyes widening as they raised their gazes to the tops of the high stone walls, mottled and pocked with mosses and lichens, and draped with encroaching creepers, then looked further, gazes sweeping over a wide expanse filled with the remnants of tumbled-down walls.

Henrietta slipped her hand onto James's sleeve; the chill of the shadows—and doubtless all that looming rock—sent a shiver through her, and she shifted closer, nearer to James's warmth.

He turned his head and smiled, closing his hand over hers on his sleeve, then he looked past her and drew her on, to the side, as others of the party rounded the curve and, as they had, stopped to stare.

"It's a sight worth gawping over," Henrietta murmured, looking again at the columns and the curves of arches that rose, skeletal memories of grandeur, here and there among the walls. After a moment, she said, "Come on. Let's explore."

They did, as did all the others. They paced around long-forgotten cloisters and strolled down stone-paved corridors now open to the sky. Navigating through what, from the arches distinguishing it, appeared to be the old priory church was an exercise in slipping between massive carved rectangular stones strewn like children's blocks by some giant's hand.

James and Giles met on what both agreed had to be the front porch of the church. Both stood and looked around while Henrietta, picking her way through the ruined nave, and Miss Findlayson, clambering up from below, joined them.

"I'd take my oath," Giles said, pausing to give Miss Findlayson his hand up the last steep step, "that when they built this place, that hill"—releasing Miss Findlayson with a smile, he turned to survey the hill behind them, the one the ruins appeared to be built into the side of—"wasn't there."

Hands on his hips, James nodded. "I agree. That wall"—he pointed to a wall at the rear of the ruins, the top of which showed just above the hillside as if it were a retaining wall holding back the mass of the hill—"looks to be the central wall of the main priory building, the building that would have housed the dormitories and living quarters. See?" He pointed to the rim of the wall. "Those are capstones, so that was the top of the wall." Lowering his arm, he looked around once more. "And Violet was right—this appears to be only half the priory. The rest, presumably, lies beyond the main building—beyond that wall and now buried under the hill."

Giles was nodding. "So the hill couldn't have been there, not back when this place was in use."

Scanning the wall in question, Henrietta said, "I know it's been centuries since the priory was inhabited, but I wonder how and why the hill came to form there?"

They speculated at length—given the age of the trees growing over the hill and in some places overhanging the top of the wall, some act of disrespect at the time of the Dissolution became their favored theory—then James and Henrietta parted from Giles and Miss Findlayson and plunged back into the maze of ruined walls, making their way to the rear of the ruins, to what James had hypothesized had been the central wall of the main building.

"If we look closely, there should be a pattern of rooms lying on this side of the wall." He gave Henrietta his hand to help her over a fallen rock.

They enjoyed themselves, with a certain sense of triumph discovering the remains of long-ago rooms, tracing the outlines, comparing each room's relationship to the main wall and the other rooms, and speculating as to what each room might have been used for. The sun's rays were angling through the surrounding trees when the sudden sound of voices—not chatting but arguing violently—reached them.

A gentleman's voice and a lady's voice.

James looked at Henrietta; she'd heard them, too. Quietly, he walked a short distance along the corridor to where an archway allowed him a restricted view into the next section of the ruins.

He halted abruptly, then held still, looking out at the vignette framed by the ancient stone.

Silently, Henrietta glided up and stopped beside him; placing her hand on his arm, she looked out, too.

Rafe Cunningham had finally cornered Millicent Fotherby. He was arguing . . . or was it pleading? James and Henrietta could hear the voices, the tones, but not the words. Millicent was wringing her hands and shaking her head; her expression stated she wasn't going to be moved, no matter the violence of Rafe's feelings.

Abruptly, Rafe threw his hands to the sky, then looked down at Millicent.

And Millicent finally spoke. Whatever she said, it struck Rafe like a blow—James and Henrietta saw the jerk of his spine, the jolt of his head.

But then Rafe shook his head and growled—one word of utter denial.

And swept Millicent into his arms and kissed her.

James tensed—he couldn't allow Rafe to assault Millicent—but Henrietta's fingers curled in his sleeve. "Wait!" she whispered.

James wondered what he was supposed to wait for . . . but then Millicent's arms, at first lax by her sides, slowly rose. And tentatively, so gently and warily it was difficult to watch, she raised her arms and her hands stole up to Rafe's shoulders, then slowly slid to cup his nape.

And Millicent was kissing Rafe back.

James relaxed. "Ah."

After a moment—long enough to confirm that Millicent wasn't about to change her mind—he turned away. Catching Henrietta's hand in his, he met her eyes and grinned. Then he lifted her hand, pressed a kiss to her fingers, and they headed back along the corridor. "Where were we?" he murmured.

Henrietta glanced around. "About here, wasn't it?"

"Halloo!"

The call rang out from the front of the ruins.

It was Channing. He yelled, "Come on, you lot—time to start back."

Calls came from various places, most a great deal closer to the path than James and Henrietta. James looked at Henrietta, then raised his voice. "Channing—you and the others start back. Miss Cynster and I will follow as quickly as we can."

"Right-ho! Don't dally, mind—we all have to get ready for dinner and the ball."

"We're on our way!" James yelled back. Smiling, he took Henrietta's arm, twining it with his, and they started back, following the long corridor that ran along the old wall, their fastest route back to where the path entered the ruins.

That said, they saw no reason to hurry; they ambled along, pausing so Henrietta could study the tiny ferns sprouting from the fissures in the wall.

They'd been virtually on the other side of the ruins from the path; they'd traveled about half the distance back when a sharp crack sounded, emanating from behind them, from the general area in which Rafe and Millicent Fotherby had been. James halted and, releasing Henrietta, turned.

Henrietta halted, too. They both looked back, but saw nothing. She pressed his arm. "Go and look—just in case. We should make sure they're returning as well—they didn't reply to Channing."

Which gave him an excuse if Rafe and Miss Fotherby spotted him. James nodded and retraced his steps.

He was almost back to the archway when Rafe stepped through it into the corridor, with Millicent on his arm.

"Ah, there you are." James halted. "I heard a crack."

Rafe nodded. "A rock fell." He looked down the corridor toward Henrietta. "This seemed the fastest way back to the path."

"We thought the same." James turned back to Henrietta.

A grating sound dragged his gaze upward.

Dust, then fine stones rained down from the top of the wall above Henrietta.

A massive capstone, five feet long and at least two feet high and deep, shifted, tipped, then fell.

Henrietta had looked up, but dust had got in her eyes and she'd looked down again. She hadn't seen the stone falling.

James opened his mouth, but panic locked his lungs. Then he was running.

Boots striking the corridor's floor, legs pumping hard, eyes tracking the falling capstone, he raced—and knew he wouldn't be in time.

Desperate, he summoned every ounce of his strength—and flung himself forward.

He hit Henrietta, caught her—held her to him, protecting her as best he could as his flying tackle carried them several feet down the corridor and onto the ground.

They landed, skidding, in a tumble of clinging limbs.

The horrendous *whump-thud* of the stone smashing down physically jarred them.

Silence—shocking and absolute—fell over the scene.

Then, somewhere, a blackbird trilled.

Slowly assimilating that they were still alive, they cautiously raised their heads and looked back down the corridor. Henrietta clung to James and he to her. They stared, disbelieving, at the fate that had nearly been hers.

No, nearly theirs; the capstone lay embedded in the floor mere inches from James's boots. The stone had cracked on impact, blocking the corridor and hiding them from the others.

Henrietta could barely breathe. Her heart was thudding so heavily that she wasn't sure she could hear.

Turning her head, she met James's eyes.

A smothered cry reached them, then Rafe scrambled onto the fallen stone.

The instant he saw them, he stopped, stared, then his shoulders sagged and he blew out a breath. "My *God!* I thought you were both done for."

Millicent scrambled up beside him, looked, then

clapped a hand to her chest. "Thank *heaven* you're all right!" Then she seemed to collect herself. "You are all right, aren't you?"

James slowly sat up, then helped Henrietta to sit up, too. He met her eyes, then replied, "Apparently."

Rafe dropped over the stone, helped Millicent down, then, his expression grim, turned to James. "I saw it all—that stone didn't just fall." He held out his hand and, when James grasped it, pulled him to his feet.

Rushing to help Henrietta up, Millicent glanced sharply at Rafe. "Nonsense! How can you suggest such a thing? It had to have been an accident. The stone must have been loose and something nudged it the last little way."

Rafe snorted. "Something like what? A clan of badgers acting in concert wouldn't have been able to dislodge that stone."

James knew that was true, but he held up a hand to stay further argument. "Regardless of how it happened, let's get moving." Meeting Rafe's eyes, he flicked his own upward. *There are more stones up there.*

Rafe shut his lips and nodded. "Right. Let's get on."

Henrietta and Millicent brushed and straightened Henrietta's walking dress while James vaguely dusted off his coat and breeches, then, with Millicent walking beside Henrietta and Rafe and James hovering close, glancing up and around frequently, they walked on.

Millicent, Henrietta noted, was wringing her hands again and was understandably wide-eyed, nervy and ready to jump at the least little noise. Henrietta suspected she should feel the same, but . . . she decided she must be in shock. She was simply too glad to be alive, glad to be able to breathe, to be able to glance along her shoulder and see James walking close beside her.

After being nearly squashed to death, being alive felt too good. She would worry about what had happened later, now that she was sure she would have a later.

They found the path and started along it, but a few yards on, James halted. When the others stopped, too, and faced him, he briefly studied Henrietta's eyes, then looked at Millicent. "Why don't you two ladies sit on the bank here and catch your breaths? I want to take a quick look at the spot from where the stone fell, just in case the hillside there is crumbling and we need to warn the Ellsmeres."

Rafe nodded. "Sound idea. I'll come with you."

Henrietta might not have wanted to think too hard about how she had nearly died, but she wasn't having that. "No." She glanced at Millicent and saw her own resolution reflected in Millicent's brown eyes. Looking back at James, she stated, "We're coming, too."

James hesitated, but, truth be told, he'd rather have Henrietta with him. "Very well." He reached for her hand, turned, helped her clamber up the bank, then led her steadily on, onto the hill overlooking the ruins.

Rafe and Millicent climbed up behind them.

They found the wall and followed it along—to the gap where the lighter hue of the stone on either side identified the original position of the recently fallen capstone.

Halting in a semicircle around the spot, they stared silently down at the evidence imprinted in the soft moss growing in the lee of the top of the wall. It wasn't hard to guess what had caused the capstone to fall.

Crouching, Rafe examined the smeared tracks left by a man's large boots. After a moment, he grunted. "He slipped too much to be able to guess the size."

"But," James said, forcing his voice to remain calm

and even, "it wasn't a work boot." He glanced at his own feet, then at Rafe's. "Something more like riding boots."

Rising, Rafe nodded, his face grim. He met James's gaze, then waved down the hill. "We'd better get on, or we'll be late for dinner."

Subdued, each a prey to disquieting thoughts, they made their way back to the path and set off to return to the house.

Chapter Eight

After watching Henrietta and Millicent ascend the stairs on the way to their rooms to change for dinner, James and Rafe exchanged a glance, then went hunting for Lord Ellsmere.

They found him in his library, already dressed for the evening and enjoying a quiet brandy; Lord Ellsmere took one look at their grim faces and promptly offered them both a glass. After only the minutest of hesitations, both accepted.

Sinking into the chair his host waved him to, James took a revivifying sip of the fiery liquid, then, as Lord Ellsmere sat again, caught his lordship's eye. "We were out with the others at the ruins. We were the last to head back and . . . there was an accident."

"Accident? Good God—what?" Lord Ellsmere sat up. "Here—no one's dead, are they?"

"No," Rafe said, his deep voice rough, "but it was a very near-run thing." He tipped his glass at James. "If it hadn't been for Glossup there, and a frankly amazing tackle, Henrietta Cynster would be dead as a doornail, crushed under a fallen stone."

Lord Ellsmere paled and fell back in his chair. "Good Lord!"

"But that's not the worst of it." James drained his

glass. Aware of the look Lord Ellsmere bent on him, as if unable to believe that there could possibly be anything worse, James lowered the glass, met his lordship's gaze, and disabused him of that comfortable notion. "Someone—most likely a gentleman in riding boots—deliberately pushed the stone off the wall. And he had to have known Henrietta was beneath it—we'd been talking just before."

Lord Ellsmere stared, then looked at Rafe, who confirmed James's words with a grim nod. "But," his lordship all but sputtered, "you're not saying it was anyone here?"

James met Rafe's eyes, then, frowning, slowly shook his head. "It doesn't seem likely. We were all in groups."

"Thank heaven for that." After a long moment of silence, Lord Ellsmere said, speaking slowly and carefully as if trying out the words, "There has to be some explanation. No one would want to kill Henrietta, so . . . it must have been something else. Perhaps . . . a prank gone wrong, or . . ." His lordship looked from James to Rafe and back again, but neither came to his rescue. "Well," his lordship asked, "what else could it be?"

Another long moment of silence ensued, then James set down his glass, met Rafe's gaze, and rose. "I doubt there's anything anyone can do—there was plenty of time for whoever it was to simply walk away. We just thought you should know."

Lord Ellsmere looked up at them as if wishing they hadn't thought anything of the sort, but on meeting James's eyes, he nodded. "Yes, well . . . as you say, nothing to be done."

With polite, if somewhat stiff, nods, James and Rafe parted from their host and left the library.

They paused in the front hall.

James glanced at Rafe, who looked back at him, then James sighed and reached for the banister. "We'd better get changed."

They climbed the stairs and walked to their rooms.

While he stripped and quickly washed, then shrugged into his evening clothes, James heard Lord Ellsmere's observation and resulting question repeating endlessly in his mind.

No one would want to kill Henrietta, so . . . what else could it be?

James was starting to have a bad feeling about that. A very bad feeling indeed.

For James, the dinner and ball passed in a bland blur of faces and polite conversations. Briefly meeting in the drawing room before the company had gone into dinner, he, Henrietta, Rafe, and Millicent had agreed that there was nothing to be gained by creating a sensation among the other guests by spreading the tale of Henrietta's near brush with death.

In a private aside, Rafe had baldly asked, and James had confirmed that he would be sticking to Henrietta's side throughout the night. Later, during the ball, Rafe had paused beside James to quietly report that he'd discreetly checked with the others from the house party who had been at the ruins that afternoon, and none of the gentlemen had been unaccounted for over the critical minutes.

"So it had to have been someone from outside," James had concluded.

Rafe had nodded. "And 'outside' could mean anywhere. There's a decent lane on the other side of the woods that joins the road to London."

A waltz had started up, and Rafe had left to whirl Millicent down the floor. James had watched Henrietta waltz with Channing, then had reclaimed her, and thereafter hadn't let her go.

But finally the ball ended, and after dallying in the front hall, on the stairs, and in the gallery until all the other guests had gone ahead, James escorted Henrietta down the corridor to her room.

Pausing outside the door, he opened it and waved her through.

Glancing at him, faintly puzzled, she went.

Swiftly glancing around and confirming that the corridor was empty, he quickly followed her and closed the door behind him.

Expecting to bid him good night, Henrietta swung to face the door; she fell back a step, brows arching in surprise. She met his eyes, a clear question in hers.

He met her gaze, then surveyed the room. An armchair stood by the fireplace. Stepping past Henrietta, he walked to the armchair and dropped into it.

She followed. Halting beside his boots, she looked down at him; the question in her eyes had grown even more pronounced.

He sighed, leaned back, and held her gaze. "I'm staying here tonight. All night."

Head tipping slightly, she studied him. "Why?"

"Because I can't leave you alone." When she frowned at him, he reached out, caught her hand, and tugged her down to sit on the broad arm of the chair.

Henrietta obliged, leaving her hand in his, lightly returning the pressure of his fingers. "I can see that you're worried, but . . . I don't quite understand why, at least not to this extent." She drew breath, then added, "I haven't thought—haven't allowed myself to think—too much about what happened today, but . . . even so, I can't see what we can possibly make of it. I don't know of anyone who might wish me dead, much less act on that wish."

"But someone did." He looked up at her, meeting her eyes, his concern on open display. "Henrietta, someone tried to *kill* you today—we can't overlook that. But"—his lips twisted—"there's more. I learned something I haven't yet told you, about your horse. I checked with your stableman. He's convinced, and so am I, that someone darted your mare."

When she blinked uncomprehendingly, he explained, "Someone threw a dart at her rump. That was why she screamed, reared, and then bolted." He paused, then added, "Someone hoped you'd fall to the cobbles and die."

She stared into his eyes, searched, but saw nothing but absolute conviction. She quelled a shiver. "But . . . why?"

Lips grimly set, he shook his head. "I can't begin to guess, but . . ." He tightened his grip on her fingers. "That wasn't the start of it, if you recall."

When, too shocked by what he was implying, she remained silent, he continued, his eyes steady on hers, "You fell off the bridge into the stream at Lady Marchmain's rout. We assumed it was an accident—but what if it wasn't? Anyone who was there might have seen the opportunity—you were by the side of the bridge, and all of us were distracted by the fireworks. A stumble, a quick, anonymous push, and the stream was running swiftly and it was dark . . ."

Held trapped in his gaze, reluctantly, she added, "And not many young ladies of the ton know how to swim, not even a little."

"Exactly. And the Thames was close, only yards away." He paused, then after a moment continued, "So we have three near-fatal accidents—the bridge, your horse, and now the falling stone. Any of those incidents might have seen you dead, and all of them, even the last, might well have passed for accidents. If it wasn't for the dampness of the moss by the wall, we wouldn't have seen your would-be murderer's boot prints. We would simply have been left wondering how the stone had come to fall, but meanwhile, you would have been dead."

"But . . ." The first shock of realization was fading; annoyance, spiced with a definite dollop of belligerence, swelled, and she embraced the strength it offered. She frowned. "Who the devil could it be?"

James was relieved by her reaction; he'd worried she wouldn't want to see, to acknowledge that someone might wish her ill. That much ill. "I think we can be sure it's a man, and that he's a member of the ton. He would have to be to have been on the bridge at Marchmain House. Anyone with a purpose in Brook Street that morning, from a street sweeper, a delivery boy, a costermonger, to a strolling gentleman, could have darted your horse, and the falling stone could have been any man who wears decent riding boots, but the incident on the bridge could only have been caused by a gentleman of the haut ton."

"Or a lady." Henrietta wrinkled her nose. "But no lady pushed that stone, so I concede your point." She blew out a breath. "So some gentleman of the haut ton is trying to kill me." Brows knitting, she tilted her head. "Which brings us back to why."

He studied her face, her expression. "Could it have anything to do with some past activity of yours as The Matchbreaker?"

She gave the suggestion serious thought but ultimately shook her head. "Other than you, no gentleman has ever protested my findings, and"—she met his eyes— "if they had wished to, I would think they would have protested to my face, at least at first, as you did, but none have."

He conceded the point with a tip of his head. "True enough." After a moment of studying her eyes—and her studying his—he sighed and sat back, fingers gently caressing the back of the hand he still held. "So that's why I have to stay with you tonight. This would-be murderer is a gentleman. He's not at the house party, but he knows you're here. He's familiar with our world. It's perfectly possible he's familiar with this house, and he'll certainly know that few doors will be locked, just in case guests wish to wander."

For a long moment, she stared at his face, then said, "I can see your reasoning. More, I don't dispute it—I agree." She paused, then drew breath and said, "Yet I ask again: Why?"

Looking into her eyes, he didn't pretend to misunderstand. Instead, very conscious of her fingers beneath his, in the simplest, most direct words he could find, he gave her the truth. "Because you're mine."

She held his gaze for a heartbeat, then nodded decisively. "Yes, I am."

Then she swiveled on the chair's arm, leaned over him, framed his face, and tipped it to hers—paused to look into his eyes as if to confirm that he was following *her* reasoning—then she bent her head, set her lips to his, and kissed him.

From that first touch of her lips, there was never any doubt what she intended or where this would end; the kiss went from definite, to scorching, to incendiary in mere seconds. Hardly surprising then, she being her and he being him, that thereafter matters rapidly spiraled out of control.

Or, more correctly, were with ruthless determination and unwavering will driven forcefully toward one paramount goal.

Mutually ravenous, mutually greedy, the kiss ignited a conflagration that spread flames beneath their skins, that incited, razed and burned. Heat surged in a wave of molten hunger, of fiery yearning.

On a muted gasp, she shifted, and then her hands were everywhere, racing over him, tugging at his coat, urging him up out of the chair so she could strip the restricting garment away.

Engaged himself, absorbed and caught, distracted and enthralled, his tongue dueling with hers, his lips rapaciously devouring hers while his hands shaped and weighed her sumptuous breasts, he had to haul sufficient awareness from those all-consuming, senses-stealing tasks to oblige—to bodily lift her to her feet and rise to his, and release her long enough to shrug his coat and waistcoat off—and once he had, nothing could hold her.

Nothing he did seemed capable of reining her in, of reining her back—of reestablishing any degree of supremacy in a world fired by unexpectedly rampant need, and flooded with burgeoning passions, with violently surging desires that only had to rise to be given full expression, only to be offered—in the next heartbeat—immediate gratification.

He felt giddy—as reckless and unrestrained as she as they wrestled each other free of their clothes, as silk whispered over flushed and dewed skin, as palms and fingers flagrantly explored, sculpted, traced. As the cool caress of the night air was banished by the first touch of heated skin to heated skin, naked and burning, and sensation, sharp and potent, rocked them.

Jolted them into a new level of fiery flames, into a new level of consuming awareness.

Of utterly consuming passion.

He closed his arms about her and locked her tight against him, evocatively molding her body to his. And still she didn't pause, not for thought or modesty; she wriggled and urged him on, seemingly hell-bent on plunging into the act—one she'd never indulged in before—with a reckless enthusiasm that left him reeling.

His problem was that her wishes were his; everything she wanted—to do, to feel, to explore—precisely coincided with his own ravenous hungers.

As she desired, so, too, did he; everything she demanded with such flagrant abandon, he was eager and aching to give her.

To lavish on her, to pleasure and delight her.

The only disagreement they might have had, had he been able to summon his wits from the whirling maelstrom she'd engineered, lay in the tempo, the timing; he would have gone slowly, easing her through each step, but she wanted to race, and rush, and fling herself through each stage.

And straight into the next.

Henrietta had never felt so free, so powerfully sure of herself and her destiny. Realization of the faceless threat and her brush with near death had forged a honed edge to her desire. To her consuming need to step forward and seize and reach for all she could be, to stake her claim to the role she now knew to her soul was her birthright.

She wanted him. Yes, she was his, but, to her mind, that translated to he being hers. Hers to engage with as she wished, to the swirling depths of passion and the giddy heights of desire.

And she'd never been one to do anything by halves.

So she let herself free, free to be as she wished to be, to do as she wanted, to desire and explore and demand as she would, to yearn and seek satisfaction.

To take all she would, to give all she could, and find the holy grail she was sure was there for the finding.

Yet despite the compulsion, beneath her driven purpose she was fascinated, intrigued, and enthralled. By him. With him. With the physical reality and the ephemeral connection, with how he, his body, felt, to her, against her, about her, and the emotions she sensed ran like a raging river beneath his smooth surface.

His lips, his mouth, the broad width of his chest, the heavy muscles sculpting his shoulders, all tempted and lured her closer, lured her to caress, to touch and possess, to taste . . . which much to her delight made him shudder.

That, she discovered, was a potent joy, reducing him to the point where he had to close his eyes and ride out the pleasure she lavished on him . . . only for her to be forced to close her eyes and do the same as he returned the delight in full measure.

His touch, the evocative sweep of his fingers over her skin, the hot brand of his mouth on her naked breasts, the possessiveness that drove his more ardent caresses, threatened more than once to sweep her away, to leave her gasping and reeling, awash on a surging tide of sensation, but each time she found her anchor to the here and now in him—in the hard, muscled, irredeemably masculine, godlike beauty stripping him had revealed.

Not just to her eyes, but to all her senses.

Yet despite the potent allure, the intense attraction, she didn't have time to spend on further exploration. Not tonight, not while the driving need to reach the culmination of their mutual desire had already sunk its spurs so very deep, and need beyond bearing, awakened and stirred, provoked and incited, thundered, a heavy compulsive beat in her veins.

She might be twenty-nine, but she hadn't wasted her time. What whispered confidences and overheard gossip hadn't told her, books had. So she palmed his rigid erection and went to her knees. Stroked slowly, then bent and caressed the broad head with her lips, then with her tongue.

And gloried in the taste, and even more in his reaction, the sharp, intense, searing response she provoked.

She set herself to reduce any lingering resistance he might have felt to ash.

Succeeded well enough that he groaned, a guttural sound that sent pleasure cascading through her, that drove her to experiment with touch and tongue . . . until he softly cursed, slipped a thumb between her lips, withdrew his rigid member from her mouth, then he swooped, swept her into his arms, strode to the bed, dropped her on it, and followed her down.

The sensual wrestling match that ensued was *exactly* what she'd wanted. She wanted—needed—to feel his strength, to provoke it, explore it, and ultimately meet it with her own supple surrender. A surrender that was nothing of the sort, that was more in the nature of unadulterated incitement.

Delicious.

The pressures, the tension, the shifting give of her body against his was sensational in the truest sense. She grasped his head between her hands, raised her head and planted her lips on his, and showed him her delight, her unfettered appreciation.

Enough was enough; James knew it was past time he exercised his wolfish expertise, his customary dominance, and seized—urgently regained—control.

Yet they were already rolling, limbs tangling, naked and oh-so-heated in her bed.

His cock was already on fire for her, yet the touch of her silken skin, of her supple limbs sliding over and against and around the muscled hardness of his, made him shiver. The dual sensations were exquisite, the urgent anticipation they fired even more so; the sexual promise she embodied as she wrestled and rolled and he finally lay back and allowed her to sit up and straddle him was beyond anything he'd previously known.

He stared up at her in wonder.

He'd known so many women, yet she was unique. Unique and infinitely precious, so precious he wanted to seize and devour while simultaneously worshipping and protecting her, even from himself.

She made his head spin.

She made him feel like he'd never felt before.

His chest was already working like a bellows. His hands as he grasped her waist and steadied her already shook with rampant desire.

Panting, her hands spread on his chest, fingers greedy and clutching, she unblushingly visually and tactilely possessed, then, bracing her arms, the pendant of the necklace she still wore about her throat swinging between them, she hung over him, met his eyes, and brazenly asked, "So . . . what's next?"

He looked into her eyes, and from somewhere found the strength to ignore the wanton invitation etched in the blue, enough to grit out, "I wanted to give you more—to take more time and court you properly."

She studied his eyes, then shook her head. "No need." She dragged in a shaky breath, her breasts, swollen and full, nipples tightly furled, rising before his avaricious eyes. "For us, there's no need for any careful wooing."

Tipping her head, she looked down at him, then her already well-kissed, luscious lips curved. "I've waited for years, although I never truly knew what I was waiting for. What I was searching for." She glanced down; he thought she looked at her pendant, a curious many-faceted pink crystal, then she raised her head and, smiling, met his eyes. "But now it seems I simply know. Here." Briefly, she touched her fingers between her breasts. "In here, I know. I didn't think it could happen like that—that such a certainty of knowing would simply come to be—but it has, and so I know."

She held his gaze steadily. He couldn't have dragged his gaze from hers had the bed been in flames. He waited, everything he was hanging on her next words; when they came . . . his heart stood still.

"I know," she said, her gaze wide and open and locked with his, "that for me . . . it's you. What I've been waiting for is you."

My hero is you.

Henrietta heard the words and felt their truth, absolute, immutable, irrefutable. The words and the knowledge behind them, the knowledge that was now an intrinsic part of her, pushed her to say, in a voice so sultry she barely recognized it as her own, "So . . . this, you and me, here and now—tell me how. Or, better yet, show me."

His chest swelled as he dragged in a breath, then his grip about her waist tightened and he eased her back, down his body. Then he half sat and kissed her, touched and caressed her; his fingers tracing through the slickness at the apex of her thighs, stroking, then probing, he readied her, then he lay back again and, as she'd demanded, showed her how.

Held her while she positioned his erection at her entrance, then he simply steadied her and let her ease down at her own pace—let her discover the indescribable sensation of his flesh, hot and iron-hard, parting hers, then pressing in, forging steadily fraction by fraction into her body . . .

She closed her eyes, savoring each second, each scintillating heartbeat of sensation.

He was large.

He felt larger.

Quite unbelievably huge.

Eyes closing tighter, her heart thundering heavily, with desire a scalding whip urging her on, she caught her lower lip between her teeth and eased down a fraction more, caught her breath—had it stolen—by the mind-numbing impression of him stretching her, impaling her. . . .

His hands urged her up a touch, and she rose a fraction, then eased down again, a smidgen further this time, but . . .

She wanted more, wanted him. All of him.

Desperately.

And he wanted her in the same way; she could feel the fraught tension thrumming through his body.

Opening her eyes, she caught his, panted, her voice nothing more than a hoarse whisper, "I can't—not like this. Just . . . do it, and take me. Make love to me."

She didn't have to ask twice.

Stifling a groan—he'd known trying it the first time

that way hadn't been a good idea, but she'd wanted to try, and who was he to argue, and he hadn't wanted to deny her even that—James lifted her, rolled, and had her beneath him, thighs widespread, his hips wedged between with the throbbing head of his erection poised at her entrance, in a blink.

Braced above her, he looked down into her mesmerizing eyes, hazed with passion, with desperate desire. Despite the scalding heat of her beckoning sheath, he clung to sanity enough to grate, "Trust me. This will hurt at first, but—"

"I know!" She glared and wriggled beneath him, enough to press her slick heat over the head of his erection. "Just do—"

He thrust in and filled her, and it was the most glorious sensation he'd ever experienced. Her maidenhead ruptured and she didn't even flinch; instead, the honey-eyed walls of her heated sheath clamped tight around his rigid member, the ultimate velvet vise. Lids involuntarily falling, he tipped his head back, caught his breath on a shocked hitch, and hung on to the fleeting moment as hard as he could.

But primitive instinct wouldn't be denied, not for long; finally forced to obey its dictates, he flexed his spine, withdrew almost to the point of losing her clinging heat, then thrust in again.

Deeper, harder.

She gasped, shuddered, clung.

Then reached up with one hand, dragged his head down, found his lips with hers, kissed him voraciously, and flagrantly, brazenly, commandingly urged him on.

He surrendered—to her, to the whip of her passions and the lash of his—and withdrew again, thrust deep again, in an escalating crescendo repeating the age-old dance of retreat and possession, again, and again, until she caught the rhythm and they were riding freely.

Then wildly.

Then desperately urgently.

And ultimately beyond thought in a pounding rhythm that rocked and razed and compulsively drove them both. Clinging, gasping, utterly in thrall, they raced for the peak, the thunder in their veins escalating, the thudding of their hearts a single beat that swept them on, whipped them higher.

Until they broke through the clouds and ecstasy beckoned, as hot as the sun and more brilliant than the stars.

And fingers compulsively twining, clutching tight, together they raced for it, harder, more powerfully, until as one they reached for the glory.

Found it—and completion found them.

Shattered them.

She cried out and convulsed around him, fingers sinking deep as her sheath contracted powerfully and drew him irresistibly on, pulling him with her into a wild, surging cataclysm of sensation; on a groan, he surrendered and went with her.

Into the full flush of ecstasy's possession.

That elemental tide of pure sensation wrecked them, wracked them, wrung them out, then, like flotsam, flung them high and far, out and into the void.

To where glory rolled in and filled them, healed them, sealed them, fused and remade them.

Then, with a gentle hand, set them floating free, bliss-filled, on a golden sea.

Hours later, or so it seemed, James regained sufficient muscle control to lift and roll off Henrietta. With a heartfelt—gloriously sated—groan, he slumped alongside her.

Somewhat to his surprise, she stirred, stretched like a cat, then turned and curled against him. He lifted his arm and she snuggled closer, nestling her head into the hollow below his shoulder.

With an inward sigh of impossible contentment, he settled his arm around her. And, to his amazement, knowing she was awake, found words on his tongue, waiting to be spoken. He examined those words, their implication, but then inwardly shrugged, opened his lips, and let them out. "You'll have to marry me now."

He squinted down at her face and saw her smile.

"Yes, I suppose I will." She was toying with the pink crystal pendant, a smile of feminine mystery laced with sensual appreciation flirting about her lips.

He wasn't so sure about the mystery, but that acknowledgment of pleasure warmed him. And her ready acceptance of his statement only underscored what he'd already divined; she might be intelligent, but she was refreshingly without guile.

When he said nothing more, she glanced up at him, read his expression, then widened her eyes. "Was that your proposal?"

"No . . ." He studied her expression, then more warily said, "I haven't done this before. Shouldn't I wait to gain your father's approval before I formally ask you?"

Her smile grew intent. "Not in my family."

"Ah." Summoning the full force of his charm, he smiled back. "In that case." He caught the hand she'd spread on his chest, raised it to his lips, and, trapping her gaze, reverently kissed the backs of her fingers, then asked, "Will you marry me, Henrietta Cynster, and make me the happiest of mortal men?"

The quality of the smile that washed over her face was, to him, heaven and paradise rolled into one.

Then she pushed up in his arms, stretched up as if to kiss him, but just before their lips met, she whispered, "Yes, I will. With all my heart, and with all that is in me, I will marry you, James Glossup."

Then she pressed her lips to his and sealed their pact.

Later, much later when they finally settled to sleep, James lay slumped on his back, with his wife-to-be a warm weight in his arms, and turned his mind to the next phase in his grandaunt-induced quest. He'd found his bride and secured her hand—now all he needed to do was keep it.

All he needed to do was discover who was trying to kill her, expose them, stop them, and all would be well.

Eyes closing, he sighed and relaxed.

Tomorrow.

Tomorrow he would buckle on his armor and sally forth and slay her dragons, but, for tonight, all was well.

Chapter Nine

Along with the rest of Lady Ellsmere's houseguests, James and Henrietta quit Ellsmere Grange after a leisurely breakfast the next morning. No lurking danger had surfaced to disturb their sated slumber, yet James remained alert and on edge, although he made an effort to rein in any overly protective impulses.

Especially as Lord Ellsmere gave every indication of having already forgotten their previous evening's conversation.

James knew what he knew, and his first concern was to get Henrietta safely back under her parents' roof. To his mind, and even more to his instincts, she was now his—his to protect, to keep safe. As he'd driven his curricle to the grange, he rolled sedately along behind the Cynsters' carriage, much to his horses' dissatisfaction; only by traveling behind the coach could he be sure of spotting any threat, even if that meant eating a certain amount of dust.

Once they reached the cobbled streets of Mayfair, he turned off the direct route, tacking down several side streets to reach Upper Brook Street before the carriage; when it drew up before the Cynsters' steps, he was standing on the pavement waiting to hand Henrietta down.

When he opened the door, Henrietta was sitting poised on the seat, eager to give him her hand; as he assisted her to the pavement, eyes bright, expression alight, she said, "It's only just eleven. Mama and Papa should still be at home."

Lips curving in an impossible-to-suppress response, he gave her his arm. "Let's go in and see."

The butler, Hudson, on admitting them to the house, confirmed that Lady Louise was in the parlor with Miss Mary, while Lord Arthur was in his study.

James exchanged a look with Henrietta, then drew a suddenly tight breath and said, "Please inquire if I might have a few minutes of Lord Arthur's time."

Hudson glanced from James to Henrietta, then beamed. "At once, sir."

Hudson returned in less than a minute with the news that Lord Arthur was prepared to bestow as many minutes as James wished.

Henrietta met his gaze. "I'll be in the parlor with Mama." She squeezed his arm, then released him.

Feeling as she imagined a cat on a hot tin roof might feel, Henrietta watched James disappear in Hudson's wake down the corridor to her father's study. Then, dragging in a huge breath, she held it, paused for a moment to define what—how much—to reveal to her mother and sister, then she determinedly walked down the other corridor to the parlor the ladies of the family used for informal relaxation.

Opening the parlor door, she saw her mother and Mary sitting on the window seat, flicking through a stack of ivory cards—doubtless deciding which of the various morning teas they would attend that day. Both had glanced up; the instant they set eyes on her both straightened, alert, their gazes locking on her face.

Realizing she still wore her traveling cape and was clutching her reticule rather tightly, Henrietta went in, closed the door, then walked, carefully, almost tentatively, to stand before the window seat.

Her mother's eyes searched her face, then Louise reached out and took one of her hands. "What is it?"

Henrietta dragged in a breath past the constriction that had suddenly cinched tight about her chest. "James . . . is asking Papa for my hand."

For an instant her mother and sister stared, then both shot to their feet and enveloped her in simultaneous scented hugs.

"Excellent!" Releasing her, Mary all but bounced with delight.

"My dear, dear girl! This is wonderful!" Louise drew back to look into Henrietta's face. "I'm so glad for you both."

Henrietta smiled back, aware of the relief lurking behind her mother's pleased and thoroughly satisfied expression; she knew Louise had started to worry that her activities vetting gentlemen for other young ladies would influence her view of gentlemen as a whole to the point that she wouldn't accept any gentleman herself.

Glowing with maternal benevolence, reassured and expectantly thrilled, her mother released her and stepped back to the window seat, waving Henrietta to join her. "Come, sit, and tell us all about it."

Henrietta obliged. Flanked by her mother and Mary, both eager to hear every last detail, she related an edited account of her and James's association, repainting what her mother at least had taken to be a platonic friendship into something more closely resembling their reality. "So, you see, because of James's grandaunt's will, we'll need to hold an engagement ball all but immediately, and we have to marry before the month is out."

"Well," her mother said, "you always did like to be different. And getting engaged and marrying in three weeks is definitely something different for this family." Her mother beamed at her, then at Mary. "So we'll all need to dive in and work together to ensure we pull it off."

"I don't want a big wedding," Henrietta hurried to state. "We've had a surfeit of those—something nice and comfortable would better suit me—and James, I daresay, and our situation. Speaking for myself, I would prefer not to feel overwhelmed on my wedding day. I really don't know how the others all coped."

"Hmm." Her mother tapped her chin with one fingertip. "Comfortable is as comfortable might be, at least in this family, but"—she nodded—"I'll speak with the others and Honoria, and see how quiet we can make it."

Mary had been jigging, waiting to ask something. She opened her lips, but a sound at the door had them all looking that way.

The door opened and Henrietta's father preceded James into the room; one look at her father's face told her that James's suit had met with unqualified approval.

Beaming jovially, her father met her mother's eyes, then focused on Henrietta.

She rose as he approached.

Her father took her hand and patted it. "Well, my girl, I understand celebrations are in order. Glossup here tells me you and he wish to tie the knot, heh?"

Henrietta's smiling gaze shifted to James's face; in her eyes, James saw nothing but unalloyed anticipation for, and confidence in, their joint future. In their shared life.

"Indeed, Papa, we do." Closing her hand over Arthur's, Henrietta smiled at her father. "I'm so glad you approve."

"Approve? Of course! James here has told me everything I need to know." Lord Arthur cast a paternally approving glance at James. "Very good job he did of it, too. No obfuscation and all aboveboard. I have no hesitation in bestowing your hand on him, my dear—none at all." Lord Arthur tugged her closer. "Here—come and give your father a hug. This is a happy day for us all."

Henrietta laughed and obliged.

"Indeed, this is a joyous event!" Louise pressed forward to hug James, then drew his head down to kiss his cheek before stepping back to meet his eyes. "Welcome to this family, James—and it's simply a delight that we already know you so well. Simon will be thrilled."

James smiled back, pleased everything had gone so smoothly, so relatively easily; Lord Arthur had been encouraging and understanding. Being a friend of Simon's and long known to the family had significantly eased his path. "Thank you, ma'am." Placing a hand over his heart, he bowed. "I will do everything in my power to live up to yours and Lord Arthur's expectations."

Louise beamed, patently pleased, and stepped back to allow Mary to hug him.

Henrietta's sister was jigging up and down, it seemed with sheer exuberance. She planted a quick peck on his cheek—and insouciantly whispered, "Good job!"

The door opened and Hudson swept in with a bottle of champagne and glasses. In an expansive mood, Lord Arthur handed around the glasses, then offered a toast, "To James and Henrietta!"

They all duly sipped, then Lady Louise set down her

glass and sank onto the window seat. She looked up at James and Henrietta, who had moved to stand beside him. "Henrietta has told me of your need to marry by the end of the month, which means your engagement will have to be announced and celebrated before that."

Lord Arthur humphed. "The wedding will have to be by special license, but there'll be no difficulty there."

His wife quelled him with a look, one that, to James, suggested that the arranging of his and Henrietta's betrothal and wedding was Lady Louise's domain and she wasn't about to brook any interference. "Naturally." Her tone was faintly haughty. "However"—she looked back at James and Henrietta—"that means we have no time to waste in setting matters in train." She focused on James. "I'm assuming you'll be placing a notice in the *Gazette* forthwith?"

He nodded. "I'll go to their office from here. The notice will appear tomorrow morning."

Louise nodded. "Excellent. So"—she arched her brows—"when would you like your engagement ball to be held?"

Henrietta glanced at James, met his eyes, then turned back to Louise. "How soon can we host such an event?"

Without waiting to be asked, Mary rushed to the escritoire, retrieved an appointment book, and brought it to her mother.

Receiving the book, Louise opened it and flicked through the pages, eventually pausing on one, fingertip tapping, then she looked up. "A week. Seven days from today. We don't want your ball to clash with too many of the major events, but that evening will do admirably." She looked at Arthur. "You may start spreading the word to the male half of the family and your friends. Meanwhile"—Louise rose—"I'll speak with

Honoria immediately, and all the others, too." She met Henrietta's eyes and smiled with anticipatory relish. "It'll be a rush, but we'll manage it."

Turning to James, Louise added, "As for deciding the wedding day, as I understand it, as long as your marriage occurs before the first day of June, all will be well—is that correct?"

"Yes, ma'am."

"I'll have to consult more widely before we can decide on a date"—Louise caught his eye—"but the family will want to informally celebrate your betrothal, so we'll see you for dinner tomorrow evening, my dear."

James inclined his head. "I'm hoping to meet with Simon today—I'm going to enjoy seeing his face when I inform him I'll shortly be his brother-in-law."

Louise laughed and patted James's cheek. "He'll be as delighted as we are."

They left the parlor. Arthur returned to his study. James took his leave, bowing over Henrietta's hand, then, his eyes meeting hers, he raised her fingers briefly to his lips before releasing her, finally dragging his gaze from hers, and walking out of the door a beaming Hudson held wide.

As Hudson shut the door, Henrietta sighed, amazingly happy and content, then she turned to see her mother dispatching her dresser, whom she'd summoned to fetch her cloak, bonnet, gloves, and reticule.

Turning to survey Henrietta, her mother said, "You'll do as you are—the others would never forgive me if I didn't give them this news as soon as humanly possible." She turned to survey Mary.

Who was waltzing, twirling, a delighted smile curving her lips, a dreamy expression on her face.

Louise's eyes narrowed. "I can understand that you

might feel happy for Henrietta, but why, my darling Mary, are you so very overjoyed?"

Mary's smile didn't waver, but she halted. "Because I'm thrilled that Henrietta will now be able to pass on the necklace to me, and I'll be able to get my search for my own hero properly underway."

"Ah." Louise nodded. "Well, in the meantime, I believe you should accompany us to St. Ives House—your aunt Helena will want to be informed straightaway, as will Honoria—so go and fetch your bonnet and cloak."

"Yes, Mama." Her exuberance undimmed, Mary rushed up the stairs.

Henrietta watched her go, and wondered. Mary rarely if ever lied, not outright, but she was a past master at deflection, and even though, as Henrietta understood it, Mary already had her hero in her sights, who knew what her little sister meant by *"properly"*?

Henrietta turned to her mother to hear Louise confirm for Hudson that "Miss Henrietta is, indeed, engaged to Mr. Glossup." Her mother went on to sketch their current thoughts on the engagement ball and the wedding.

Hearing the words—words she'd heard so many times before about others, about her older twin sisters, her numerous female cousins—and knowing that this time those words referred to her, Henrietta again felt a species of amazement well.

The Matchbreaker had met her match, and was getting married.

It suddenly occurred to her that it was a very good thing that their wedding would take place as soon as could be. She seriously doubted her patience would bear with the quips and comments that would inevitably rain down upon her; luckily she would only have to grin and bear it for at most three weeks.

Not for the first time, she offered up a silent prayer of thanks for James's Grandaunt Emily and her farsighted will.

On leaving the Cynster house, James drove his curricle the short distance to the mews behind the house in George Street he'd inherited from his grandaunt. Handing horses and curricle into the care of his grandaunt's stableman—now his—he crossed to the house and found replies from both Simon and Charlie Hastings already waiting.

Reading the short notes, James snorted. He wasn't surprised by the alacrity expressed; his request for them to meet with him at Boodles to discuss a major development had been intriguing enough, and the fact that his messages had been delivered by Lord Arthur's footmen would have made the lure irresistible. Folding both missives, he quickly climbed the stairs; he needed to wash away the dust and change before showing his face in Boodles.

Earlier that morning, while he'd been dressing prior to leaving Henrietta's room, she'd asked him not to tell her father about her "accidents." While he'd wanted to oblige—she'd asked, and his first impulse was, apparently, to grant her whatever was in his power to grant—the application of a little thought had forced him to admit that he didn't feel able not to inform her father of all that had happened, and, more, of what he now feared.

What she now feared, too, yet she'd argued her point, opening his eyes to the likely outcome seen from her perspective, one he'd never before considered. They'd ended discussing the pros and cons at some length.

Eventually, he'd agreed to consider carefully how he presented the subject to her father, while she'd reluctantly conceded that he couldn't conceal the matter entirely.

The drive from Ellsmere Grange to London had afforded him plenty of time for cogitation. Once ensconced with her father in his study, he'd told Lord Arthur all—he couldn't ask the man to trust him with his daughter and her future while keeping the very real threat to both back—but he'd also explained Henrietta's understandable reaction to the prospect of being so hemmed in by protectiveness that she wouldn't be able to enjoy said future. She'd made a strong case that as the victim of the attacks, it was unfair to force her to bear the consequences, especially as they could not know when, or even if, another attack would come.

Lord Arthur had been understandably concerned, and James had made no bones about his own agitation over Henrietta's safety. Perhaps because Lord Arthur had seen that James's concern was, if anything, even more acute than his, his lordship had suggested that, for the moment, they might proceed with a simple protective strategy, one Henrietta might not even notice.

As soon as he'd repaired the damage that travel had wrought on his person and changed into attire better suited to St. James, James quit the house, hailed a hackney, and rattled off to Boodles.

Simon and Charlie were already there, waiting at a table tucked away in an alcove at the rear of the club's dining room. They rose as James arrived; the three shook hands, Simon's and Charlie's gazes examining every tiny facet of James's expression for some clue as to his news.

He'd expected that, and wore an expression of utter

inscrutability, even though his lips were impossible to force straight.

Waving them back to their chairs, he sat, too, met Charlie's gaze across the table, then looked at Simon. "I've just come from your parents' house. I've offered for Henrietta's hand and been accepted."

Simon's slow grin broke across his face. "Henrietta's accepted you?"

That, James had to admit, was a pertinent clarification. He nodded. "We spent the last few days at Ellsmere Grange, and . . ." He shrugged. "We decided we would suit."

"Wait, wait." Charlie, although beaming, also managed to look confused. "I thought she was helping you find your necessary bride? That you'd persuaded The Matchbreaker to turn matchmaker?"

"That was how it started," James allowed, "but the more time she spent in my scintillating company, the more she came to understand that she wanted to marry me herself."

Both Charlie and Simon made rude, scoffing sounds.

Simon noticed the head waiter passing, hailed the man, and ordered a bottle of the club's best burgundy, a wine the three of them preferred. Turning back, he said to James and Charlie, "To celebrate." Looking again at James, Simon, still grinning delightedly, shook his head. "God knows how you did it, but you do realize, don't you, that you're going to be the toast of the ton's gentlemen? Ah." Simon turned as the head waiter proffered a bottle for inspection, then, at Simon's nod, poured three glasses.

After passing the filled glasses around, the waiter set down the bottle and withdrew.

Simon raised his glass. "To James—the man brave

enough, with fortitude enough, to beguile The Match-breaker into matrimony."

"To James," Charlie echoed, raising his glass, too. "The Matchbreaker's fate."

"The Matchbreaker's mate," Simon offered, setting his glass to Charlie's.

James shook his head, raised his glass to both of theirs, and corrected, "The Matchbreaker's match."

"Yes—that's it!" Charlie clinked his glass against the other two. "The Matchbreaker's match—that's you."

Of course, their ribbing didn't stop there, but as it was all good-natured, and his friends made no secret of how pleased and happy they were over his news, James put up with their more ribald jokes until, finally, they reached the point of asking about the engagement ball and the wedding.

Their meal had arrived by then. While they ate, James told them what he knew, and Simon confirmed that when it came to weddings in the Cynster family, the men were expected to do as they were told and other-wise leave all to the females of the clan.

"It's not worth trying to get a word in," Simon warned.

James shrugged. "As long as we front the altar before the first of June, I'm happy to leave it all in their hands."

Eventually, they pushed their plates aside, refilled their glasses, then relaxed in their chairs, sipping contentedly. Turning his glass in his fingers, James studied the red glints gleaming in the wine and more quietly said, "So I've told you all my good news, but, I fear, there's a more disturbing tale to tell."

"Oh?" Simon studied his face. "What?"

James told them of Henrietta's "accidents," and why he no longer believed they were accidental at all.

Simon and Charlie listened without comment; by the

time James reached the end of his report, both were entirely sober.

"Good God," Charlie said, his wine forgotten, "a massive capstone? You would both have been killed!"

James grimly nodded. "If we'd still been under it when it reached the ground, without question."

A long moment of silence ensued while Simon and Charlie digested the facts, then Simon said, "So . . . some unknown gentleman, a member of the haut ton, is trying to kill Henrietta and make her death look like an accident. We have no idea who he might be, or why he wants her dead."

James lowered his glass. "Correct."

"Clearly we have to expose this beggar and hand him to the authorities." Charlie looked from James to Simon and back again. "So what's our next move?"

"Our first priority," James said, "is to keep Henrietta safe." He looked at Simon. "I told your father all, of course, and he and I felt that if we can ensure that Henrietta is guarded whenever she isn't surrounded by the females of your family, then this blighter, whoever he is, will find it difficult to approach her. He seems set on making her death appear an accident, so as long as there are others with her, she should be as safe as we can reasonably make her."

Simon grunted. "*Reasonably* being the critical word—Henrietta will hate being 'guarded.' "

"True, but as long as we're not overly obvious about it, she's unlikely to get her back up. Luckily, what with our about-to-become-public engagement, with our wedding to follow quickly thereafter, no one—including Henrietta—will think it odd if I'm constantly by her side when she's in public, and on the few occasions I might not be there, for one of you two to be there instead."

Both Simon and Charlie nodded.

"The timing of your impending nuptials is helpful," Simon agreed. "We should be able to pull that off without abrading Henrietta's feminine sensibilities."

James nodded. "And your father is going to speak with your mother, so she will ensure that female members of your family are always around while Henrietta is with them, attending their various daytime entertainments. Enough people will know to ensure that she's never left alone."

Simon nodded. "All right—we've got Henrietta covered, as protected as we can make her in the circumstances."

James grimaced. "Short of sealing her up in a tower, I can't see what more we can do. And as she's been quick to point out, whoever this madman is, we can't be certain that he'll try again."

Charlie's gaze sharpened. "But we need to find out who he is, just in case he does."

"True," Simon said. He met Charlie's gaze, then James's. "Any thoughts as to how we might do that?"

They revisited the three incidents again, trying to draw what they could from the facts, but that was precious little. Wine gone, they rose from the table and made their way out into St. James Street.

On the pavement, Simon halted and slid his hands into his pockets. "The incident in Upper Brook Street holds little hope, but I wonder if I can persuade Lady Marchmain to part with her guest list?" He met James's eyes. "If you're right about the incident at Marchmain House, then the villain was there, and almost certainly one of her ladyship's guests."

James slowly nodded. "It's a place to start. There must have been a hundred or more there, but only half of those will be men, and from the incident at the ruins, we know we're looking for a man."

"More," Charlie put in, "there'll be a lot of gentlemen on Lady Marchmain's list we can immediately exclude. You, Lord Marchmain and his cronies, and probably a host of others."

"You're right." Simon nodded. "We're looking for a reasonably strong, able-bodied, fit and healthy blackguard—"

"Who's masquerading as a gentleman of the ton." James met his eyes. "Exactly."

After agreeing to share anything they thought of or learned that might help identify Henrietta's would-be murderer, they parted, Simon sauntering off to see if he could locate Lady Marchmain and inveigle her guest list from her, while Charlie strode off to keep an appointment with his barber.

James headed back to George Street, strolling and wracking his brains, trying to think of what more he could do.

That afternoon, Henrietta was the toast of an impromptu gathering of all the Cynster ladies and the family's close female connections presently in London. Eschewing the more formal setting of the St. Ives House drawing room, the ladies, one and all, crowded into the more comfortable back parlor, into which footmen had ferried additional chairs, love seats, and sofas.

Every seat was taken, because everyone was there— from Louisa, the young daughter of the house, still in pigtails, to Louisa's grandmother, Helena, and her even older bosom-bow, Therese Osbaldestone. The younger ladies, Henrietta included, stood chatting in groups wherever there was space between the chairs and occasional tables and behind the sofas. Their elders frequently engaged those standing, especially Henrietta, who was passed from group to group, each clutch of ladies wanting to hear her story—how she came to have decided on and enticed James Glossup to the point of him offering for her hand—directly from her lips.

Although Henrietta normally found such gatherings wearying, to her very real surprise she discovered she enjoyed being caught up in the hubbub of excitement engendered by the news of her unexpected engagement, and the even greater excitement provoked by the demands of organizing her engagement ball and then her wedding, all at such short notice.

Not that she harbored the slightest anxiety on that score; she'd seen these same ladies in action many times before. She had every confidence her engagement ball and her wedding would pass off without a hitch; her mother, her aunts, Helena, Horatia, and Celia, let alone her cousins' wives, would simply not allow anything else.

Of her cousins' wives, Honoria, Patience, and Alathea were presently in London, but letters had already been dispatched to all the others, and their ranks would swell as soon as those others could get their horses hitched to their carriages. Henrietta's sister-in-law, Simon's wife, Portia, was presently standing by Henrietta's side, beaming with delight.

Beaming almost as much as Mary, but, viewing her sister as she stood chatting with Louisa, Henrietta honestly didn't think anyone could possibly be more ecstatic than Mary.

Studying her sister, and wondering yet again which gentleman Mary had in her sights, Henrietta became aware of the necklace about her throat, felt the pendant touching the sensitive skin above her décolletage.

She hadn't believed in the necklace, but she had worn it, and . . . here she was, betrothed to James and planning her engagement ball and her wedding.

After a moment's hesitation, she excused herself from Portia and Caro Anstruther-Wetherby, with whom she'd been chatting about the latest style in veils, and made her way across the room to Mary.

Louisa had just been summoned by her mother, which, Henrietta reflected, was just as well; after Mary, the necklace was due to return north to Scotland, and she had no idea whether it would come south again— that was in The Lady's hands.

Mary turned to Henrietta, and her smile grew brighter. "How are you holding up?"

Henrietta arched her brows. "Surprisingly well."

"I daresay it's different when it's your engagement, your wedding, and you at center stage." Mary's tone suggested that while she didn't begrudge Henrietta the position, she was nevertheless looking forward to the day when it would be her turn to stand in the glow.

"I thought," Henrietta said as she drew the necklace free of the modest neckline of her day gown, "that as we have reached this stage—me betrothed, with Mama and the others arguing about how many musicians should play at my wedding breakfast—then perhaps it's time for me to give you this." She let the pendant dangle from her fingers, swinging before Mary's gaze, which had fixed on the rose-quartz crystal.

Covetousness shone clearly in Mary's cornflower blue eyes, but her lips slowly firmed, then pressed into a line, and, slowly, she shook her head; Henrietta got the distinct impression that it took effort for Mary to force herself to do the latter.

Then Mary dragged in a breath and tipped up her head. "No. I want it—obviously—but it has to be right. It has to be passed on to me exactly as it's supposed to be—as Angelica passed it on to you—at your engagement ball. If I don't get it in *exactly* the right way, it might not work as it's supposed to, and what use will it be to me then?"

An unanswerable question. Henrietta sighed and tucked the necklace back inside her bodice. "In that case, seven evenings from tonight." She hesitated, then asked, "Why are you so impatient to have it? Why now?"

Mary's gaze had drifted past Henrietta; looking over the room, she replied, "I told you and Mama this morning. I want to start searching properly for my own hero."

Henrietta narrowed her eyes on Mary's face. "But you've already started searching, haven't you? Just without the necklace. So you're impatient to get the necklace now because—"

"I *might* have started searching, but I'm not going to say anything more at this point—so don't ask." Mary shot her a warning glance.

Henrietta held up her hand. "Very well—seven nights from tonight, the necklace will be yours, and then . . ."

Mary nodded in her usual determined fashion. "And then we'll see."

Henrietta saw Honoria waving, trying to get her attention. Quitting Mary's side, she picked her way across the room to where Honoria, Duchess of St. Ives and wife of the head of the family, Devil Cynster, sat flanked by Patience, Vane Cynster's wife, and Alathea, the wife of Gabriel Cynster. Now in their forties, all three were stylish matrons accustomed to wielding significant social and familial power, yet to Henrietta they were nearly as close as her older sisters, the twins, Amanda and Amelia, both of whom had yet to reach town. Since their marriages over ten years before, the twins had spent much of their time on their husbands' estates, administering to said husbands and their bountiful broods. Henrietta frequently visited both households, but Honoria, Patience, and Alathea were usually in London, and usually attended the same entertainments Henrietta did, so they had in large part become her "London sisters"; certainly, that they viewed her in the light of a younger sister was not in any doubt.

Consequently, she wasn't the least surprised when Alathea caught her hand, tugged her down to sit on a footstool they'd commandeered and had placed before them, then, when Henrietta had settled, stated, "It's time to tell us the best part—how he proposed."

When she hesitated, Patience chuckled. "You don't need to tell us the setting—just give us the words."

Fighting to straighten her lips, Henrietta said, "Just let me think, so I remember it properly . . . oh, that's right. He asked if he shouldn't wait and ask for Papa's approval first."

Honoria nodded. "Very proper."

Henrietta grinned. "But when I told him that wasn't considered necessary in our family, he said, 'In that case, will you marry me, Henrietta Cynster, and make me the happiest of mortal men?' "

Patience and Alathea sighed.

Honoria smiled approvingly. "That's very nicely put—James does, indeed, sound as if he'll do. Given he's such a close friend of Simon's, I did wonder." The last was said with a teasing look.

"It's so very comforting when they profess their undying love." Alathea heaved another sigh, then blinked, misty-eyed. "I still remember the rose in a crystal casket that Rupert sent me, with a note saying I held his heart—I still remember how I felt when I opened the casket and read that note."

"I know just how you feel," Patience said, in a similar, fondly reminiscent tone. "Although I rather suspect I had to work harder than you to hear the words."

Honoria snorted. "I never *got* the words—not as such."

Patience, Alathea, and Henrietta stared at her.

"Devil never told you he loves you, never vowed undying, unending love?" Patience sounded incredulous.

"Not in words," Honoria stated. Her lips weren't entirely straight. "Mind you, years later"—she tipped her head toward Henrietta—"around the time Amelia married, he did ask me, much in the manner of checking that someone hadn't missed something obvious, whether I did, in fact, know that he loved me."

"Ah, but wait!" Alathea raised a finger. "I recall hearing something about Devil delivering himself up in front of some madman and allowing said madman to shoot him in order to save you." Alathea met Honoria's eyes. "I daresay, after that, you didn't really need further words."

"Indeed." Regally, Honoria dipped her head, but her own gaze, normally so incisive, had softened. "After that little exercise, words were quite redundant. If, combined with all the rest, a man is willing to risk his life for you, there's not much more that needs to be said." Focusing on Henrietta, Honoria said, "From what I've heard, James has already risked his life for you in leaping to your rescue at Marchmain House."

And later, and then again; Henrietta smiled back. "And combined with all the rest, yes, it's true—I really don't need the words, either. I know he loves me."

Before they could question her further, or she them, Helena called the four of them to join the conference that was taking place on the other side of the room, principally concerned with fixing the date for the pending wedding.

Henrietta allowed herself to be drawn into the discussion, although her opinion was not as informed as those of the others, all of whom were up with the latest news regarding ton events. She largely left them to it, while Patience's and Alathea's words, and even more Honoria's, circled in her head.

Honoria was right; Henrietta knew beyond doubt that James loved her. He might not have used that precise word, but the reality was there, undeniable and unquenchable. That reality showed in his eyes, in his tone, in the way he'd made love—yes, love—to her. It was very clear in her mind that making love was what they'd done the previous night, just as it had been transparently clear at the time, even to her untutored senses, what emotion had driven them both.

She'd heard that a brush with death could strip aside the veils and reveal love as the powerful emotion it was, compelling and demanding. That was what had happened with them; it was love that had pushed them into intimacy last night, and then further, into their betrothal.

So yes, she knew James loved her, and therefore she did not need further words, yet . . .

By the time the gathering broke up and she was walking the short distance to Upper Brook Street, flanked by her mother and Mary, Henrietta had accepted that while she didn't *need* to hear the words, she would nevertheless *like* to be on the receiving end of an avowal of undying love from James, one impossible to mistake or misconstrue.

Because even though she hadn't uttered the words either, she was, definitely, absolutely, and irredeemably, in love with him.

Chapter Ten

The following morning, Henrietta, accompanied by Louise and Mary, attended a well-publicized at-home at Celia Cynster's house in Dover Street.

The notice of James and Henrietta's betrothal had duly appeared in the *Gazette* that morning. The Cynster ladies had chosen Celia's long-scheduled event as Henrietta's first foray into the wider ton as a formally affianced young lady. Several of those Cynster ladies—Honoria, Patience, and Alathea among them—were there in support, but the older ladies had deemed their presence unnecessary, and potentially too overwhelming; no one wished to deny Henrietta her moment.

As the steady stream of guests ascending Celia's front steps attested, the announcement in the *Gazette* had been noted at many a ton breakfast table that morning. Matrons and their daughters flocked to Dover Street, correctly divining that there they would learn everything—all the relevant details—behind the unexpected engagement, and would thus be best placed to spread the news through the upcoming luncheons, promenades, and afternoon teas.

On gaining Celia's drawing room, all the ladies made a beeline for Henrietta; standing with her back to the fireplace, facing the long room, she almost felt besieged.

But as soon as they'd passed on their felicitations, the matrons fell back, circling to join Louise or one of the other Cynster ladies, hoping to extract further pertinent details from them. Meanwhile, the younger ladies, those not yet betrothed and those recently engaged or married, remained in a knot about Henrietta, excitedly asking about her engagement ball and speculating over when she and James would wed. The latter was something Henrietta and her mentors had decided to keep private for the moment, not that that deterred those speculating in the least.

The company was in constant flux; groups arrived, remained for twenty minutes, then departed, well primed with facts to share.

Once again to her surprise, Henrietta found herself swept up in the giddy whirl. She felt particularly gratified when several young ladies she'd helped through the years to make up their minds to accept or decline various offers arrived to press her hand and enthusiastically congratulate her on having found her own true love.

Phillipa Hemmings was typical of those who gathered to wish her well. Clasping Henrietta's hands, Phillipa beamed. "You helped me when I needed it, and many others, too, and steered us away from unhappiness. Now that you yourself stand on the brink of the ultimate happiness, I couldn't be more happy were it me in your shoes."

A chorus of "Hear, hear" echoed around the group.

"Thank you!" Beaming back, Henrietta squeezed Phillipa's hands and released them, then scanned the bright faces surrounding her. "I had no idea you would all feel so . . . delighted on my behalf."

Constance Witherby, now the younger Lady Hume, laughed. "Henrietta, my dear, you're twenty-nine—

you've been helping young ladies like us for nearly a decade and you've never, to my knowledge, steered us wrongly. *Of course* there are many who wish you well. Heaven help you, you've earned it!"

Everyone laughed, and the pleasant exchanges continued.

Later in the hour, several grandes dames arrived, haughtily sailing in, agog to discover how such a development had escaped their notice. Henrietta was pleased to leave the task of enlightening them to the other Cynster ladies, who swiftly stepped in to divert the armada-like attack.

Eventually the flood of incoming guests slowed to a trickle; the event was nearly at an end when Mrs. Wentworth and Melinda Wentworth came in. Smiling happily, both made straight for Henrietta. With not a hint of insincerity, Mrs. Wentworth congratulated her, then moved on to speak with Louise and Celia.

Melinda beamed at Henrietta and very prettily wished her well.

Henrietta felt distinctly awkward, but she kept her politely delighted façade in place and chatted inconsequentially . . . until Miss Crossley, by then the only other young lady standing with Henrietta and Melinda, was called away by her mama.

The instant Miss Crossley was out of earshot, Henrietta turned to Melinda. She searched her friend's face; there was no less-frank way to phrase it, so she bluntly said, "I do hope you don't feel that I stole James from you—I assure you it didn't happen like that."

Melinda blinked, clearly taken aback, then her smile rebloomed. "Of course I don't think that, silly." Reaching for and squeezing Henrietta's fingers, Melinda searched her face in turn. "It honestly never occurred to me. I know you told me the truth, and you were perfectly correct—James and I wouldn't have suited. But if making you consider him on my behalf was instrumental in opening your eyes, yours to him and his to you, then I can only say I'm delighted to have been of service—so there."

Henrietta let her relief show. "Thank you. I'm so glad you're not upset."

"Not a bit of it." Melinda glanced at her mother, still engaged with Louise and Celia, and lowered her voice. "Indeed, I can't thank you enough for being so honest with me over James, and forcing me to look to my own motives. If you hadn't done so, I don't know where I would be now, but . . ." Melinda's voice rose on a note of excitement. Shifting closer to Henrietta, tightening her grip on her fingers and leaning near, Melinda whispered, "I'm not supposed to talk about it because discussions are still going on, but I expect to be where you now stand in a week or so's time."

"You're getting engaged, too?" Henrietta felt her own happiness well. "Truly?"

Melinda nodded, lips compressing as if she could barely contain her joy. After a moment, she went on, "I always liked Oliver—he's a distant cousin—but he's nowhere near as handsome as James, and while I had James on my string, so to speak, I refused to even look at Oliver." Melinda met Henrietta's gaze. "But once you forced me to turn from James and look elsewhere, I saw Oliver much more clearly, and then he made a push, and, well . . ." Her joy threatening to break free, Melinda smiled dazzlingly. "Here I am." She shook Henrietta's hands. "Here we both are!"

Henrietta smiled back, unrestrainedly joyous. "Indeed. How wonderful! You must let me know the

instant"—Henrietta glanced at Mrs. Wentworth—
"that I'm allowed to know."

"Oh, I will," Melinda assured her.

They stood for a moment, side by side, absorbing the
news that they were both soon to be wed.

Abruptly, Melinda shivered. "Oh—I meant to tell
you, but all this happiness, both yours and mine, simply
swept it from my head."

When Henrietta looked at her in question, Melinda
lowered her voice and went on, "That evening you
joined us in Hill Street, to tell me what you'd learned
about James?"

"What of it?"

Eyes rounding, Melinda whispered, "There was
murder done next door!"

Henrietta stared at her friend—and remembered the
gentleman she'd bumped into on the pavement outside
the Wentworths' house. A chill swept through her, but
then she grabbed hold of her wits and asked, "Who was
killed? And when? Do you know when it happened?"

"It was Lady Winston. She lived next door. She was
a widow, and apparently she was killed sometime that
evening. No one's certain exactly when because she was
in the habit of sending her staff off for the night every
now and then—they all assumed she was entertaining
some gentleman friend, very privately."

"I see." Henrietta fought to bring order to the stream
of thoughts cascading through her mind.

"Melinda!"

They both turned to see Mrs. Wentworth beckoning
Melinda to join her, clearly preparing to depart.

"Coming, Mama." Melinda wound her arm in Henrietta's, and together they followed Mrs. Wentworth,
Celia, and Louise as the three ladies headed for the

door. "Remember," Melinda whispered, her gaze on her mother's back, "you must pretend that I haven't told you anything about my pending engagement, or, for that matter, the murder. Mama was even more insistent that I keep my mouth closed over that. Well . . ." Melinda blew out a breath. "A horrible murder just next door—mere yards away from where I sleep." She shivered again.

Henrietta patted Melinda's hand absentmindedly; in something of a stunned daze, she went through the motions of farewelling the Wentworths, thanking her aunt Celia for hosting the event, and climbing into her mother's carriage for the journey back to Upper Brook Street.

With a contented sigh, Louise settled back against the squabs. "That went well, I thought."

Mary, seated opposite Louise and already engaged in looking out at those strolling the pavements, made a sound of agreement.

"Hmm." Seated alongside her mother, Henrietta stared unseeing at the empty seat opposite while her mind raced, juggling possibilities . . .

By the time the carriage halted outside her parents' house, she'd worked out enough to realize she needed to speak with James as soon as she possibly could.

Much to Henrietta's disgust, what with the demands of her day and, apparently, his, she and James didn't manage to meet until she walked into the front hall of St. Ives House that evening and found him waiting.

Smiling with his customary charm, debonair and, to her at least, riveting in his evening clothes, he lifted her cloak from her shoulders and handed it to Webster, Devil's butler, then, capturing her hand, raising it to his lips and trapping her gaze, James pressed a kiss she felt to the tips of her toes on the backs of her fingers.

Then he smiled into her eyes. "My butler told me you'd sent a footman with a message while I was out. What did you want to see me about?"

She'd lectured herself that maintaining an appropriate façade throughout the evening, and allowing herself to genuinely enjoy the informal family dinner party Honoria and the others had arranged to celebrate their betrothal, was essential, but every time she thought of what Melinda had told her, maintaining her smile and her air of pleased delight required significant effort . . . and once she told James what she'd learned, she had little doubt that he would find enjoying the evening appropriately while concealing his reactions near impossible. So she smiled back and murmured, "Not now. I'll tell you later."

He studied her eyes, trying to decide if he should push.

She arched a brow, then, sliding her hand into his arm, she turned to the archway leading to the drawing room. "Come along—it's our moment to face the family."

He humphed, but obliged, and walked by her side into the drawing room, into the waiting storm of congratulations and felicitations, smiles and good-natured laughter.

The evening went well, a comfortable, relaxed gathering of the immediate Cynster family, all those presently in London coming together to do what they most enjoyed doing—celebrating another alliance, another, as Devil put it in his toast, twining of branches on two old family trees that would, in the fullness of time, lead to new buds and more branches in the future.

The company drank to their health. Several times.

James was entirely at ease in this milieu. It helped that, just as he was Simon's oldest and closest friend, other members of his family, both male and female, were longtime friends with their Cynster peers; the Glossups and the Cynsters numbered among the oldest families in the ton, so the connections were many, and solid and sound.

He had no difficulty navigating these waters; in many ways, he felt more at home among the socially active Cynsters than in his own family, who had largely retreated from the wider ton.

After due discussions with Lord Arthur, and subsequent meetings with both James's and the Cynsters' men-of-business, the settlements had been decided on, and after a day James deemed well-spent, he and Lord Arthur could join with Louise and Henrietta to announce to the assembled company the date for their official engagement ball, which, in keeping with Cynster tradition, would be held in the ballroom of St. Ives House.

Seated around the long table, the family cheered and applauded, then cheered even more when Lord Arthur added that the wedding would follow on the thirtieth of May, two days before James's grandaunt Emily's deadline.

Later, when the company returned to the long drawing room, with Henrietta on his arm, James went from group to group, renewing acquaintance with those Cynsters he knew less well.

"I gather," Henrietta confided as they left one group, "that all the others not in London are on their way. Most—like Lucifer and Phyllida—will be here in time for the engagement ball, but those further north might not be able to reach town in time. We're hoping Richard and Catriona, at least, will be here for the wedding, but, of course, no one's heard back as yet, and Celia and Martin are hoping very much that Angelica and Dominic can make the journey."

The following hour passed in cheery, often jovial conversation. Henrietta bided her time; there was no sense in disrupting their evening by telling James of her unnerving discovery prematurely. She was safe in St. Ives House, surrounded by family; no matter who the gentleman-villain was, he wouldn't be able to reach her there . . . and she definitely didn't want to risk being overheard and the disquieting information spreading to the rest of the family—not until she'd had time to discuss the situation and how to deal with it with James.

At last, the company started to thin. On James's arm, she weighed her options while James and Simon chatted. Soon, her mother would summon her and she would have to leave with her parents; she couldn't afford to wait much longer, but Simon and James showed no signs of parting—indeed, from what she'd overheard, they intended to leave together to meet with Charlie Hastings at some club.

Did she really care if Simon learned about what was going on?

Even as the question formed in her mind, she realized that—with James and Simon being so close—it was more than likely that Simon already knew about her three "accidents."

Seeing Louise leave Helena and glide over to speak with Honoria, Henrietta drew breath and turned to join James's and Simon's conversation.

Both looked at her; both sensed she had something momentous to say.

Simon wrinkled his nose at her. "Do I have to leave?"

Henrietta narrowed her eyes. "You can stay if you promise to be good."

Simon's smile flashed. "I'm not sure I can promise that, but"—he gestured encouragingly—"do tell."

She shot him a warning look, then transferred her gaze to James. "I met Melinda Wentworth this morning."

"Oh." James's expression blanked. He swiftly searched her eyes. "Was she difficult?"

Henrietta shook her head dismissively. "No, not at all. That isn't it." She paused to draw breath and order the revelations in her mind. "She told me that on the evening I visited the Wentworths' house in Hill Street to tell Melinda and her parents my findings about you, Lady Winston, a widow who lives—lived—next door, was murdered."

Both James and Simon visibly stiffened. His expression abruptly sober, James nodded. "Go on."

"As one might expect, Melinda doesn't know much—just that the murder was thought to have been committed sometime that evening, and most likely by the gentleman Lady Winston was in the habit of entertaining in secret. She habitually sent her staff away for the night, so no one knows who said gentleman is."

A pause ensued while James and Simon digested that. It was Simon who, frowning, said, "I don't see how that involves you." He sent a swift glance around, confirming no one else was near enough to overhear, before he met Henrietta's eyes and said, "I'm assuming you think this has something to do with the recent attacks?"

So James had told Simon, which meant Charlie most likely knew, too. Tight-lipped, Henrietta nodded. "I'm coming to that." She switched her gaze to James's eyes. "It was cold and foggy, but my carriage was waiting just across the street. Melinda saw me out, and I told her to go in and shut the door—the groom and coachman were there and watching—then I went down the steps . . . and a gentleman ran into me. He would have knocked me over, but he caught me and steadied me. I think he did that instinctively. He had on a cloak, and the hood was up. He apologized—his voice, his diction, was exactly what I expected from his clothes. Then Gibbs—my groom—called out, and the gentleman released me, nodded, and walked quickly off. I thought nothing more of it . . . until Melinda told me about the murder."

Neither James nor Simon was slow. Both shifted, but, glancing around, immediately reined their reactions in. James's gaze refixed on her face. "You think he was the murderer?"

Henrietta met his gaze steadily. "I'm almost certain he was. There was one thing I registered at the time, one thing I didn't understand, but subsequently I forgot about it."

"What thing?" Simon asked.

"When I started down the steps, I glanced around—instinctively, as anyone would—and the pavement was clear. Yet mere seconds later, the man nearly mowed me down, so where did he come from? Why hadn't I seen him when I looked?" When James and Simon frowned, understanding the point but not immediately realizing the answer, she gave it to them. "He had to have erupted, moving at speed, from the area steps of the house next door—the one in which Lady Winston died. That was why he didn't see me, and why I didn't see him. He was running away from what he'd done."

Both men stared at her, and she stared back. She

could see in both pairs of eyes trained on her—one pair warm brown, the other sharply blue—that they were putting things together, linking the facts.

Lips thin, James said, "He thinks you can identify him."

"But," Simon put in, "you can't, can you?"

Slowly, she shook her head. "Since this morning, I've gone over those seconds countless times in my mind, but there was nothing I saw that could in any way tell anyone who he was."

James's expression grew to be the definition of grim. "But he, unfortunately, doesn't know that."

"I suspect not." Fingers instinctively tightening on James's arm, Henrietta looked at Simon. "Which I suppose means my accidents were, indeed, not accidental at all."

"No. But that also suggests," Simon said, his face now coldly expressionless, "that he believes that you do know but haven't yet realized the significance of what you know. He must be living in fear that you'll hear about the murder, and suddenly realize . . . and expose him."

James had been thinking. Now he looked at Simon. "I haven't heard anything about this murder, have you?"

Simon shook his head. "Not a whisper." Raising his gaze, he looked across the room. "Which means Portia hasn't heard of it, either."

"Melinda said her mother had told her not to speak of it," Henrietta said.

"Perhaps the authorities are, for some reason, holding back the news." Simon shrugged.

"Possibly so they don't scare the horses," James cynically said. "Can you imagine the outcry such a crime in Hill Street, in the heart of Mayfair, will provoke?"

Simon grimaced. "Very true. So . . ."

"How can we learn more?" James asked. "Clearly, if that is the reason behind the attacks on Henrietta, then there's no reason to suppose the blackguard will stop."

Not until she's dead didn't need to be said.

Henrietta shivered anyway. James closed his hand over hers on his sleeve.

Simon humphed. "Barnaby Adair, and through him, Inspector Stokes." Simon met James's gaze. "You've met Adair, haven't you?"

James nodded. "Here and there, and I already know Stokes from that time at Glossup Hall."

"Not something I'm likely to forget," Simon said. "But Adair and Stokes joined forces, so to speak, in another matter later, and subsequently they've often worked together, with the higher-ups' blessings, whenever there's a difficult serious crime within the haut ton."

"I remember," Henrietta said. "Stokes was the policeman who helped Penelope and Barnaby with that matter about the orphan boys going missing."

Simon nodded. "Yes—and that case was a social and political mess, which is where the Adair and Stokes combination comes into its own. Stokes isn't just any old policeman. He understands enough about us—the haut ton—to know how to navigate our shoals, and Barnaby's father has significant political clout."

Increasingly grim, James said, "This murder has the hallmarks of just such a case." He looked at Simon. "Can you speak with Adair?"

Simon nodded decisively. "He'll be interested, I'm sure. I doubt we'll find him out tonight, but I'll invite myself to breakfast tomorrow—such useful things, family connections—after which I'll bring him around to Upper Brook Street." Simon met Henrietta's eyes. "He'll want to hear everything from your lips."

She nodded. "I'll stay in."

James squeezed her hand. "I'll call and wait with you."

Simon said, "Barnaby will want to hear all about the accidents, too."

They all spotted Simon and Henrietta's aunt Horatia sweeping regally down on them; the three exchanged glances, then turned and smiled welcomingly.

Horatia halted before them, eyes scanning their faces. "Now what are you three planning?"

"A wedding, as it happens," Henrietta said. "Do you think Simon will do as James's best man?"

It was the perfect distraction, and then the evening was over. Those still present gathered in the front hall, confirming plans for the next days and making their farewells.

They were the last to leave; Henrietta quit the house with her parents and Mary, while James left with Simon to hunt down Charlie Hastings, then put their heads together and revisit the now even more urgent necessity of keeping Henrietta safe.

From a murderer who, in order to escape justice, was apparently convinced he needed to murder again.

It was ten o'clock the following morning, and Henrietta was pacing, restless and distracted, before the windows in the back parlor in Upper Brook Street.

Leaning against the back of the sofa, James watched, and otherwise worked at maintaining an outwardly calm façade. He had no idea how long breakfast in the Adair household might take, much less if Adair would be free to speak with them today—

The door opened; James turned and saw Simon walk in. His friend and soon-to-be brother-in-law presumably still had a latchkey to this house, his childhood home. A gentleman with curly fair hair, whom James recognized as the Honorable Barnaby Adair, followed Simon through the door.

Straightening, James rounded the sofa.

Simon stepped back and closed the door, then waved at Barnaby. "Behold, the very man we need."

"Glossup." Barnaby shook the hand James offered, smiling self-deprecatingly. "Anyone would think he'd had to bend my arm, while in reality, nothing could have kept me away." He smiled at Henrietta as she joined them; married to Penelope, who was sister to Portia and also to Luc, Henrietta and Simon's older sister Amelia's husband, Barnaby was a connection several times over, and was well known throughout the Cynster clan. "Henrietta." Barnaby took her hand, gently squeezed her fingers. "It seems you've unexpectedly become the target for a murderer." His expression sobering, he glanced at James before saying to Henrietta, "I hope you don't mind, but given the seriousness of the situation, I sent word to my colleague from Scotland Yard, Inspector Basil Stokes."

Barnaby looked at James. "Glossup here, as well as Simon, and indeed, Portia, can add their recommendations to mine—they worked with Stokes during the incident at Glossup Hall several years ago." Refocusing on Henrietta, Barnaby continued, "Stokes is a sound man, and I fear we'll need him and his people to help us with this."

Henrietta summoned a smile, although it felt weak at the edges. "I've already heard much about Inspector Stokes from Penelope—she's sung his praises more than once. I'll be happy to make his acquaintance."

Barnaby was, she realized, studying her face, as if to gauge how upset she was—or, perhaps, was likely to become; she straightened her spine and looked him in the eye—and he faintly smiled. "Excellent. In that case—"

The doorbell jangled. They looked at the parlor door.

"That'll be Stokes," Barnaby said.

Simon cast him a glance. "That was quick. He must have set out the moment he got your note." Simon went to open the parlor door.

"If you had any idea how much of a confounding problem Lady Winston's murder has become," Barnaby said, "you would be more surprised if he hadn't come at the run."

Brows rising, Simon opened the door and stepped out. "Stokes! This way. Thank you, Hudson." Simon paused, listening to a rumble from Hudson, glanced at Henrietta, then looked up the corridor. "No tea just yet—perhaps later."

"Tell Hudson I'll ring," Henrietta said.

Simon relayed the message, then stepped back to allow a tall, dark-haired man, with slate gray eyes and a rather brooding expression—as if he was constantly observing all about him and didn't expect to be favorably impressed—to enter the room.

Barnaby made the introductions. Stokes clearly remembered James and Simon; the quick flash of his smile lightened his face. Then Barnaby introduced Henrietta, and Stokes's gray gaze fastened on her.

When she offered her hand, he shook it with an easy, understated elegance that belied his working-class station in life. "I understand, Miss Cynster," Stokes said, his voice deep, his tone even but with an autocratic edge, "that on departing the Wentworths' house in Hill

Street nine evenings ago, you encountered a gentleman leaving the house next door."

Henrietta nodded. "Although it would be more accurate to say he encountered me." Turning, waving Stokes and the others to the armchairs, she walked to the sofa and sat.

James sat alongside her; Simon took the armchair to her right, Barnaby the armchair to the left of the sofa, leaving Stokes to take possession of the large armchair directly across the small table from Henrietta.

After drawing a notebook from his pocket, along with a pencil, Stokes sat, opened the notebook, balanced it on his knee, and looked up at Henrietta. "I would appreciate it, Miss Cynster, if you would tell me what happened—all that you can remember, every little detail no matter how small or apparently inconsequential—from the instant you stepped onto the Wentworths' front porch." Stokes met her gaze and smiled encouragingly. "Take your time, as much time as you like."

Henrietta drew in a deep breath, fixed her gaze past Stokes's left shoulder, and called up the scene in her mind. "It was cold—chilly—and there was fog, enough so I couldn't see the end of the street. That made the light from the streetlamps seem dimmer than usual, so overall the light wasn't strong." She paused, but no one interrupted her, so she continued, "It was bitter, so I told Melinda—the Wentworths' daughter—to go inside and shut the door. My coachman had halted the carriage—my parents' carriage—on the other side of the street, and both my groom and the coachman were there, and—" She broke off, then said, "There was no one else nearby. I just realized—I'd already looked up and down the street by then, because that was why I felt so confident about being left alone to cross to the carriage." She met Stokes's eyes. "At that point, there was no one on the nearer pavement close enough to reach me—to intercept me—before I crossed the road."

Stokes asked, "Did you see any others further along the road?"

She thought back, bringing the memory to life in her mind. . . . "Yes. There were two gentlemen walking away toward North Audley Street, and in the other direction, much further away, there was a couple who had just come out of a house and were getting into a hackney."

"Very good." Stokes was busy making notes. "So what happened next?"

"With the chill in the air you may be sure I didn't dally. I walked down the steps—I was holding my cloak around me, and I had my reticule in one hand. I was looking down, placing my feet. Then I reached the pavement and lifted my head—and that's when he barreled into me."

"You didn't hear footsteps?" Barnaby asked.

She thought back, then, frowning, shook her head. "Not coming along. I heard maybe two quick steps, but by the time I'd even registered them, he'd already run into me." Frowning more definitely, she looked at Barnaby. "That's odd, isn't it? If he'd come up the area steps, wouldn't I have heard him?"

Barnaby glanced at Stokes. "Not those area steps. The staff had put down matting because the steps got too slippery in winter. The matting's quite thick, more than enough to muffle the sound of footsteps." Barnaby looked back at her. "That you didn't hear him coming only makes it more likely that the gentleman who ran into you did, indeed, come up those steps."

Head down as he jotted notes, Stokes was nodding. "If he came from anywhere else, you would have heard enough to have been aware of his approach before he collided with you. But even more telling, if he hadn't come up very quickly from those particular area steps, *he* would have seen *you* in good time to avoid any collision." Pencil poised, he looked up at her. "Did your groom or coachman see where the man came from?"

"I don't know—I didn't think to ask. I doubt Johns, the coachman, saw anything—he was looking at his horses—but Gibbs should have."

"Leave them for now—I'll speak with them later. Let's go on with what you saw." Stokes looked down at his notebook. "The gentleman's just run into you—go on from there."

She did, recounting as best she could exactly what she'd seen of the mystery man. Between them, Stokes and Barnaby questioned each of her observations.

"He wore gloves?"

"Yes, very nice gloves. Cordoba leather at a guess—Bond Street, definitely."

"The silver head of his cane—describe that. Was it a flat top, engraved, or . . . ?"

She hesitated. "It was some sort of heraldic design." She glanced at James, then Barnaby. "You know the sort of thing. An animal, most likely—I know Devil has an old cane of our grandfather Sebastian's that has a silver stag's head on the top." She looked at Stokes. "The stag is the animal on the family crest."

"I see," Stokes said. "Did you see what animal it was?"

"No." She thought, picturing the scene again in her mind, then grimaced. "The light was poor and . . ." She raised her right fist and pressed it to her upper left arm.

"He had it clutched in his right hand, so it was at the corner of my vision and the head was tipped away. And when he released me and straightened . . ." She examined the moment carefully in her mind, then sighed. "His hand covered the cane's head, of course, so I never did get a clear look at it."

Stokes humphed. "That would have been too easy." He read through his notes. "Let's move on to his face. What did you see of it?"

"Very little." She considered her mental image. "He had the hood of his cloak up—right up and over his head, so that the cowl shaded his face. The nearest streetlamp was to my left, a little way along the pavement and somewhat behind him, so the light fell obliquely across his jaw." She refocused on Stokes. "Only the part of his face below his lower lip was lit enough for me to see. All the rest was just shadow. I couldn't see his eyes at all, nor even his cheeks enough to tell you the shape of his face. And I didn't see his hair—color or style—at all."

"Was there any identifiable mark on the part of his face you did see? A scar or mole—anything like that?"

She shook her head. "Nothing at all. It was a perfectly ordinary face." She grimaced. "Nothing I saw would allow me to pick him out from any group of tonnish men of similar height and build—and even his height and build were unremarkable."

"What about his voice?" Barnaby asked. He met her gaze. "Close your eyes and replay what he said in your head. Listen to the cadence and rhythm of his speech. Was there any discernible accent—any hint at all?"

She did as he asked. The room remained silent for a minute, then she opened her eyes and grimly shook her head. "All he said was, 'My apologies. I didn't see you.' He had no obvious accent, but those are too few words to say he doesn't have one. All I could say was that his diction was definitely tonnish—I couldn't see him even as a wealthy merchant. From his appearance I took him to be a gentleman, and his voice fitted perfectly."

Stokes nodded. He looked through his notes again. "Now tell me about these 'accidents' of yours."

James took the lead in recounting the details of the three incidents.

While Stokes scribbled, Barnaby listened intently; when James came to the end of his recitation, eyes narrowed, gaze unseeing, Barnaby murmured, "So putting everything together, he's a gentleman of the ton—that's absolutely certain—and further, is currently moving among the upper echelons, the haut ton."

"He has to be to have been on Lady Marchmain's guest list," Simon said. "I'd intended to see if I could extract that list from her ladyship. We know the villain's name will be on it, and while we won't be able to pick him out of the ruck, it'll at least give us a place to start."

"Or finish." Stokes looked at Simon. "If nothing else, that will be corroborative evidence. Think you can persuade her ladyship to let you have it?"

Simon grinned grimly. "I can but try."

"I'll leave you to that, then, but if she won't, I'll ask officially, but I'd prefer to do it your way—discreetly— without having to explain my reasons for wanting it."

James exchanged a look with Simon, then said, "It seems we're all in agreement that it's the gentleman who killed Lady Winston who is now attempting to kill Henrietta, presumably because he believes she saw enough to be able to identify him, thus putting a noose around his neck." James studied Stokes, then glanced at Barnaby. "What I don't understand is why there has been no hue and cry. None of us had heard that Lady Winston had been murdered, and it seems the whole affair has been hushed up." He refocused on Stokes. "And now you don't want to explain to Lady Marchmain why you want her guest list." Again he glanced at Barnaby, then looked back at Stokes. "What's going on?"

Stokes met James's gaze, then looked at Henrietta, then glanced—faintly questioningly—at Barnaby.

Barnaby hesitated, then nodded. "We need to tell them all of it." He met James's and Henrietta's gazes. "We can't risk leaving you operating in the dark and not understanding what we're up against with this villain."

Stokes grimaced, but nodded. He cleared his throat. "Right then. What I'm going to say now . . . I won't say it can't go past this room, but be careful who you tell. We can't afford panic in Mayfair—that's why you haven't heard about Lady Winston's murder."

Stokes paused as if gathering his facts, ordering his thoughts, then he said, "Lady Winston was murdered sometime that evening. She'd sent her staff off for the night—they were not to return until midnight. She'd been in the habit of doing this for the past several months—since late January, at least. The staff don't know precisely why, but they concluded her ladyship was entertaining a gentleman, and their view was that it was he who had insisted on that level of secrecy. Her ladyship was a widow of long-standing, and had entertained lovers at her home before, but never before had she ordered her staff away. None of them have any idea who the gentleman was. They never saw or heard or found any hint or clue to his identity.

"So—that night, he killed her. He beat her near to death with his bare fists, then strangled her." Stokes paused, then, his voice rougher, added, "Seemed like he'd enjoyed doing it, too." He glanced at Simon and James. "If you know what I mean."

Meeting Stokes's eyes, understanding what he was trying to convey, James felt ill.

"So . . ." Stokes drew in a breath. "He killed her ladyship—and left via the area steps. He stepped onto the pavement and bumped into Miss Cynster, which must have been a shock."

"Oh . . ."

Everyone looked at Henrietta, only to discover she'd paled. She was staring at Stokes.

James reached for her hand, held it.

"What is it?" Stokes asked.

She blinked, then softly said, "I just remembered. There was an instant—a pause. He ran into me, steadied me—then he looked at my face. I had my cloak on, but my hood wasn't up, and the light came from over his shoulder. He must have seen my face quite clearly. He was holding me—one of his hands gripping each of my upper arms—and he . . . hesitated. I remember wondering what he was going to do—whether he'd recognized me and was someone I knew, or . . . and then Gibbs called out and the man released me, nodded, and quickly walked away."

An instant of silence ensued, then Stokes cleared his throat. "You might want to give that groom of yours a tip. Whoever this blackguard is, he likes to hurt women, and you met him at a very . . . fraught moment." Stokes sighed. "Which probably helps explain why he thinks you've seen too much." He paused, then rather glumly said, "But there's more. We questioned all the staff the next day, of course, and I'd swear all of them told us the truth, told us all and everything they knew." Stokes glanced at Barnaby, tipped his head his way. "Adair was there."

Barnaby nodded; his expression had grown even grimmer. "And I agree—I'd take my oath all the staff, including her ladyship's dresser, told us everything they knew—which in terms of identifying the villain amounted to nothing."

"But," Stokes said, "two days later, her ladyship's dresser—she'd gone to stay with her sister in Clapham— was murdered, too. Same way as her ladyship—beaten near to death, then strangled. Her sister went out just before noon and came home later in the afternoon, and found her."

Quiet horror engulfed the room, then Simon said, "So he killed her, too, in the same god-awful way, even though she knew nothing?"

Stokes's lips tightened. "It's possible she did know something and had contacted him—tried to black-mail him—but . . ." He glanced at Barnaby. "Neither Adair nor I think that's the case. The woman—the dresser—was an honest sort. She was devoted to her ladyship—had been with her from when her lady-ship was a bride. If the dresser had known anything about this beast, she would have tripped over her own tongue to tell us."

"So yes," Barnaby said, "Stokes and I, at least, feel certain this blackguard killed her just in case. Just to make sure there was no chance she knew something she hadn't yet thought of."

Stokes nodded grimly. "He's covering his tracks, re-gardless of whether he actually needs to or not. Which brings us to the attacks on Miss Cynster."

James glanced at Henrietta, tightened his grip on her hand. "He thinks you know something—"

"Or that you might know something even if you haven't realized it yet," Barnaby put in.

"Or," Simon said, his tone hard, "that you might have seen enough of his face that if you see him—come upon him at some event—you'll recognize him then."

"Any or all of those." Stokes shut his notebook. "It won't matter to him. He wants you dead, and the fact that you haven't any information that might identify him won't stop him."

"He views you as a potential threat." Barnaby met Henrietta's gaze. "And he'll keep on until he succeeds in silencing you."

James felt the moment grow heavier as they absorbed that apparently incontestable fact. After a moment, he said, his tone cold, "To return to my earlier question— why no hue and cry? How on earth are we to find this villain without going after him?"

Stokes looked at Barnaby.

Barnaby leaned forward, speaking to Henrietta, James, and Simon. "There's been discussions aplenty at the highest levels about how to handle this case. The excuse of not wanting to cause panic in Mayfair, at the height of the Season no less, is true enough, but that's a more minor consideration. The truth is that laying hands on this villain is not going to be easy—we knew that after investigating Lady Winston's death and find- ing nothing to identify him—but when he murdered her ladyship's dresser, he told us one thing we hadn't known before."

Barnaby met James's and Henrietta's gazes. "To wit, he intends to stick around. He intends to remain a part of the ton—the haut ton, almost certainly—and has no intention of quitting the scene. That's why he's now turned his sights on you—and, more, is trying to make your death look like an accident, or at least the result of an attack not specifically aimed at you. He doesn't want to create more noise within the ton, or to focus attention on you—on why someone might want you dead. But if, at this point, we raise a hue and cry and openly try to pursue him . . . we have nothing. He simply has to sit tight and wait us out, and if he's wary of you, simply avoid you for a time—which, all in all, would be easy enough."

"But ultimately he wants to be able to move freely among the upper echelons of the ton," Stokes said, "so at some point, when he feels safe again, he'll come after you again. He isn't going to let you live, even if he has to be careful for a time."

James held Stokes's gaze. A moment passed, then he said, "What you're saying is that the only way to keep Henrietta safe—permanently safe—is to conceal the fact that we're aware of this gentleman-villain, aware of his intention to kill her, and to . . . what? Let him have a chance at her?"

"Not exactly," Barnaby said. "We need to keep Henrietta safe and thoroughly protected—that goes without saying—but we need to play our hand quietly, stalk this man silently, and let him think it's safe enough to have another try at her. But when he does, we'll be there, and then we'll have him."

"As it stands," Stokes said, "regardless of what any of us might wish, the only way we can permanently ensure Miss Cynster's continued health is to identify and catch this man. And the only way we can do that is to let him think it's safe enough to step out of the crowd and show us his face."

Chapter Eleven

They spent the rest of the morning discussing the most pertinent question, namely how to keep Henrietta safe. To James's relief, his lady love, once she'd recovered her composure and her customary poise, deigned to agree with him and the others; they were given to understand that, in light of the seriousness of the situation, she was willing to suspend her usual independence and endure being guarded, essentially twenty-four hours a day.

After defining ways to achieve that, and agreeing over who needed to be apprised of the situation, Stokes and Barnaby departed.

Along with James, Simon stayed for luncheon. As luck would have it, both Lady Louise and Lord Arthur were also lunching in; over the dining room table, James, Henrietta, and Simon shared all they knew, and, after the inevitable shock and exclamations, outlined how they all needed to proceed.

Lord Arthur wasn't happy, but he accepted that their plan was the only sure way forward.

Lady Louise was eager to support any move by Henrietta to repair to the safety of the country—to Somersham Place, perhaps—but was reluctantly persuaded by Henrietta, who most effectively capped her argument by reminding her mother that, aside from avoiding being murdered, she had an engagement ball coming up, and a wedding shortly thereafter.

Mary, also present, listened to the tale wide-eyed, then, in typical Mary fashion, swung the discussion to the subject of how best to organize everyone into doing what they needed to do.

While James would normally have found Mary's bossy nature trying, in this case, he was grateful. She soon had her mother and father organized to spread the word; they'd decided to limit the information, at least in the first instance, to members of the family and the staff of the Upper Brook Street house. Between those two groups, along with Charlie Hastings, Barnaby, and Penelope, Henrietta could be sure of always having others about her. That she readily accepted the need for being so constantly guarded was balm to James's soul.

He, of course, was designated as Henrietta's most frequent guard, a role Mary glibly assigned to him and with which he had no argument at all. In that capacity, once luncheon was over and Lord Arthur left to hunt down his brothers and his nephews, Simon left to find Charlie and later speak with Portia, and Lady Louise and Mary set out for Somersham House to speak with Honoria and from there to spread the word, to keep Henrietta amused James suggested that he and she do something useful with their afternoon and visit his house in George Street. "You can take a look around and see what you might like to have changed."

With very real gratitude, Henrietta agreed. Although James's house was only a few blocks away, she bowed to his request and ordered the smaller town carriage, the one she usually commandeered, to be brought around.

As Hudson, and via him the rest of the staff, had already been informed of the need to keep her constantly guarded, she wasn't surprised to discover not only Gibbs and the coachman on the box but also Jordan, one of the footmen, up on the step behind.

She merely nodded at the trio, all stern-faced and looking watchfully around, and allowed James to hand her up into the carriage.

The house in George Street was a surprise; she'd expected a narrow town house, but instead James led her up the steps of a substantial older house with wide windows on either side of a porticoed front door. The front door itself was painted to a high gloss, and the brass knocker gleamed; James opened the door with a latchkey and held it wide . . . stepping over the threshold, eyes widening, she looked around, drinking in the elegant sweep of the staircase, the detailed moldings around the doors and arches, the oak half-paneling, and the paintings—lush landscapes—that hung on the green-papered walls.

"My grandaunt Emily's, but I rather like them." Closing the door, James came to stand by Henrietta's side. Head tipping, he tried to see the scene through her eyes. "The paintings have grown on me."

"They suit the place." She swiveled in a circle. "This has a nice feel, a nice sense of balance. Elegant, but not overdone."

He smiled, then the door at the rear of the hall swung open and his butler, Fortescue, came through.

"Good afternoon, sir." Fortescue saw Henrietta, and his ageing eyes lit.

James introduced Fortescue; his staff knew of his betrothal and were eager to meet the lady who would be their new mistress.

Somewhat rotund, but turned out in impeccable style, with a regal demeanor and an innate stately air, although well past his prime Fortescue had forgotten more about butlering than most butlers ever learned; his low bow was nicely judged. "Welcome to this house, miss. The rest of the staff and I look forward to serving you in whatever way we may."

"Thank you, Fortescue." Henrietta looked questioningly at James.

"I'm going to take Miss Cynster on a tour of the house, but I suspect, this time, we'll restrict ourselves to the principal rooms." Meeting Henrietta's gaze, James reached out and twined his fingers with hers. "We'll start with the reception rooms on the ground floor, and then head upstairs." He looked at Fortescue. "Perhaps you would warn Mrs. Rollins—we'll have tea in the drawing room when we come down."

"Indeed, sir." Fortescue bowed to them both, then walked back to the staff door.

Retaining his hold on her hand, James drew Henrietta to the double doors to the right of the hall. "Mrs. Rollins is the housekeeper. Like Fortescue, I inherited her. Indeed, other than my man, Trimble, all the staff date from Grandaunt Emily's day."

"Fortescue appears perfectly personable, and he seems assured and experienced."

"He is, as are the rest."

"In that case," Henrietta met his eyes and smiled, "they'll do nicely. Do you have any idea how hard it is to find experienced staff in London?"

"None at all." Releasing her hand, James opened the double doors and set them wide. He waved her in. "Behold—your future drawing room."

Over the next hour, he learned that while his bride-to-be projected the image of a young lady sometimes distressingly practical, with no overt liking for the usual feminine fripperies, there was another Henrietta lurking inside; as he showed her around his grandaunt's house—now his and soon to be theirs—another side of her emerged, one he found enchanting.

Henrietta was delighted—far more than she had thought she would be—with the house. The house she was soon to be mistress of; doubtless that fact sharpened her interest and made her more aware, certainly more prepared to be critical, yet, instead, she found herself walking by James's side through rooms that, in a nutshell, felt like home.

Like *her* home.

They inspected the formal drawing room, neither overly large, nor cramped in the least, but a perfect blend of comfort allied with fashionable formal simplicity. Clean lines dominated, with Hepplewhite furniture arranged on a silky Aubusson rug spread over mellow oak boards, and the green and ivory color scheme met with her complete approval.

The dining room behind it was impressive in its richly paneled, restrained sumptuousness, while the long library, and the smaller connected parlor that lay at the back of the house, its windows overlooking the rear garden, were simply a delight.

Standing before the window looking out into the lushly planted garden, she spread her arms wide and, with a thoroughly silly smile on her face, spun in a slow circle. "I can see us here." Even she heard the happiness in her voice. "You in the library, sitting at the desk working on your papers, and me, here, sitting at that escritoire and writing letters."

James smiled back, one of his lazy, charming smiles. "I can pop in and visit whenever I wish—or you can come and interrupt me."

She grinned back. Hand in hand, they returned through the library to the front hall and started up the curving staircase. The balustrade was smooth, polished wood; there was not a speck of dust to be seen, even though the house had lacked a mistress for nearly a year. "How many staff are there?"

"As well as Trimble, Fortescue, and Mrs. Rollins, there's Cook, two maids, a footman, a kitchen boy and a scullery maid. But we can hire more staff if you wish."

She shook her head. "That sounds ample, at least to start with. I'll bring my maid, Hannah, with me, of course." She glanced at him as they stepped into the gallery. "Did your grandaunt spend much time here?"

"Actually, she spent almost half the year here—she was always in town for the full Season, and she would return for the Autumn Session. She was quite interested in politics, strange to say, and kept abreast of everything going on."

Henrietta insisted on looking into all the rooms on the first floor. "It will be helpful if I have some idea of the accommodations in case we need to put up any extra guests for the wedding." She halted in the corridor and looked at James. "Do your parents have a house in town? Or will they and your brother put up here, with you?"

"They have a house in Chesterfield Street, and although it's been more or less shut up for several years, I think my brother, if not my parents, need an excuse to use it again, so I'm not going to offer to put them up here. Besides"—James caught her eye—"if you and I are to return here after the wedding, then we won't want to have houseguests."

"Ah." Lips lifting, she nodded. "I take your point." Then she flashed him a grin, whirled, and walked on to the last door at the end of the corridor. "What's in here?" Opening the door, she crossed the threshold into what was clearly the master bedroom.

Larger than all the other bedrooms, the room was L-shaped. Directly before the door lay a wide sitting area with comfortable armchairs covered in tan leather angled before a hearth. A large autumnal landscape in a heavy gilt frame filled the wall above the carved oak mantelpiece, and the walls and furnishings were decorated in muted shades of gold and warm browns.

The sitting area ran the length of the longer arm of the L; windows flanked the fireplace, and when Henrietta turned toward the base of the L, she found herself facing another wide window overlooking the rear gardens. This room, she realized, ran above part of the library and all of the adjoining parlor.

She walked on to where she could better view the massive, carved oak, four-poster bed that dominated the shorter arm of the room, its ornate head against the end wall. The warm, autumnal decor continued, with cream sheets, gold satin bedspread, and russet-and-gold brocade canopy and curtains tied up with tasseled gold cords.

The tallboys and dressers were all oak, all substantial; with the heaviness of the furniture offset by the soft tones of the decor and the rich detail of the landscapes again decorating the walls, the room was a curious blend of male and female.

James was studying her face as if trying to gauge her reaction. "Grandaunt Emily wasn't overly fond of frills and lace."

Henrietta met his eyes and smiled. "That's probably why her style so appeals to me—I'm not overly fond of frills and lace either."

He breathed out, and she allowed her smile to deepen. "What's through there?" She pointed to two doors spaced along the inner wall. There were clear pathways along both sides of the bed, the one further from the windows, giving access to those two doors, ending at another, third, closed door.

James strolled across, opened the nearer door and set it swinging. "My dressing room."

Following him, Henrietta peeked in, glimpsing more tallboys and chests, with the usual paraphernalia of brushes and grooming implements laid out neatly on top.

Then James walked on to the next door, opened it, and waved her in. "This will be yours."

She walked on and entered a lady's closet with extensive wardrobes and cupboards, and a dressing table with adjustable mirrors. "Are these from your grand-aunt's day?"

James nodded. "Despite her age, she liked to keep up with the latest improvements." He caught her eye and tipped his head toward a door at the far end of the narrow room, opposite the door through which they'd entered. "Speaking of which, take a look through there."

She cast him a curious glance, then walked on, opened the door, looked in—and laughed. "It's our bathroom."

The long narrow room had a large skylight. She spent several minutes examining the amenities and appurtenances, noting that James's dressing room also had a door to the bathroom, while a third door gave onto the main corridor, then James waved her back into the bedroom. "We have one more room to inspect."

Back in the bedroom, he opened the last door, the one alongside the head of the bed, and ushered her through—into the most beautiful lady's sitting-room-cum-boudoir she'd ever seen.

"Oh, my!" Eyes round, she drank in the wide windows, the Hepplewhite chairs, the well-stuffed armchairs and chaise. Care had been taken, to an even greater extent than elsewhere, to ensure that every last little detail matched and contributed to the ambience of the room; not a single touch marred the overall impression of being surrounded by a warm, autumn wood. Trailing her fingers along the butter-soft tan leather of the chaise's raised back, Henrietta murmured, "Your grandaunt loved these colors, didn't she?"

Sliding his hands into his pockets, James leaned against the mantelpiece. "Yes, she did." After a moment, he went on, "These are the colors she chose for her rooms up here. Downstairs is mostly woodland greens and browns, and the other bedrooms, you'll have noticed, are in brighter shades—more yellows and light greens, more summery."

He paused, but when Henrietta turned and looked at him—as if sensing there was more to it than that—he went on, "She was an artist, old Emily." He tipped his head toward the painting above the mantelpiece, a rich tapestry of greens and golds and subtle browns depicting a scene of a path through a wood. "I told you she spent half the year in town, but her heart remained in the country, in Wiltshire, at her estate there. She loved the walks, the woods, so she painted them and brought them with her here."

Henrietta searched his eyes, then looked at the painting. Drawing—drawn—nearer, she asked, "So when we're there, I'll be able to see this—the real this?"

He nodded. "All the paintings in the house are hers, and you can see all of the views, all of the scenes, in real life, at Whitestone Hall."

Henrietta studied the painting, then looked at him. "You'll have to take me to see each of the places depicted in her paintings."

He held her gaze. "If you'd like that."

She smiled and nodded decisively. "I would." Returning to his side, she cast the painting one last glance. "It'll be like making contact with your grandaunt, and I rather think, had I ever met her, I would have liked her."

"She would have liked you." He caught her gaze as she turned to him, then smiled. "More to the point, she would have approved of you."

Henrietta opened her eyes wide and stepped closer. "Do you think so?"

Drawing his hands from his pockets, he nodded. "Definitely."

"Why?" She tipped up her face as he grasped her waist and drew her nearer still.

Bending his head, he murmured, "Because you're mine—but even more because you've made me yours."

Their lips met.

Later, he would wonder whether it was he, or she, either by conscious act or through unconscious need, who initiated the next step—or whether they were both driven, captive to some elemental, intrinsic command, mere actors engaging under the direction of a power greater than them both.

Or whether, given the situation, the threat hovering over her and therefore over the shared future that was hourly taking more definite shape, it was inevitable that they would end in his bed, and that the afternoon—that particular afternoon—would be filled with the heated tangle of limbs, with provocative caresses, evocative groans, and the sibilant sounds of smothered gasps as together they reexplored, reclaimed, and reaffirmed all they'd previously discovered.

All they'd previously uncovered. Reassuring, restating, revisiting, and reiterating, they dived in again, plunged in again, seized and surrendered and shared the scintillating delights once again.

He couldn't remember quite how they'd returned to the bed; he vaguely recalled the heated duel of their tongues, the frantic melding of their mouths, followed by an even more driven rush to rid themselves of all physical barriers between them. Clothes shed, fell away, vanished—banished. And then they were naked, hot skin to hot skin, and they both paused, eyes closed, senses stretching wide to absorb the delirious pleasure of that sharply intense moment. To savor it.

Then the flames rose, hungry and greedy, and wouldn't be denied, and they gave themselves up to the fire, to the conflagration of their senses. Falling across the bed, in the warm afternoon light they reveled and rejoiced.

And it grew stronger. More assured, more powerful.

The force that rose up and claimed them both, that flashed through them and possessed them as, joined and together in body and in mind, they raced up the peak, then soared high.

And fractured.

They clung and slowly fell, spiraling back to the real world, to the heavy thud of each other's hearts, to the soft, ragged rush of each other's breaths.

To the joy and comfort of each other's bodies embracing, holding, accepting, and enveloping.

Protecting. Holding on.

In the soft golden light, in the warmth of his bed, one fact rang crystal clear. Neither had any intention of retreating.

Of backing away, no matter the challenge.

They wanted this, both of them, this and all it could lead to.

Slumping back onto the pillows, as she crawled into his arms, their gazes met and held . . . and he read in her eyes the same resolution that resonated inside him.

Without words, without further thought, in that moment they made a binding commitment.

To each other, to themselves, to their future lives.

To this.

For this they would battle any foe.

Because *this* was worth any price.

It was that simple. That fundamental.

She lowered her head to his shoulder, let her body, her limbs, relax against his.

Eyes closing, he cradled her close.

As all tension fell away, he inwardly smiled, and sent a prayer winging heavenward—to his grandaunt Emily.

He was entirely reconciled to her manipulation.

Chapter Twelve

Atop Marie, Henrietta trotted into the park early the next morning. Two grooms rode at her back, both alert and watchful, there to ensure no one attempted to accost or otherwise threaten her.

The morning was cool and damp, light wisps of fog clinging to the trees and wreathing the bushes deeper in the park. No sun had yet struck through the pale gray clouds, and the birdcalls were muted.

"At least there's no wind," Henrietta murmured. For her and Marie, this was a regular outing, one of their customary biweekly morning rides; while she'd readily agreed to the extra guards, she hadn't felt inclined to allow her villainous would-be murderer to dictate how she lived her life.

Yet in deference to the threat, James had insisted on joining her, and with that she was perfectly content; they'd arranged to meet by the start of the tan track along Rotten Row. Conscious of the warming spark of anticipation the prospect of seeing James provoked, she clung to it and rode at a quick clip down toward the track.

Beneath her outward calm, she felt restless, discomfited. She felt almost itchy, her nerves abraded by the constant scrutiny that had surprisingly quickly escalated once the rest of the family had been informed of the threat against her life.

She hadn't expected to feel quite so "under observation," to the extent that the three hours she'd spent at a ball last night had ended feeling like time to be endured, rather than enjoyed. Even having James constantly by her side hadn't alleviated the oppressive feeling.

"But until this damned villain is caught and hung by the heels," she muttered, "it appears I'm going to have to put up with it."

She reached the start of the tan track and wasn't all that surprised to find no James waiting. Drawing rein, she leaned forward and patted Marie's glossy neck. "We're a trifle early, I fear."

She and James had agreed to ride extra early, but, restless, she'd left home as soon as she'd been ready, and as yet there were few others abroad. She could see only two groups of riders, one threesome of rakish gentlemen, and two older gentlemen out for their morning constitutional. Both groups were already using the track; their members noted her escort and gave her a wide berth.

She shifted in her saddle; Marie pranced as the three rakish gentlemen set their mounts facing down the tan track, then swept past and on in a thunder of hooves. The mare loved to run and didn't at all appreciate Henrietta holding her back.

"James will be here soon." Henrietta gentled the mare, settling her. Along with Marie, she looked longingly down the track. "We'll be able to run when he comes."

Then again, she had two guards, and the track wasn't that long . . . and other than the five riders, all of whom she recognized, there was no one else around.

The mare danced, jiggling her.

"Oh, all right." Easing the reins, she swung Marie toward the start of the track and called over her shoulder, "I'm going down for one pass."

Her guards quickly brought their horses up; when she sent Marie at an easy gallop down the tan, the grooms kept station just behind her.

They were galloping fluidly by the time they reached the end of the track. Laughing—feeling considerably better, freer, lighter of heart—Henrietta reined in and turned, bringing Marie around in a wide arc preparatory to riding back to the start of the track.

Looking up and ahead, she saw James emerging from the misty distance. She waved and called a halloo.

He spotted her, smiled, and raised a hand in salute.

Grinning, she leaned forward—

Crack!

James saw Henrietta jerk, then start to crumple a fraction before the sharp report of a pistol reached him. Shock hit him like a fist to the chest.

Digging in his heels, he sent his mount racing over the sward.

Fear sank icy talons around his heart and squeezed. . . .

Then he was hauling his gray in alongside the confused and skittish black mare. He was vaguely aware of the two grooms milling close, putting themselves, horses and bodies, between Henrietta and the thick bushes from where the shot must have come. But his focus, all his awareness, all his senses, were locked on Henrietta. She lay slumped forward, arms limply embracing the mare's glossy neck. Blood was trickling down the side of her face, disappearing into the black hide.

She looked pale as death, but her back rose slightly and fell.

Throttling his panic, dropping his reins, he reached for her. It took a moment of juggling to free her from her sidesaddle, then he lifted her across and into his arms, settling her before him.

Cradling her close, he felt her chest expand and contract. Rhythmically and repeatedly. Carefully moving her head, he gently examined her wound, an ugly furrow above one ear, then he blew out a breath. Sucked in another as his reeling wits steadied. "She's alive." He glanced at the anxious grooms. "She'll live. It's only a bad graze."

He looked down at her face. Pain and shock had knocked her unconscious, and she was losing copious amounts of blood, but she wasn't going to die.

Relief swamped him; if he'd been standing, it would have brought him to his knees.

Awkwardly searching for, then folding, his handkerchief, he pressed it firmly to the angry wound, then glanced at the grooms. Meeting their worried gazes, he realized they were torn—should they try to catch the villain or stay and help with their mistress?

"I'll take her straight home." Lips tightening, he nodded at the bushes. "Take the mare, and see what you can find."

They didn't need further urging; one seized the mare's reins, then they both raced off.

He didn't dally to see where they went; managing his gray with his knees, he cantered as fast as he dared straight out of the park, then up Park Lane to Upper Brook Street.

He picked his moment." A glass of brandy in his hand, James stood before the fireplace in the drawing room, his gaze locked on Henrietta; in a fresh day gown with her wound bathed and bound, she was seated on the chaise flanked by a pale-faced Louise and a grim-faced Mary, each clutching one of her hands. Lord Arthur sat in the armchair facing the chaise, his pallor verging on ashen.

The rest of the room was full of Cynsters. Other members of the family, alerted, James assumed, by Lord Arthur and Lady Louise, had started arriving within half an hour of him carrying Henrietta, unconscious and still bleeding, into the front hall.

Pandemonium had, unsurprisingly, ensued.

Now, nearly two hours later, the room was awash in stylish day gowns and morning coats, their owners overflowing with concern or bristling with protectiveness, or, in some cases, both.

Henrietta had, to his intense relief, quickly recovered her wits and a degree of her composure, at least, but as was to be expected, she was shaken and shocked.

As was he. Taking another sip of brandy, he continued his report—for her benefit as much as that of the others in the room. "At the time of the shot, the other riders who'd been there had left. I could see them in the distance, but they didn't even hear the shot. It was just plain luck that he had such a window of opportunity, but given where he'd hidden, he would have been able to take his shot regardless of whether anyone else was around."

"Nevertheless," Devil Cynster said, his deep voice just above a growl, "that point's important. It was early—did anyone else notice you while you were riding back?"

James hesitated, then replied, "Not that I was aware

of, but"—he met Devil's gaze—"I wasn't looking around to see who we shocked."

"Just so." Helena spoke crisply. "But what you are wanting to know, I think"—she caught her son's eye—"is whether it is likely that the whole ton now knows of this incident, or if it is still only us"—with a regal wave, she indicated the family gathered around—"who know of this cowardly attack."

Devil nodded. "Correct. We agreed to keep the attacks—that they were attacks and not accidents—to ourselves, but no one's going to label being shot in Hyde Park an accident."

"Indeed, but"—Helena glanced at the other ladies—"I believe we, the ladies, are best placed to learn what the rest of the ton knows, so . . . who has luncheons to attend?"

Several ladies admitted to having such engagements; in the end, fully half the skirts and several of the morning coats departed the room, their owners sallying forth on their fact-finding mission.

The door had barely closed behind them when it was flung open again and two ladies rushed in, making a beeline for the chaise.

"Good God, Henrietta! Are you all right?"

"Mama's note just said you'd been shot!"

A pair of near identical eyes, having taken in Henrietta's relative health, swiveled to fix almost accusingly on Louise.

She flung up her hands, then opened her arms to her elder daughters. "I'm sorry, my dears, but I knew you would want to know immediately you reached town, and I was a little distracted."

The twins, Amanda and Amelia, hugged their mother, then moved on to greet all the other family members. James found himself being hugged, his cheek kissed, then introduced to the twins' husbands, Martin Fulbright and Luc Ashford, with both of whom he was passingly acquainted.

"This sounds like a bad business," Martin said as the ladies moved on.

"You'll need to fill us in," Luc said. "We thought we were coming down for your engagement ball, only to discover we've landed in the middle of attempted murder. Why on earth would anyone want to shoot Henrietta?"

By the time James and the other males had answered Martin's and Luc's understandable questions, it was time for luncheon; the entire gathering transferred to the dining room, where a cold collation lay waiting.

Everyone took seats around the table, filled their plates, and were just settling to eat when the front doorbell pealed. Urgently. Everyone looked at each other, wondering . . . then swift footsteps were heard and the door opened and Angelica, Countess of Glencrae, and her husband, Dominic, swept in.

Greetings, exclamations, and explanations started all over again. Angelica's older sisters, Heather and Eliza, and their husbands, had arrived with the earlier troops, but both ladies had left with the company that had gone forth to assess the ton's knowledge of the latest incident, and their absences, too, had to be explained. . . .

James cast a long-suffering look at Devil, seated across the table. The Duke of St. Ives, a nobleman powerful enough to command instant obedience in many other spheres, merely shrugged and looked resigned.

Eventually, at last, everyone was seated, and eating, and the gathering finally quieted.

From the faint frowns in most eyes, the distracted expressions, while they ate most were thinking. Reviewing all they knew, and thinking of what next they might do—of how to identify the blackguard who had so nearly claimed one of their own.

James glanced at Henrietta, seated alongside him, then looked back at his plate. He had no difficulty comprehending, indeed, fully shared, the barely restrained aggression emanating from all the Cynster males; had the ball passed one inch to the right, Henrietta would have been dead.

He was, now, perfectly ready to do murder himself.

But first he—they—had to identify the madman.

Gradually, discussions started up, here and there down the long table. What if . . . ? Perhaps . . . ? Maybe if . . . ? The cold collation was whisked away and replaced with fruit, nuts, and cheeses, served with a fruity white wine. As the platters were passed along the table, the swell of speculation rose.

"It's not going to be easy." Henrietta glanced up and met James's eyes. "Is it?"

He hesitated, then replied, "I can't see any simple way to learn who he is."

From across the table, Devil asked, "What did the grooms find? Anything?"

James shook his head. The two grooms had returned half an hour after he and Henrietta had reached the house. "They hunted high and low, but while they found the place where the man had been—in that dense stand of bushes about fifteen yards from the end of the tan—they didn't see anyone about. They think he must have had a horse waiting."

Devil grimaced. "At that hour, once he was away from the immediate area, there'd be no reason for anyone to pay any attention to him. He'd be just another gentleman out for an early morning ride."

"True, but that wasn't a bad shot." Seated beside Devil, Vane Cynster said, "Think about it." He met Henrietta's eyes. "You must have been a good twenty yards away, and riding away from him."

Henrietta thought back, then felt what little color she'd regained drain from her face. "I leaned forward just as he shot. . . ." She met Vane's eyes, then glanced at James. "He wasn't aiming for my head."

Devil growled, "He was aiming for your heart." Abruptly he reached out, seized a salt cellar, and rapped it like a gavel on the table. "Quiet!"

All the discussions cut off. Everyone looked at Devil.

Lips thin, he smiled, not humorously. "Let's go back to the drawing room. We need to pool everything we know and decide what steps we're going to take to bring this blackguard down."

No one argued with either the directive or his tone. Everyone seemed in a belligerent mood as they found seats or took up positions around the drawing room.

Feeling a trifle unsteady emotionally as well as physically, Henrietta drew James down to sit on the arm of the chaise, the corner of which she—as the lady most likely to be feeling frail—was instructed to take.

Devil claimed his usual position before the fireplace, flanked by his cousins Vane and Gabriel. Her father sat in an armchair alongside; his brothers, George and Martin, occupied chairs next to his. The other males ranged around the walls, or leaned against the backs of chairs and sofas. The ladies, not the full complement as the others had yet to return, disposed themselves around the circle of available seats.

Henrietta watched as Devil scanned the faces. This

was just the family, all of them connected directly by blood or marriage. The connections weren't present. What was discussed in this room would be family business, and unless agreed otherwise, would be restricted to the family only.

"Let us assume," Devil began, "that the rest of the ton don't know about the shooting this morning. Given there've been no inquiries made at the door here, I suspect that's a reasonable assumption, but the rest of our number will return shortly and bring confirmation. So . . . the question we currently face is what to do next, specifically how we can identify the gentleman who, quite aside from already being a double-murderer, apparently thinks it's wise to take aim at a Cynster."

A rumble, a ripple of instinctive response, ran around the room. Ignoring it, Devil turned to James. "It might be helpful if the two of you would outline for the rest of us the earlier incidents—what exactly happened at Marchmain House, in Brook Street, and at the ruins at Ellsmere Grange."

James nodded. Henrietta was holding his hand tightly, so he stayed where he was and addressed the company from there, outlining the three incidents, describing what had happened from his point of view; Henrietta chipped in with her observations as they went along.

Everyone listened in attentive silence, broken only by a few shrewd questions put by some of the gentlemen.

When they'd finished describing the morning's events, Devil stated, "Scotland Yard, in the form of Inspector Stokes, knows everything bar this morning's happenings. Before we inform him of those, however, I suggest we discuss what steps we intend to take to catch this blackguard. There are things we might do that Stokes might have difficulty condoning, and we don't need to place him in any unenviable position. So let's decide what we're going to do first."

There was general agreement with that sentiment, and also with the need to bring the matter to a head sooner rather than later.

"We don't want him taking any more potshots at Henrietta," her uncle Martin growled.

The ladies and gentlemen who had gone out over luncheon to assess the ton's state of knowledge returned with the news that, overall, the ton remained oblivious.

"It seems," Heather, now Viscountess Breckenridge, said, as she sat on a straight-backed chair her husband had fetched for her, "that it was simply too early and no one was about."

"Or if they were, they weren't awake enough to take proper notice." Jeremy Carling set a chair for his wife alongside Heather's; Eliza swept her skirts close and sat. Jeremy looked at Devil. "There wasn't so much as a whisper at any of the clubs."

"Good," Devil said. "So the blackguard will most likely think that this morning's incident is the first we've got wind of him and his lethal intentions, and that not having any idea what might be behind them, we're in the dark and"—he waved around the room—"gathering in a panic and not yet actively doing anything. The longer he remains ignorant of our intention to trap him the better—the easier our task will be."

The door opened and Simon entered; he'd gone to see if he could winkle Lady Marchmain's guest list from her. Everyone looked at him hopefully. He grimaced. "She's happy to share it, but it's at Marchmain House. She'll send it by rider the instant she gets home."

James nodded his thanks but pointed out, "We need

to remember that, given the number on it, at best all that list will do is narrow our field. It won't get us all that much closer to identifying the killer."

"True." Devil looked around the room. "So who can think of a plan to draw the blackguard out?"

Various options—some rather fanciful—were aired. Henrietta sat back and let the discussions rage . . . until they started to peter out. Then, speaking more strongly than she had to that point, she stated, "We all know there's really only one way."

The look Devil cast her told her very clearly that he'd understood that from the first but had chosen to exhaust every other avenue before even considering it.

Before he could take charge again, she said, "The only way to trap him, to lure him into stepping out of the ton crowd, is to use me as bait."

She wasn't surprised by the resulting furor.

Under cover of the arguments being tossed back and forth, James, her hand trapped in his, leaned closer to say, "I don't want you to do it—to risk yourself like that."

Henrietta looked into his eyes. "I know. I don't want to take the risk—but it's the only way." She squeezed his hand, held tight. "The only way we'll get to live in your grandaunt Emily's house, the two of us together, free of any threat, the only way I'll ever be able to see the scenes she painted in real life, at Whitestone Hall." She held his gaze for a moment more, then quietly but determinedly said, "I don't wish to take any risk, but to have the future we both want, we need me to do this, and so I will. Please don't make it more difficult."

He returned her regard for a long moment, then . . . with palpable reluctance, he nodded and looked up, at Devil. "St. Ives."

When Devil glanced his way, James said, "Let's cut to the chase. Henrietta's right. There is only one way."

His eyes on James's, Devil hauled in a huge breath, then he glanced at Henrietta, saw her resolution, and sighed. Nodded. Then Devil raised his voice, called the family conclave to order, and stated, "There's no point arguing. This has to be done. So how, exactly, do we do it?"

Silence fell as everyone paused and drew breath.

Then step by step, point by point, layer of protection upon layer of protection, acting in concert, bringing their collective experience to bear, the Cynster family formulated a plan to trap Lady Winston's murderer, the malefactor who had had the temerity to target one of their own.

Later that night, James climbed through the back parlor window of Lord Arthur Cynster's house. "Thank you," he whispered to the shadowy figure who had opened the window and waved him inside.

"If you want to thank me, just make sure Henrietta gets through this, happy and alive." Mary closed the window, locked it, paused, then amended, "In reverse order will be perfectly acceptable."

Wrapped in a thick robe with a shawl knotted about her shoulders, without further words she crossed to the door, opened it, glanced out, then impatiently beckoned him to follow.

James made his way across the room, stepped quietly into the corridor, and shut the door. Mary held a finger to her lips, then proceeded to lead him through the silent house. Into the front hall and up the main stairs, she walked confidently but made little sound; James did his best to emulate her, praying they wouldn't encounter any members of the household on some midnight excursion.

Mary led him around the gallery, then down a corridor; she halted outside a door, glanced at him, and tipped her head toward the panels. "That's her room. Everyone's been in bed for an hour, so she might be asleep. Make sure she doesn't scream."

James inwardly frowned. Before he could respond, Mary blithely went on, "I assume you can find your way back out?"

"Yes. Of course." It hadn't been a complicated journey.

"Good. You'd better make sure you leave early enough to escape notice—I don't want any repercussions over this. Just leave the window closed—I'll lock it when I go down in the morning."

There really was no limit to her brassy bossiness, but she had helped him tonight, and for that he was grateful; she hadn't had to agree, but beneath her self-assured schoolma'amish arrogance, James sensed she really was anxious over Henrietta, and he could find no fault with that.

Closing his hand about the doorknob, he inclined his head.

With a regal nod, Mary glided on and away.

He didn't wait to see where she went but turned the knob, opened the door, slipped through, and quietly closed it behind him.

Although no candle burned, there was enough light to see. Two wide windows were uncurtained, and moonlight washed across the polished boards to lap about and across a large tester bed. The head of the bed and the pillows remained in shadow, but even as he started across the floor, James heard a rustle, then saw the covers move.

Mary's admonition about making sure Henrietta didn't scream blared in his mind.

"James?" Henrietta sat up; instinctively holding the sheets to her chest, she peered past the spill of moonlight into the gloom beyond. "Is that you?"

Even as she whispered the words, the thought that it might not be him, the fear of who it might be instead, flared in her mind but was immediately doused by some rock-solidly sure part of her that—somehow—knew beyond question that the indistinct figure shrouded in gloom was James.

"Yes." He walked into the moonlight and crossed to the bed.

She looked up at him, drank in the sight. He halted beside the bed and looked down at her in the same way—as if just seeing her, setting eyes on her face, looking into her eyes, was an end in itself, a balm to both mind and emotions. They both took the minute, used it, then she held out a hand. "I'm glad you came."

He closed his fingers firmly around hers. When she tugged, he obliged and sat on the side of the bed, facing her. "I had to see you. I needed to speak with you. I asked Mary to help me, and she let me in."

Henrietta smiled fleetingly. "I must remember to thank her."

His gaze rose to her head, to the bandage still circling it. "How's your head?"

"Sore where the ball grazed, but otherwise it doesn't hurt." Curling her legs beneath the sheets, leaving her hand in his, she shifted closer, propping on her other arm, letting the covers slide to her lap. She was wearing a fine lawn nightgown; regardless, she had no reason to hide from him. Leaning closer, head tipping, she murmured, "Indeed, otherwise, I'm perfectly all right."

Because she was watching, she saw the shadow that passed across his face. He drew a tighter breath, then met her gaze. "That was just luck. Pure luck that you leaned forward."

She held his gaze, gripped his hand tighter. "True, but fate took a hand and . . . I'm still here."

His voice lowered. "*We're* still here—as I see it, as I feel it—there's no longer any me or you, only we and us."

She studied his eyes, then her lips lifted. "I'm glad you feel that—think that—because I do, too."

A minute ticked by while they simply looked at each other, while they drowned in each other's eyes, marveling anew, reveling again in the connection, in the power of what now bound them.

The flaring intensity peaked. Moved by it, compelled, she shifted, fluidly coming up on her knees to lean closer; placing her hand on his shoulder, she tipped her head and set her lips to his, and kissed him.

She parted her lips and drew him in, then let the kiss spin out, and he kissed her back; releasing her hand, he raised his and gently, so gently, framed her face, careful not to press against her wound, and held her steady, balanced on her knees before him, so the kiss could extend, could stretch and evolve, so they both could savor.

So they could calm their inner demons, exorcise their fears, and through the caress, through the intimate sharing, be once again assured—of the other, of them.

That they were still there, were hale and whole and still together. That their joint future was still there, theirs to claim, waiting for them to own it.

Her lips supped from his, then his from hers. Passion and desire swirled in the darkness, subtle flames licking over their skins, teasing their senses, tantalizing their nerves.

Tempting them.

Eventually, she drew back; breasts rising, she filled her lungs on a slow, deep inhalation, then, eyes locked with his, mere inches apart, she murmured, her tone low, a blatant, sultry, unequivocal invitation, "You are going to stay, aren't you?"

His lips softened, fractionally curved. His eyes didn't leave hers. "That would be my preferred option."

She laughed soft and low, and drew him down to the bed.

Drew him into her arms as he tipped and they rolled, and passion swelled. But in instinctive accord they caught it, reined it back. Tonight was theirs—no threat could reach them, no would-be murderer touch them, not there. They had no need to rush, and much more reason to loiter.

To linger, and savor, and rejoice.

James had rolled to his back, had settled her atop him. Cradling her head in one large hand, he looked up into her eyes. "We'll have to be careful not to hurt your head."

"We will be, and we won't." Settling her elbows on his chest, she stared down into his eyes, then seductively smiled. "Just kiss me." As she bent her head to teasingly brush her lips over his, she murmured, "Make love to me."

He needed no further invitation; cupping the back of her head, he waited, let her play and script the kiss for several heartbeats, then he took over and let the kiss turn hungry.

Hungry, but leashed.

Tongues tangled, dueled; their lips parted only to meld and fuse again as the exchange grew more heated. More intent.

Their breathing grew ragged; soft sounds of passion floated in the air.

Clothes fell, flew, vanished. Hands grasped, then caressed and sculpted.

Weighed and flagrantly possessed.

Their lips parted only so they could savor the other's skin, so they could taste the other's passion.

So they could drive each other on.

They both knew what they wanted; they both wanted the same thing. Tonight even more than previously they were in perfect accord.

In perfect empathy.

What followed was a symphony, one orchestrated by them both, with first him directing, then her conducting, then, hand in hand, body to body, skin to skin, they let passion and desire and all that flowed from the physical and emotional conflagration sweep them up and away.

Together.

As one their hearts seized as he entered her and joined them; as one they paused, senses wide, to drain every last scintilla of heightened pleasure from that critical second . . . then with flawless rhythm they started the dance, their journey to completion.

They were as one in their grasping desperation, in their giddy, reckless, passionate joy, as one with their hoarse, rasping breaths as they rode, skins damp, senses burning, for the ultimate distant peak.

And found ecstasy waiting, powerful and sure, to embrace them, shatter them, and once again remold them.

To once again fuse them, but at an even deeper level, in an even more unbreakable bond.

As they tumbled back to earth, to the dark bliss of the bed and the warmth of the other's arms, even as the golden glow of satiation spread through them both, they found each other's eyes.

Breaths mingling, gazes locked, neither needed to ask what the other thought.

They would defy hell for this. For this joy, this passion.

This unbounded togetherness.

No one—no murderer, no villain of any stripe—would take this from them. They wouldn't let it go. Not willingly, not even if death threatened.

They read the truth in each other's eyes, then let their lids fall. They needed no words to repledge their troth; for this, for their chance to live with this, to devote their lives to living the promise of this, they would, unhesitatingly, stake their lives.

Nothing needed to be said. Sliding deeper into the bed, dragging up the covers, they turned into each other's arms, and slept.

Chapter Thirteen

The following evening, Sir Thomas Grenville, Trustee of the British Museum and prominent bibliophile, had elected to host a gala to raise funds for the continuing construction of the new museum. Sir Thomas had had the happy notion of staging his gala in the part of the new East Wing known as The King's Library Gallery, a completed section of the new works until that evening forbidden to any but the curators, hence assuring attendance by all those of the ton lucky enough to receive an invitation.

As most of the upper echelon of the ton was presently in residence for the Season, the event was destined by design to be the most horrendous, albeit select, crush—literally everyone who was anyone could be counted on to be there.

"It truly is the perfect venue for our trap," Henrietta murmured. On James's arm, she stood just behind her mother and father in the reception line; tall though she was, she couldn't see over, much less through, the sea of heads and shoulders bobbing and nodding as those in the line ahead of their party chatted excitedly. Everyone was anticipating a highly memorable evening. Sir Thomas, an old hand at staging fund-raising events, had been extremely cagey over the entertainment he intended providing, letting speculation build and do his job for him.

As a consequence, all those invited had turned up *en masse*.

"I heard," James said, bending his head to murmur in her ear, "that those senior hostesses who had intended to host events tonight have, by and large, cancelled them."

Henrietta nodded. "There was no point persevering. Everyone is going to be here, and as it's a gala, few will be likely to leave until it's over."

"Which, again, will presumably play into our hands." Raising his head, James glanced around. "I can see St. Ives ahead, and Gabriel and Alathea are ten yards behind us." He swept his gaze ahead, then back along the densely packed line of would-be revelers again. "I can't see any of the others."

"They'll be here, somewhere, although with such a crowd I'm relieved we don't have to meet up with any of them. Finding anyone will be well-nigh impossible."

"Unless you're watching and waiting." James felt his jaw set. After a moment, he relaxed it enough to ask, "Remind me again—who are the ones elected to supply our façade of obliviousness?"

Henrietta glanced around, but the noise generated by the crowd was already such that she seriously doubted even her mother, directly ahead of her, would hear anything she said. Nevertheless, she leaned nearer to James and lowered her voice. "Devil and Honoria, Vane and Patience, Gabriel and Alathea, Lucifer and Phyllida, and Demon and Flick, as well as Simon and Portia, Amanda and Martin, and Amelia and Luc." She shifted her gaze forward. "And my parents, of course—and Mary, too." Her sister was standing on Arthur's other side. "Plus all the older generation—Aunt Helena, Martin and Celia, and George and Horatia. They'll all be here, and all will be playing their part."

They'd all agreed that her would-be murderer would definitely know enough to be wary of those named. He would watch them for their reactions, possibly even be bold enough to test them, and if they showed any hint of being alert and on guard, then no matter how tempting the lure they cast, he wouldn't step free of the crowd to pursue it. Consequently, the above-named members of the wider company who had come there that night intent on capturing the murderer would project a façade of supreme unawareness of any potential threat. That was their role—to convince the murderer that no one was expecting him to do anything so outrageous as to strike again that night, certainly not at the gala, and that therefore no one was maintaining any particular watch on Henrietta.

"So," James said, "we have Adair and Penelope, Charlie Morwellan and Sarah, Dillon Caxton and Pris, Gerrard Debbington and Jacqueline, your cousins Heather, Eliza, and Angelica, and their husbands, and Charlie Hastings playing the part of the surreptitious watchers."

They shuffled forward in the line and Henrietta nodded. "Along with Christian and Letitia, Wolverstone and Minerva, and other members of that special club of theirs, as well as some of their army friends, and all their wives." She glanced up at James. "There'll be many more watching me than the murderer could possibly guess."

James fought not to let his inner grimness show. He was supposedly there to enjoy what was widely expected to be the highlight of the Season, with his newly affianced bride-to-be on his arm, but projecting the correct image was proving a difficult task given his preordained role in their drama.

He still didn't know how he'd come to agree to it—to agree to stage a disagreement with Henrietta of sufficient intensity to support the fiction of them parting, of her storming into the crowd and him turning on his heel and stalking off in the opposite direction.

Facing forward, Henrietta added, "And don't forget Stokes and his men waiting outside."

James wasn't about to forget that the nearest the police could get was the outside of the building. If anything, Stokes liked their plan even less than James did, but, like James, he'd been largely helpless to prevent it being carried out, so had elected to lend his support as best he could. With a small cohort of his junior detectives and several eager constables, Stokes had set up a continual watch on all the exits from the building. If something occurred and the villain attempted to flee, he would run into the waiting arms of the Metropolitan Police.

James glanced at Henrietta. She appeared entirely calm, her attention focused outward, exchanging smiles and nods with others in the crowd.

Only he was near enough to detect the wary watchfulness lurking in her soft eyes; only he could feel, through her hand lying on his sleeve, the tension thrumming through her. She was wound as tight as he.

They reached the head of the reception line, and Sir Thomas greeted them with jocular good cheer. After exchanging the usual brief pleasantries, and receiving Sir Thomas's congratulations on their engagement, James led Henrietta in Louise, Arthur, and Mary's wake. All of them looked about them as they walked, tacking around other couples and groups likewise caught in admiration of the elegance of a room reputed to be the finest in all of London.

The gallery, built to house the King's library, was three hundred feet long; over most of that length, it was thirty feet wide, but the central section, delineated by four spectacular columns of polished Aberdeen granite, was said to be nearly double that width.

"Just look at that ceiling." Head tipped back, Henrietta stared upward at the ornate plasterwork in creams, pale yellows, and gold. "That must be at least forty feet high."

"At least." Grasping her hand, James wound her arm in his and started them on a course separate from her parents and sister. "Those balconies all around will afford an excellent view of the room."

"Hmm." Henrietta glanced his way, caught his eye. "Anyone on them, up there above the crowd, will also be in easy view of anyone watching them."

James's lips twisted. "Precisely my thought." He dipped his head to murmur, "Up there would be the perfect place to stage our disagreement. We should keep an eye out for the stairs leading up."

Henrietta nodded. The balconies in question ran above the bookcases lining the long sides of the room; about halfway up the forty-foot-high walls, the balconies formed narrow walkways that ran over the top of the deep bookcases and in front of the long windows set in the upper halves of the walls. Delicate, gilded, rail-type balustrades gave the balconies an airy appearance, as if they were suspended over the body of the room.

"According to Adair," James said, "there are only two doors—the one we came in and another at the far end of the room." They paused beside one of the beautiful polished desks situated along the room. Examining it, then the marble statue beside it, James shook his head. "I can't believe this room is intended purely for the use of scholars, and the wider public wasn't supposed to ever get a chance to appreciate it." He glanced around as they started off again. "I can see why they've claimed it's the finest room in London."

Still engrossed in drinking in the architectural magnificence, Henrietta nodded, then added, "Which, I suppose, all but guarantees that whoever we're after, they will be here."

They were nearing the middle section, where the room doubled in width. Glancing back toward the door through which they'd entered, Henrietta saw the polished oak and mahogany floor fast disappearing beneath a tide of elegant skirts as the rest of the guests poured in. "How long do you think we should wait before we enact our scene?"

"Adair and Devil both pushed for us to wait a full hour—all of the guests should be in the room by then."

"All right." Plastering on a brighter smile, Henrietta tightened her arm around his. "In that case, we can mingle freely and forget about the plan until then."

They did precisely that, stopping to chat with others, receiving congratulations on their engaged state with appropriate modesty. Nevertheless, as they promenaded around the central section, then continued down the long room, both continued to assess the possibilities the room afforded in terms of carrying out their plan.

When they reached the other end of the room, James drew Henrietta aside, into one corner. Dipping his head, he spoke quietly; the room was now so crowded, the guests so densely packed, that despite the cacophony of a thousand voices they needed to be wary of being overheard. "I'm sure Adair will send some of those watching you up onto the balconies." Barnaby had been delegated to oversee that arm of the plan—those of their company delegated to watch over and ultimately protect Henrietta while the rest of her family pretended obliviousness.

"I can already see Dillon and Pris up there, on the right, nearer the middle." Henrietta nodded at the pair. "Pris is expecting, so Dillon won't leave her, but they're both very sharp eyed."

"Doubtless Adair is standing at some point from where he can see all the watchers, so they can alert him to anyone approaching you."

Henrietta quelled a shiver; the only way she was going to get through the evening was to *not* think about the man who wanted to murder her. Hannah had dressed her hair to conceal the wound along the side of her head, but she could still feel it, a constant reminder of the pistol ball tearing through her skin. "Is it time yet?"

James consulted his fob watch, then tucked it back into his pocket. "At least another fifteen minutes."

"Lady Holland mentioned that the first entertainment to be offered was to be that Italian soprano from Milan. I assume she'll perform beside the grand piano in the middle section, and as her ladyship said the soprano was the first of three acts, then I assume she'll perform soon, most likely on, or just after, the hour." Henrietta met James's eyes. "Should we wait until after she performs, or enact our scene before?"

"Just before, and staged on the balcony above the piano will gain maximum attention, but . . ." James grimaced, then met Henrietta's eyes. "There's no reason the entire ton needs to witness our 'disagreement.' If our man is here, and he should be by then, he'll be watching you anyway—we don't need to make a major production out of it, so after the soprano's performance might be better."

Henrietta nodded decisively. "Yes, it will be—aside from anything else, making too big a show of it might tip the blackguard off. I wouldn't be so gauche, and neither would you. We can't act out of character and make our parting too obvious—it has to be believable." She met James's eyes. "Quite literally a temporary disagreement and nothing more."

He held her gaze, then nodded. "Yes, you're right. But I still think we should make it easy for him to see us disagree and part." He looked up and along the balcony running above the left wall of the section they were in. "We could position ourselves toward the end of this balcony, just above the piano, above where the soprano will stand."

Henrietta turned to the delicate spiral staircase that led up to the balcony in question. "We can go up here and promenade along, then take up position to listen to the singer." She glanced at James. "That will look entirely natural."

With a nod, he followed her to the nearby stairs, then up them. Gaining the balcony, he retook her arm, and they commenced a slow promenade back toward the central section of the room.

They found the perfect spot at the end of the balcony, where another spiral stair led down to the gallery's floor just a little way from one of the four massive granite columns that supported the ceiling of the long room's central section. The piano was being positioned at the foot of that column.

Henrietta stood beside the balustrade, one gloved

hand on the smooth rail, and looked down, watching as five liveried staff muscled the piano around under the direction of a dapperly dressed but currently harassed-looking individual. She glanced at James, beside her. "I think that's Sir Thomas's secretary."

James, who had been scanning the room below them, focused on the poor man, then snorted. "I don't envy him his job. Bad enough having to organize all this, but on top of that to have to deal with temperamental artistes . . . I can't imagine there's many lining up for that honor." Gossip had painted the soprano who was to perform as having the voice of an angel and the temper of a demented devil.

"I gather he—the secretary—has been with Sir Thomas for years, so no doubt he's grown accustomed to the drama." Henrietta leaned further over the railing to peer down.

James had to quash a sudden impulse to seize her and drag her back; he was already so tense, so much on high alert, that his instincts were searching for any excuse to drag her into his arms.

To seize her and keep her safe, to remove her from any danger. Gritting his teeth, he reminded himself of his role and that, from his instincts' point of view, the evening was going to get significantly worse before it got any better.

"Good!" Henrietta said. "Here's the soprano now."

James heard the barely restrained impatience in her voice, and also the underlying tension. There was nothing worse than waiting to act, holding off putting their plan into motion, but now the moment was nearly upon them. . . .

In the crowd below, he saw many of their company—those pretending to obliviousness as well as the others who were hanging back and very much more surreptitiously keeping their eyes glued on Henrietta.

The accompanist took his place at the piano, and with word quickly spreading, the crowd shifted and re-formed the better to hear and appreciate the performance. The pianist ran his fingers over the keys, then paused, and the soprano swept dramatically forward as if she were on a stage. Taking up position before the piano, she nodded to the pianist, then visibly drew in a breath, opened her mouth, and sang.

Her voice was so powerful that it filled the room, reaching to the furthest corners. The rise and fall of the music, the song, was captivating, and effortlessly held the audience spellbound. James toyed with the notion of staging his and Henrietta's charade right then— while all those below were distracted—but even as the thought formed, he discarded it; the singer was so very good there was a definite chance the murderer might be distracted, too, and might miss their performance.

So he waited. Even though the singer was so engaging, he couldn't appreciate her talent; he was too on edge, too focused on what he and Henrietta had to do next. On the image they had to successfully project.

When the soprano concluded her performance, the applause was thunderous. As it faded, Sir Thomas stepped forward to announce that a celebrated tenor would perform for the gathering in half an hour, and then later in the evening, the diva and the tenor would return to send the attendees home with a duet.

After further accolades and applause, the soprano retreated, along with the pianist and the secretary, and the guests returned to their previous occupation. Noise rose in a wave and crashed over the scene.

Her expression reflecting something akin to

rapture—a common enough expression on many ladies' faces at that precise moment—Henrietta turned to James, met his gaze. "We do it now." Her expression altered, sobering—as if he'd said something to bring her jarringly back to earth.

He nodded curtly, lips already a thin line. "So we're having an argument."

She tipped up her head. Chin firming, lips tightening, she flatly stated, "Yes. You've said something horrible—God only knows what."

They'd rehearsed through the afternoon, but that hadn't been in their script. He narrowed his eyes, tipping his face downward to meet her militant gaze, an aggressive frown hovering over his face. "Don't you dare make me laugh."

In response, she tipped her nose higher and all but tossed her head. "Nonsense. A laugh will do you good."

He scowled blackly; it was easy to make light of what they were doing—their "disagreement" charade. This was the simple part of the plan; what came next was the bit neither of them felt the least inclined to do.

"So I'm going," she pronounced, turning away, but pausing, as if to allow him one last chance to apologize, or to otherwise say the right thing.

"Take care." He had to grip the balustrade to stop himself from reaching out to her.

She swung fully away with an almost violent flounce and, her back to him, head high, took the two steps to the spiral stair and, nose still elevated, went very deliberately down.

Stone-faced, jaw clenching, he tightened his grip on the balustrade, then, forcing himself to slowly let go, he turned on his heel and stalked, slowly, rigidly, back along the balcony.

It took effort, real effort, not to turn and glance back at her; it took almost as much effort not to check on the others, especially those who would, by now, he hoped, be trailing her, sticking close by as she made her way through the crowd. They'd reasoned the murderer, unless he had studied the family's connections, wouldn't realize the link between, for example, Gerrard Debbington and Henrietta Cynster.

Gerrard and Charles Morwellan were two of those who would shadow Henrietta wherever she went in the crowded room, waiting to see if any gentleman approached her. They'd hypothesized that if the murderer saw her, his target, believably alone, he wouldn't be able to resist and, under cover of the crowd, would approach and seek to inveigle her out of the room.

So now James had to wait on tenterhooks, wait and suppress every instinct he possessed, all of which, knowing Henrietta was swanning into danger, were desperately urging him to react, to go after her, protect her, to do his all to keep her safe. . . .

Sadly, in this instance, keeping his distance and playing out their charade was the only way he could, ultimately, ensure her safety. Only through capturing her would-be murderer would she ever be safe again.

He paused on the balcony, swiftly scanned the crowd below, then walked down the spiral stair at the balcony's end, far from where Henrietta had joined the crowd near the room's center. He'd noted several friends with whom he could pass the time, as he'd be expected to do had their disagreement been real. To preserve the fiction, he would speak with his friends and avoid all members of her family, which was what he proceeded to do.

Of course, all his acquaintances had heard of his

engagement and wanted to meet his fiancée. He had a glib answer prepared—that she'd paused to speak with some elderly relatives and would no doubt catch up with him soon.

The effort it cost him was more than he'd expected, yet he held to his role, stayed at that end of the room, and doggedly fought the impulse to search the crowd.

Henrietta, meanwhile, made her way through the throng milling in the room's center. It was easy to stop and chat, and even to accept the felicitations on her betrothal. Even though James was not by her side, people were so accustomed to her drifting through ton ballrooms alone that few remarked on his absence, and those who did were easily deflected. If they'd just had an argument in reality, she would behave with a high hand and allow no signs of any disturbance to mar the façade she presented to the world.

But as the minutes ticked by and James did not come after her, she might be expected to seek out a quiet place to stop and think. To take stock.

After half an hour of chatting inconsequentially, noting the members of their company who were close by in the throng, she started easing toward the edge of the crowd, slipping toward the rear of the wider central section that was opposite the piano.

When the tenor came out to sing, and the crowd reformed and focused their collective attention on the diminutive man, she was able to step back, into the relative shadows at the rear of the throng, into a space that was far less crowded.

She stood facing toward the tenor, but more or less alone. The nearest couple was standing in front of her, their backs to her. There was clear space on either side of her, the best invitation she could manage for a gentleman to approach her, especially with everyone else absorbed with the tenor, transfixed by his soaring voice.

As she stood there, waiting, fighting not to allow any of her nervousness to show, she was acutely conscious of feeling exposed. What if he'd brought a gun, or a knife . . . but no. They'd discussed those possibilities, and everyone had agreed that trying to kill her in the gallery itself would be futile; the murderer would never be able to get out, get away, without being recognized.

Which was precisely the reason he wanted to kill her, to protect his identity, so . . . he would approach her, and, one way or another, get her to leave the gala with him.

One part of her mind wondered in an academic sort of way what arguments he might use to accomplish that, but most of her nerves were dancing, taut, twitching and twisting with an unnerving blend of impatience and fear.

From the corner of her eye, she could see Gerrard and Jacqueline Debbington at the rear of the crowd to her right, their gazes and their full attentions fixed, supposedly, on the tenor.

Ahead and a little to her left, further into the crowd, stood Jeremy and Eliza Carling, but they, too, had their backs to her.

Rather closer to her left stood a gentleman and lady she'd met but didn't know well, Rafe and Loretta Carstairs. There were others, too; she wasn't alone, yet her lungs tightened and she had to fight not to grip her reticule overly tightly.

She waited. Waited.

The tenor ended his performance, and no gentleman had approached her. Stifling a sigh, she forced herself to plaster on a smile and move into and through the crowd again. She chatted with friends, smiled and nodded to acquaintances as she made her way across the wider central section of the room. Several gentlemen, spotting her alone, halted and smiled and passed the time, but all were known to her, and none made any attempt to engage with her other than in mundane social ways.

Eventually, she circled back behind the pillar opposite the piano, as if seeking refuge from the constant chatter and press of bodies; when the soprano and tenor came out together for their final duet, she was standing in the lee of the pillar, as concealed from the body of the crowd as she could get even had said crowd not been focusing on the singers. Once again, everyone's back was to her.

Once again, she waited.

Waited.

And, once again, no gentleman or, indeed, anyone else, approached her.

"I don't believe it," she muttered beneath her breath as the tenor and soprano ended their aria and the crowd again burst into thunderous applause. Grimacing faintly, she put her hands together and politely clapped, but the truth was she'd heard not a single note.

The crowd started to shift, to drift, its focus dissipating; presumably the singers had departed.

Henrietta looked around. "What now?" she whispered. They'd been so sure the murderer wouldn't be able to resist her as bait that his refusing the lure was the one eventuality for which they hadn't planned.

As if in answer to her question, Sir Thomas raised his voice, thanking all for their attendance, then informing them that, as this was the museum and the event was at an end, they were now free to leave via the doors at either end of the room.

The crowd started to break up. People searched for others of their party, then headed toward the doors. As the bodies thinned, Henrietta dithered, unsure, then she heaved a sigh, marched around the pillar to the side fronting the central part of the room, and, somewhat glumly, took up station there, waiting again, but this time for James. He, she had no doubt, *would* come for her.

James didn't know what he felt as he realized the gala had come to an end and no disturbance of any kind had marred the evening. Disbelief, relief, and frustration all vied for dominance in his mind; jaw setting, he stepped free of the stream of guests heading for the nearer door and turned back up the room, scanning for someone who could confirm their failure.

Devil saw him first and hailed him. James waved and they met, Devil with Honoria on his arm, by one side of the room.

"Nothing." Devil bit off the word; he looked as disgusted and deflated as James felt. "Perhaps, after all, he wasn't here." Devil tipped his head toward the furthest of the four granite pillars. "Henrietta's waiting at the base of that pillar. I'd suggest you make it appear as if you've both come to your senses and wish to make up, rather than allow whoever this cursed villain is to guess that we'd planned anything."

"We're holding a debriefing in Upper Brook Street." Honoria smiled faintly, then stretched up and planted a kiss on James's cheek. "Don't worry. We'll think of something." Drawing back, she nodded regally. "We'll expect to see you soon—don't dally."

James's lips twisted wryly and he bowed. "Yes, Your Grace."

Then he turned toward the far pillar.

Henrietta was, as Devil had said, standing at the base of the pillar, waiting. What Devil hadn't said was that she was looking lost, even forlorn.

That made his own approach—and the fiction Devil wanted them to promulgate—rather easier.

Smiling ruefully, he approached. Eyes on hers, he halted, then, after a moment, held out his hand. "Pax?"

"Yes, please." Henrietta placed her hand in his, then shifted closer as he twined her arm with his, then she sighed and tipped her head so it rested fleetingly against his shoulder. "That was one hellish waste of time."

All their supporters who had attended the gala congregated in the drawing room in Upper Brook Street. Tea was dispensed and distributed, along with sweet biscuits. Everyone partook, putting off revisiting their failure for as long as they could.

But Royce, Duke of Wolverstone, arguably the one person there most experienced in such intrigues, cut directly to the heart of the matter. "So it didn't work, but I fancy I know why."

Devil narrowed his eyes at Royce. "Why?"

Royce's lips twitched, but he immediately sobered. "Your plan was sound, but it was a plan designed to catch a different type of villain." Across the room, he met James's and Henrietta's gazes. "A different sort of murderer. If our villain in this instance had been a typical ton gentleman who had, for whatever reason, found himself murdering not just Lady Winston but then her dresser as well, and now attempting to kill Henrietta, all out of panic, out of blind fear of his identity becoming known . . . then he would have, almost certainly, approached Henrietta at the gala. Even if he made no move to harm her there, or to remove her, because he hadn't planned it, nevertheless he would have approached her and spoken with her and assessed his chances, maybe tried to establish himself as someone she might, next time they meet, trust." Royce set down his cup. "But he didn't do any such thing."

"But can we be sure he was there?" Gabriel said.

"Oh, I think so." Royce steepled his fingers before his face. "I do think the assumption that he would have been there was sound, but you can check that by comparing the guest lists from Marchmain House and tonight."

"I know Sir Thomas quite well," Horatia said. "I can ask him for his list."

Royce inclined his head. "Please do. At this stage, we need every little piece of intelligence we can gather." He glanced around the room. "Because I have to warn you that the fact the murderer didn't take the bait tonight does not bode well."

Silence hovered for several seconds, eventually broken by Lucifer's growled "How so?"

Royce paused, then said, "Because I don't think he saw through our plan." He looked at James and Henrietta, seated on the sofa opposite. "Your charade was"—Royce smiled faintly—"exquisitely gauged. It was not too much, not too obvious. You kept in character. No one who was watching, as I was, would have thought anything other than what you intended them to think—so that wasn't the reason he didn't act."

Letting his gaze travel the room, Royce went on, "And I watched everyone else, too—we all played our roles to perfection. No one gave our game away."

"So why didn't he take the bait?" Barnaby asked.

Royce glanced at Devil, then looked at Barnaby. "I

believe the reason he didn't act was because he evaluated the possibility and found it wanting. He walked through it, both in his mind and at least in part in actuality. As you'd theorized, he couldn't murder Henrietta in the gallery itself—he had to get her to leave with him. *But*, and you couldn't have known this before we arrived there tonight, there are only two doors to that room—and because of the valuables stored in the gallery, the doors were manned by museum staff. There were at least six staff at each door throughout the evening. In addition, because of the gala and the peculiar structure of the room with the doors being at either end, none of the guests were going in and out. Hardly any left during the event, only at the end.

"So there was no way our man could have left the room with Henrietta and not have been seen, not have been noted." Royce paused, then added, "It was too great a risk. He wanted to take the bait, but he resisted because he evaluated the chance and decided the odds weren't in his favor."

Once again, Royce looked around the small crowd disposed about the drawing room. "And that," he continued, "is what's so disturbing. A murderer who, despite his most desired bait being dangled before him, can resist acting, more, can resist reacting at all, is a very dangerous man."

"Ah." Barnaby grimaced. "So we have ourselves an *intelligent* murderer."

Royce glanced at Barnaby. "As I said, a profoundly dangerous man."

If they'd felt deflated before, that realization, one no one could dispute, cast a further dampener on the debriefing.

As no one had any further insights to offer, much less any new and better plan, and it was already late, the gathering soon broke up. The key players agreed to meet, not the next day but the morning after, to plot their next move; Henrietta promised to, in the meantime, take all reasonable care.

Both she and James stood in the front hall to farewell all those who had answered their call, thanking them for their help, unproductive though the evening had been. Her disappointment was somewhat ameliorated by the unwavering resolution universally displayed, reflected in Amanda's staunch reassurance, "Don't worry. We're not going to stop until we catch this blighter."

With a swift, hard hug and a kiss on Henrietta's cheek, Amanda allowed her husband, Martin, to escort her down the steps to their waiting carriage.

They were among the last to leave. Minutes later, Arthur waved Hudson to close the door, then turned to his wife and daughter. He smiled a trifle wearily, but before he could speak, Louise did, squeezing Henrietta's hand as she said, "Amanda put what we all feel into words. Don't lose heart, my dear. We'll find this blackguard, and catch him, too."

Releasing Henrietta's hand, Louise patted her cheek, then smiled at James and patted his shoulder as she passed on her way to the stairs. "Come along, Arthur. Leave the two of them to their good-byes."

Arthur snorted, leaned down, and bussed Henrietta on the cheek, clapped James rather more vigorously on the shoulder, then followed his wife up the stairs.

Leaving Henrietta facing James, looking into his lovely brown eyes; he looked as tired as she felt.

His gaze traveled slowly over her face, then his lips lightly lifted. "We're both wrung out—it was all that tension. I'll head home. I want to let everything settle in my mind overnight." Raising his hands, he gently framed her face and kissed her.

A gentle, inexpressibly sweet kiss.

Lifting his head, he smiled into her eyes, then released her and stepped back. "Get a good night's sleep, and I'll come by in the morning. A turn about the park might do us both good."

She managed a smile. "That would be refreshing— I'll look forward to it."

Rather than summon Hudson, who had discreetly withdrawn to give them privacy, she opened the front door herself. With a last, lingering brush of his fingers over hers, James stepped out, went quickly down the steps, then strode away into the night.

Henrietta watched him go, then sighed, stepped back, and shut the door. She would have preferred him to stay, but he was right. Tonight, they would be no good company, not even for each other; better they rest and regroup. Stifling another sigh, she turned and headed for the stairs, and her cold and lonely bed.

Head down, his hands in his pockets, James walked along Upper Brook Street, then turned left into North Audley Street.

He couldn't stop mentally juggling facts, turning over every detail of the four attempts on Henrietta's life, searching for some clue they'd missed, anything that might give them some inkling or any type of hint as to who the murderous villain was.

Hostage to his thoughts, he crossed North Audley Street and several paces later turned right down Brown's Lane, a habitual shortcut to his house in George Street. As usual, the narrow laneway was lit only by reflected light shining down from the high sides of the buildings to either side, and shafting in from the streets at either end. The relative darkness barely registered; he'd walked this way countless times before, very often late at night. He paced along, the echo of his footsteps a reassuringly familiar beat.

Was there anyone he could remember as definitely being at the Marchmain event, anyone who had paid particular attention to Henrietta? Wrack his brains though he did, no one stood out clearly in his memories.

There were two small courts along Brown's Lane. Frowning to himself, James walked through the first, the cobbles illuminated by two small lamps above narrow doors, then plunged back into the, in contrast, deeper darkness of the section of the lane between the courts.

Simon had received the Marchmains' guest list. Hopefully, tomorrow, Horatia would secure Sir Thomas's list, and they'd be able to compare the two, and perhaps make a shorter list of possible suspects.

A faint sound registered, the scrape of a shoe on the flags.

There was someone behind him. James started to turn—

Pain exploded through his skull.

Blackness engulfed him.

He fell and knew no more.

The first thing he realized when the blackness thinned, then receded, was that he was sitting awkwardly slumped in a chair, his head—throbbing mightily—hanging forward, his arms pulled back.

He tried to frown, but even that hurt. He tried to shift in the chair and realized his arms were lashed; his body was, too. Then his senses cleared and he felt the rope chafing his wrists. He was sitting in a straight-backed chair, with ropes around his torso, and with his hands tightly bound behind the chair's back.

He blinked, forced his eyes open, then squinted against the glare cast by a nearby lamp. Glancing aside, he waited; when his vision cleared and focus returned, he found himself staring at a rough stone floor.

His feet were flat on the floor; whoever had left him there hadn't bound his legs.

Letting his gaze slowly rise, he followed the floor to a nearby wall; it, too, was of rough stone.

Slowly, feeling as if his neck might break if he moved too fast, he raised his aching head; someone had struck him across the back of the skull with something heavy—a cosh, most likely.

Finally, breathing in shallow pants, he sat upright, easing his shoulders against the raised back of the chair. Biting back a moan, he briefly closed his eyes as the room spun, but then his senses settled. Swallowing, he carefully raised his lids and, without shifting his head, looked around.

"Ah—excellent." The deep fashionable drawl came out of the dense shadows behind the shielded lamp. "You've survived."

The matter-of-fact tone sent a chill down James's spine; the speaker hadn't cared whether he'd lived through the attack. Squinting, he tried to see past the flaring light from the lamp, positioned two yards away atop several old crates and trained full on his face. "Who are you?"

"Obviously you have a hard head." The speaker paused for a second before reflecting, "I'm not sure if that's a good thing or a bad thing, but no matter. At least this way, should your fiancée prove difficult, I'll have all the bait *I* might need."

If James had harbored any doubts that the speaker was indeed Henrietta's would-be murderer, that little speech had slain them. More, the taunting amusement laced through the last words confirmed that the blackguard had seen through their plan . . . and, James realized with a jolt of icy shock, had gone one step further and turned their plan back on them.

Instinctively, he tested the bindings about his wrists, but the ropes held tight. Worse, he still felt wretchedly weak and woozy. He slumped against his bonds. "You won't get away with this."

"You think not?"

James could hear the smile in that cultured voice.

"Well," the speaker went on, "we'll see."

James hauled in a breath, moistened his dry lips. "What the devil do you think to gain?"

A pause ensued, then, in a more pensive vein, the voice replied, "I would have thought that was obvious. After tonight's demonstration of how very wide the Cynsters' net can be cast, I was left wondering what might induce the delightful Miss Henrietta to leave the overprotective circle of her family and come to me—clearly that's the only way I'm going to be able to lay my hands on her—and then . . . there you were. Leaving the Cynsters' house late, walking home alone through the night, lost in your thoughts . . ." The speaker chuckled softly. "It really was too easy."

Another pause, as if the man was reflecting. James struggled to get his mind to function past the throbbing ache in his head.

"I was considering sending one of your fingers, perhaps the one carrying your signet ring, but that does seem a trifle gruesome, at least as an opening gambit, and all in all it might be wiser to keep that option in reserve, just in case the lovely Henrietta needs further inducements to come to your aid." The speaker shifted; a gloved hand appeared in front of the lamp, turning something in the beam so James could see. "Besides, I suspect this"—the man rolled a thin piece of gold-colored metal with a shiny head between his gloved fingers—"will do, will be sufficient to bring her flying to your rescue."

James stiffened as he recognized his cravat pin. Again, this time surreptitiously, he tested his bonds, but they gave not at all. Raising his gaze to where he thought the speaker's face must be, he asked, "And then what?"

"And then . . ." James couldn't see anything of the man's face, but he could clearly hear the cold relish in the blackguard's voice, could sense his chilly smile of anticipation.

"I intend to stage a double murder." The villain paused, then went on almost eagerly, "I haven't done one of those before. Killing Henrietta Cynster will, clearly, start a manhunt, but what if it appears that you—her fiancé—killed her, then committed suicide? Better still, what if it appears that you've killed Henrietta in the same way Lady Winston was murdered?" Cool satisfaction laced the man's voice as he went on, "And then, naturally, overcome by grief, or perhaps by fear of the consequences, you shoot yourself?" Self-congratulation welled, ringing clearly as the man continued, "Oh, yes, that will fit nicely. After all, Lady Winston lived next door to the young lady you were thinking of offering for. Perhaps that was how you noticed Melinda Wentworth— because she lived next door to your lover?"

James tasted bile; raising his head, he swallowed and said, "I would never hurt a woman like that—like you hurt Lady Winston." Gaze steady on where he judged the murderer's face to be, lips tight, he shook his head. "You'll never get anyone to believe that. Aside from all else, I barely knew Lady Winston."

Unperturbed, the murderer replied, "Oh, I grant you there may be questions in the minds of some, but you would be surprised how easily the general populace can be led."

James caught a shift in the shadows, then the gloved hand appeared and closed about the lid of the lantern.

"And who, after all," that suavely chilling voice murmured, "can know the torments of another man's mind?"

Before James could respond, the lamp was doused, plunging the room into inky darkness.

Searching for any spark, straining his ears, James heard soft footsteps retreating, strolling away. Then came a *scritch,* and a match flared, a tiny flame at the far end of the room. The flame and the bulky shadows about it traveled upward at an angle; the murderer was using the match to light his way up some stairs.

The man reached the head of the stairs, and the flame waved and died.

James waited, listening hard to hear what sort of locks or bolts were on what he assumed would be the door into the room . . . was it a basement?

"Incidentally"—the murderer's disembodied voice floated through the empty space—"you can roar and even scream, but no one will hear you. This house is deserted, as are those on either side, and all the walls are sound, solid stone." A pause ensued, then the murderer moved. "Sleep well."

James heard the scrape of wood on stone; a waft of fresh air barreled down the room, then a heavy door thudded shut.

A second later, he caught the metallic scrape of a large bolt being slid home, first one, then another.

Silence fell. The darkness seemed to thicken.

After several moments, James settled as comfortably as he could, gingerly easing his head, still pounding, back on his neck.

He stared upward into the blackness. "Now what?"

He waited, but no answer came.

Chapter Fourteen

"Miss Henrietta."

Stepping off the stairs onto the tiles of the front hall, Henrietta turned to see Hudson approaching; juggling a silver-domed platter, he was fishing in one pocket as he came.

"This"—Hudson pulled out a letter—"was lying on the tiles by the door this morning." He tipped his head toward the front door. "Presumably someone delivered it very early this morning or very late last night."

"Thank you." She took the note, a neatly folded sheet of parchment with her name inscribed across the front in a bold hand. There seemed to be something enclosed within the folds.

Hudson hovered. "Will you be breakfasting, miss? Would you like fresh tea and toast?"

She flashed him a smile. "Yes, please. I'll be in in a minute."

He bowed, turned, and magisterially swept down the corridor and into the breakfast parlor, whither she'd been heading.

Remaining where she was, she broke the plain seal, unfolded the parchment, and caught the small item that fell from the folds . . . stared at it as it rested on her palm.

James's cravat pin. She recognized it—she'd removed it several times. . . .

Closing her hand around the pin, she smoothed out the parchment and read the words inscribed thereon.

I commend you, Miss Cynster—your charade last night was excellent. However, I was rather more surprised and somewhat disappointed that you and your supporters imagined that I might fall victim to such a ploy. That was presumptuous, not to say insulting, but, on the other hand, I fully appreciated the strategy of employing live bait.

Consequently, my dear Miss Cynster, if you wish to see your fiancé, James Glossup, alive and well, you will follow my directions and do so without fail. You will tell no one of this contact, or of my demands, and yes, I will be watching, just as I was last night. Rest assured I will know if any in your family are alerted—you must take all and every care to do nothing throughout the day to raise anyone's suspicions. If I judge that you have succeeded in that, and have made not a single wrong move through the day, then over dinnertime, I will send word again as to where you will need to come this evening if you wish to set eyes on Glossup again.

I am prepared to trade your life for his, but only if you follow my instructions to the letter.

The missive was unsigned, of course.

Henrietta read it through a second time, then, moving very slowly, shaking inside, she refolded the parchment and tucked it into her skirt pocket. She looked down at James's cravat pin, turned it in her palm, then, lips tightening, carefully pinned it to the inside of her bodice, above her heart.

Straightening her spine, she drew in a deep, deep breath, held it for a second, then she forced her lips to ease, found and plastered on an unconcerned expression, and walked down the corridor to the breakfast parlor as normally as she could.

From the cheery, comfortable sounds emanating from within, the rest of her family was already present.

She was, of course, going to rescue James, but . . . she would play the role the murderer had scripted for her until she'd worked out how.

Morning sunshine eventually slanted through the grimy windows set high in the wall of the basement in which James was imprisoned. He woke, blinking in the faint light. Gradually his senses refocused, informing him that his head was still pounding, albeit not as painfully as it had been, but to add to his woes he was stiff in every joint.

His shoulders ached; his neck felt tortured. But he could stretch his legs. He concentrated on flexing and lifting them, working the muscles until they felt reasonably normal.

By then he'd realized what he would have to do. He'd arranged with Henrietta to meet that morning and go for a drive in the park. When he didn't arrive, she would, eventually, send to his house, and then . . . but the murderer had proved beyond question that he was intelligent enough to have anticipated that.

Easing his shoulders, trying to loosen the bonds, James muttered, "He'll have already sent her word that he's captured me, because otherwise she would raise a hue and cry, and that's the last thing he wants. He wants her, so he'll offer to spare my life for hers, and get her to go to him somewhere." Settling back on the chair, he narrowed his eyes and tried to think like their villain. "He'll get her to meet him somewhere, but he's already decided he's going to stage this double murder, which he needs to do to throw everyone off his scent, so he'll bring her here."

He glanced around. He couldn't afford to sit and wait in the chair. "When he brings Henrietta in here, I have to be free and able to save her."

She would come to save him, that he didn't doubt, so he would have to be in a position to return the favor.

"So . . ." He looked around again, this time with greater concentration, searching for anything that might help his cause. He didn't see it at first, but a glimmer of light, of sunlight slanting off glass, drew his gaze to the area beneath the second window, the one further from his present position.

He squinted and, eventually, made out the shards of a broken bottle. "Perfect. Now . . ." He assessed his strength, debated, but he needed to get free as soon as possible; he had no idea when the murderer would bring Henrietta to the house, to the basement.

Summoning his will and his still-wavering strength, he planted his feet and slowly tipped forward, until he was standing, still lashed to the chair and bent over at a peculiar and rather painful angle. But, glory be, he had just enough freedom to shift his legs and feet and shuffle, foot by foot, across the floor.

Once he was standing over the shattered remains of the bottle, he had to work out how to get his hands on a suitable piece of glass—there were at least three he thought would suffice—without risking slashing himself in the process.

Eventually, he used the tip of one shoe to nudge one shard along the floor until it lay well clear of the rest. Then he went down, first on one knee, then on the other—a complicated maneuver that had him swearing—then, kneeling with his knees pressed together, he gauged the distance to the single shard, wriggled into position, and then tipped onto his shoulder.

The move jarred his head so badly he saw stars. He lay on the floor, panting, until the spinning stopped, then, carefully, he stretched his fingers, feeling, searching.

He had to shift a trifle further, but finally his fingers brushed the shard. He teased it nearer, into his hand, careful not to cut himself. Blood would only make the glass harder to hold, harder to work with.

Exhaling, he filled his lungs and waited until his heart slowed and his mind sharpened again, then he turned the shard and set what felt to be the sharpest edge to the rope—

Wait, wait, wait!

What if the murderer didn't bring Henrietta down to the basement?

James lay awkwardly twisted on the floor and tried to think. Forced himself to put himself in the murderer's shoes, at least as far as he was able.

The murderer wanted to stage a double murder and make it appear to be a *believable* murder-suicide, with echoes of Lady Winston's murder thrown in, and chances were he intended to carry out the foul deeds in the order he'd described, namely killing Henrietta first . . . and given the murderer's cold-bloodedness, James had no difficulty believing that the blackguard intended to kill Henrietta in front of his own eyes.

From all Barnaby and Stokes had said, the murderer was more than sadistic enough for that.

But killing Henrietta and James in the basement wouldn't support the fiction of a murder-suicide; such a setting would strike a discordant note, especially if Henrietta's murder was supposed to be a replay of Lady Winston's. The basement was hardly the place for a lovers' rendezvous, and this murderer was very intelligent, and very aware of how the ton thought. So he would shift James to some more believable location.

"For instance, a room upstairs." Twisting his still aching head, James glanced at the basement stairs, closer to him now; in the strengthening morning light he could see them clearly. There was no landing at the top, and the door opened inward. If he were free and ready to engage, and standing on the stairs when the murderer opened the door . . . James grimaced. "He'll have plenty of time to shoot me, and if we grappled, I would be the one most likely to end falling down the stairs and breaking my neck."

While that might put a crimp in the murderer's plans, it wasn't how James wanted this to end.

And such an end wouldn't save Henrietta, and that, after all, was his principal and dominant aim.

From his strained position on the floor, he glanced at the windows, then sighed. Even once he was free, there was no way he could break out of the basement; the door was bolted on the outside, the windows were small, too small to fit through even if he could break their thick glass, and the murderer had told him the houses were deserted, so there was no reason to suppose that there would be anyone passing outside the windows for him to hail.

It took him a little while to convince his brain of what

would have to be, and even longer to get his body to cooperate. Getting up onto his legs again was an excruciating feat, but eventually he managed it, and managed to laboriously work his way back across the room and set the chair down, with him still lashed to it, in exactly the same place where the murderer had left him. There was, thankfully, enough dust layered on the floor, smudged not just by the murderer's boots but by countless others previously, for his shuffling progress across it to have left no obvious trail, and the murderer must have dragged him in, because his evening clothes were already too filthy for his recent brush with the floor to have made any additional impression.

Shifting on the chair, James settled again; closing his eyes, he concentrated, and managed to ease and inch the glass shard up beneath his shirt cuff, along the inside of his right wrist. He wriggled his fingers, shifted his hands, but the shard remained safely tucked away, ironically held in position by the rope that bound his hands.

Slumping in the chair, he ran through the possible scenarios again, but there was nothing more he could think of to do.

Closing his eyes, he worked at relaxing his muscles and getting what rest he could—until the murderer returned to fetch him to wherever the blackguard intended to bring Henrietta.

Henrietta kept her distressing news entirely private all through the morning. Not because she wished to but because she had to; given that James's life was at risk, she had to take the murderer at his word and assume he would know if her family was alerted to his plan. So she couldn't allow anyone who might react precipitously to know of the murderer's demand. And she had to go about her life as if nothing at all was wrong.

It was early afternoon before, by dint of a whispered word at this at-home, at that morning tea, she managed to arrange a meeting restricted to those she felt sure she could trust—her three sisters and her sister-in-law. They, she knew, would understand her predicament; at the very least she could rely on their advice.

After reassuring her mother that she would remain safely indoors and would be sufficiently well entertained by the other four, all of whom, having answered her summons, seconded that assurance, Henrietta watched Louise leave on her usual afternoon social rounds, then she shooed the others, all curious as to why she was suddenly so intent, into the back parlor and firmly shut the door.

Turning, she watched as Amelia and Amanda sank onto the old chaise, and Portia sat in one armchair, while Mary curled up in her usual position on the love seat. Walking to the armchair facing the chaise, as the others settled and focused their attention on her, Henrietta surveyed their expressions, intrigued, expectant, and eager to hear what she had to tell them.

Looking up at her, Amanda blinked her eyes wide. "Well? You perceive us agog, as Lady Osbaldestone would say."

Henrietta felt her composure falter. "I need your help." She twitched the folded letter from her pocket and held it out to Amanda. "Read that, and tell me what you think."

Taking the letter, Amanda smoothed it out, briefly scanned, then, her expression abruptly somber and serious, returned her gaze to the top of the letter and read the villain's message aloud.

Hearing the words, flatly rendered in Amanda's clear voice, underscored the dread Henrietta felt, crystalized the threat to her life, to her and James's future. She abruptly sat, hands clasping tightly in her lap.

Amanda reached the end of the letter and its chilling closing sentence.

A brief moment of silence ensued, then Mary looked sharply at Henrietta. "You haven't told anyone." Statement, not a question.

Henrietta gestured at the letter. "How can I? If I tell Papa he'll send word to Devil, and then . . . well, you all know what will happen."

"Heaven help us, but we can't have that," Amelia said. "They'll be roaring around rattling sabers in the streets."

"Exactly." Grim-faced, Amanda decisively stated, "They—Devil and the rest—cannot be allowed to know."

Portia leaned forward and laid a hand over Henrietta's tightly twined fingers. "You've done the right thing—come to the right people. We'll help—of course we will."

Henrietta managed a genuine, albeit weak, smile. Looking from Portia's earnest expression to her elder sisters' faces, she watched them grimly, determinedly nod, the same sisterly support lighting their eyes. She glanced at Mary.

Just as Mary stated, "The first thing we need to do is to work out a plan to defeat this villain, and then"— eyes narrowing, she went on—"decide what help we require to make our plan work, and *then* decide who we can trust to assist us. And then make it happen."

They all studied Mary for a moment, then Amelia said, "That's true enough, but I think we can agree from the outset that whatever our plan is, we cannot—simply *cannot*—let Devil and Vane and the rest of that lot know anything about this at all."

"Indeed," Portia said. "And if you think of who this villain must be—a gentleman of the ton, of the right age for Lady Winston to have had as a lover, and the right sort to have been present at the gala—then his way of monitoring whether you tell others and alert the family will almost certainly be via watching them—Devil, Vane, and your older male cousins."

"Indeed," Amanda said. "They—our male cousins—are the ones he'll be watching to see if you keep his secret. If they know of it, they'll give it away instantly—he'll only need to look at their faces, at the set of their jaws, the way they stalk about."

"And most likely he belongs to the same clubs as they do," Mary put in.

"That," Henrietta said, "is why I haven't told anyone else." She glanced around at their faces. "Only you four. Mama or Papa would insist on telling Devil—to their minds, that's the way difficulties are always dealt with."

"Precisely." Amanda nodded. "So let's all agree that, while we appreciate that they're going to be very unhappy about not being told of this, we cannot tell anyone who will involve Devil and the others, and that in meeting this challenge we can't call on their aid. We have to go forward and deal with this ourselves. So"—she glanced at Mary—"as Mary said, let's work out our plan."

"Obviously," Amelia said, resetting her shawl, "you're going to wait for the villain's next note, and then go and meet him wherever he stipulates. Until you learn where he's keeping James, you'll need to do exactly as the blackguard says."

"Once we know where James is," Mary said, "we can act against the villain, but not before."

They fell silent, all thinking. Eventually Portia said, "That's our first hurdle—working out how Henrietta can go and meet with this murderer in safety, without us doing anything that will alert him to others knowing. He has to believe that you"—she glanced at Henrietta—"are quite alone. Only then will he lead you to wherever he's keeping James."

No one argued, just vaguely nodded in agreement. Henrietta waited, glancing around the faces, all faintly frowning as they tried to see how . . .

Portia drew in a deeper breath and said, "I'd like to suggest that we seek advice from someone who knows more about dealing with villains than we do. Someone we can trust with this, who'll understand our situation."

Amanda opened her eyes wide. "Who?"

"Penelope," Portia said. "If anyone can help us devise a workable plan to capture a murderer, it'll be she."

"Of course." Amelia looked at Henrietta. "Penelope will know how to manage this."

Amanda raised her hand. "I third the motion." She glanced at Mary, then looked at Henrietta. "What say you two?"

"I'm in favor," Mary said. "I don't know enough about villains, and Penelope assuredly does."

Henrietta pressed her lips together, but she really had only one question. She looked at Portia. "How can we arrange to see Penelope without alerting our villain?"

"That's easy enough," Amelia said. "It's early afternoon—the perfect time for us as a group to pay a family call on Penelope to see her baby son, little Oliver."

"We can make it appear that you're reluctant," Mary said, standing and shaking out her skirts, "but that the four of us are dragging you out, insisting that you can't sit at home alone."

"Projecting the right image will be easy," Amanda said, "and we can make our diversion to Albemarle Street appear spontaneous, an unplanned visit—one with no ulterior motives—just in case the blackguard has people watching this house." She glanced at Portia. "Do you think Penelope will be in?"

Portia nodded and rose. "Knowing my little sister, at this hour, with Oliver so small, Penelope's sure to be at home, most likely consorting with some ancient Greek."

Ancient Mesopotamian, actually." Penelope ushered the five of them into her drawing room half an hour later. Following, she shut the door. "Jeremy's given me some of his translations to read. Quite fascinating."

The others, engaged in taking seats on the twin sofas, exchanged glances but didn't respond.

Waiting until they all sat, then resuming her position in the armchair angled to one side of the fireplace, a massive old tome lying open on a small table alongside, Penelope surveyed them. "But what brings you here?" Her gaze sharpened as she looked from one to the other. "Has something happened?"

"Yes." Henrietta, seated between Amanda and Amelia on one sofa, decided to take charge before anyone else did. "The blackguard has seized James and is dangling him as bait to force me to give myself up to him—to the villain."

"Well!" Penelope looked simultaneously shocked and intrigued. "That certainly is a development." She paused, then said, "Do you mean to tell me he saw through our plan last night, and rather than fall into our trap, refashioned it for his own use?"

Henrietta nodded decisively. "That, indeed, is how it appears."

Penelope blinked. "How very impertinent." She refocused on Henrietta. "So tell me all."

Henrietta proceeded to do so, punctuated by various belligerent and militant comments from the other four. She concluded with, "So we've come to you for advice and any help you can give."

"We walked from Upper Brook Street and through Grosvenor Square," Portia put in, "all the while making it appear that we were dragging Henrietta along for an outing, and that diverting here was purely an impulse, a spontaneous female family call."

Penelope was nodding. "Excellent. You've done exactly as I would have—exactly as you should have."

Henrietta caught Portia's eye and, despite all, struggled to keep her lips straight; they all understood that from Penelope, the words "exactly as I would have" were high praise indeed. It was widely accepted that in a family well-endowed with intelligence, Penelope nevertheless took the cake.

"We thought," Amanda said, "that, clearly, Henrietta has to go to this rendezvous and meet with the villain."

"And she has to go along with whatever he says until she learns where James is being held," Mary added.

Penelope looked around the circle of faces, at the last considered Henrietta, then nodded. "I agree. I can't see any way around that—not if we want to rescue James, and, of course, we do."

"Yes, but we can't just let Henrietta swan off all alone to meet this murderer who wants to kill her," Amelia said, "but equally we have to make it appear that she is, indeed, all alone."

"And more," Amanda said, "we cannot allow even the slightest whisper of this to reach our male cousins, or the elders, who will promptly refer it to said male cousins."

"Oh, no." Penelope waved a hand. "I quite agree. Telling them, or letting them learn of it, would be entirely counterproductive in this case."

"So . . ." Eyes on her younger sister's face, Portia gestured for her to go on. "How do we manage it—what should we do?"

Penelope gazed unseeing at the narrow table between the sofas for several moments, then she looked up and met the others' eyes. "We're going to have to recruit a small and highly select army—those we can trust to do what we need them to do and to keep quiet while they're about it. We need sufficient numbers, but we also need a degree of expertise." She paused, her gaze resting on Henrietta, then said, "I would strongly advise that we involve Barnaby, of course, but also, through him, Inspector Stokes. Both already know of the murderer and his previous attempts on your life. I believe if we present this correctly to them, both will see the necessity for secrecy, and the sense in the plan we propose."

Mary opened her eyes wide. "We have a plan?"

Penelope smiled intently. "We will have by the time they arrive." She looked at Henrietta. "In the circumstances, it's your decision, but I know Barnaby and Stokes are at Scotland Yard at this moment, and I can send word and have them come here via the mews and the back door."

Henrietta knew she needed help, and this was the sort of help she'd come there to find. She nodded. "Yes, please do send word. And meanwhile"—she glanced at her sisters, sister-in-law, then at Penelope—"perhaps we can work on our plan."

Penelope nodded and rose to tug the bellpull.

By the time Barnaby Adair led Inspector Stokes into the drawing room, the five ladies had settled on the bare bones of their plan.

After performing the necessary introductions for Stokes, then waiting while both men fetched straight-backed chairs from by the wall and joined the gathering, Penelope stated, "Before we can tell you anything, you must swear to hold everything we say in the strictest confidence, to be revealed only to those others we agree need to be informed."

Now seated, both men stared at Penelope for an instant, then exchanged a long glance weighted with unvoiced male communication. But, eventually, both reluctantly nodded and gave their word, Barnaby with his customary urbanity, Stokes in a rumbling growl.

Penelope smiled approvingly at them both, then invited Henrietta to relate the day's developments.

She did. When he heard of what had occurred and read the villain's letter, Barnaby looked grave.

Stokes looked blackly grim.

Before either man could speak, Penelope said, "What we've decided must happen is this." She proceeded to outline their plan.

Henrietta watched as both men digested Penelope's words. She'd expected them to argue, but neither did; that, she supposed, was one benefit in recruiting Penelope, a lady with established credentials in the dealing-with-dangerous-blackguards sphere. There could be no doubt that Stokes as well as Barnaby treated the situation, them, and their plan seriously, and gave each aspect due consideration. That was apparent in both men's expressions as they followed the outline of their plan to its, at present rather nebulous, conclusion.

When Penelope fell silent, both men remained silent, too, transparently thinking, assessing and evaluating.

Eventually Barnaby stirred and refocused, first on his wife, then he glanced at the other ladies. "I agree we need to do something along those lines, but . . . frankly, this puts both me and Stokes in a difficult position. You insist that Devil and your other cousins can't know, and"—he held up a hand to stay their comments—"I understand and agree entirely that we can't afford to allow them to know, much less be involved with this. However, to ask me, and even more, Stokes, to assist you without anyone—any male—of the family knowing . . ." He looked around at their faces and grimaced. "You can see my point, can't you?"

Portia, Amanda, and Amelia all grimaced back. "Sadly," Amanda said, "yes. I see your difficulty."

"But," Mary said, sitting up in her corner of the sofa opposite Henrietta, "as long as one relevant adult male of the family knows and approves"—she looked at Stokes, then Barnaby—"that would do, wouldn't it?"

Stokes frowned. "Who . . . ?"

"Simon." Portia met Mary's eyes and nodded. "We can tell Simon and make him understand. He might not like it, but he will understand—he knows how the others will react as well as we do."

"That would be enough for you, wouldn't it?" Amanda looked at Stokes, then Barnaby. "Simon is, after all, Henrietta's older brother."

Barnaby nodded decisively. "Yes, and I'm sure he'll

agree with us—with your reasoning as to why this has to be kept secret from Devil and the rest."

Stokes had raised his brows, considering; now he, too, nodded. "Miss Henrietta's older brother's involvement would absolve me of having to inform His Grace."

"Well," Mary said, "that's a relief."

Which summed up everyone's reaction.

Penelope and Portia arranged for a message to be sent to Simon.

By the time Simon arrived, also entering via the back door and bringing Charlie Hastings with him, their plan had evolved considerably, with Stokes adding a great deal, not only from his extensive experience but also by way of the personnel he could command.

Simon and Charlie sat, and Simon listened as Henrietta related what had occurred since the previous evening, then Barnaby explained the outline of their plan, and Stokes filled in various details of how the plan would have to be executed.

Amanda then explained the dilemma they faced in that they could not allow any of the above to come to the attention of Devil and the older members of the Cynster clan.

Henrietta concluded their arguments with, "We have to remember that it's not only my life at risk in this, but James's, too, and at present he's in this blackguard's hands."

Simon met her eyes, blue meeting blue of a similar shade, for a long-drawn moment, then he sighed. Nodded. "You're right. If we let the others know, James's life will be at even greater risk than it already is. It might even be forfeit due to their reactions, and that we cannot have. And the truth is, if we're successful in laying hands on this villain and rescuing James, while they'll grumble and grouse about not being told, it'll be more in the vein of not being involved and so missing out on the excitement, but beyond that they won't really care. Just as long as we all come out of this with a whole skin and in good health, that's all they'll truly care about."

Amanda nodded. "Well said. So"—she looked about the gathering—"let's get down to sorting out the details. First point—who else do we need to inform and involve?"

Barnaby drew out a notebook, as did Stokes, and the company settled to walk through the entire plan, from the preparation necessary to ensure Henrietta could respond to the villain's summons when she received it, to the ultimate end of what was, as Charlie put it, "Rather like a treasure hunt of sorts."

They discussed and drafted in more husbands and others to help; when they paused for refreshments, Henrietta glanced around the group. And felt hope well; with so many behind her—the small, select army Penelope had decreed—she was starting to feel the first seeds of confidence that by the end of the night, all might be well.

A dangerous confidence. The whisper slid through her thoughts. She took due note of it, acknowledged that Lady Winston's murderer was far too intelligent, and far too cold-blooded, to be taken lightly, yet . . . she had to cling to hope.

Turning back to the discussion, raging still, she gave herself up to their plan to rescue James.

As long as she got him back, nothing else mattered.

James had dozed throughout the day, waking to shift as much as he could, easing cramped muscles as far as he could, which, with respect to his arms and torso, hadn't been very far at all.

But he was awake, and wondering, when he heard muffled footsteps approach the basement door, then the bolts were drawn back and the door swung inward.

Judging by the quality of the light slanting through the small windows, it was early evening. James watched as the man he assumed to be Lady Winston's murderer came down the stairs. Studying the man closely, he confirmed that the man was the one who had left him in the basement the previous night—the same height, the same build, the same gait. Today the villain wore a plain black suit, with a black cloak over all, and with his head and face concealed beneath a wide-brimmed hat, the lower half of his face further masked by a black silk scarf.

Other points of difference were the sharp knife the man held in one fist, and the pistol he held in the other.

James watched as the villain strolled toward him, then halted several yards away. The villain's eyes fixed on him, studying him with a certain dispassion. Dark, perhaps black, brows, brown eyes paler than James's; that was all James could see.

After a long moment, unable to help himself, he arched a weary brow.

Behind the scarf, the villain's lips shifted. "Indeed. I fear you must have been atrociously bored. My apologies." What little expression had been discernible in his eyes leached to blankness. "But it'll all be over soon."

The man's voice had lowered, growing both softer and harsher, more rasping. James quelled a sudden shiver.

The blackguard stirred, paused, then said, "I'm here to move you upstairs. I'm going to undo the ropes tying you to the chair, and then you're going to stand." Slowly, keeping his distance, he started to pace around the chair. "You will not turn around. Once you're steady on your feet and I give the word, you will walk, slowly and steadily, over to the stairs and up them. I'll give you directions from there." He passed out of James's field of vision. "I'll be walking behind you, far enough that you won't have any chance to reach me before I pull the trigger, but also close enough that should you try to make a bolt for it, I'll have no difficulty shooting you, and then, if necessary, finishing you off with the knife."

Now standing behind James, the man continued, in the same calm, deadly tone, "While I'm sure by now you realize the futility of your position, I'm equally sure you'll do everything—cling to every hope—of living to at least see your betrothed alive and well, and to try to get her free. Your best chance of doing that is to co-operate in moving to the room upstairs—the room to which I intend bringing her, regardless of whether you are alive to see it or not." He paused, then, voice hardening, asked, "Do I make myself clear?"

James pressed his lips tight, holding back the various responses that leapt to his tongue. Rather than trust himself to speak, he nodded.

"Excellent."

He sensed the murderer draw closer, then felt the rope about his chest tighten and tug as the blackguard undid the knots.

Then the rope loosened and the murderer stepped back, drawing the rope away. "There. You can stand."

Slowly, feeling his balance teeter, his joints and muscles realigning, James eased upright. Eventually, he straightened to his full height; he closed his eyes in blessed relief as he stretched his spine as well as he could, given his hands were still lashed behind his back.

The murderer gave him a few moments to ease his back and properly regain his balance, then ordered, "Start walking. To the stairs and up them."

James obeyed. Climbing the stairs, he was curious to see what he could of the building as they moved through it; the more he could learn about the house or whatever it was the better—who knew what might happen once Henrietta arrived?

"Turn left at the top of the stairs."

Following that and subsequent directions, James walked through a long-deserted kitchen, down a corridor, and into a narrow front hall wreathed in cobwebs. Through various open doorways, he saw that although the place was clearly abandoned, some furniture still remained. As, at the murderer's direction, he started up the narrow stair, he asked, his tone purely curious, "As I understand your plan, you want to make it appear that Henrietta and I both came here willingly, but why on earth would we be meeting here?"

"For a tryst, why else? You certainly can't share any intimate interludes at her parents' house, and for what will appear to be your . . . shall we say, esoteric tastes?—your own house would be too dangerous, so you and your fiancée have been meeting here." After a moment, the villain added, his voice holding a darker note, "Trust me, I know how to set a stage."

James wondered what he meant by that—how the comment could possibly relate to Lady Winston's or her dresser's murder, neither of which had been made to appear as anything but the violent if not frenzied attacks they were—but had reached no conclusion by the time he gained the top of the stairs and the villain directed him along the gallery, then told him to stop.

James did, then heard the door he'd already walked past being opened.

"Turn to your right, toward the wall, and so, slowly, turn around, then walk back to the open door and go in."

James did as he was bid, noting that the murderer circled behind him as he turned. A grimy skylight high above the stairwell let in light, more light than he'd yet had; clearly the murderer was taking no chances of him getting any reasonable look at the man's face. Even now. Even though the villain planned to kill him in just a few hours.

A cautious beggar to the last, James mused.

Walking through the open doorway, he found himself facing a large four-poster bed. The room was of reasonable size, but not huge. If this was the main bedroom of the house, it was a terrace house, not a mansion. That fitted with what he'd seen of the front hall and stairs.

The room was clean, the bed made, but without any counterpane. The curtains over the windows were drawn. A swift glance around confirmed that the furnishings included a washstand and basin, as well as various other little touches that reinforced the image of this being a place currently in use for intimate trysts.

A straight-backed chair had been set to the right of the bed, three yards away and facing it. A stout rope lay coiled behind the chair. A lamp had been lit; turned very low, it sat atop a tallboy set against the wall immediately to the right of the door.

James halted.

"Further." The end of the pistol barrel prodded his spine. "Walk to the chair and halt, facing it."

James did, wondering. The villain again told him to turn slowly, this time to his left, allowing the blackguard to circle behind him, confirming that the man was taking extraordinary care to ensure that James saw as little of his face—his largely concealed face—as possible.

Which, James concluded, meant that, if he did get a clear view of the devil's face, he would know him.

"Sit."

James did; a second later, the rope looped about him and cinched tight, then looped around him again, lashing him very effectively to the chair.

He waited, saying nothing, trying to think if there was anything more he might ask, might hope to learn. There was really only one more piece of information he needed.

After testing the rope, and that his hands were still securely bound, the murderer stepped back, then walked to the door, showing James nothing but the back of his cloak.

But on reaching the door, with his hand on the knob, the villain turned. And told James what he wanted to know. "I'm off to arrange to meet with your fiancée, and then . . . I'll bring her here."

Although he couldn't see the man's lips, James knew they were curved when the blackguard added, "And then I'll bring this whole sorry tale to an end."

The murderer's pale eyes gleamed briefly in the lamplight, then he opened the door and went out, closing the door gently behind him.

James stared at where the man had stood. By the door, the lamplight had been strong enough for James to clearly see that part of the blackguard's face above the band of the black silk scarf. . . . "He's right." James frowned. "If I could see more of his face, I would know him—would recognize him." As it was . . . he knew he'd seen the man before, but he couldn't put a name to the face.

Setting the puzzle of the man's identity aside, James waited—counseled himself to patience even though his instincts were urging him to act, and act swiftly.

Presumably the man would send a note to Henrietta and she would come to rescue him. She would accompany the murderer back here, to this house, to this room, and then . . . if James read the man and his ghastly intentions aright, the blackguard would violate her and beat her to death in front of James, and then kill James, staging his murder to appear to be suicide driven by anguished remorse.

"Well," he muttered, "if Henrietta did die like that trying to save me, I *would* kill myself out of anguished remorse."

But that wasn't going to happen.

Once the devil's footsteps had receded, then died away down the stairs, after the front door had closed and remained closed for, James judged, long enough to be sure that the fiend wasn't about to have second thoughts and for whatever reason come back to check his bonds, he carefully eased the long glass shard down from its position under his cuff.

Gripping it carefully between his fingers, he started sawing.

Hudson was waiting to deliver the second note from Lady Winston's murderer when Henrietta walked out of the dining room after dinner that evening.

As they'd arranged that afternoon, dinner had been

transformed into an impromptu family gathering, with Amanda and Martin, Amelia and Luc, and Simon and Portia joining Mary, Henrietta, Louise, and Arthur about the table.

Arthur and Louise had been delighted to have their family all together, the only minor blemish being that, as Henrietta had explained, James had had a prior engagement that had prevented him from joining them.

Expecting the murderer to have been as good as his word, after an hour and a half of concealing her fraught state, assisted by the others, who had done their best to keep her parents' attention fixed elsewhere, Henrietta led the exodus from the dining room, leaving Martin, Amanda, Luc, and Amelia to delay Louise and Arthur enough for her to accept the note, swiftly read it, then tuck it away in her pocket.

Looking up, she met Simon's eyes; he and Portia had followed her and Mary from the dining room. Simon arched a brow. "As expected?" He kept his voice low.

Raising her head, Henrietta nodded. "Just a place and a time, and some instructions. Nothing more."

The rest of the company joined them; they all stood milling in the front hall, talking of the engagements they were about to leave to attend.

Arthur held Louise's evening cloak for her.

Shrugging into it and settling the folds, Louise glanced at Henrietta. "You're coming with me and Mary tonight, aren't you? I know James is otherwise engaged, but—"

"Actually, Mama," Mary cut in, "I'm feeling rather queasy." She grimaced and pressed a hand to her stomach. "It must have been something I ate."

Louise was at once solicitous, but Henrietta stepped in to say, "I'll stay with Mary. I'm really not enthused by the prospect of another night socializing—I could do with a quiet night in. And I know you're looking forward to seeing Lady Hancock, and you really can't cry off Mrs. Arbuthot's soiree."

Louise grimaced. She glanced at Mary, then nodded. "All right. You two girls have a quiet night and get to bed early." She looked inquiringly at the twins and their husbands, at Portia and Simon. "So where are you all bound for? Can I drop any of you off on my way?"

The others all had their stories rehearsed; Martin, Luc, and Simon were off for an evening at Boodles—not White's, wither Arthur was bound. Amanda, Amelia, and Portia were supposedly planning to attend a ball at Hilliard House, but on hearing of Mary's indisposition, and Henrietta's, too, the three elected to spend an hour with them before heading out for the evening.

"Very well." Turning to the door on Arthur's arm, Louise waved to them all. "Have a pleasant evening, and we'll catch up with you all tomorrow at the meeting at St. Ives House."

They all called their farewells; poised about the front hall, on the tiles, on the lower steps of the stairs, they all watched, smiles in place, as Hudson opened the door, then Arthur swept Louise out, waved a cheery farewell, and escorted Louise down the steps to the waiting carriage.

As Arthur shut the carriage door on his wife, then headed for the hackney summoned earlier, Hudson closed the front door and turned. He surveyed all those remaining in the front hall, none of whom made any attempt to move, listening, as they all were, to ensure that Arthur's carriage as well as Louise's was well away and unlikely to turn back.

A puzzled frown in his eyes, Hudson studied Henrietta, then, as if making some decision, turned to Simon. "What would you like me to do, sir?"

Simon met his eyes. "They're not coming back, are they?"

"I wouldn't expect your parents to return until the end of their evenings."

"Good." Simon glanced at the others. "In that case, Hudson, you're delegated to hold the fort here, and otherwise don't pass on anything you see or hear, not unless asked directly."

"Naturally not, sir." Hudson gave a small bow. "Like the best of my breed, I will endeavor to be deaf and dumb while seeing and hearing all."

That drew chuckles and grateful smiles from all, but then Luc looked at Henrietta. "What does the note say?"

She drew in a tight breath, fished the note from her pocket, unfolded it, and read, " 'Meet me at the corner of James Street and Roberts Street, in Mayfair, at ten o'clock. It should take you no more than fifteen minutes to walk there from Upper Brook Street. Make sure you are alone and that no one follows you. Should you fail to keep this appointment, or think to trap me in any way, your fiancé will die, slowly and painfully. And so will you.' "

Henrietta stared at the note, then shivered and folded it again, as if by doing so she could contain the malicious intent that oozed from the page. Looking up, she met the eyes of those around her—her nearest and dearest—all grave, but determined.

"Buck up." Amanda squeezed her hand. "We're going to get James back safe and sound, and catch this madman."

Murmurs of agreement came from all around.

"Right then," Simon said. "We all know what we have to do. Let's get to it. I'll send a note to Barnaby—as arranged, he'll alert Stokes. Henrietta, whatever you do, don't leave until you need to. The longer we have to get everyone in place, the better."

There were nods all around. Henrietta turned and led the way up the stairs. Simon walked off to the parlor to write his note, but everyone else followed Henrietta, hurrying up the stairs in her wake, eager to change and sneak out to take up their assigned positions.

Chapter Fifteen

At precisely fifteen minutes before ten o'clock, cloaked and veiled, Henrietta descended the front steps of her parents' house and set off, walking briskly along the pavement toward Grosvenor Square. She felt keyed up, nerves tight, but, surprisingly, her principal emotion wasn't fear, not even trepidation.

They would get James back, and catch the murderer, and all would be well.

She knew there were any number of things that might go wrong, but her brain had, it seemed entirely of its own volition, shut them out, denying failure any purchase whatever in her mind. She was so determined that it was an effort to walk normally and not march militantly along.

The night was unhelpfully black, with little moon to light her way. Luckily, her path to the appointed rendezvous was along well-lit Mayfair streets; the streetlamps were all burning, and it wasn't yet so late that there was any real danger, not in that area.

Knowing that, courtesy of their plan, she wasn't actually alone no doubt contributed to her combative mood. She spotted a familiar street sweeper loitering along one side of Grosvenor Square—directly opposite St. Ives House; Luc was prone to taking such risks. Henrietta didn't dare look more closely to see where Amelia was, but she knew her sister would be near.

Also comforting was the pistol weighing down her reticule; Penelope had loaned it to her and instructed her in how to fire it. As, along with all the Cynster girls, Henrietta had insisted on being taught about guns along with their brothers, a little instruction was all that had been necessary; the small, American muff pistol felt nice and snug in her grasp.

Penelope had assured her that despite its size, the pistol would put a sizeable hole in the murderer.

Of course, none of the ladies had considered it wise to mention the pistol to any of their menfolk.

Head up, gaze fixed forward, Henrietta walked purposefully along, ignoring the hackney, and its driver, who rolled past as she crossed Duke Street, leaving Grosvenor Square to walk on along Brook Street.

James Street was the second street on the left. She crossed the street, staring up it to the opening of the much narrower Roberts Street, a poorly lit dark maw, but she could see no figure waiting. Resisting the urge to nod in greeting to the apparently old man in a frieze coat who shuffled past, she turned up James Street and walked briskly to the designated corner.

The old man shuffled on across the mouth of James Street, then, placing one foot tentatively in front of the other, turned up the street on the opposite pavement. At the rate he was moving, she would meet the murderer and be long gone before Barnaby reached the spot directly across from Roberts Street.

Taking up position at the corner, closer to the edge of the pavement so she could more easily be seen, she put back her veil and looked around again, searching the shadows. She even turned and peered into the deeper shadows of Roberts Street; courtesy of the light from the lamps in the street at the other end, she could see that there was no figure lurking along the pavements in Roberts Street, either.

Turning back to face James Street, and Barnaby, still puffing and wheezing along, she heaved a sigh and settled to wait.

Two minutes later, the hair at her nape lifted. She stiffened.

"Don't turn around. Not yet."

He—the murderer—was standing directly behind her. Her senses screaming, she battled the primitive impulse to whirl about. Gripping her reticule tightly, she raised her head higher, then stiffly nodded. "Very well. Now what?"

"Now I'm going to turn around and walk down Roberts Street, and when I give the word, you will turn and follow. We're going to walk the streets—I will lead and you will follow, remaining a good yard behind me at all times. If all remains well, I will eventually take you to where I'm holding Glossup." He paused, then asked, "Is that clear?"

She'd heard him speak before. Not often, and she couldn't remember where, but there was a faint echo of some shire accent hidden beneath the polished vowels . . . she shook aside the distraction and nodded. "Yes. I'll stay behind you so I won't be able to see your face."

Amusement laced his voice. "Precisely." Then his tone hardened. "Wait for my word, then follow."

She did as he'd ordered, holding still when she sensed him moving away; across the street, Barnaby had drawn back into the shadows of a doorway, but he was there, watching.

"Now."

Turning, she walked into the darkness of Roberts Street and fell in behind the tall, broad-shouldered male figure who steadily paced down the shadowy pavement ahead of her; he was wearing a dark cloak, a wide-brimmed dark hat, plus a dark scarf wound about his neck, and most likely about his lower face, but tonight he carried no cane. Nevertheless, even in the gloom of Roberts Street, very little observation was required for her to confirm that he was, indeed, the man she'd collided with in Hill Street all those evenings ago.

She debated questioning him, and while she didn't hold much hope he would be overly forthcoming, she asked, "Was it you behind all the attacks—at March-main House, then my horse being darted, the stone falling in the ruins at Ellsmere Grange, as well as the attack in the park?"

He didn't reply for several paces, then said, "Yes. You don't need to know more than that."

"Well, at least I now know I don't have more than one mystery attacker," she muttered at his back.

"Be quiet. No more talking."

Yes, sir. Grimly, she set her lips and, for the sheer hell of it, glared at his black back. The weight of the pistol in her reticule was tempting; she could pull it out and shoot him now, and he'd have no chance to stop her, and then he'd be stopped for all time . . . but Penelope had assured her the pistol would put a *very* big hole in him at close range, which would almost certainly kill him, and then they'd never be able to find and rescue James. Tied up in a room somewhere in London . . . even learning the identity of the murderer wouldn't guarantee they'd be able to find James.

They were more than halfway down Roberts Street; Davies Street, much better lit, lay ahead. Realizing that walking ahead of her as he was, the villain couldn't see what she did, she kept her pace steady but turned her head and looked back.

Twenty paces behind her, Barnaby, no longer shuffling, was slipping from dense shadow to dense shadow; he raised a hand in brief salute.

Henrietta faced forward and kept walking. As they neared the better illumination of Davies Street, she realized her lips were curved in an intent and determined, and potentially revealing, smile, and promptly wiped her face of all expression. She wasn't all that good at charades; she wasn't sure she could creditably fake the sort of fear the murderer might be expecting her to be experiencing. Better to appear expressionless than to make him suspicious.

They stepped into Davies Street, crossed it, and turned right. South. Another hackney rolled slowly past. Charlie Hastings, disguised as a jarvey, was driving; from the corner of her eye, Henrietta caught a glimpse of Mary's face as her sister observed her—and even more closely studied the man ahead of her—from inside the hackney.

The villain thankfully didn't notice Mary; he continued walking, and Henrietta continued following. And the others continued to shadow them wherever they went.

She hadn't really thought of what he—the murderer—had meant when he'd said they would "walk the streets," but that was precisely what they did; although he avoided the busier parts of Mayfair, those streets where they might encounter members of her family leaving one event or going to another, he led her along streets she knew, heading east and south toward Bond Street, tacking through narrow mews and then walking short distances along wider streets, before turning into another alley or lane.

Whoever he was, he knew the streets well. From the way he halted every now and then to search their surroundings, even looking back, risking her seeing more of his face—not that she ever got a decent look—it was clear the entire exercise was designed to ensure no one was following them.

He was cautious, in her view to the extreme. And the longer they walked, the more she worried that he might notice her protectors, or, worse, might succeed in losing them.

She'd already seen Barnaby in three different locations, but at least he was changing his appearance each time. The hackneys, driven by Simon, Martin, and Charlie, with, respectively, Portia, Amanda, and Mary as passengers, were harder to disguise; even if the drivers changed hats and coats, the carriages themselves, and even more the horses, remained the same. Against that, the sight of a hackney on a Mayfair street was so unremarkable they were counting on the villain not truly registering the coaches at all.

Luc was with Amelia on foot, and Penelope had paired with Stokes's wife, Griselda, and Stokes and several of his constables and junior inspectors were also part of the net of protectors scattered about the streets.

Henrietta didn't fully understand the logistics, but Barnaby, Penelope, and Stokes had assured her that at least one observer, if not two, would have her in their sights at all times but would rotate constantly to limit the chance that the murderer would notice them.

The problem was he was choosing certain streets—those with very limited concealment and also limited in length—to pass through again and again; the shorter streets gave those following her very little time to see them go into the street, then get someone into position to watch her come out again and see where he led her next.

Twice, he started down a short, featureless lane, only to turn around halfway along and retrace their steps.

When, more than an hour after he'd met her at the rendezvous, he led her down the short length of Blenheim Street to Woodstock Street, paused at the corner to glance back, then turned left and led her into an unexpected, and largely invisible, little court, she had no idea if any of her protectors were still with her. And no way of checking.

He led her to a row of houses that were clearly all abandoned and empty, most likely due for demolition.

Despite her resolve, her earlier belligerence, her heart was thudding heavily, too rapidly, as she followed him, her would-be murderer, through an ancient wrought-iron gate and up an uneven path to a set of worn, cracked stone steps leading up to a narrow front door.

Would this dark, abandoned house be where her life ended?

The unexpected thought shook her; suddenly flustered, she bundled it from her mind.

Yet there was no denying her instinctive aversion to meekly following him like a lamb to the slaughter.

Pausing on the wide last step, the murderer drew a key from his pocket and unlocked the door. He pushed it wide, then he turned and looked at her, still standing on the path a yard behind him.

The streetlamp in the court was too distant to cast any light on his features, those visible between the low brim of his hat and the black silk scarf swathing his jaw. As in Hill Street, she simply couldn't see enough of his face to form any real picture.

"Who are you?" The words fell from her lips without conscious thought as she stared, frowning, up at him.

She sensed his smile, heard the satisfaction in his voice as, with one last glance over the empty pavements, the deserted court, he said, "You'll find out soon enough."

Stepping back, he waved her in, a mocking courtesy. "If you will, Miss Cynster, walk into the hall and halt at the foot of the stairs."

About to start forward, she halted. Eyeing the narrow, heavily shadowed hall, she asked, "Is James here?"

That and only that would get her over the threshold; only for James would she enter a murderer's lair.

Again she sensed a certain gloating amusement as the murderer replied, "He is. He's tied up, but he's hale and whole. I intend taking you to him directly."

There was something behind those last words that made her skin crawl, but she forced herself to nod and, raising her skirts, walked calmly up the steps, past him, and on into the darkness of the narrow front hall.

The house smelled dusty, faintly musty. As she halted at the foot of the stairs, unlit and unwelcoming, and looked upward, primal panic gripped her, a clawed hand closing about her throat, sharp nailed and choking.

She whirled. Looking back along the hall she saw her captor bending over a narrow hall table and lighting a small lantern. The familiar clop and rattle of a hackney reached her. The lantern lit, the murderer straightened, playing the lantern's light over her so she couldn't easily make him out.

Reaching back, he caught the doorknob and slowly closed the door.

Before he did, a hairsbreadth—a heartbeat—from breaking and running, Henrietta looked out of the door as the hackney she'd heard rolled slowly past.

Simon, on the box, looked directly at her.

She stood at the foot of the stairs, bathed in the lantern's light, as the door shut.

The instant it did, she drew in a huge, shuddering breath, then she blinked, squinted, held up a hand to shield her eyes and turned her head aside as the murderer walked slowly closer. He'd been focused on her, but it appeared she hadn't given their game away.

The sight of Simon had acted like a shot of the purest courage tipped directly into her veins. As the effect burned through her, she had to remind herself she couldn't sneer at the coward before her—not yet.

He halted a good yard from her, then, with the lantern, gestured to the stairs. "Go up."

Turning, she raised her skirts and started climbing; she couldn't wait to find James and get this over with. The sooner she could see this man in Stokes's hands and safely away from her and hers, the better.

As she neared the top of the stairs, the murderer, following a few steps behind her, said, "Turn left and walk along the gallery. Stop at the second door."

She turned as directed, but once he was walking directly behind her, she raised her reticule and slipped the catch free, opened the neck wide, and, reaching inside, closed her hand firmly about the grip of the small pistol. She didn't yet pull it free but used her cloak to conceal what she'd done.

Halting as instructed, facing the second door, she drew in a deep breath and steeled herself for what she might find beyond it. Lady Winston's murderer had a reputation for brutality. He'd said James was alive, hale and whole, but that didn't mean he hadn't beaten James badly.

Regardless, James would be tied securely and unable to help her. She would have to rely on herself, on her own resources, until the others burst into the house—which, she was praying, they would do any minute now. . . .

Her senses revolted again, skin crawling, nerves skittering, as the murderer drew close enough to reach around her and open the door.

He set it swinging. "Go in. Your fiancé is waiting to see you . . . one last time."

The tone of those last words sent a shudder down her spine, but, raising her head high, she stepped into the room and halted.

By the shaft of light cast by the lantern behind her and the weaker glow coming from a lamp on a tall-boy beside the door, she saw a bed, but it was empty. She looked further and saw a chair set deeper in the room, to one side of the bed, but she couldn't see James anywhere. Then she realized there were ropes lying discarded about the chair—

Hard fingers gripped her arm and yanked her sideways—behind the door.

James! Her heart leapt even while he bundled her behind him, into the lee of the door, and swung to face the murderer in her stead.

Only to get the lantern flashed in his face.

The full light of the lantern in his eyes made James instinctively recoil and raise an arm to shield his eyes.

Realizing he'd lost the advantage, he cursed. Lowering his arm, he tried to see, but the light was so bright that he wasn't even sure exactly where the villain was standing.

Then, ominously, the lantern beam slowly lowered, falling from his face to center on his body.

"Step back, Glossup, or I'll shoot you now. In front of your bride-to-be."

James finally managed to focus—and discovered that, yes, the villain now held a pistol aimed directly at his heart.

But . . . thinking furiously, James held his ground. "Me getting shot in the chest won't fit with your plan. How will your story run if I have a hole in my chest, instead of the side of my head? Not many men commit suicide by shooting themselves in the heart."

Silence held for a moment, then the murderer replied, amusement and more lacing his words, "That won't discomfit me in the least. I'll just turn my story around the other way. You beat Miss Cynster nearly unconscious, and in desperation she grabs the pistol and shoots you in the chest, then, in despair, she shoots herself. It's all one to me—who gets shot in the head and who in the heart." The murderer's voice strengthened. "So why don't you just step back toward the chair—*now*."

James hesitated.

Stunned by the murderer's intentions, made even more nauseating by being stated aloud, Henrietta clapped a hand over her lips, smothering her spontaneous rebuttal. She could see James thinking, trying to decide what he should do; the noble idiot would sacrifice himself for her, and then where would she be?

Living out the rest of her life alone.

She had to make her next words sound believable. Gulping in a breath, she discovered she didn't have to try all that hard to make her voice quaver. "James, please . . . do as he says."

His gaze flicked to her; she opened her eyes wide at

him and showed him the pistol she'd pulled free of her reticule.

Understanding held James motionless for a second, then the murderer drawled, "Do as she says, Glossup, and who knows? After I tie you up again, I might let you have one last kiss."

Henrietta was perfectly certain she could not hate a man more. Settling her weight evenly, she grasped the pistol in both hands, simultaneously making her voice weak and wavery. "Please, James, do what he says. I don't want him to shoot you—and perhaps he'll change his mind. We really don't know who he is, so perhaps he'll believe us and let us go . . ." She ended with a passable sob.

James met her eyes, then, his lips a thin line, looked back at the murderer and took one step back.

"That's right." The murderer was gloating. "Keep going."

James moved slowly, backing one defined step at a time; Henrietta realized he was keeping his gaze locked with the murderer's, and his slow, deliberate—clearly reluctant—retreat was keeping the murderer focused on him.

Step by step, James retreated, and, step by step, the murderer came further into the room.

At last, he cleared the open door; his gaze still on James, the villain reached back and caught the edge of the door with the hand holding the lantern and pushed it closed.

He was standing precisely where Henrietta was aiming.

Squeezing her eyes shut, she pulled the trigger.

Two shots roared out, one immediately following the other, the combined sounds deafening in the enclosed space.

On a gasp, Henrietta opened her eyes. Heart thudding, she slowly lowered her pistol. As the echoes of the shots faded, she saw the lantern on the floor near her feet—and the murderer sprawled awkwardly across the floor, his upper back against the tallboy, one hand clamped to a massive hole in one shoulder.

"James?" She couldn't see him. Panic surged.

Had he been shot?

Killed?

To get around the bed she had to pass the murderer. His pistol lay beside him, spent; she kicked it away from him regardless. She could see he was trying to gather his strength. Drawing back her foot, she kicked him squarely between the legs; he howled and curled up on himself.

Satisfied, she rushed around the bed. "James?"

Then she saw him. "Oh, my God!" He *had* been shot. He was struggling to sit up, to prop himself against the side of the bed. She rushed to help. "How bad is it?"

James blinked at her as she crouched beside him. He could barely believe it—they were both alive. He drank in her concern and managed a crooked, albeit pained, grin. "Not that bad. I flung myself aside and his ball clipped my arm. It probably looks worse than it is."

He wasn't sure she heard him over the thunderous cacophony of God only knew how many people pounding up the stairs. But all he cared about was her; his gaze feasted on her, devoured her face, her beloved features, then settled on her eyes. Lost in the blue, he murmured, "I assume that's the cavalry. I'm glad you didn't come alone."

With his unbloodied hand, he gently touched her cheek, then cupped it. Just that touch was the most wondrous relief.

She looked fierce as a tigress as she raised a hand to cradle the back of his. "I would have come alone if that's what it took, but I didn't have to." She glanced up as a horde of people rushed into the room.

James didn't care about anyone else; for him, there was only her. Gently, he turned her face back to his, found her gaze, those lovely soft blue eyes, and held it. "I love you. God, how much I love you." He let himself sink into the blue. "While I was tied up here, all I could think about was that I hadn't told you that. In facing possible death, that was my one real regret."

She smiled stunningly—a beauteous sight, sunshine banishing the darkness—and caught his hand in both of hers. "I love you, too. I truly do." Raising his hand, she kissed his knuckles, held as tightly to his gaze as he was holding to hers. "I am *so* relieved that you're alive."

She leaned in and their lips touched. Softly lingered. Just that, a simple caress that meant the world to them both.

She drew back and, eyes closed, sighed, then, her grip on his hand tightening, she leaned her forehead against his, and for an instant they both clung—to the moment, to each other. To the inexpressible joy of being together and alive.

Then Stokes arrived. They both looked up as he swept in to join the crowd already standing around the murderer, retribution in their eyes.

Stokes humphed, then bent over the villain and stripped away the black scarf and lifted off the wide-brimmed hat.

The others crowded around to look, to study the murderer's face, to divine the identity he'd been willing to kill again and again to conceal.

While they were thus engaged, Henrietta rose and

helped James to his feet. He was clutching his left arm just below his shoulder. His sleeve was torn and bloodied, but when she got him to ease his grip, the wound bled only sluggishly. As far as she could see in the poor light, as far as he could tell, the ball had passed through and wasn't lodged in his flesh. Pushing him to sit on the edge of the bed, she stripped the case off one pillow and used the fabric to bind his arm. He smiled more strongly, more definitely at her, and murmured his thanks.

They turned to the others just as Stokes shifted and looked around the circle. "Anyone know who the bastard is?"

"He's vaguely familiar," Barnaby said.

"Hmm." Simon, frowning, nodded. "But I can't quite place him."

"I know I've seen him about," Charlie said.

Henrietta realized that, somehow, none of the ladies had made it up the stairs. Linking her arm with James's uninjured one, she helped steady him on his feet, then they rounded the bed to join the others about the fallen villain.

The others took that as a sign that they could now bombard them with questions, most of which were devoted to confirming that they were, indeed, as well as they appeared. The circle parted to include them, finally allowing them a clear look at the villain who had tried to take their future from them.

Said villain was still half curled, slumped on his side before the tallboy, his face partly in shadow. Someone had roughly bound his wound; it was, Henrietta realized, too high on his shoulder to be fatal. She looked down at him, then pointed to the lantern. "Shine that in his face and let me see."

Simon was only too ready to oblige. The villain flinched away from the brighter light, turning his head up and away.

Henrietta gasped. "Good God! It's Sir Peter Affry."

Stokes grunted.

Charlie stared. "Sir Peter Affry, the MP?"

"Yes." Henrietta nodded decisively. "He's been lionized in political circles this Season. He's certainly been at all the major functions."

"He was at Marchmain House," James said. "Someone pointed him out to me there."

"And he was definitely at the gala," Barnaby said.

"Doesn't matter," Stokes said. "He's done his dash. He's not going to be able to escape the gallows over this." Reaching down, Stokes hauled Sir Peter unceremoniously to his feet, then, with a distinct lack of gentleness, propelled the injured MP through the door into the waiting arms of two burly constables. "Take him to the Yard and charge him. Get the doctor to bind him up properly, but keep him under lock and key at all times. I'll be along shortly."

"Yes, sir." The constables looked thoroughly thrilled with their captive. They cinched a rope around his wrists, then, each taking one arm, ignoring Sir Peter's moans and weak protests, they half carried, half dragged him away toward the stairs.

James felt light-headed, but he didn't think it was from blood loss; euphoric relief was nearer the mark. But he remembered enough to turn to Stokes and say, "He admitted to killing Lady Winston."

"Good." Stokes met James's eyes. "Will you testify, if it comes to that?"

Grimly, James nodded. "Yes. Definitely. I want him to get his just deserts."

"Don't we all," Barnaby said. "At least we now know why he was so hell-bent on hiding his identity. M'father mentioned something about him being considered for Cabinet."

Stokes looked around the circle, his gray gaze coming to rest on Henrietta and James. "I'm going to need statements from all of you, but if you like, we can put it off until tomorrow."

They all looked at each other—Simon, Barnaby, Charlie, Martin, and Luc, as well as James and Henrietta—then Martin grimaced, and put what they were all thinking into words. "The others—and the elders—aren't going to appreciate that they were left out of this. I vote we adjourn to somewhere more comfortable and get all the statements and explanations cleared away tonight, then we can tell the others about it tomorrow, when it's all done and finished with."

Agreement was unanimous. Stokes nodded. "I'll need to go back to the Yard and see him charged, and make sure they understand to hold him regardless of what he says, then I'll come and interview you." He glanced at them inquiringly. "Where?"

They decided Barnaby and Penelope's house in Albemarle Street would be best.

Stokes left, and the others all gathered around. James was amazed at their disguises, while they wanted to know what had happened to him.

Henrietta cut all explanations short with the demand, "What I want to know is what took you so long?" She looked pointedly at Simon. "You knew we were here—I expected you to arrive and overpower the fiend much sooner."

"Yes, well." Simon looked sheepish. "He'd put an extra lock on the front door—a bolt. We were intending to pick the lock and creep up on him in case he had a gun—which, as it transpired, he did—but the bolt meant we had to break the door down, which he would have heard . . ."

Barnaby crisply stated, "We were arguing the merits of breaking down the door over forcing a window when we heard the two shots, and nearly died ourselves." He eyed the pistol as Henrietta, reminded of it, retrieved it from where she'd left it on the bed. "But I see Penelope took her own precautions."

"Just as well." Henrietta tucked the pistol back into her reticule. "But speaking of Penelope, where is she? And the others—Mary, Amanda, Amelia, Portia, and Griselda?"

All the men except James exchanged wary, resigned glances, then Luc admitted, "We insisted they stay in the carriages outside. Speaking of which, we'd better go down and explain."

And grovel, Henrietta thought, but men like these would always act true to their natures, and, at base, all of them were protective to a fault.

The others clattered down the stairs; she and James followed more slowly, using the lantern to light their way.

In the front hall, they left the lantern on the table, turned down the wick, then walked out of the door and pulled it shut behind them. Or as shut as it would go, given it was hanging half off its hinges.

The small court was filled with the three hackney coaches they'd hired for the night. In the light of the streetlamp, various couples were talking, the men reporting, the ladies reprimanding, yet curious to hear every detail.

Arm in arm, Henrietta paused with James on the top

step and looked out at the small army of friends who had helped them. She leaned lightly against James, so very grateful to feel the warmth and strength of him beside her again. "They might not have been there at the critical moment, but knowing they were close and would come to our aid gave me the courage to do what I did."

"Friends. Family." James closed his hand over hers, twined his fingers with hers and gripped, met her gaze as she glanced at him. "On both fronts we've been blessed."

Henrietta searched his eyes, then softly smiled. "They're watching us, you know—all the ladies. They don't want to interrupt, but they're dying to speak with us, to fuss over us."

James let his smile deepen. "I suppose we'd better let them—it's only their due—but before we do . . ." Lifting her hand, he raised it to his lips and, eyes locked with hers, brushed a kiss across her knuckles. "Let me say it again—I do so love you."

Henrietta's heart overflowed—with love, happiness, gratitude, and relief. And with joy. Simple, unadulterated joy. She held his gaze and, stars in her eyes, gave him back the words. "And I love you. Forever and always."

His lips lifted in a smile that held the same joy she felt. "I can barely believe it, yet despite all the hurdles, despite the determination of a murderous villain, we have won through."

"We've won our future." Henrietta beamed. "And now we get to live it."

Together, they faced forward, and, arm in arm, went down the steps, out of the gate, and onto the pavement, where, as Henrietta had foretold, they were immediately mobbed by a coterie of curiously garbed ladies. After hugging them both, and oohing and aahing over James's wound, said ladies dismissed their husbands' reports as inept and insisted on hearing all in James's and Henrietta's own words—once they'd repaired to the comfort of Penelope's home.

No one argued. Instead, everyone piled into or onto the hackneys, and the company adjourned to Albemarle Street.

Chapter Sixteen

It was after midnight before, between them, James and Henrietta had related their stories to the assembled company, and had in turn heard the tales of the amazingly complex, and at times quite mad, scrambling the others had had to do to follow Affry and Henrietta around the Mayfair streets.

"Keeping you in sight was one thing," Barnaby said. "Doing it while staying out of *his* sight was another. He was the hardest quarry I've ever had to trail."

"Still," Martin said, leaning back in the corner of one sofa, his arm around Amanda, "at least we now understand why he was so desperate to kill you. He would never have been able to have a moment's rest, forever knowing that at any time you might see something, or hear his voice at some ball, and make the connection."

"And" Luc said, from his position perched on the arm of the chair in which Amelia sat, "while it would be bad enough for anyone to be convicted of such heinous crimes, for a Member of Parliament . . . the government, the entire ton, and all of society are going to be baying for his blood."

Stokes walked into the room in time to hear those words. "Actually, impossible though it might seem, it appears his case is even worse than that."

Various people made disbelieving sounds. Accepting a cup of coffee, Stokes sat beside his wife, Griselda, sipped, gave Griselda a small smile, then looked around at the inquiring faces. "I could barely believe it myself, but it's true. When I got back to the Yard, it was to find one of the other senior inspectors, Mullins, waiting to collar me. He'd been about to leave when he'd seen Sir Peter brought in. Mullins is in charge of any investigations involving elected officials, and in that capacity he asked me what the charges were to be. I told him about Lady Winston's murder, her dresser's murder, and what I'd gathered Affry had planned for Miss Cynster and Glossup here."

A sardonic smile flirted about Stokes's lips. "Mullins went so pale, I thought he would faint, but then he asked me to wait and rushed away to his office, and returned with a file, which he handed to me. The file contained a report from the local constable of the town outside of which Sir Peter used to live with his aunt. Sir Peter's current wealth, more or less all of it, was inherited from this aunt—he was her sole living relative and, unsurprisingly, her nominated heir. The aunt was, by all accounts, a hearty, healthy, country lady, but just after Sir Peter won his seat in Parliament and was wanting to move up to London, his aunt was murdered. Brutally beaten to death in very much the same fashion as Lady Winston and her dresser."

"Good Lord," Barnaby said. "He's murdered before?"

"Looks like it." Stokes paused to take another sip of coffee. "However," he went on, "Sir Peter was close friends with the local magistrate, as anyone might suppose of an up-and-coming politician, and the aunt's murder was blamed on some passing vagabond—a convenient itinerant no one saw. The constable was suspicious because the staff at the house, all loyal to the old lady, said Sir Peter was there, in the house, over the time his aunt was killed, but Sir Peter said he'd gone out riding. No one had seen him out riding, even though there are numerous farms nearby and people had been out in the fields, but, equally, none of the staff had actually seen him in the house over the relevant time, so . . . but the constable remained suspicious, and to give the man his due, knew he had reason to be. He, the constable, knew of another murder, just like the old lady's, that had occurred nearly a year before in a neighboring parish. A farmer's lass who, rumor had it, had been walking out with a gentleman, one she'd never named and who had never been seen by anyone else. There were no other suspects for the lass's murder, not even a convenient vagabond, so the death was put down as murder by persons unknown, but everyone agreed the secretive gentleman was the one who had done the deed."

"So," Penelope said, "the constable in the country had two mysterious murders that looked identical, and in one Sir Peter was the prime suspect, and in the other, an unknown gentleman was the only real suspect?"

Stokes nodded. "So the constable did the right thing. He sent the file to the Yard, and as Sir Peter's name was in it, it was handed to Mullins for careful consideration."

"Meaning," Luc said, "that nothing would be done?"

Stokes smiled one of his quick, sharklike smiles. "That's not quite how it works. Mullins sits on the case—it remains active—until we see if Sir Peter makes any further mistakes. But, of course, the file's contents aren't bruited about, so I didn't know about the similarities in the killings, and, as we'd kept Lady Winston's murder and that of her dresser secret, too, Mullins hadn't heard about them. We wouldn't have connected the cases if Sir Peter hadn't been caught."

"Which he now has been," Portia said. "So will he be tried for all the murders?"

Stokes nodded. "Without doubt. I took a quick look at the descriptions of the bodies—there can be no question that it was the same fiend who committed all the crimes." He looked at his wife, reached out, and grasped her hand. After a moment, he glanced at the others. "I've sent my fair share of villains to the gallows, but this will be one I'll be *glad* to see hang."

Agreement was universal.

When he'd finished his coffee, Stokes got down to business. Assisted by Penelope, who acted as his secretary and wrote down all that was said, Stokes formally interviewed and took detailed statements from Henrietta, James, Barnaby, Martin, Simon, Charlie, and Luc.

Once the statements had been reviewed and signed, Stokes nodded. "That should do it." Gathering the papers, he stood. "I haven't yet interviewed Affry. I'll do that tomorrow, now I have all the facts, but from what little he let fall, I gather he couldn't believe that you"—Stokes nodded at Henrietta—"wouldn't recognize him, all but instantly, if you ever got a clear view of his face."

She frowned. "But I never *saw* his face—I only saw him as the murderer that once in Hill Street, and his face was almost all in shadow . . ." Eyes on Stokes, she tipped her head. "Perhaps that was it? He didn't know—and couldn't tell—where the shadow fell across his face. He thought I saw more than I did."

Stokes nodded. "Most likely. He's got a scar that runs between his upper lip and his nose. If you'd seen that, chances are you would have recognized him the next time you came face-to-face with him in some ballroom, or over a dinner table."

"And from his point of view, that would have happened at some point, and he couldn't have that." Barnaby rose, along with all the others. "So it was misplaced ego, in a way, that brought Affry down. If he'd just waited patiently to see if Henrietta ever said anything, and did what he could to avoid her meanwhile, he would have got away cleanly."

"Overweening ego," Simon said, "seems to be a trait that brings down a lot of villains."

"For which," Stokes said, "I, for one, am perennially grateful. The ego of villains—long may it be their Achilles' heel."

On that rousing note, the company broke up. Buoyed by collective satisfaction and unalloyed triumph, they exchanged farewells and drifted off, in the hackneys or on foot, to find their respective beds.

Henrietta asked Charlie to drive her and James to George Street. Very happy to oblige, Charlie left them on the steps of James's house and, with a flourish of his whip, drove away.

"He'll have to return the hackney to its stable, I suppose." James hunted in his pocket for his latchkey.

"I'm sure it will all have been arranged." Her arm still supportively twined with his, Henrietta waited patiently by his side. "Penelope's organizing is always very thorough."

James grunted. Fitting the key to the lock, he opened the door, then waved Henrietta in. Walking into the hall, she paused by the central table and set down her reticule.

James shut the door, waited until she glanced his way, then arched a brow.

She smiled. "Set the locks. I'm staying."

"If you're sure." Which wasn't really in question. Using his good arm, he slid the bolts home.

"Aside from anything else"—she studied the way he moved while she shrugged off her cloak—"your wound needs tending. I'm certainly not about to leave you alone with such an injury."

James glanced at his bound arm. Grimaced. "I would say, if that's the case, then I'm almost glad he shot me—but it hurts too much."

Smiling in sympathy, she crossed to take his good arm and steer him toward the stairs. "Come along—I'm sure Mrs. Rollins will have left all the supplies we'll need waiting."

"Speaking of which." Allowing Henrietta to guide him onto the stairs and up, James glanced frowningly down into the hall. "Where is everyone? Seeing I didn't return home last night—"

"I sent around a note, of course." Henrietta met his gaze. "It was one of the first things I did after I got Affry's note this . . . no, yesterday morning. He threatened to kill you if I raised any alarm, any hue and cry, and, of course, the same applied to your household, except Affry didn't know you didn't just have lodgings. I realized I needed to reassure Fortescue and Mrs. Rollins, and make sure they didn't make any fuss, either, so I did." Facing forward, she went on, "Then when we reached Penelope's this evening, I sent another note to tell them all was well, but that you had been shot in the arm, a flesh wound, and I would need cloths and hot water and bandages to tend it, but we wouldn't be home until late and they shouldn't wait up for us."

Reaching the top of the stairs and stepping into the gallery, she halted and faced him. "I told them we'd see them tomorrow, meaning this morning." She tipped her head. "I hope that's all right?"

James smiled—found he couldn't stop smiling. "It's more than all right. Did you realize you just called this house 'home'?"

She lightly shrugged but didn't take her eyes from his. "I suppose that's because I already think of this house as my home."

He felt—literally felt—every last iota of tension, of uncertainty for their future—fall from him. Holding her gaze, he raised her hand to his lips, kissed. "That makes me beyond happy."

She smiled at that, one of her radiant, glorious smiles. "Good." Linking her arm with his again, she turned them toward the master suite.

They went in, and sure enough, Mrs. Rollins had left all the required supplies laid out on the chest of drawers, along with a samovar of hot water. Henrietta helped him remove their rough bandage and ease out of his coat, then cut him out of his shirt and dampened the fine material that had stuck to the wound in order to peel it away.

The gash looked ugly, red and raw; she bathed it, then applied the salve Mrs. Rollins had left, and between them they bound the wound tightly.

"With luck," he said, testing his arm, "there won't be too much of a scar."

Standing by the chest of drawers and drying her hands, Henrietta drank in the sight of him, seated on the low table, naked to the waist, his magnificent chest bared to her gaze, and smiled, then she considered the bandage and softly said, "I don't mind if there is a scar. Every time I see it, I'll think of how you got it." She met his eyes. "How you worked to keep Affry's gaze, his attention, fixed on you—his pistol trained on you— away from me, so that I could shoot him. Even though that put you in danger of being shot, even knowing you very likely would be." She held his gaze steadily. "Don't think I didn't see that. Don't think I didn't appreciate that for what it was."

Transparently uncomfortable, he shrugged the words away, then rose and came toward her. Prowled toward her, intent edging his features, his approach designed to distract, but she kept her gaze on his face, drank in the now familiar, well-beloved features, and thought, *I know you now.*

Outwardly, he remained a wolf of the ton—an ex-wolf, perhaps, yet the pelt was still there—but beneath the glamour he was a man who moved quietly through life, who did what needed to be done, what should be done, what was right. He didn't see that as any distinguishing feature, as anything special, but . . . that made him the right man for her.

So she smiled and opened her arms, opened her heart and embraced him.

He studied her eyes, then he closed his arms about her, bent his head, and set his lips to hers, and together, step by step, whirling stride by stride, they stepped out together, reached for and found the ineluctable rhythm, and gave themselves up to the unutterable pleasure of their own, private celebration.

It started as that, as a compulsively necessary worshipping of life, of living, in the aftermath of escaping death's shadow.

A simple matter of acknowledging they still lived, that they still breathed, still desired, still needed.

But as they shed their clothes, as their skins met and the flames flared, then raced over and through, claiming them, and they fell, limbs tangling, on the big bed, the engagement transformed into something more. Something broader, grander, more wild and joyous and passionately enthralling—a true celebration of their wider triumph.

Built on the joy of having found each other, of having discovered, uncovered, and learned. Of having grasped the challenges that fate had sent them, of having met those challenges and succeeded beyond their wildest dreams.

Of having forged a relationship, sound and true, a partnership that had seen them through the last fraught hours and brought them safely home.

To *home*.

To having won through to that blessed place.

They came together with open hearts, with passion driving them, and desire filling them, but, above all, with love fusing their souls. Recognized, acknowledged, and freely given, it bound them, held them, and made them more, forged in its fire into the very best they could be.

"I love you."

"I love you."

The words fell from their lips again and again, in soft murmurs and gasps, in passion and in frenzy.

Then the cataclysm caught them, wracked them, and they flew, then they knew no more, were blind and senseless to all but the ecstasy.

To the glorious, scintillating, coruscating delight.

Gradually, the sensual nova faded, and the golden pleasure that was love made all but tangible wrapped them in its succoring folds, and held them safe, protected and cared for, shielded from the world in each other's arms.

Epilogue

The engagement of the Honorable James Glossup and Miss Henrietta Cynster had titillated the perennially jaded interest of the ton. No one had seen it coming; not one of the grandes dames could claim to have predicted it, nor anything like it, for either participant.

Consequently, despite the short notice, their engagement ball, held in the magnificence of St. Ives House, was viewed as an event of signal significance, one everyone honored with an invitation braved hell and high water to attend. But prior to the ball itself, a formal family dinner was held to toast the engaged couple; every Cynster—even Catriona, Richard, Lucilla, and Marcus—gathered in the long formal dining room to feast, drink, and delightedly commend the pair. And, of course, to hear the tale of their brush with a madman, and their role in bringing one of the more heinous villains of recent years to justice.

The news of Sir Peter Affry's arrest and incarceration pending trial, a trial those lords and parliamentary dignitaries who had been permitted to view the evidence had confirmed could have only one end, had deeply shocked the ton. So many had welcomed Sir Peter into their homes, so many had shaken his hand, so many had judged him worthy of support that on learning of his perfidy, all of society felt deeply disturbed and, indeed, betrayed.

From up-and-coming politician and potential minister, he became a pariah in a matter of hours.

But within St. Ives House on that happy evening, the talk rarely strayed into darker spheres. Indeed, possibly in reaction to the darkness Sir Peter represented, everyone attending turned their minds and their hearts to embracing the shining hope and expectations for a joyous future embodied by the engaged couple.

In many ways, they, and the promise of their upcoming union, were the perfect and most appropriate antidote to lift the shaken spirits of the ton.

The family dinner ended with a traditional round of toasts to the affianced couple—ending with a warning to all, delivered by Honoria, that they would soon be summoned back to St. Ives House for the wedding breakfast. The date for the wedding was confirmed by Arthur, a beaming Louise by his side, then the gathering broke up to repair to the ballroom upstairs with everyone in a mellow mood and a delighted, expectant frame of mind. Every lady had more than enough fact and speculation to never be at a loss for conversation over the next several weeks, while as they climbed the stairs, the gentlemen traded opinions and quips on the benefits of a rapid engagement, and an even more rapid wedding thereafter.

Recalling one last duty she had to perform before taking her place in the receiving line upstairs, Henrietta drew her hand from James's sleeve and, leaving him chatting with Gabriel and her father, turned—to discover Mary standing directly in her path, looking pointedly at her.

Henrietta laughed. "Yes, I have it." Catching Mary's hand, flown with her own happiness, she drew her younger sister—the last of the Cynster girls of their generation yet unwed—to the side of the room. "Here. This is where Angelica gave it to me, so . . ." Opening her silver reticule, Henrietta fossicked inside, then drew out the gold links and amethyst bead necklace, with its long, tapered, rose-quartz pendant.

She held it up, dangling from her fingers; both she and Mary studied it for a moment, then Mary reached for it—but Henrietta whisked it away. "No." She met Mary's eyes. "Let me put it on for you."

Mary smiled delightedly and presented her back. Henrietta was significantly the taller—Mary was, if anything, shorter than Angelica—so looping the necklace into position was a simple matter.

Fiddling with the clasp, Henrietta softly said, "I didn't believe, and if it weren't for your pushing I never would have worn it—and I honestly don't know if I would ever have found James, if he and I would ever have found our way to the happiness we now have, without it. Without The Lady's help."

Raising one hand, Mary touched the fine necklace, holding it against her skin. On her, the pendant hung fully between her breasts. "But you believe in the necklace now."

"Oh, yes." Henrietta was still fiddling. "If anything I would say I believe in it, in its power, even more than you. I've seen what it can do, experienced what it can bring. There!"

Feeling Henrietta pat the clasp at her nape, Mary turned, looking down at the necklace, at how it sat against her creamy skin; the cornflower blue of her satin ball gown, chosen to match her even more vivid eyes, echoed the purple hues of the amethyst beads. Looking up, she met Henrietta's gaze. "Thank you."

"No." Henrietta held her gaze steadily. "Thank *you*. I know you've been waiting for this—to receive the necklace and be able to wear it and so find your own hero—literally for years. Even though you're generally so impatient, you waited patiently—and then you pushed at just the right moment. I truly believe you were influenced by The Lady in that, that you've already felt Her hand, for you certainly played a major part in bringing me and James together."

Henrietta paused to draw in a huge breath, then she smiled one of what Mary privately dubbed her over-the-moon-joyous smiles. "For that—for all of that—I wish you the very *best* of success in finding your own hero."

Mary felt the warm wash of affection as Henrietta swooped and embraced her. She returned the hug with equal joy; she was sincerely happy, from the depths of her heart happy, to see Henrietta so perfectly matched. This was her sister's fairy-tale ending; now it was her turn to go out and find hers.

"Henrietta!"

Releasing each other, they both straightened. Turning, they saw Louise beckoning imperiously. "Come along—we need you in the receiving line. And Mary, too—*you* should already be upstairs."

Mary and Henrietta shared a glance, then they laughed and hurried to where Louise waited. Together, they swept their harried mother up the stairs.

"Really, I don't know what's got into you," Louise said to Mary once the receiving line had been reached. Louise noted the necklace around Mary's throat, hesitated, but then said, "But off you go and enjoy yourself." With one hand, she made a shooing motion. "Just behave."

"Yes, Mama!" Delighted—with the evening, with life in general—Mary was only too ready to obey. Her first task was to quarter the room, to see who was there and note the new arrivals as they streamed into the fabulous white, pale green, and gilt ballroom.

Very soon, the room was pleasantly crowded. Then more guests arrived, and the event became a certified crush.

Mary tacked through the groups, stopping to chat as the mood and the company took her; as a Cynster young lady raised very much in the bosom of the ton, such an event held no terrors. She'd cut her eyeteeth on the correct way of doing things, and knew every possible way around any social situation. Even the grandes dames, after observing her over the past four years, had accepted that she was entirely at home in this sphere and unlikely to put her dainty foot wrong, even while stubbornly following her own path.

Tonight, however, there was no advance to be made on her already defined way forward; the name of the gentleman she'd set her sights upon had not appeared on the guest list. Consequently, she had no particular aim beyond obeying her mother and enjoying herself.

Then the violins started playing the engagement waltz, and James and Henrietta circled the floor, so lost in each other's eyes, with James so blatantly proud and Henrietta positively glowing with joy, that the company was held spellbound. When the affianced couple completed their circuit and other couples started to join them on the floor, Charlie Hastings, with whom Mary had been conversing, solicited her hand, which she happily granted.

Waltzing with Charlie was pleasant; Mary viewed him as an older brother. He had his eye on Miss

Worthington, a young lady Mary was acquainted with, and she was pleased to encourage him by telling him all she knew.

But as the evening wore on, she drifted closer and closer to the wall. While she could chatter and converse with the best of them, and usually, when she had some end in view, she found the exercise stimulating, now, when she knew there was no point—when there was nothing she could or wished to gain from any conversation—she found her interest flagging.

She couldn't, she decided, risk slipping out of the ballroom. Even though it had happened years ago, her cousin Eliza had been kidnapped from this very house during her sister Heather's engagement ball. If Mary appeared to have vanished from Henrietta's engagement ball . . . that was the sort of error Mary did not make.

But there were two alcoves, one at either end of the long room, both housing large nude statues and consequently, for the evening, screened by large palms. She elected to make for the alcove between the pair of double doors, the one less likely to have been appropriated by anyone else.

She was nearing that end of the room, several yards short of her goal, when, abruptly, she was brought to a quivering halt, nose to lower folds of an exquisitely tied cravat. To either side of the cravat stretched a wall of black-clad male chest.

"Good evening, Mary."

She recognized the deep, drawling, sinfully seductive voice. She looked up—up—all the way up to Ryder Cavanaugh's ridiculously handsome face. She'd decided years ago that such godlike male perfection was patently ridiculous, certainly in the effect it had on the female half of the ton. No, make that the female half of the species; she'd never met a woman of any class whom Ryder Cavanaugh did not affect.

In exactly that ridiculous way.

She'd made it a point never to allow even the smallest hint that she was aware of his charisma—the attraction that all but literally fell from him in waves—to show.

His late father's heir, and now the Marquess of Raventhorne, he was considerably older than she was, somewhere over thirty years to her twenty-two, but she'd known him all her life. Nevertheless, she'd been surprised to see his broad shoulders moving about the drawing room before dinner, and to later see him seated a little way along the dinner table on the opposite side, but then she'd learned that he was a connection of the Glossups' and had attended the dinner as the senior male of his line.

Ignoring the distraction of his gold-streaked, tawny-brown hair, a crowning glory too many ladies had compared to a lion's mane, not least because it held the same tactile fascination, a temptation to touch, to pet, to run one's fingers through the thick, soft locks, that had to be constantly guarded against, she fixed her eyes on his, a changeable medley of greens and golds framed by lush brown lashes, and baldly asked, "What is it, Ryder?"

From beneath his heavy hooded lids, his eyes looked down into hers. One tawny eyebrow slowly arched. He let the moment stretch, but she was too wise to let that tactic bother her; she held her pose, and let faint boredom seep into her expression.

"Actually," he eventually murmured—and how he managed to make his voice evoke the image of a bed was a mystery she'd never solved—"I wondered where you were making for so very doggedly."

She realized that with his significant height—Ryder would vie with Angelica's husband, Dominic, for the title of tallest man in the room—he might well have been able to see her making her way through the crowd.

But why had he been watching her?

Most likely he was bored, and her determined progress had captured his peripatetic attention. She'd heard matrons uncounted bemoan the fact that Ryder grew bored very quickly. She'd also heard him described as "big, blond, and definitely no good," except for his performance in the bedroom, which, by all accounts, was not just satisfactory but exemplary beyond belief.

Yet she'd always recognized the steel behind the languid lion's mask, and knew he could be as dogged as she if he decided he wanted something—for instance to enliven an otherwise boring evening by toying with her.

Which, she had to admit, held a certain attraction. He was rapier-witted, and his silver tongue held a lethally honed edge, and he was utterly unshockable, yet there was a . . . she'd never been sure quite how to describe it, but . . . a *deepness* of strength in Ryder that, his ridiculous beauty aside, had always made her shy away from him.

She'd always thought that if ever he was moved to actually pounce and seize, even she would find it impossible to escape.

And she entertained no illusions about Ryder; she might be one of the strongest of ton females, even among the Cynster clan, yet not even she could ever hope to manage Ryder Cavanaugh.

*Un*manageable was his middle name.

Given the point along her path at which she was presently poised, having Ryder Cavanaugh, of all the gentlemen in the ton, take any interest whatever in her—no

matter how mild and, relatively speaking, innocent—
was not just unnecessary but also could prove distinctly
counterproductive, and might possibly give rise to unexpected hurdles.

For her, not him.

Given that she'd finally got her hands on the necklace
and could now move forward along her path apace, she
was even more adamantly disinclined to offer herself up
as Ryder's amusement for the evening.

She'd kept him waiting for her reply; that he had,
indeed, waited, not shifting in the least, his hazel gaze
locked on her face, meant that every second of further delay risked fixing his attention, a heavy, feline,
weighty sensation, distinctly predatory, even more definitely on her . . . she tipped up her chin. "I don't want
to play, Ryder, at least not with you." He would accept
a straightforward—shockingly blunt—dismissal, while
anything less definite might further pique his interest,
so she held his gaze and simply stated, "You'll only com-
plicate things. So please, go and chase someone else."

Brazenly, she patted his arm, pure steel beneath fine
fabric, then stepped past him and pushed on, into the
crowd.

Leaving Ryder Cavanaugh, Marquess of Raventhorne, utterly flabbergasted. "I must be losing my
touch." He said the words aloud, confident that, in the
hubbub around him, no one would hear. Turning his
head, he watched Mary slip through the crowd, tacking
around this group, then that, halting whenever someone wished to chat, but not dallying. "What the devil
was that about—and where the hell is she going?" And
why?

"Clearly, I've grown rusty." Either that, or . . . but he
knew the advantages with which he'd been born hadn't

failed him yet. He wasn't such a coxcomb as to believe that every woman in the land should come flocking to his lazy smile, yet . . . most did.

Mary hadn't flocked. She'd run. No—worse—she'd calmly turned on her heel and marched off.

He wasn't entirely sure what he thought of that, but . . . he recognized that she'd chosen her words, her way to dismiss him, deliberately. In that, she'd read him aright. Normally, if things had been normal for him, he would have smiled, mentally saluted her frank speaking, and moved on to more amenable prey.

Heaven knew, there was plenty of the latter about.

Except he'd decided to change his diet.

Which meant . . .

Because he was still watching Mary's dark head, he saw another lady, of similar height with tumbling red-gold locks, intercept her. Angelica, now Countess of Glencrae, caught Mary by the arm, smiled as she spoke—and drew Mary to the side of the room.

Just beyond the alcove and its screen of tall palms.

Even before he'd thought, Ryder was moving toward the alcove. He'd long ago mastered the knack of cleaving his way through a crowd. If he walked purposefully in a straight line, because of his size people instinctively got out of his way, almost without conscious thought. His progress created very little by way of disturbance, and as long as he didn't stare at Angelica or Mary, with luck neither would notice him drawing near. . . .

He slid into the shadows of the palms without either Mary or Angelica noticing.

They stood just beyond the far edge of the alcove; sinking back into the shadows, Ryder leaned his shoulders against the wall beside the statue and tuned his excellent hearing to their conversation.

Mary inwardly sighed as her cousin Angelica, a few months older than Henrietta and the previous wearer of the necklace, fixed her hazel eyes on Mary's face and demanded, "What are you up to?"

"Why do you imagine I'm up to anything?"

"Because, sweet Mary, I know you." Angelica snorted, glanced over her shoulder at the crowd in the ballroom, then turned back to Mary. "You might as well face it—you and I are the most alike of all the family, and Henrietta told me about you all but forcing her to wear the necklace—which, incidentally, was a very good thing, and I would have done exactly the same—but, quite clearly, you did it because you now have an agenda of your own. You didn't push Henrietta to wear the necklace earlier because you didn't need to, because, until recently, you didn't have your eye on anyone."

Mary opened her mouth, but Angelica held up an imperious hand. "No, don't bother trying to tell me that you merely decided that at twenty-two it was your time—your turn to search for your hero. That won't wash." Angelica trapped Mary's gaze. "So confess. You've got your eye on some gentleman, haven't you?"

Mary narrowed her eyes, pressed her lips tight, but then, knowing Angelica far too well, admitted, "Yes. But it's no one's affair but my own. My hero—my choice."

Angelica regarded her for several seconds, then her expression turned thoughtful, even intrigued. "Hmm . . ."

Mary waited, then, irritated but unable to resist—it was entirely true that she and Angelica were the most alike, and therefore most able to get under each other's skins—prompted, "Hmm, *what*?"

Still regarding her, Angelica raised her brows. "It's just that, to my knowledge, the necklace has never worked like that—with you deciding, and then, essentially, using it to verify your choice. That's what you're proposing to do, isn't it?"

"Yes. But I don't see why it won't work like that." Mary looked down at the necklace, at the section that supported the crystal pendant, which was currently trapped beneath her bodice and wedged between her breasts. The pendant, she realized, felt pleasantly warm, presumably from absorbing the heat from her flesh. "I'm perfectly certain I've found the right gentleman for me—I just . . . want confirmation."

When she glanced up, Angelica searched her eyes, then more gently said, "You're not sure. And if you aren't . . ."

Mary tipped up her chin. "It's not that—I *am* sure. If you knew who I have in mind, you'd agree he was perfect for me, too. I just need to have The Lady's imprimatur—Her seal of approval. I fully expect Her to agree with my assessment."

Angelica held Mary's gaze for an instant more, then smiled and touched her arm. "Very well. I truly hope all goes as you wish. But . . . now don't poker up at me, but *if,* now you're wearing the necklace, you don't . . . well, *feel* something special for this mystery gentleman of yours, if he *doesn't* sweep you off your feet, or get under your skin to the point you simply can't shrug him off, then please, promise me you'll listen to The Lady's advice. Trust me, it's sound. No matter what, She won't fail you."

From where he was situated, Ryder could see enough of Mary's face to guess her expression; her chin had firmed and her lips had set. Her stubbornness was legendary.

But, somewhat to his surprise, after a moment, she

inclined her head. "Very well." She paused, then said to Angelica, "Thank you. I know what you said is the truth." Mary glanced down at the curious necklace encircling her slender throat. "If I want to find my hero, then I have to accept whatever verdict The Lady deigns to give."

Angelica chuckled. "There—that wasn't so hard, was it?" Laughing, she linked her arm with Mary's, and together they turned to face the crowd. "Believe me, I know all about accepting The Lady's decrees, but it worked for all of us, so trust me, it'll work for you, too. Now come and talk to Dominic—he was saying he hasn't had a chance to speak with you yet."

Arm in arm, the pair moved into the crowd, heading down the room.

Leaving Ryder to mull over all he'd overheard.

It seemed that fate, almost always his willing mistress, was once again smiling, helpfully and benevolently, on him.

Mary Cynster was searching for her gentleman hero, and he was looking for an engaging wife. He'd wanted to interact with her to see if she might suit—quite why he wasn't sure, but she'd always caught his eye and, more telling, his awareness—but she'd summarily dismissed him, so . . .

Apparently, he, Ryder Cavanaugh, Marquess of Raventhorne, didn't measure up to her hero standards, whatever they might be. . . .

Pushing away from the wall and stepping out from the cover of the potted palms, Ryder smiled a distinctly leonine smile and ambled back into the fray.

As anyone who knew him was well aware, he never backed away from a challenge.

Following is a chat with

#1 **New York Times** *bestselling author*

Stephanie Laurens

Toward the end of *The Capture of the Earl of Glencrae* we saw a newly engaged Angelica Cynster hand over to her cousin Henrietta the necklace The Lady, a Scottish deity, had gifted to the Cynster girls to assist them in finding their true heroes—and the necklace resurfaces in the first scene of Henrietta's book. What role does the necklace play in Henrietta's story?

The necklace provides the critical imperative that starts Henrietta's story off—think of it as the spark that starts the fire. In that first scene, it's Mary who, for her own reasons, insists that Henrietta must wear the necklace. Mary believes in the necklace, but Henrietta does not. In fact, although, like all Cynster females, Henrietta firmly believes that love is the best basis for a marriage, and the only acceptable basis for her, she nevertheless does not believe that love will come to her. Will find her. Well, you can see her point—she's now twenty-nine, and love hasn't found her yet. Henrietta has no faith in the necklace—which translates to no faith in love finding her—but to keep the peace with Mary, Henrietta agrees to wear the necklace that evening . . . and everything changes. In these two books, Henrietta's, then Mary's, we see the necklace come into its own as a real force, as a more obvious facilitator of love.

Henrietta has been nicknamed The Matchbreaker. How did that come about?

Ah—Henrietta's nickname has come about through her chosen way to fill in her time. Her social status, the circles into which she's been born, the connections, the ready access to the grandes dames, and indeed to all the female power brokers within the ton, combine all that with her natural tendencies to the pragmatic and practical, and from her earliest years of being out in society, she has assisted other young ladies of the haut ton—her peers—to answer the fateful questions: Does the gentleman who has or is about to offer for my hand love me? Or does he have some other reason for wishing to marry me? Henrietta knows who to ask, and how, and consistently gets the right answers. Consequently, certain disgruntled gentlemen of the ton, having failed to secure the brides they'd thought to inveigle into matrimony, have dubbed Henrietta The Matchbreaker. Where other ladies, the chaperons and the mamas, foster matches, Henrietta disrupts them—or more specifically, disrupts those not based on love.

James Glossup is a character who readers have met before. Did you always intend him to feature in his own book one day?

James Glossup previously appeared in *The Perfect Lover*. He was and still is Simon Cynster's oldest and closest friend—and Simon is Henrietta's brother, only a few years older than her. When I finished *The Perfect Lover*, I suspected I would have to, at some point, write James's story, but I didn't know at that time that it would be Henrietta his eye would light upon. And he didn't know that, either. In many respects, this book,

Henrietta and James's story, is an outcome of the action of *The Perfect Lover*, in which Simon and Portia finally realized they were meant for each other. Through the subsequent events surrounding Simon's engagement and wedding, James and Henrietta naturally spent more time together; they had met before and were aware of the other's existence, but had not before had occasion to spend any real time in each other's company. So the events of Simon's engagement and wedding provide the essential groundwork that allows James to react very directly to Henrietta's disruption of his matrimonial plans.

What is it that makes James the perfect match for Henrietta?

This was something that came out in the telling—as I wrote the book—that these two people truly were made for each other. Henrietta—practical, pragmatic, and, courtesy of her years as The Matchbreaker, very aware of all the negative aspects of gentlemen of the ton with respect to marriage—was never going to fall for the usual alpha hero. She would instinctively distrust such a man. But although James is very definitely a "wolf of the ton," definitely an alpha male as might be expected of Simon's closest friend, he has a quiet side to him, a deeper side that values the same ideals that Henrietta herself most fundamentally values, and it's that side of him that connects most strongly with her. They are not so much two sides of the same coin, but rather a male and a female who are strongly complementary—they fit together well.

The stories in your previous three books (The Cynster Sisters Trilogy) were dominated by country settings, but Henrietta's story takes place entirely in or around London. How do you choose your settings?

I don't define settings first, and then evolve a story to fit the setting. Rather the story, which is largely dictated by the characters, defines the setting. For instance, The Cynster Sisters Trilogy books had a lot of "out in the country" involved, including a lot of Scotland, because of who the primary motivator of all three stories was, namely the Highland Earl of Glencrae. Because he was the driving force behind the actions and London was dangerous for him, he shifted the girls out of London as fast as he could. But Henrietta's story is about James finding his necessary bride, and quickly, so the action will clearly take place during the ton Season, which means in the ballrooms, drawing rooms, and country houses in and around London.

The villain in this tale is particularly heinous. How real was such a villain to the times?

Very real, actually. Although my villain isn't drawn from any particular real-life incident or person, such malefactors existed then as they do now—sadly, villains of this stripe appear to be a constant in any civilized society. While the bulk of society plays by civilized rules, there are always those who believe such rules don't apply to them. My villain in this book bears all the typical traits of a self-absorbed, power-hungry, yet charismatic character. The one aspect that distinguishes then from now is that then it was so much harder to catch and unmask such villains—they really did get away with dreadful crimes very often— because, of course, there was none of the CSI that modern crime fighting relies on to identify perpetrators. Back then, it was all a matter of careful deduction, and very often engineering a trap.

It seems that Mary, Henrietta's sister, plays a pivotal role in her older sister's love life—and Mary's romance is to follow. Are these two books connected?

First, yes, Mary does indeed play a pivotal role in Henrietta's story by insisting that Henrietta wear the necklace—and keep wearing it until she's engaged, and can, properly and correctly, pass the necklace on to Mary, which in Mary's eyes must happen at Henrietta's engagement ball. Mary wants that necklace for her own reasons, but it has to come into her hands in the proper way, or it might not work as it's supposed to. So from the very first scene in Henrietta's book, we have Mary pushing Henrietta toward the altar— doing everything she can to get Henrietta to Henrietta's engagement ball. And, of course, Henrietta finally gets there, and in the Epilogue we see Henrietta hand the necklace on to Mary. Essentially, the short scenes in Henrietta's book, where she and Mary discuss Mary's desire for the necklace and the reasons behind that and what happens in the Epilogue once Henrietta fastens the necklace around Mary's throat, provide the back story to Mary's romance. So yes, these two books are connected, but, as usual with my books, it's perfectly possible to read them separately, or even in reverse order. The reader will simply have a more chronological view of events if they read them one after the other—Henrietta's first, then Mary's.

And read on for an excerpt from

THE PERFECT LOVER

by Stephanie Laurens
Available wherever books are sold

Late July, 1835
Near Glossup Hall, by Ashmore, Dorset

"Hell and the devil!" Simon Cynster reined in his bays, his eyes narrowing on the ridge high above Ashmore village. The village proper lay just behind him; he was headed for Glossup Hall, a mile farther along the leafy country lane.

At the rear of the village cottages, the land rose steeply; a woman was following the path winding up the berm of what Simon knew to be ancient earthworks. The views from the top reached as far as the Solent, and on clear days even to the Isle of Wight.

It was hardly a surprise to see someone heading up there.

"No surprise she hasn't anyone with her, either." Irritation mounting, he watched the dark-haired, willowy, ineffably graceful figure steadily ascend the rise, a long-legged figure that inevitably drew the eye of any man with blood in his veins. He'd recognized her instantly—Portia Ashford, his sister Amelia's sister-in-law.

Portia must be attending the Glossup Hall house party; the Hall was the only major house near enough from which to walk.

A sense of being imposed upon burgeoned and grew.

"Damn!" He'd yielded to the entreaties of his long-time friend James Glossup and agreed to stop by on his way to Somerset to support James through the trials of the house party. But if Portia was going to be present, he'd have trials enough of his own.

She reached the crest of the earthworks and paused, one slender hand rising to hold back the fall of her jet-black hair; lifting her face to the breeze, she stared into the distance, then, letting her hand fall, gracefully walked on, following the path to the lookout, gradually descending until she disappeared from sight.

She's no business of mine.

The words echoed in his head; God knew she'd stated the sentiment often enough, in various phrasings, most far more emphatic. Portia was not his sister, not his cousin; indeed, she shared no blood at all.

Jaw firming, he looked to his horses, took up the slack in the reins—

And inwardly cursed.

"Wilks—wake up, man!" Simon tossed the reins at his groom, until then dozing behind him. Pulling on the brake, he stepped down to the road. "Just hold them— I'll be back."

Thrusting his hands into his greatcoat pockets, he strode for the narrow path that led upward, ultimately joining the path from the Hall that Portia had followed up the rise.

He was only buying himself trouble—a sniping match at the very least—yet leaving her alone, unprotected from any wastrel who might happen along, was simply not possible, not for him. If he'd driven on, he wouldn't have had a moment's peace, not until she returned safe and sound to the Hall.

Given her propensity for rambling walks, that might not happen for hours.

He wouldn't be thanked for his concern. If he survived without having his ego prodded in a dozen uncomfortable places, he'd count himself lucky. Portia had a tongue like a double-edged razor—no way one could escape being nicked. He knew perfectly well what her attitude would be when he caught up with her—precisely the same as it had been for the past decade, ever since he'd realized she truly had no idea of the prize she was, the temptation she posed, and was therefore in need of constant protection from the situations into which she blithely sailed.

While she remained out of his sight, out of his orbit, she was not his responsibility; if she came within it, unprotected, he felt obliged to watch over her, to keep her safe—he should have known better than to try to fight the urge.

Of all the females he knew, she was unquestionably the most difficult, not least because she was also the most intelligent, yet here he was, trudging after her despite his certain reception; he wasn't at all sure what that said of *his* intelligence.

Women! He'd spent the entire drive west considering them. His great-aunt Clara had recently died and left him her house in Somerset. The inheritance had served as a catalyst, forcing him to review his life, to rethink his direction, yet his unsettled state had a more fundamental genesis; he'd finally realized what it was that gave his older cousins and his sisters' husbands their purpose in life.

The purpose he lacked.

Family—their own branch of it, their own children— their own wife. Such things had never seemed critical before; now they loomed as vital to his life, to his satisfaction with his lot.

A scion of a wealthy, wellborn family, he had a comfortable lot in life, yet what worth comfort against the lack of achievement he now felt so acutely? It wasn't his ability to achieve that was in question—not in his mind, nor, he'd warrant, in any other—but the goal, the need, the reason; these were the necessities he lacked.

Crucial necessities for a satisfying life for such as he.

Great-aunt Clara's legacy had been the final prod; what was he to do with a rambling country house if not live in it? He needed to get himself a wife and start building the family he required to give his life its true direction.

He hadn't accepted the notion meekly. For the past ten years, his life had been well run, well ordered, with females intruding in only two arenas, both entirely under his control. With countless discreet liaisons behind him, he was a past master at managing—seducing, enjoying, and ultimately disengaging from—the wellborn matrons with whom he habitually dallied. Other than that, the only females he consorted with were those of his own family. Admittedly, within the family, they ruled, but as that had always been the case, he'd never felt constrained or challenged by the fact—one simply dealt with it as necessary.

With his active interest in the Cynster investment business together with the distractions of tonnish society, with his sexual conquests and the customary family gatherings to season the whole, his life had been pleasantly full. He'd never seen the need to linger at those balls and parties graced by marriageable young ladies.

Which now left him in the unenviable position of wanting a wife and not having any useful avenue through which to acquire one, not without setting off alarm bells that would resonate throughout the ton. If he was foolish enough to start attending the balls and parties, the fond mamas would instantly perceive he was on the lookout for a bride—and lay siege.

He was the last unmarried male Cynster of his generation.

Stepping up to the top of the earthworks' outer wall,

he paused. The land fell away in a shallow sweep; the path continued to the left, leading to a squat, covered lookout set into the earth wall some fifty yards on.

The view was magnificent. Sunshine winked on the distant sea; the silhouette of the Isle of Wight was distinguishable through a soft summer haze.

He'd seen the view before. He turned to the lookout, and the female presently in it. She was standing at the railing, gazing out to sea. From her stance and stillness, he assumed she hadn't seen him.

Lips setting, he walked on. He wouldn't need to give any reason for joining her. For the past decade, he'd treated her with the same insistent protectiveness he applied to all the females of his family; doubtless it was her relationship—the fact she was his brother-in-law Luc's sister—that dictated how he felt about her despite the lack of blood ties.

To his mind, Portia Ashford was family, his to protect. That much, at least, was unarguable.

What tortuous logic had prompted the gods to decree that a woman needed a man to conceive?

Portia stifled a disgusted humph. That was the crux of the dilemma now facing her. Unfortunately, there was no point debating the issue—the gods had so decreed, and there was nothing she could do about it.

Other than find a way around the problem.

The thought increased her irritation, largely self-directed. She had never wanted a husband, never imagined that the usual path of a nice, neat, socially approved marriage with all its attendant constraints was for her. Never had she seen her future in such terms.

But there was no other way.

Stiffening her spine, she faced the fact squarely: if she

wanted children of her own, she would have to find a husband.

The breeze sidled up, whispering, coolly caressing her cheeks, lightly fingering the heavy waves of her hair. The realization that children—her own children, her own family—were what in her heart she truly yearned for, the challenge she'd been raised, like her mother, to accept and conquer, had come just like the breeze, stealing up on her. For the past five years, she'd worked with her sisters, Penelope and Anne, in caring for foundlings in London. She'd plunged into the project with her usual zeal, convinced their ideals were both proper and right, only to discover her own destiny lay in a direction in which she'd never thought to look.

So now she needed a husband.

Given her birth, her family's status and connections, and her dowry, gaining such an encumbrance would be easy, even though she was already twenty-four. She wasn't, however, fool enough to imagine any gentleman would do. Given her character, her temperament, her trenchant independence, it was imperative she choose wisely.

She wrinkled her nose, her gaze fixed unseeing on the distant prospect. Never had she imagined she would come to this—to desiring a husband. Courtesy of their brother Luc's disinterest in pushing her and her sisters into marriage, they'd been allowed to go their own way; her way had eschewed the ballrooms and salons, Almack's, and similar gatherings of the ton at which marriageable young ladies found their spouses.

Learning how to find a husband had seemed beneath her—an enterprise well below the more meaty challenges her intellect demanded . . .

Recollections of past arrogance—of all the chances to learn the hows and wherefores of husband selection and subsequent snaring at which she'd turned up her nose—

fed her aggravation. How galling to discover that her intellect, widely accepted as superior, had not forseen her present state.

The damning truth was she could recite Horace and quote Virgil by the page, yet she had no real idea how to acquire a husband.

Let alone the right one.

She refocused on the distant sea, on the sunlight winking off the waves, constantly vacillating. Just as she was, had been for the past month. That was so unlike her, so at odds with her character—always decisive, never weak or shy—her indecision grated on her temper. Her character wanted, nay *demanded,* a decision, a firm goal, a plan of action. Her emotions—a side of herself she'd rarely been swayed by—were far less sure. Far less inclined to jump into this latest project with her customary zeal.

She'd revisted the arguments ad infinitum; there were no further aspects to be explored. She'd walked here today determined to use the few hours before the other guests arrived and the house party got under way to formulate a plan.

Lips setting, she narrowed her eyes at the horizon, aware of resistance welling inside, of a shying away from the moment—so aggravating yet so instinctive, so powerful she had to fight to override it and push ahead . . . but she was not going to leave without a firm commitment.

Grasping the lookout's railing, she tipped her chin high and firmly stated, "I will use every opportunity the house party provides to learn all I can and make up my mind once and for all." That was nowhere near decisive enough; determinedly, she added, "Whoever is present of suitable age and station, I swear I will seriously consider him."

There—at last! She'd put her next step into words.

Into a solemn vow. The positive uplifting feeling that always followed on the heels of decision welled within her—

"Well, that's heartening, I must say, although of suitable age and station for what?"

With a gasp, she whirled. For one instant, her mind boggled. Not with fear—despite the shadows in which he stood and the brightness of the day behind him, she'd recognized his voice, knew whose shoulders blocked the entrance arch.

But what in all Hades was *he* doing *here*?

His gaze sharpened—a disconcertingly acute blue gaze far too direct for politeness.

"And what haven't you made up your mind about? That usually takes you all of two seconds."

Calmness, decisiveness—fearlessness—returned in a rush. She narrowed her eyes. "*That* is none of your affair."

He moved, deliberately slowly, taking three prowling steps to join her by the railing. She tensed. The muscles framing her spine grew rigid; her lungs locked as something within her reacted. She knew him so well, yet here, alone in the silence of the fields and sky, he seemed larger, more powerful.

More dangerous in some indefinable way.

Stopping with two feet between them, he gestured to the view. "You seemed to be declaring it to the world at large."

He met her gaze; amusement at catching her out lurked in the blue, along with watchfulness and a certain disapproval.

His features remained expressionless. "I suppose it's too much to hope there's a groom or footman waiting nearby?"

That was a subject she wasn't about to debate, especially not with him. Facing the view, she coolly inclined her head. "Good afternoon. The views are quite magnificent." She paused for only an instant. "I hadn't imagined you an admirer of nature."

She felt his gaze slide over her profile, then he looked at the view.

"On the contrary." He slid his hands into his pockets; he seemed to relax. "There are some creations of nature I'm addicted to worshipping."

It required no thought at all to divine to what he was alluding. In the past, she would have made some tart remark . . . now, all she heard in her mind were the words of her vow . . . "You're here for the Glossups' house party."

It wasn't a question; he answered with an elegant shrug. "What else?"

He turned as she drew herself up. Their eyes met; he'd heard her vow and was unlikely to forget . . .

She was suddenly sure she needed more space between them.

"I came here for the solitude," she baldly informed him. "Now that you've arrived, I may as well start back."

She swung toward the exit. He was in her way. Her heartbeat accelerating, she glanced at his face.

In time to see his features harden, to sense him bite back some retort. His gaze touched hers; his restraint was almost palpable. With a calm so deliberate it was itself a warning, he stepped aside and waved her to the door. "As you wish."

Her senses remained trained on him as she swept past; her skin prickled as if in truth he posed some potential danger. Once past him, head high, she glided out of the archway; with a calm more apparent than real, she set off along the path.

Jaw setting, Simon ruthlessly quelled the urge to stop her, to reach out, catch her hand, reel her back—to what end he wasn't sure. This, he reminded himself, was what he needed, her on her haughty way back to Glossup Hall.

Drawing a long breath, he held it, then followed her out into the sunshine.

And on down the path. The sooner she got back to civilization and safety, the sooner his own journey would end. He'd driven straight down from London—he was thirsty; a glass of ale would not go astray.

With his longer strides he could easily overtake her; instead, he ambled in her wake, content enough with the view. The current fashion for gowns with waists that actually fell at a woman's waist suited her, emphasizing the svelte lines of her figure, the slender curves, the very long lines of her legs. The purply blue hue of the light summer walking dress complemented her dramatic coloring—raven black hair, midnight blue eyes, and pale, almost translucent skin. She was taller than the average; her forehead would brush his chin—if they ever got that close.

The thought of that happening made him inwardly, grimly, laugh.

Reaching the crest of the rise, she continued over and on—and only then realized he was following her. She threw him a black glance, then stopped and waited, swinging to face him as he halted before her.

Her eyes like shards of dark flint, she glared at him. "You are *not* going to follow me all the way back to the Hall."

Portia didn't ask what he thought he was doing; they both knew. They'd last seen each other at Christmas, seven months before, but only distantly, surrounded by the combined hordes of their families. He hadn't had a chance then to get on her nerves, something that, ever since she'd turned fourteen, he'd seemed absolutely devoted to doing, if possible every time they met.

His gaze locked on hers. Something—temper? decision?—flashed behind the deceptively soft blue of his eyes. Then his lips firmed; he stepped around her with his usual fluid grace, unnerving in a man so large, and continued on down the path.

She whirled, watched. He didn't go far but stopped a step beyond the fork where the footpath to the village led down to the lane below.

Turning, he met her gaze. "You're right. I'm not." He waved down the path.

She looked in that direction. A curricle—his curricle—stood in the lane.

"Your carriage awaits."

Lifting her gaze, she met his. Directly. He was blocking the path to the Hall—quite deliberately.

"I was intending to walk back."

His gaze didn't waver. "Change your mind."

His tone—sheer male arrogance laced with a challenge she hadn't previously encountered and couldn't place—sent a peculiar shiver through her. There was no overt aggression in his stance, yet she didn't for a moment doubt he could, and would, stop her if she tried to get past him.

Temper, wild willfulness—her customary response to intimidatory tactics, especially from him—flooded her, yet this time there were other, powerful and distracting emotions in the mix. She stood perfectly still, her gaze level and locked in silent combat with his, the familiar struggle for supremacy, yet . . .

Something had changed.

In him.

And in her.

Was it simply age—how long had it been since they'd last crossed wills like this? Three years? More? Regardless, the field had altered; the battle was no longer the same. Something was fundamentally different; she sensed in him a bolder, more blatantly predatory streak, a flash of steel beneath his elegance, as if with the years his mask was wearing thin.

She'd always known him for what he was . . .

Her vow echoed in her head. She mentally shook aside the distraction, yet still she heard . . . recognized the challenge.

Couldn't resist.

Head rising, she walked forward, every bit as deliberate as he.

The watchfulness in his eyes condensed, until his attention was focused exclusively on her. Another tingle of sensation slithered down her spine. Halting before him, she held his gaze.

What did he see? Now she was looking, trying to see past his guard, only to discover she could not—odd, for they'd never sought to hide their mutual dismissiveness—what was it he was hiding? What was the reason behind the veiled threat emanating from him?

To her surprise, she wanted to know.

She drew a deliberate breath, evenly stated, "Very well."

Surprise lit his eyes, swiftly superceded by suspicion; she pivoted and looked down, stepping onto the path to the village, hiding her smile. Just so he wouldn't imagine he'd won, she coolly added, "As it happens, one of my shoes is pinching."

She'd taken only one more step when she sensed him shift, then he was sweeping down on her, moving far too fast.

Her senses leapt. Uncertain, she slowed—

He didn't halt; he bent, and scooped her up in his arms.

"What—?"

Without breaking his stride, he juggled her until he

had her cradled, carrying her as if she weighed no more than a child.

Her lungs had seized, along with her senses; it took serious effort to draw breath. "What do you think you're *doing*?"

Her total incomprehension invested every word. Never before had he shown the slightest sign of reacting to her gibes in any physical way.

She was . . . what? Shocked? Or . . . ?

Thrusting her confusion aside, she met his gaze as he briefly glanced her way.

"Your shoe's pinching—we wouldn't want your delicate little foot to suffer unnecessary damage."

His tone was bland, his expression guileless; the look in his eyes would even pass for innocent.

She blinked. They both looked ahead. She considered protesting—and discarded the notion in the next thought. He was perfectly capable of arguing until they reached the curricle.

As for struggling, she was intensely aware—far more than she liked to be—that she was physically much weaker than he. The arms supporting her felt like steel; his stride never faltered, powerful and assured. The hand clasping her thigh just above her knee—decently protected by her full skirts—grasped like a vise; the width of his chest and its muscled hardness locked her in. She'd never regarded his strength as anything she needed to consider or weigh, yet if he was going to bring physical contact into their equation, she would need to think again.

And not just on the basis of strength.

Being this close, trapped in his arms, made her feel . . . among other things, light-headed.

He slowed; she refocused.

With a flourish, he set her on the curricle's seat.

Startled, she grasped the railings, out of habit drawing her skirts close so he could sit beside her—noting the equally startled face of Wilks, his groom.

"Ah . . . afternoon, Miss Portia." Wide-eyed, Wilks bobbed as he handed the reins to Simon.

Wilks had to have witnessed the entire performance; he was waiting for her to explode, or at least say something cutting.

And he wasn't the only one.

She smiled with perfect equanimity. "Good afternoon, Wilks."

Wilks blinked, nodded warily, then hurried back to his place.

Simon glanced at her as he climbed up beside her. As if expecting her to bite. Or at the very least snarl.

He wouldn't have believed a sweet smile, so she faced forward, serenely composed, as if her joining him in the curricle had been her idea. His suspicious glance was worth every tithe of the effort such sunny compliance cost her.

The curricle jerked, then rolled forward. The instant he had his bays bowling along, she asked, "How are your parents?"

A pause greeted that, but then he replied.

She nodded and launched into an account of her family, all of whom he knew, describing their health, their whereabouts, their latest interests. As if he'd asked, she continued, "I came down with Lady O." For years, that had been their shorthand for Lady Osbaldestone, a connection of the Cynsters' and an old friend of her family's, an ancient beldame who terrorized half the ton. "She spent the last weeks at the Chase, and then had to travel down here. She's an old friend of Lord Netherfield, did you know?" Viscount Netherfield was Lord Glossup's father and was presently visiting at Glossup Hall.

Simon was frowning. "No."

Portia smiled quite genuinely; she was fond of Lady O, but Simon, in company with most gentlemen of his ilk, found her perspicaciousness somewhat scarifying. "Luc insisted she shouldn't cross half the country alone, so I offered to come, too. The others who've arrived so far . . ." She rattled on, acquainting him with those present and those yet to arrive, precisely as any friendly, well-bred young lady might.

The suspicion in his eyes grew more and more pronounced.

Then the gates of Glossup Hall appeared, set wide in welcome. Simon turned the bays in and set them pacing up the drive.

The Hall was a sprawling country house built in Elizabethan times. Its typical redbrick facade faced south and boasted three stories with east and west wings set perpendicular to it. The central wing housing the ballroom and conservatory made up the middle stroke of the E. As they neared, sunlight glanced off the rows of mullioned windows and glowed on the tall chimneys with their ornate pots.

By the time he swung the bays into the circular forecourt, Simon felt thoroughly disconcerted. Not a common feeling, not for him; there wasn't much in tonnish life that could throw him off-balance.

Other than Portia.

If she'd railed at him, used her sharp tongue to its usual effect, all would have been normal. He wouldn't have enjoyed the encounter, but neither would he have felt this sudden disorientation.

Rack his brains though he might, he couldn't recall her ever behaving toward him with such . . . feminine softness was the description that sprang to mind. She was usually well armored and prickly; today, she'd apparently left her shield and spears behind.

The result was . . .

He reined in the bays, pulled on the brake, tossed the ribbons to Wilks, and stepped down.

Portia waited for him to come around the carriage and hand her down; he watched, expecting her to leap down in her usual, independent, don't-need-you way. Instead, when he offered his hand, she placed her slim fingers across his palm and let him assist her to alight with stunning grace.

She looked up and smiled when he released her. "Thank you." Her smile deepened; her eyes held his. "You were right. My foot is in an unquestionably better state than it otherwise would have been."

Her expression one of ineffable sweetness, she inclined her head and turned away. Her eyes were so dark he hadn't been able to tell if the twinkle he'd thought he'd seen in them was real, or merely a trick of the light.

He stood in the forecourt, grooms and footmen darting around him, and watched as she glided into the house. Without a single glance back, she disappeared into the shadows beyond the open front door.

The sound of gravel crunching as his curricle and pair were led away jerked him out of his abstraction. Outwardly impassive, inwardly a trifle grim, he strode to the door of Glossup Hall. And followed her in.

Watch for

The Taming Of Ryder Cavanaugh

The next historical romance
From #1 New York Times bestselling author
Stephanie Laurens
Coming in July 2013
From Avon Books

Don't miss these passionate novels by #1 *New York Times* bestselling author

STEPHANIE LAURENS

Viscount Breckenridge to the Rescue

978-0-06-206860-6

Determined to hunt down her very own hero, Heather Cynster steps out of her safe world and boldly attends a racy soiree. But her promising hunt is ruined by the supremely interfering Viscount Breckenridge, who whisks her out of scandal—and into danger.

In Pursuit of Eliza Cynster

978-0-06-206861-3

Brazenly kidnapped from her sister's engagement ball, Eliza Cynster is spirited north to Edinburgh. Determined to escape, she seizes upon the first unlikely champion who happens along—Jeremy Carling, who will not abandon a damsel in distress.

The Capture of the Earl of Glencrae

978-0-06-206862-0

Angelica Cynster is certain she'll recognize her fated husband at first sight. And when her eyes meet those of the Earl of Glencrae across a candlelit ballroom, she knows that he's the one. But her heart is soon pounding for an entirely different reason—when her hero abducts her!